PRAISE FOR LOUISE VOSS

'A cracking page-turner that sucks you straight into the dark heart of human behaviour. I couldn't put it down!' Marnie Riches, author of *Born Bad*

'A twisty, thrilling read with engaging and complex characters' Sarah Ward, author of *In Bitter Chill*

'I loved the subtlety and style of Louise Voss's writing; the slow reveals and hints at the darkness to come in *The Old You* will make it impossible to put down!' Sarah Pinborough, author of *Behind Her Eyes*

'I'm a huge fan of Louise Voss's novels and this one did not disappoint. Cleverly plotted and beautifully executed, a must-read for fans of emotionally driven, dark and twisted thrillers' Susi Holliday, author of *The Damselfly*

'The way the plot unfolds, unfolds – and unfolds again – is brilliant. Poignant, clever and terrifically tense' William Shaw, author of *A Song from Dead Lips*

'A top-notch thriller, with seams of doubt and illusion sewn through the plot with total skill. I love books where you wonder who to trust, and keep changing your mind' Hayley Webster, author of *Jar Baby*

'If I'm looking a bit sleep-deprived right now it's because this one is keeping me up way past my bedtime. A really original and compelling story from Louise Voss that will keep you turning the pages' Howard Linskey, author of *The Drop*

'A disturbing, brilliant tale of lies and psychological manipulation, with a gutsy, believable heroine' Kate Rhodes, author of *Crossbones Yard*

'A brilliant tale of deception with a twist that took my breath away' Mark Edwards, author of *Follow You Home*

'One of the twistiest books I've read for a while. Completely gripping' Cass Green, author *The Woman Next Door*

'It's immense! I loved it! Couldn't put it down' Jane Isaac, author of *The Lies Within*

'Brilliantly unsettling, a gripping, clever novel where nothing can be taken at face value' Jane Casey, author of *After the Fire*

'This novel was so creepy it kept me awake. I was guessing right to the end' Katerina Diamond, author of *The Teacher*

'Grippy and twisty, this one will keep you guessing' Melanie McGrath, author of *White Heat*

'An ingeniously twisty tale of simmering resentments, long-hidden secrets and murderous intent – a must-read for all psychological thriller fans' Steph Broadribb, author of *Deep Down Dead*

'An ingeniously plotted and totally addictive psychological thriller about identity and deception. The killer twist left me reeling' Paddy Magrane, author of *Disorder*

'*The Old You* has a unique vibe that makes it stand out, and is also a truly twisty yet believable tale with memorable characters and a cleverly woven, atmospheric narrative' Liz Loves Books

'*The Old You* provoked an uneasy feeling inside me from beginning to end, as I worried about what was to come, yet I couldn't tear myself away from it. I wasn't sure what was real and what wasn't, whether everything was as it seemed or something more sinister was going on ... Filled with jaw-dropping revelations, I had no idea where the book was heading and I was certainly surprised as I followed this twisty rollercoaster journey' Off-the-Shelf Books

'One of the most moving books about friendship I've ever read' Lisa Jewell, author of *Ralph's Party*

'Louise Voss hooks you from the first page and doesn't let go' Lauren Henderson, author of *Dead White Female*

The Old You

Over her eighteen-year writing career, Louise has released books through pretty much every publishing model, from deals with major traditional publishing houses (Transworld and Harper Collins), to digital-only (the Amazon-owned Thomas & Mercer) and self-publishing. In 2011 she and co-author Mark Edwards were the first UK indie-published authors to hit the No. 1 spot on Amazon. She has had twelve novels published in total, six solo and six co-written, a combination of psychological thrillers, police procedurals and contemporary fiction. Louise has an MA (Dist) in Creative Writing and also works as a literary consultant and mentor for writers at www.thewritingcoach.co.uk. She lives in south-west London and is a proud member of two female crime-writing collectives, The Slice Girls and Killer Women.

You can follow Louise on Twitter: *@LouiseVoss1*.

The Old You

Louise Voss

ORENDA
BOOKS

Orenda Books
16 Carson Road
West Dulwich
London SE21 8HU
www.orendabooks.co.uk

First published in the United Kingdom by Orenda Books 2018
Copyright © Louise Voss 2017

A catalogue record for this book is available from the British Library.

ISBN 978-1-912374-11-3
eISBN 978-1-912374-12-0

Typeset in Garamond by MacGuru Ltd
Printed and bound in Denmark by Nørhaven

For sales and distribution, please contact *info@orendabooks.co.uk*

Dedicated to Julia Cripps, an absolute warrior whose courage, stoicism, kindness and humour are a shining example to all who know and love her.

1

Ed's condition was formally diagnosed on the same afternoon I had my interview for the job at Hampton University. A probable ending and a potential new beginning, all on the same day.

I'd rushed home and picked him up – there wasn't even time to change out of my interview suit – and now here we were, in the Memory Clinic of the local mental health centre. We were with the consultant, whose name was Mr Deshmukh; the three of us crowded together in such a small side room that our knees almost touched.

'Spell "world" backwards,' Mr Deshmukh instructed, gazing intently at Ed as though Ed was in the spotlit black chair in the *Mastermind* final, not in this tiny windowless office in Mountain Way.

'D,' Ed began, confidently.

There was a long pause.

L, I silently urged him. This was the man who did the quick crossword and the Sudoku in the *Guardian* every day without fail, rarely leaving any blanks – or at least, he had done for years. It occurred to me that I hadn't seen him even pick it up for a couple of months now.

'Um,' Ed said, and the breath stopped in my throat.

He couldn't really have dementia. It was unthinkable. He wasn't even sixty yet! My heart sank as I remembered all the qualms I'd dismissed about marrying an older man. The fourteen-year age gap hadn't seemed insurmountable back then.

'Go on.'

'Um – D, L...'

I mentally cheered. He was fine! That, surely, was the trickiest part of the task.

But then Ed corrected himself. 'Wait, no: D, R, L, O, W.'

He looked pleased with himself, like a shy child winning a prize on sports day. This was not the Ed I knew. The Ed I knew was political, clever, confrontational.

Mr Deshmukh shook his head. He was a smooth-cheeked Indian guy with the sort of thick, glossy, black hair that wouldn't look out of place on a luxury cushion. It undulated gently, like the movement of wind through a cornfield.

'Try again,' he urged.

Ed was puzzled and then annoyed. 'Why? That's correct!'

'I'm afraid not.'

My husband made his exasperated face – a face I was very familiar with. 'D, R, L, O, W! What the hell is wrong with that?'

'It's not quite right,' the consultant said. 'Let's come back to it.'

He slid a blank sheet of paper across his desk towards Ed and handed him a pencil. 'Please draw me a clock face, with the numbers, and draw the hands indicating that the time is twenty to four.'

I saw the swoop of Ed's Adam's apple as he swallowed. He thought for a moment, then, with decisive movements drew something almost recognisable as a circle. It was more of an oval, and the ends didn't meet properly, but it wasn't bad, I thought.

Then I thought, not bad? A kid in infants' school would have done a far better job.

The tip of Ed's pencil hovered over the oval. He wrote a 1 at the top, where 12 should be, then, far too close together, 2, 3, 5, 7 and 9. He'd only got as far around the clock face as 4 should be.

'There's something wrong with that,' he admitted miserably.

There was something wrong full stop, I thought. I'd never be able to take the uni admin job if I was offered it. I'd have to stay home and look after him. And how, dear God, were we ever going to break it to Ben? He adored his dad.

Mr Deshmukh scribbled something on a pad. 'In the light of the knowledge that your father died of Pick's Disease, an MRI scan would be by far the best way to diagnose you; much better than these neuropsychological tests. Plus, it would exclude other reversible causes of dementia like hydrocaephalus or brain tumour. I'll refer you.'

'No way,' Ed said, jumping up in agitation. 'There is absolutely no chance whatsoever of me going into one of those scan things.'

'He's developed claustrophobia,' I told Mr Deshmukh. 'He can't be in small spaces, and he won't fly any more either. I don't know if that's related.' I paused. 'Is there any likelihood it might be something reversible?'

I barely remembered Victor Naismith, Ed's father. He died soon after Ed and I met, a tiny catatonic shell hunched in a nursing-home vinyl armchair, doubly incontinent, unable to recognise anybody, speak, or do anything at all for himself. Years of misery, guilt, pain and vast expense for all of their family.

Victor had only been seventy-four when he died. Was this what was in store for Ed? For me? All our plans! Travel, hobbies, the helter-skelter whiz into retirement I'd envisioned, rather than a slow plod gravewards. I would have to shelve everything and stand by watching as Ed's brain gradually shrivelled and his intellect crumbled daily, until there was nothing left but a breathing corpse that would probably cling to endless long, expensive years of a useless life ... I wasn't sure I could do that, and it made me feel terrible.

Deshmukh ignored my question, which didn't make me feel any better. Instead he turned to Ed: 'If you're really adamant about not wanting an MRI, I suggest you get a lumbar puncture instead. That will also rule out any unusual infections or cancer. And an EEG, although with FTD – sorry, frontotemporal degeneration – that may be inconclusive, especially early on in the disease.'

Ed suddenly sat up straight, the light back in his eyes making them flash a startling, piercing blue. 'What are you saying? Is this a diagnosis?'

Mr Deshmukh opened a cardboard folder in front of him and didn't meet Ed's gaze – which I thought was fairly poor, as bedside manners went. He held up a sheet of paper that I hadn't seen before.

'Dr Naismith, this is your second visit. We've already diagnosed mild cognitive impairment and that was – when? – Hmmm, yes, six months ago.'

I held up my hand. 'Wait – what? What do you mean? This isn't Ed's second visit!'

Ed looked sheepish. He reached over and gently pushed down my outstretched fingers. 'I didn't tell you, honey. I came before. I was worried because of Dad. Hugh Lark at the surgery referred me.'

I stared at him. Now he was Ed again, not a little boy with milk teeth drawing a wobbly circle, but a strong man; a medical man, wise and insightful. My husband, the man for whom I'd given up my career, my reputation, my friends…

He squeezed my fingers and a lump came to my throat.

'Why didn't you tell me? You've been worried for six months and you didn't tell me?' My voice was high and tight, veering dangerously towards being out of control as I remembered the numerous times I'd felt infuriated by him recently, accused him of 'not listening' when he repeated things or forgot arrangements or made odd claims that people had stolen personal possessions that it transpired he'd just mislaid.

'You've been worried too,' he said in a sulky voice.

This was true. But I had convinced myself that he was just being annoying – a natural corollary of his advancing age.

'If we compare the tests, I'm afraid that it's fairly obvious there has been a significant decline in mental capability since then, and in tandem with the information you have already given me, and your GP's report stating his belief that the damage has not been caused by an infection, or thyroid malfunction or vitamin deficiency, I'm sorry to say that I do believe you to be in the early stages of either Alzheimer's or Pick's Disease – most likely the latter, given your family history. Please do not assume that this is a death sentence…'

He was going to say more but Ed cut him off. 'Please remember that I was a GP myself, Doctor…' – Ed had to look at the brass nameplate on the doctor's desk – 'Dekmush. I don't need to make any assumptions. It could be a fluid build-up in my, um…' He gestured towards his head. 'Or a lump thing. Or a bleed.'

The doctor scribbled something on a pad. I noticed how hairy his knuckles were, like a werewolf. 'It's Mr Deshmukh,' he corrected gently. 'Of course, but unless you agree to brain scans then we can't find out much more, clinically.'

'Can you give him some medication, to improve his memory?' I felt desperate. 'What's that drug – Aricept?'

Mr Deshmukh gazed levelly at us both. 'I'm afraid that the usual drugs for dementia really don't work with Pick's disease; in fact they can be quite counterproductive.'

Ed snorted. 'Even when they do work, they only work for about fifty percent of parents ... patents ... patients, and only for about a year. What's the point?'

I was aghast. 'Is that the best that medical science can offer? Drugs might buy him a year if they work at all, which they probably won't?'

I had a sudden, unbidden mental image of Ed's dad the last time I saw him, being hoisted out of the wingback chair in which he spent the majority of his days, into a wheelchair to be taken to be 'toileted', as the staff euphemistically referred to it. His nappy had been clearly visible above the waistband of his stained tracksuit trousers, and there had been an enormous lump at his groin where the nappy – or 'continence aid', another euphemism – had got wet and bunched up. The brightest man Ed said he'd ever known was drooling, his hands curled into claws, his teeth turning black and dropping out because nobody had been able to clean them for weeks.

Poor Victor. Poor *Ed*. And poor me, I thought, suddenly angry. This was not what I'd risked everything for.

2

We left Mountain Way in shock, a fistful of leaflets on support groups, phone numbers of counsellors and cards with dates for follow-up appointments and lumbar punctures stuffed into my handbag.

I glanced sideways at Ed as I drove home, worried about the blankness of his expression. It was as if he hadn't taken it in at all.

'It'll be OK,' I said. 'We'll get through it.'

Ed ignored me.

He came into our bedroom later, as I was changing out of my interview suit. The thick elastic waistband of the tight skirt had left striations on the skin of my hips and stomach, as though I'd been wearing bandages all day. I peeled it off, struggling to keep my balance as I hopped around the room.

'How are you feeling, darling?'

He sat down heavily on the bed, causing it to creak under his weight. 'I don't want to talk about it. Not yet.'

'OK,' I said. I put my arms around him and he wrapped his own around my hips, burying his face in my stomach. I could feel his breath on my skin, through the thin mesh of my tights. His lilac cashmere jumper was soft under my hands.

Ed only ever wore cashmere sweaters – he had one in every single colour. I never knew a straight man that liked clothes as much as he did – he also owned over fifty pairs of jeans. We had a separate wardrobe for them; stacked in piles on shelves as if our spare room was a shop, many still with the cardboard designer labels attached. Just yesterday I'd teased him that if he'd only stop shopping, I might not need a job.

'I'm sorry. I'm so sorry, Ed.' My voice cracked.

'I said, I don't want to talk about it. Anyway. I didn't ask you how your job thingy went. You don't want to take it, do you?'

I balled up the skirt and threw it with some force into the laundry basket, wanting to cry. I *did* want it.

'It was great, actually,' I said. 'Office with a view to die for, in this amazing old Regency house on campus – apparently Florence Nightingale's aunt used to live there –and it's more about organising concerts than a secretarial job. Colleagues seem nice. Slightly mad boss, but mad in a good way, you know?'

'Hmm,' said Ed, as if he didn't believe a word. 'Can't see it being your sort of thing though really, can you? Working in a college.'

'Why not? I can totally see myself there. It was fantastic to be around so many people again; all that music. It'd be like *Fame*. Much more interesting than working for Henry.'

Henry was the financial advisor I'd bored myself rigid working for.

'"I wanna live for ever"', Ed quoted, deadpan, sounding so like his old self that the breath caught in my chest, fluttering like minnows.

'I won't take it though, if they offer it.'

'Why not?'

'Isn't that obvious?'

We gazed at each other for a minute, his expression unreadable.

'No,' he said. 'It's not obvious. Of course you should take it, if you want it. We could use the money. I just didn't think you'd be that into it.'

I hesitated, aware that he didn't want me to talk about it – but I had to. Unclasping his arms from round my waist I sat down on the bed next to him. 'I don't want to be so far away from you. I know it's only part-time but...'

He leaped up as if I'd scalded him. 'So, what, now you don't want to leave me on my own? Don't you dare treat me like a, like a...'

I didn't supply the missing word but it hung between us like a rotten fruit: invalid. In-valid. Ed had been diagnosed as an invalid person. No wonder he was angry. Normally if he used that tone of voice on me, I'd rise to the bait and we'd be yelling at each other within seconds. But how could I blame him for being angry?

I was torn. If I was offered the job and didn't take it, he'd be upset. But if I did take it, I had no idea how I'd be able to enjoy it, if I was worrying about him the whole time...

Hopefully I wouldn't be offered it. That would just be easier. I flopped back on the bed, my arms spread wide in surrender.

'When will you know?' Ed asked, calm again.

'Soon. Alvin – the boss – said in the next couple of days if not before. They need someone to start ASAP. The new students have already arrived for Orientation Week, and next week is Induction. Lectures start the week after that.'

At that very moment my mobile rang. I picked it off the bedside table and answered it, Ed leaning close to me so that he could hear too.

'Lynn? Professor Cornelius; Alvin. We all loved you, you walked it. Can you start next week? We're happy for you to do Mondays, Wednesdays and Fridays, if that suits. HR will email you some details.'

I bit my lip and turned to face Ed. To my surprise the clouds had cleared from his stubbly face and he was laughing at me, nodding his approval and giving me a thumbs-up. I'd meant to ask for a day or two to think about it, but Ed's reaction sealed the deal.

'Brilliant,' I said. 'Thank you so much! See you on Monday morning.'

When I finished the call, Ed kissed me effusively.

'Hey, well done you. I knew you'd get it!'

By the time I put our lamb chops on the table at seven-thirty that night, I'd changed my mind again, several times. It wouldn't be fair for me to take the job if Ed's health suddenly went downhill and he couldn't be left alone.

But it might be a year or two before he got worse...

Suzan next door could keep an eye on him, she worked from home. I could have a discreet word with her.

The job was only three days a week, and we did need the money. Ed's pension wasn't enough for us to live on comfortably, and our savings were in case of emergencies. Now they'd most likely all have to be used for his residential care, at some point in the future.

I called up the stairs. 'Dinner's ready!'

Ed appeared, took one look at the food on the table, and turned around again. He was wearing his pyjamas.

'I'm going to bed. Not hungry.'

He stomped back upstairs, in sulky teenager mode again. I heard him crash about in the bathroom, the flush of the toilet and the buzz of his electric toothbrush then, finally, the decisive bang of our bedroom door.

Suddenly I had no appetite either.

When I crept up about half an hour later to check on him, I could hear him snoring through the closed door. All his clothes had been discarded on the landing in an untidy pile, so instead of disturbing him, I draped them over the banister and went back downstairs.

I couldn't concentrate on the TV, so I poured myself a large brandy instead and sat in the armchair in the conservatory with my socked feet up on the radiator, staring out at the dark garden, until the tumbler contained nothing but fumes and my eyelids were heavy with worry. I was just nodding off over a programme on the radio about the miners' strike when a sudden noise made me jerk awake. The miners' programme was still on, so I couldn't have been asleep for long. The noise sounded like the front door clicking shut, but Ben was the only other one with a key, so it couldn't have been that.

'Hello?' I called, sitting bolt upright, every sense awake and tingling. 'Ben? Is that you?' I knew it wasn't, though, because he and Jeanine were on their way back from a safari in South Africa.

I reached over and switched off the radio, straining my ears into the silence. I'd have assumed it was the cat, knocking something off a shelf – except that Timmy was here with me, curled up on one of the other chairs, one ear twitching.

I got to my feet, looking around for something to use as a weapon. Our house was so isolated, ours and Suzan's next door, two halves of a whole, standing alone on the towpath. We'd been the target of burglars in the past when we'd been away on holiday.

The knife block in the kitchen felt too far away, and there were no heavy lamps or anything in the conservatory. Outside, the darkness still pressed against the windows and I felt a shiver play up my spine, a finger across harp strings. Had someone just been standing out there, watching me? Perhaps they knew that Ed was asleep upstairs and I was alone down here.

Our conservatory was, unusually, at the front of the house so that we had a direct view of the Thames, with only the muddy towpath and our front garden in between. Hardly anybody came along there after dark, so I'd never minded sitting in the lit room before.

Heart thudding, I grabbed a table mat I had made myself, gluing and varnishing pebbles from Jersey beaches onto an old heatproof mat. It was heavy – I'd used far more pebbles than I'd anticipated and I'd ended up supplementing them with gravel from our own driveway. As I stared at it, in a weird kind of mental synchronicity I was sure I could hear the faint crunch of a footstep outside on that same gravel.

Maybe it had been one person who had just left, or maybe there were two of them; one inside and one out? My imagination was going into overdrive. I raised the mat high in the air, holding it with both hands, ready to bring it crashing down on the head of an intruder. Slowly pushing open the door from the conservatory with one foot, I crept into the hall. There was nobody on the stairs and no sound from above. The hall was quiet and empty and felt cold, and I tried to work out if it had been like that earlier or if it felt cold because the front door had recently been opened. It was closed now, but not Chubb-locked. Ed usually did that before we retired to bed.

I checked the front room, then the kitchen and back doors – all secure – and then padded up the stairs in my socked feet, still brandishing the mat. Bathroom, study and spare room were all empty. Finally I pushed open my bedroom door. It was pitch dark and silent, not even any green light coming from the digital display on the clock. Ed always leaned a coaster against it because it bothered him when he was trying to get to sleep.

'Ed? Ed? Are you OK?' I went over to the bed and poked him.

'Whaaargh?' he grumbled, stirring.

I put down the mat and lay on the bed behind him, spooning him through the duvet, curling my arms and legs around his broad back. 'Did you just come downstairs?'

His voice was thick with sleep. 'Er ... no, not unless I was walk sleeping.'

'Sleepwalking.'

'Wharrever,' he mumbled before subsiding back into gentle snores.

I kissed the back of his head and went back downstairs to lock up and turn off the lamps. I must have imagined the noise. Stress, probably. Or my justifiably over-developed sense of suspicion.

3

'It's what his dad died of,' I concluded, looking away as our neighbour Suzan's eyes filled with tears. Other people's tears never failed to make me itch with discomfort, however much I empathised.

Suzan's house smelled, as always, of white spirit and oil paint. She'd answered the door with her paintbrush in her hand, and sat at her kitchen table twirling it absently while I gave her our grim news.

'Oh Lynn,' she said. 'This is awful.'

'I know. But what can we do?'

She gave a watery smile. 'I'll get you a mug with *Keep Calm and Carry On* written on it.'

'Please don't.' I tried to sound light-hearted but it didn't work.

'He's too young.' Suzan picked at an oil paint scab on the back of her hand.

'I know,' I repeated miserably. I paused. 'Suze ... were you here on your own last night?'

She nodded. 'I'm working flat out to get that finished. My art class is having an exhibition next month. Why?'

She gestured with the end of her paintbrush towards a splurgy-looking seascape on her easel. I didn't know anything about art, but to me it looked like someone had thrown up on the canvas. Similar paintings hung all around the room, crowding me, looming down on us, their smeary colours and slimy stripes unsettling me. I imagined them like the inside of Ed's brain.

'I thought I heard someone prowling round on the gravel.'

I wasn't going to tell her that the noises I'd heard had been inside the house as well; she'd been nervy enough since her husband died a couple of years before. Keeled over one Saturday morning over his cornflakes.

It had been horrendous. She'd come round screaming and crying, and Ed and I had run straight over there. Ed had performed CPR on Keith while I rang the ambulance, but it was no good.

Now she threw herself into her painting. She was in her early seventies, a former Biba model and photographer's muse, and her house was full of amazing monochrome photographs of her – I was fairly sure that was partly why Ed enjoyed going round there so much.

'I probably imagined it.'

'Darling, don't you think you should tell the police?'

Most likely, I thought. But *that* wasn't going to happen. 'I'm sure it's fine. I feel silly for mentioning it. Anyway, the other reason I came over is to tell you that I've got a new job.'

'You've got a new job – now?' Suzan looked over her glasses at me and I felt hot with guilt, which immediately made me defensive.

'It's only part-time, three days a week,' I said. 'I don't have to do it forever! Ed's basically fine on his own, it's only words and stuff that he keeps forgetting at the moment. I left Henry's eight months ago and Ed's pension isn't really enough for us both. But it would really put my mind at rest if I knew that you were...'

'Keeping an eye on him?'

I bit my lip. 'I wasn't going to say that, not exactly. I was going to say, "aware of the situation". So if he locked himself out or anything, you could let him back in. Or perhaps invite him over for coffee occasionally. As long as he doesn't *think* you're keeping an eye on him...'

'I'd be happy to,' she said, reaching over and covering my hand with hers. 'Where's the job, and when do you start?'

'Thanks, Suze. It's only up at Hampton Uni – the music department at Fairhurst House, you know? Round the corner really. I could be back in twenty minutes if there was a problem. I start on Monday.'

'I'll do what I can.'

I thanked her and said goodbye, as she gave me a turpentine-scented kiss on the cheek.

Walking back up our garden path, I glanced affectionately at the house, then paused. My gaze swept across the front door, living-room and conservatory windows – then back to the living room. That was it – the blinds were down. They hadn't been down last night because we hadn't been in there. Ed had gone to bed at seven-thirtyish and I'd spent the evening in the conservatory, until I'd heard the footsteps on the gravel. Last time I'd been in the front room had been at some point yesterday afternoon, fetching a couple of dirty coffee cups left from when we were watching TV the night before that. Obviously the blinds had been up then, because it was still daylight. So Ed must have got up in the night. Weird that I hadn't heard him. But then I had heard other noises when Ed had definitely been asleep. It was all rather unsettling ... unless Ed wasn't the only one having memory problems.

It was horrible leaving the house the following Monday morning to start work. I'd come into the kitchen to say goodbye and found Ed slowly banging his head against the fridge door, fists bunched by his sides.

'Ed! What's the matter?' I rushed over and hugged him from behind, trying to tug him away from the refrigerator.

'I. Just. Can't. Bear. It,' he said, punctuating each word with another bang. When he turned around and I saw the tears in his eyes, I felt my heart breaking.

I couldn't dwell on it, though, once I arrived at Fairhurst House and took my place at the spare desk in the music school office. Not with the brain-overload that accompanied the deluge of new information I was required to retain.

The other administrator, Margaret, was helpful and polite, in a slightly distracted way. She was a tall, slender woman with a short crop of bleached hair, who seemed to glide from filing cabinet to Xerox machine as she filled me with a stream of facts I had to scribble down in order to have the faintest chance of remembering.

I called home once, ringing Ed on my mobile from the toilet, trying to pee silently when he answered. He was fine, he said. Round at Suzan's doing a painting of some tulips with her.

'Nice one, Pablo Naismith,' I said, relieved that he sounded better than he had earlier.

My new boss Alvin appeared just as my stomach was rumbling and I was asking Margaret what refreshment options there were.

'Come on then, I'll show you the staff canteen,' he announced. 'In fact, I'll give you a tour of the campus, shall I?'

I scrutinized him surreptitiously as we walked along together. He must have been at least six foot six, with a shiny-bald tonsure, but a mass of thick, curly auburn hair and matching beard. He was ridiculously skinny, one of those people who seem entirely composed of angles and knobbles, but strangely, he somehow managed not to look like a nerd, despite the silly hair and pipe-cleaner limbs.

After a soggy panini and a tepid latte, he gave me the grand tour, ending up back at Fairhurst House, where we had a look at the computer lab, the equipment hire office and the seminar rooms. In the final corridor, Alvin showed me into a damp room full of random bits of percussion, half a drum kit, and some scuffed amps. A stepladder and tools lay around, along with a digital radio that someone had left on, and a pile of crumbled bits of plaster on the floor.

'This is one of the band practice rooms,' he said. 'We've had a work order in for months to get the damp removed. Right – that's everywhere, I think. Next stop Asda – we need to buy booze and crisps for the Freshers' party tomorrow.'

'Oh! We don't have caterers then?'

Alvin snorted. 'You must be joking. No, we do it ourselves. There's a kitchenette outside the gamelan room. Always thought it was risky, having a drawerful of sharp knives with a load of hormonal teenagers around – but how else are we supposed to cut up the cheese to have with our wine?'

We were just leaving the room when a voice from the radio stopped me in my tracks. I gasped and Alvin turned. 'Everything OK?'

I made a 'hang on' gesture and peered at the digital read-out on top of the radio. It was tuned to 5 Live – not a station that we ever listened to at home.

So what was Ed doing on 5 Live talking about cuts to the NHS?

'Sorry,' I said, not wanting to sound like a maniac, but needing to explain. 'That sounds just like my husband!'

The Ed-soundalike was spouting off about zero-hours contracts, exactly the sort of topic that he used to get very aerated about – except that Ed had shown no interest whatsoever in current affairs for several months now. He no longer read the paper or watched the news. He talked aimlessly over the top of all the radio news bulletins. It was one of the things that first alerted me to the changes in his personality. I felt a stab of overwhelming sadness that I'd never again hear him doing anything like this.

'Is it him?' Alvin enquired. I could see he was keen to get on, but I couldn't leave. It felt like I would be walking away from the man my husband used to be. The caller did sound exactly like him – if Ed had a cold; the voice was deeper and croakier than his usual one, but it had the same timbre. He was talking in an articulate, concise way, using all the cadences and expressions that Ed used to, before he began to forget how to construct sentences properly. I realised how much I already missed him.

Just as he was saying something about erosion of civil rights, the DJ cut him off: 'Well, I'm afraid we're coming up to the news now so we'll have to leave it there. Thanks very much for your input, Steve from Cheam...'

'My husband's called Ed. But he sounded so like him,' I said slowly.

Alvin looked at me. 'Been married long?'

The question seemed loaded.

'Eight years now. No kids, just a grown-up stepson.' I always pre-empted the inevitable next question about children. It just seemed better to get it out of the way, on my own terms. 'Ed's a bit older than me – he's been round the block once already.'

I didn't know why I'd said that. Perhaps deep down I knew I'd have to admit to Alvin about Ed's diagnosis sooner or later and I was sub-consciously preparing for it.

'Ed? Ed Naismith?'

Alvin had that amused 'small world' look on his face.

'Yes ... do you know him?'

'Only vaguely. Was his nickname Edna? Many moons ago, before I married Sheryl, I dabbled in a bit of am-dram with the Molesey group. Fancied myself playing Hamlet, truth be told, but they never recognised my obvious talent and the sort of parts I got were more along the lines of "second spear-carrier on the right" so I didn't last long. I'm sure Ed was the director of whatever the play was that I ended up almost doing, before I decided it wasn't for me.'

I laughed, relieved. 'Yes. Edna I. Smith, that's what they called him in MADS. That's where he and I met, actually. I joined MADS when I first moved to the area and didn't know anybody, as a way to meet people. So you know him? What are the chances of that?'

A slightly hooded expression crossed Alvin's features and he looked suddenly reticent.

'What indeed?' he asked. 'Come on then, let's go and buy some cheap wine and E numbers.'

4

'So, I never thought I'd end up pushing a trolley around Asda on my first day at work,' I told Ed. 'You should've seen the cashier's face when we went through with all that wine and beer – oh, and a bottle of Jack Daniels for his office drawer. He said, "This should keep us going for a day or two, honey," to me, you know, like he was pretending we were a couple and it was all for us.'

Ed just stared at me. He had a stain of indeterminate origin on his blue cashmere and splodges of paint on his hands, which were hanging uselessly between his manspread legs as he sat on a kitchen chair. I'd found him like that when I'd come in twenty minutes ago. There were no signs of any dinner preparation and I was starving.

'Ed? Are you listening?'

I poured us each a glass of wine, waiting for him to answer me, or at least ask me something about my day, but he didn't say anything. Then, as I replaced the half-empty bottle in the fridge, something caught my attention. I rolled my eyes; it was a pair of Ed's socks, balled up next to the eggs. I discreetly removed them and stuffed them in my pocket.

'Where's the painting you did at Suzan's, then? I can't wait to see it! Are you going to do more?'

He took the wine and finally made eye contact with me. 'Might do,' he said.

'So you enjoyed it?'

'Yeah.'

'What did you paint?'

'Some flowers.'

'Was it difficult?'

'Not really.'

I remembered with a pang the days we used to stay up late into the night, debating all sorts of things, from the latest line-up of Take That to cuts in arts funding, Trident, the existence of God, and which was the most flattering style of jeans for a man in his late fifties...

Then I remembered something else. Carefully scrutinising his face as I spoke, I said, 'Hey, Ed, there was someone on the radio at lunchtime who sounded just like you, it was spooky!'

Did I imagine the tiny hostile flare of his pupils, an almost imperceptible narrowing of his eyes? Then the blank expression was back again.

'What do you mean? Of course I wasn't.'

I turned away, busied myself with emptying the dishwasher's clean contents, thoughts crowding my mind. Being on the radio was something Ed used to boast about, not try to deny. Since he took early retirement he'd often rung up radio stations. He'd booked to be in the audience of *Question Time* within minutes of hearing the announcement that it was to be filmed in Kingston a couple of years ago, and he'd been fuming when he wasn't picked to ask a question.

As I stacked cereal bowls and plates – and retrieved a second pair of socks I'd found, soaking wet, in the cutlery basket – I made a mental note to ask Suzan what time Ed left her place. If she gave him a firm alibi I'd know I had been mistaken.

But it was that flare of panic in his eyes when I mentioned it, the hard set of his lips, just for a nanosecond, that flung me into a grey cloud of doubt.

Unless the panic had been because he'd forgotten, then remembered again after already denying it? That was far more likely.

I put a clean saucepan on the hob with a clatter and changed the subject. 'So, are you looking forward to Saturday?'

'What's happening on Saturday?'

'Dinner with April and Mike. On the boat, remember?'

'I don't want to go! Do we have to?' A muscle ticked in his cheek.

'Why not?'

He and Mike used to be really friendly, but in recent years they'd been funny with each other, distant and strained. Something must have happened between them but neither man would admit to me or to April what it was, so we doggedly continued to arrange social events in the hope that it would blow over.

Ed shrugged. 'I'm not really in the ... er ... mood. Not feeling great.'

He did look tired and a bit flushed. I felt his forehead – it was warm, but not feverish.

'Come on, Ed, you know you'll love it when you get there. And it's not till the weekend. It will be a good way to celebrate the end of my first week of work.'

It was his turn to change the subject. 'By the way, a doctor rang me earlier. Deckmush. Deshmuck.'

'Deshmukh. What did he want?'

'No. Wait. It wasn't him. It was someone else. Can't remember his name but he wants me to join some sort of, er, thing, you know – trial thingy. A new treatment for whatever my silliness is.'

'Illness?'

'Yes.'

'It's all top secret though. I'm not allowed to tell anybody except you. I have to take pills, or have injections. It might be a ... fake thing, or the real drug.'

'A placebo? Sounds promising, Ed; you should do it. Can I talk to him about it?'

'He said not to tell anyone.'

'Except me, you said. Which hospital would it be based at? Or do they do it in a lab, or at the doctor's surgery?' I had no idea how clinical trials worked.

Ed shrugged. 'I think he told me but I can't remember. He said he would email me the, er, details.'

As I poured boiling water into the pan, switched on the gas and tipped in some fusilli, my instinct told me that something didn't seem quite right about the way he was trying to relay this information – but then, nothing was right about someone getting dementia in his fifties. Of course he was likely to be vague about the details – the man couldn't remember what he'd had for breakfast and was leaving socks in the dishwasher and fridge – I'd just need to wait and see what the email said.

Yet I couldn't seem to stop all my old worries from popping up again, roiling inside my head like the water in the pan. Those understandable concerns I'd had back when I first met him, about the wisdom of dating a man who'd been the main suspect in a murder investigation.

5

By the end of the first week, I felt I was beginning to learn the rhythms of the job. I was in the swing of planning and promoting the concerts; I'd learned the names of the biggest student troublemakers, and that the vending machine had ants in it. All the important stuff, as Alvin claimed.

He and I were getting on well – so well, in fact, that he'd just taken me to The Feathers for a curry and a pint or two (although I was sure this was more about him wanting a legitimate excuse for a couple of drinks at lunchtime). Back at my desk, I was feeling a bit tipsy. Tipsy, and a bit guilty, too – I'd ended up confiding in Alvin about Ed's diagnosis. I didn't fancy Alvin at all, but he was a good listener. It was just that I knew Ed would hate that I'd told my new boss anything personal, let alone something we hadn't yet told our close friends and family.

I got back to my PC and the document I'd been working on – an event plan for music at the graduation ceremonies at the Barbican the following month – but I couldn't concentrate. I'd called Ed three times to check he was OK and he hadn't picked up or returned any of the calls.

By 4pm I had visions of him falling into the river or electrocuting himself making tea. I was about to ring Suzan and ask her to pop round, when he finally called me back. He sounded very grumpy.

'What's with all the missed calls? I was in the bath!'

'Sorry, honeybun. I've been trying you all afternoon. You're OK?'

'Of course I'm OK! Why wouldn't I be?'

I didn't reply. 'Good ... well, I'll be home soon. Love you.'

It was Ed's turn not to reply. I hated it when he didn't reciprocate with an endearment.

'That your husband?' Margaret asked from across the office as she logged off her computer. I watched in astonishment as she managed to gather up a scarf, yoga mat, leggings, novel, iPod, headphones, washed Tupperware and extra cardigan and stuff them all into one bag.

I nodded, trying to discern if her tone was disapproving because I was making personal calls during office hours, or perhaps merely because I was in possession of a husband, but she sounded neutral enough.

'I'm off to yoga. With any luck, that skinny hippie in the obscene shorts won't fart every time he does a shoulder stand. But I'm not holding out much hope. You got anything good planned for tonight?'

'No. Just cooking supper.'

She looked briefly scornful and I had an urge to say, 'It's not ALL I know how to do – I'm a black belt in taekwondo! I'm not just some downtrodden housewife, you know!' but obviously I didn't. I really liked Margaret, but sometimes her willowy calm was tinged with a faint aura of superiority. 'Actually, no,' I said instead. 'We're going to my stepson's. I've just remembered.'

'Well, have a nice time. See you Monday.' She hurried out, scarf trailing behind her, and I thought, great, if she's left for the day, so can I. Alvin was teaching until six, and the office closed to students at four-thirty. I sent Ed a quick text saying I was on my way.

Half an hour later I was bumping down the potholed track towards our house. I parked at the back and went around to the front, the wide Thames streaming silently past and the leaves of the trees on the opposite bank just beginning to turn. It was a view I would never tire of.

Through her window I could see Suzan standing at an easel, head tilted to one side as she scrutinised her efforts. She waved at me as I opened my front gate, flattening myself against it to avoid the muddy splashback from two lycra-clad cyclists who whizzed past, swerving around the large puddle on the towpath that, annoyingly, was a permanent fixture for nine months of the year.

I turned the key in the lock but the door didn't open. Ed must have Chubb-locked it, and I'd only grabbed the single Yale key off the dresser in the hall that morning.

I banged the knocker, then stooped and called through the letterbox. 'Ed! Can you come and unlock the door? I can't get in!' My rectangular view showed the hallway silent and empty. 'Ed!'

Surely he had seen that I'd left my big bunch of keys behind? And why would he suddenly choose today to double-lock the door when he went out? He never usually did.

Bloody dementia. Death by a thousand tiny cuts.

Delving in my bag, I grabbed my mobile and rang Ed's, listening intently through the letterbox for its ring inside. But there was no sound, which either meant that Ed was out, or across at the lock – our house and Suzan's had once been two halves of the lock-keeper's cottage and our half had come with what the estate agents called 'The Studio', a small room on the now-redundant lock's island that Ed used as his man-cave. Or maybe he was in, but had his phone on silent for some reason. I called the landline and immediately heard its ring echo around the house's interior, on and on for the ten rings until the machine picked up. I sighed and redialled Ed's mobile. No response.

Snap out of it, Lynn, I thought, panic beginning to bubble. He couldn't have gone far.

I walked back out to the towpath and hurried across the narrow metal bridge, wrenching open the studio door – although there was no sign of him through the windows. It wasn't locked, so he must be somewhere near. What if he'd fallen in the river? There were no boats around, even on this sunny autumnal afternoon, and no hikers or cyclists, apart from the two I'd just seen. My house keys were sitting on the desk, so I put them in my jeans pocket.

He definitely wasn't in the office and the river was giving up none of its secrets. Heart in mouth, I glanced out on the far side of the studio, where there was a small patch of grass hidden from view by the building itself, visible only from the riverbank on the other side – and there he was.

He was sitting in a deckchair on the grass, stark naked, listening to music on his phone through earphones. Why hadn't he answered when I'd rung?

'Ed!' I shouted, banging on the window, but he didn't move. He must have had the volume up really loud. Irritated now I could see he wasn't in danger, I yelled, louder. 'ED!'

I walked out to him and poked his shoulder, finding that I was averting my eyes from the flaccid penis nestled in the dark hair surrounding it.

'What are you doing over here?' he asked, taking out his earphones and staring at me, astonished. 'I thought you were at work?'

'I was. I texted you to say I was coming back early. Quick, get inside the studio before someone sees you and calls the police! I've been calling you! Aren't you freezing?'

He scowled, waving a hand across the vast, empty expanse of river. There was only woodland on the far side. 'Nobody can see me! Only the, um, docks.'

'Ducks,' I corrected automatically. How long had he been sitting there with his dick out? Had those two cyclists seen him? There was no sign of any clothes around him or in the office, so he must have walked across starkers from the house. They must have seen him – they only passed me five minutes before.

I dashed into the studio and took an old oilskin off the back of the chair, throwing it over Ed's lap as though it was a fire blanket and his genitals were in flames.

He blinked. 'Thanks Mum,' he said, and I had no idea whether he was being sarcastic or whether he was actually mistaking me for his mother. I helped him up and fed his arms into the coat sleeves, giving him a kiss on the mouth.

He reciprocated automatically – then reared back.

'You've been drinking!'

'Well, not really,' I said. Ed had always had such a keen sense of smell. 'Not really?'

'I had a cider at lunchtime.' I didn't mention that it had been two pints.

'But you've been at *work*!' He looked utterly outraged.

'I know. But Alvin wanted to go to the pub, and wanted me to go with him. He's the boss.'

'*Alvin*,' Ed said as if it was a swear word. 'Nice cosy time in the pub, did you have?'

I wasn't sure if his syntax was out of whack because he was annoyed or because of the Pick's.

'It was OK,' I said cautiously, guiding him out of the studio and back across the iron bridge towards our house, checking that there wasn't anybody about. 'I think Alvin and I will be mates – but honestly, Ed, that's it. I don't remotely fancy him; he's the strangest-looking man I've ever met. When you meet him you'll see what I mean. And he definitely doesn't fancy me. He doesn't stop going on about how lovely his wife is and how much in love they are.'

This wasn't entirely true, but felt like the prudent thing to say. Then I remembered something else. I'd meant to tell Ed before but had forgotten: 'Oh, and he knows you! He used to be at MADS years ago, before you and I met. He remembered that Mike calls you Edna.'

Ed padded with me across the bridge in his bare feet. He had feet like *The Gruffalo*, I'd never liked them. I could see gooseflesh sweep over his legs causing the thick hair on them to spring up like brushed fur, so I focussed on that, because his face was like thunder.

'Don't remember him.'

He splashed barefoot through the muddy puddle, through the gate and up the garden path, then stopped suddenly. 'Wait, yeah I do,' he said. 'He auditioned for something I was directing. *Death of a Salesman*. Read so badly that when I stopped him, he chucked his, thingy – you know, the book thingy – on the floor and stormed out. He's a twat.'

I wondered if Ed really had remembered, or was making it up. It didn't sound like the sort of thing Alvin would do – but then I supposed I hardly knew the man.

'Really?' I said neutrally, unlocking the front door. 'Let's get you in the shower, you must be freezing – and your feet are filthy!'

'Oh stop going on,' he grumbled, but he allowed me to usher him up the stairs and into the bathroom. I turned on the shower and he dropped the coat to the floor and climbed in.

'I'm not having you going for any more drinks with your boss, because I know he wants to sleep with you,' he said, raising his voice to be heard over the water splattering off his head and shoulders. 'That's an order!'

I made a face that he couldn't see through the opaque shower curtain and, childishly, flicked exaggerated Vs at him from my position, seated on the bath mat. His behaviour reminded me of when Ben had been an irrational teenager, shouting in Ed's face at even simple requests to remove crusty cereal bowls from his bedroom, or to flush the toilet.

'All right,' I said, with no intention of obeying. I'd recently read a book on dementia care that stressed that the best way to deal with a deluded patient was to just agree with everything he said, unless it was a life-and-death situation.

Although it didn't work in this instance.

'You're patron – patronating me, you bitch!' he roared suddenly and before I even realised what was happening, he'd jumped out of the still-running shower, flailing at the plastic curtain, and launched himself at me, dripping and swearing, punching wildly at my head.

I rolled away from him and jumped up, immediately in a defensive position. The next time he lunged at me, I performed a double forearm block on him, then grabbed his elbow and twisted his arm behind his back.

'OW!' he yelled. 'Get off me, you evil cow!'

'Well, are you going to stop attacking me?' He was lucky I hadn't thrown him, but the room was too small and he was too big.

He struggled for a minute then went limp, sinking against me as I released my grip and hugged him from behind. Within seconds my t-shirt was drenched. The shower still spattered away and I felt weak with horror. I'd never even come close to doing taekwondo moves on him before. Was this what we'd come to already?

'I'm sorry,' he said eventually.

'It's not your fault.'

He turned then and kissed me full on the mouth. 'I love you, Lynn.'

'I love you too.'

'Let's get back in the ... thing. The shaver.'

'OK,' I said, stripping off my damp clothes so fast that I banged my funny bone on the towel rail.

6

By the time we got to Ben's flat, normal service had been resumed. Nobody would have been able to guess that there was anything at all wrong with Ed. Somehow this made it harder to contemplate what we had to tell Ben.

We'd waited until after dinner, a stodgy paella cooked by his girl-friend Jeanine. Ed and I sat together on Ben's black leather sofa, our hands just touching, looking meaningfully at each other over the top of Ben's iPad as he showed us hundreds of digital photos of his and Jeanine's safari trip. I loved Ed always, but there was a kind of magic in the post-coital connection we had.

Jeanine sat on the opposite sofa, with a slightly anxious expression on her face, as if we were an interview panel. She and Ben had been together a year, but she had only moved into his flat in Kingston a few weeks before and still had the air of a guest, as if she was about to ask his permission to make a cup of tea. Mind you, I thought enviously, the pair of them went on so many holidays that she probably hadn't time to work out where he kept the kettle.

I liked Jeanine. Although she had the appearance of one of Ben's stan-dard bimbo types – manicured and groomed to within an inch of her life, two great slabs of dark-brown eyebrow dominating her tiny face – she was really sweet, with a diffident, obliging manner. Ed, in a rare comment about his first wife, once said how like Shelagh Jeanine was, and I felt sad for Ben. I couldn't blame him for subconsciously seeking out a life partner to try and replace the mother he'd lost at such a young age.

'Look at the focus on that lion's head,' Ben boasted. 'You can see every whisker, and he was at least fifty metres away!'

I swallowed a yawn. Not from boredom – even though looking at

698 photographs of trees and wildlife was undisputedly dull, however impressive the zoom lens or exotic the landscape – but because I always yawned when I was in stressful situations. I Googled it once and discovered it was to do with lack of oxygen to the brain; the shallow breathing constricted the blood vessels, or something.

'Hey, guess what? I got a new job,' I said.

Ben looked disapproving, as if it was inappropriate to mention it during the slideshow. He paused the slides. 'Really? What is it?'

'Concert organiser at Hampton Uni,' I said. 'Part-time.'

'Congratulations!' Jeanine chirped, leaping up and clinking glasses with me. 'That sounds like fun.'

'I hope so,' I said. 'It'll get me out of the house anyway.'

I glanced at Ed as I said it, but he seemed to be concentrating on the photographs and didn't look up at me.

'That's great,' Ben said. 'Now, check out this hippo!'

I watched my stepson swipe proudly through the photographs with a practised finger. Ben had been thirteen years old when his mum Shelagh had gone AWOL, fifteen when I moved in and seventeen when Shelagh was finally declared dead, after Gavin Garvey confessed to her murder. I could forgive him a lot of his bad behaviour after going through what no teenager ever should, but even to this day Ben treated me with a vestige of the supercilious condescension that he'd already mastered when I first met him.

He turned out OK, though. Only twenty-four, he'd been promoted up the ranks until he was manager of a swanky car showroom in Thames Ditton, selling cars for the sort of money you could spend on a small house somewhere up north, feeling very pleased with himself. He never mentioned his mother.

I yawned again and Ben noticed. 'Sorry, am I boring you?'

His personality was so like his dad's. That was exactly what Ed would have said. The older Ben got, the more he looked like him too, except that Ben's sandy hair was already beginning to recede. I always thought how much that must piss him off, when his dad's hair was still a great luxuriant shock.

Ben was tall and strong as well, but his eyes were starting to look as though they were retreating into his skull, hooded like Ed's, the dark circles beneath them becoming more prominent. Yet despite this he had turned into a very good-looking man.

'Of course not, darling,' Ed said, on behalf of us both. 'We just...'

I heard the catch in his throat.

'...need to talk to you about something.'

Ben and Jeanine exchanged alarmed glances. 'I'll make some coffee,' Jeanine said, practically sprinting into the kitchen. I followed her, putting a hand on her arm and gesturing back towards the living room. 'Come back in? I think Ben might need you there too. And you're part of the family.'

'Is he ill?' she whispered.

'Let him tell you,' I said, leading her back by the hand – something that I'd never done with any of Ben's previous girlfriends, and certainly never with Ben himself. Jeanine submitted like a little girl, and I felt a pang that she was like the grown-up daughter I had never had. I had a flash of imagined memories: Jeanine as a wispy-haired toddler, a pink-obsessed tweenie, a stroppy teen glued to a smartphone. I'd have loved a daughter, however moody. I was holding out for grandchildren now.

But if Ed was going to die of dementia, I very much doubted that Ben would make much, if any effort at all, to keep in touch with me, so perhaps I wouldn't even get a step-grandchild to cuddle.

Ed and I never talk about the baby I lost.

He stood up and I hovered nearby. Ben and Jeanine were now sitting together gaping up at us.

'What, Dad? You're making me all worried now.'

Ed gazed out of the window at two motionless cranes. Ben had bought off-plan, in Priory Vale, a bland luxury apartment in a development with more identical buildings springing up every month.

Ben was getting irritated now, as was his wont. 'Dad!'

'Sorry, Benj. The thing is ... oh God, this isn't easy to say...'

I saw Ben's knuckles turn white. Poor boy, he really did love his dad.

'Is it cancer?'

'No! It's not that – it's nothing life-threatening.'

Yes, it bloody well is, I thought. I'd looked it up: the average life span of someone diagnosed with Pick's disease was eight years. If that wasn't a death sentence I didn't know what was.

I was feeling a lot more pessimistic than I had been last night. I slipped my hand into Ed's and squeezed it, feeling his big fingers squishing my diamond. My emotions were up and down every five minutes; it was exhausting.

'You're emigrating!' Ben tried, plastering a fake smile on his face. 'That's OK, don't look so stressed, I've always thought you two would end up living in a shack on a beach somewhere hot – no worries, we'll come and visit, won't we, Jeanine?'

When Ed didn't reply, Ben's shoulders drooped.

'Do you want me to tell them?' I offered. It was as if Ed couldn't physically form the words. But he shook his head and took a deep breath.

'I've got what Pops had,' he blurted. 'Pick's Disease. We found out last week.'

There was a long, long silence. Ben kept looking between Ed and me, eyes narrowed in disbelief, as if he was waiting for one of us to go, *Just kidding*! Then he leaned forward and hid his face in his hands, his elbows resting on his big thighs. His shoulders began to shake. 'Oh shit. Oh fuck, Dad. No. Not that. Not like Pops...'

My heart went out to him. He must have the same kind of traumatic memories of his grandfather as I had of the man, but so much more painful because of their close relationship – and with the added shadow cast over him of the knowledge it was hereditary.

Ben jumped up and hugged Ed tightly, sobbing into his neck like a little boy. The two of them stood there like that for a long time while I went and sat next to Jeanine. This time it was Jeanine who took my hand.

'We'll help you,' she said, and I started to cry, too.

7

Our friends April and Mike bought *Fringilla* five years ago, when Mike sold his home thermostat company for somewhere north of 300 million pounds, part of a new wave in technology called the Internet of Things – bins that told the council when they needed emptying, streetlights that measured pollution, radiators that sent you email updates; basically, connecting things instead of people to the internet. Ironically, Mike was the least computer-literate person I knew. He couldn't even cope with Facebook.

Fringilla was a beautiful thirty-foot vintage motor yacht, all varnished teak interior and chrome fittings. They had her moored up at the next lock along to ours and they took her out most weekends, until the days grew too short. I loved getting an invitation aboard, and this would probably be one of her last outings of the year. Even so, I wasn't looking forward to this one so much, though, because of what we had to tell them. They were amongst our oldest friends. Mike, April and Ed went way back, from their am-dram days.

Fringilla's white hull appeared round the bend downstream at the appointed time as we were walking along the towpath – Mike was almost anally punctual.

April was at the wheel. She waved at us, her face blurry behind the plastic windows that kept the bow deck area warm and protected. Mike climbed around the edge to the prow, in preparation of mooring up by the lock. He threw the rope over towards Ed, clearly expecting Ed to pick it up and secure it around the bollard, but Ed just stared blankly at it.

'Ed!' I put down the wine carrier and lunged for the rope just before it slid into the river. 'Sorry,' I laughed fakely, as Mike raised his eyebrows.

'Too much *vino collapso* last night, Edna?' he called. Ed finally snapped out of his reverie and came to help me moor the boat.

We climbed aboard, passing April a bag with the dessert and wine down from the dock. She hugged us and gestured over to the table built into the bow, which she'd decorated beautifully with a lace table-cloth, linen napkins, a selection of olives and homemade cheese straws, and a bottle of champagne in a cooler, glistening with condensation.

April looked stunning, as usual. She had a knack with subtle make-up that always made her look about twenty years younger, giving her the same peachy bloom she'd had when I first met her. Her hair was expertly highlighted and her jeans were those expensive ones from the boutique up the road, costing about three hundred pounds. I bought all *my* jeans from Next, their 'Lift and Shape' range.

She smiled at me and I suspected she'd had her teeth bleached again – they were looking dazzlingly white. Good on her, I thought. I'd do the same if I had the sort of unlimited funds Mike's role in the Internet of Things had bestowed on them.

'Do the honours, love, would you? I've just got to help Mike with the salad and then we'll set off. We'll pootle back upriver for a few miles, shall we, then moor up by the willow tree and eat there, catch the last rays of sun. Gorgeous evening, isn't it?'

It was; like summer's last hurrah. I eased the cork out of the cham-pagne, muffling its pop with a napkin, then filled four glasses an inch at a time, so as not to waste a drop. I carried one through to April as she began to chop tiny red chillis in the galley – she was always sous-chef to Mike – then headed back to fetch two others, which I took to the boys, who were both at the stern looking out over the still river. Mike was smoking a cigarette.

'Still "not smoking", I see.' I handed him a glass. 'It'll kill you, you know.'

Mike grinned and took the fizz.

'Maybe I should take up smoking,' Ed commented to me.

I thrust the other glass into his outstretched hand. 'Here you go, misery-guts. Cheers!'

I'd been pretending that this was just one of our numerous nights on the river – but Ed's comment reminded me what we had to tell them later.

The trouble with pretending everything was fine was that, when it hit me afresh that it wasn't, it felt like a punch that took my breath away.

Mike finished his fag and went to cook the beef strips for the salad. As he squeezed past me in the doorway between the galley and the stern, I felt his belly brush briefly against mine and his nicotine breath waft in my face.

I did sometimes wonder what April saw in him, apart from his money. He wasn't handsome like Ed; he was the same height as me – just five foot seven – and his stomach looked huge and taut under his striped shirt. He was losing his hair and he had a squint. If April had seen him on a dating site, I was sure she would have clicked past him to someone taller and better-looking.

He could be a moody bugger, too, but April loved him, and that was what mattered. She treated him like a teddy bear, cuddling and fussing over him. And they'd been together for twenty-two years, far longer than me and Ed.

'How are the twins?' I asked her, as we slid on to the padded bench seat around the table. The late summer sun was low and bright in the sky, skidding across the water and massaging the back of my head with its evening fingers.

'Oh, fine. Enjoying their gap year. Monty's in London working in an architects' office and Caspar's getting ready to go and work as a ski instructor for the season.'

Sometimes I wondered how we were such good friends. We were so different. I had never been skiing in my life and wouldn't have dreamt of naming my children Caspar and Monty, if I'd ever been lucky enough to have any. April was all boarding school jolly-hockey-sticks, nine-hundred-pound handbags and, since she quit her NHS job and Mike retired, a permanent golden tan from their numerous exotic holidays.

It was hard not to envy them. Ed and I went on camping holidays and stayed in B&Bs, recently only in the UK or anywhere in Europe reachable by ferry and car, because of this weird fear of flying he had developed over the past couple of years.

Still, I wouldn't really want April's life. Until recently I had been very happy with my own choices.

'How's things with Benjy?' April enquired in return.

I laughed, because April knew full well that Ben couldn't bear being called Benjy any more. 'He's OK. Still with Jeanine. She's so lovely; I hope they get married. We saw them the other day...'

I tailed off, remembering how horrible it had been to break the news. And now we had to break the same bad news to April and Mike.

'You haven't asked me about my new job!' I teased, pretending to be huffy to disguise how I felt.

'Oh, sorry!' April laughed, threw an arm around my shoulders and kissed my cheek. 'I'm a bad friend. How is your new job?'

'Great! I love it so far,' I said, wiping off the smear of lipgloss I could feel she'd left on my face. 'My boss is a bit eccentric, but seems really nice. Good fun. Drinks too much, but don't we all? I didn't think I'd be allowed boozy lunches at work, but it seems it's par for the course.'

'Beef's marinating,' said Mike, joining us. He was blinking excessively and at first I thought he was just squinting into the low sun, until he loomed over April. 'I've got an eyelash or something, darling, can you see it? It's driving me mad.'

April tipped her shades back on top of her head and grasped his cheeks between her palms, peering into his eye, while I went to check that Ed was OK. He looked miles away, sitting gazing out at the sunset, contemplatively sipping his fizz.

There was a sudden roar of pain that made me jump: 'For fuck's SAKE, woman, you were chopping chillis! Did you not wash your hands?'

Mike started jumping around the boat as though he had a firework in his pants, clutching his eye and swearing.

April leaped up, knocking over her glass. 'Sorry, sorry, I forgot. Really sorry, honey, quick, splash water in it...'

'You STUPID COW!' yelled Mike, brushing her aside and racing to the galley to rinse his eye with a bottle of mineral water. He couldn't get enough in using cupped hands, so he stuck his head in the sink, tilted it upwards and poured the water over his face, where it flowed through his hair and splashed all around the galley.

Ed and I exchanged glances, both of us getting up to give April a brief discreet hug. She made a face. 'It's fine,' she mouthed to me. 'He doesn't mean it.'

She followed Mike into the galley, handing him a towel and soothing him until he calmed down.

Eventually they returned, Mike's cheeks the same bright red as his bloodshot eye. 'Sorry about that, folks. Didn't mean to yell at the old Trouble.'

Ed looked puzzled. 'Trouble?'

Mike slapped him lightly around the head. 'Edna! Keep up, mate – Trouble! Trouble and Strife: wife? Not like you to miss that one. Right, shall we set off upriver for a little tootle before dinner?'

I cleared my throat. Ed nodded at me and I put a hand on Mike's arm. 'Before we go, we've got something to tell you both. Will you come and sit down for a minute?'

I moved along the bench to make room for Mike and April, who looked concerned. 'Oh yes. You said on the phone you wanted to say something. You're not splitting up, are you?' April asked.

'No, nothing like that.'

A big Dutch barge chugged slowly past, making *Fringilla* rock gently from side to side in its wake, as though the little cruiser was trying to comfort us all, I thought, as I gathered my words.

I took a swig of champagne. Perhaps it was the alcohol in my system, or the charged atmosphere from Mike's outburst, but I found myself unable even to try and sugar-coat it.

'Ed's been diagnosed with dementia. Frontotemporal, same as his dad had. It's called Pick's Disease. We've been concerned he might have it for a while – Ed went to the doctor about it months ago– but we only just got the diagnosis. You're the only ones we've told, apart from Ben and Jeanine.'

And Suzan next door, I thought, and my new boss, but I didn't want Ed to know that.

There was a shocked silence around the table, broken only by the sound of the floats protecting *Fringilla*'s sides as they knocked gently against the wall of the quay. A gust of chilly evening wind blew through the gaps where the plastic curtains hadn't been fully zipped up, and I shivered.

Mike had a really peculiar expression on his face; blank and almost accusatory in the second that he stared at Ed, and I felt angry with him before I realised that it was just shock. Then his face crumpled, his bloodshot eye and downturned lips making it look as though he was already weeping, and he seemed to gather himself. He reached out and grasped Ed's hand, squeezing it so hard that Ed winced. 'Oh mate. I'm so sorry. I thought you've been acting a bit funny lately...'

'It's OK,' Ed said. 'We've all got to go some time, right? And at least this way I won't know anything about it. It's Lynn and Ben I feel sorry for.'

His eyes filled and then all four of us were crying.

'Are they sure?' asked April, who had gone very white.

'As sure as they can be without doing scans. He won't have the scans because of his claustrophobia.'

'He?' Ed interrupted, trying to smile. 'Who's "he"? The, er, dog's dinner?'

'Cat's mother,' Mike said.

Ed glossed over his mistake. 'Oh, come on, everyone. It's not the end of the world. I'm sure they'll find a cure in a few minutes anyway. No. A few ... oh fuck it, what do I mean?'

'Years,' said April, dabbing the corners of her eyes with a tissue. 'I did wonder why you kept doing that. Missing words, and so on.'

I paused. 'Listen. We don't know what's going to happen. It might develop really slowly and we'll have loads more good years. Ed's dad lived it with for about five years until he had to go into a home. We've just all got to stay positive.' The words sounded hollow even as they left my mouth. 'Can we go? We'll miss the sunset otherwise.'

'Yes, sure.' Mike jumped up and untied the moorings, clearly glad of something to do. He still had a strange dazed look on his face as he pushed the boat away from the quay and leaped back on board.

April started the engine and took the helm as *Fringilla* chugged upstream, the evening sun fracturing into a million pieces on the water as our passage disturbed its calm reflection.

It was a far more sombre evening than our boat trips usually were, and I wondered if perhaps we should have waited until the end of the night to tell them. But I couldn't imagine breaking it to them when we'd been laughing and joking and getting pissed. It was better this way.

After we had eaten, Mike navigated us back downriver towards the lock. It was pitch dark by then.

The first bang came as we were nearly back. 'Oh look, fireworks!' April called. 'Someone must be having a party.'

A huge burst of golden rain showered down almost on top of us, reflecting in the water when Mike cut the engine so we could watch.

'Look, Ed.' I nudged him, but he didn't move. He was staring away from the display, out into the darkness. Fireworks continued to explode out of the clear black sky all around in a riot of noise and colour, but Ed remained stubbornly facing the other direction.

It didn't matter. So what if he didn't want to watch the fireworks?

I realised for the first time how much of this whole dementia experience would be dictated by my own reactions and behaviour. I had to pull myself together and stop imagining that strangers were creeping round the house, for a start. It just wasn't helpful. As long as I carried on as normal, then things would remain normal. Wouldn't they?

I supposed it just came down to what my definition of normal actually was – particularly in the case of our marriage.

8

Things calmed down a bit in the couple of weeks after the madness of the naked-deckchair-sitting and Ed taking a swing at me in the shower. I convinced myself that I must have imagined the noises in the house that night, the day of Ed's diagnosis.

Even when I suggested it, Ed continued to insist that I didn't quit my job – which was a relief, as I'd have hated to admit defeat, just yet anyway; and Suzan confirmed that he was either with her during the day, or, whenever she checked on him, watching TV at home or pottering around in the garden. I still worried about him falling in the river or wandering off, but I accepted that I couldn't keep an eye on him twenty-four seven.

I asked Suzan if Ed had been with her that time I heard someone sounding like him on the radio, on my first day at work, and she looked at me like I'd lost the plot.

'Are you serious? Lynn, I can't remember what time he went home that day – not till about threeish I think – but even if it was earlier, I really don't think he's capable of taking part in a radio phone-in, do you?'

She was right. The man on the radio had been lucid and informed – there was no way it could have been Ed. He just wasn't capable of that kind of intellectual debate any longer, and it was so hard to accept. I knew it was just wishful thinking on my part.

He hadn't even been able to give me more details about this clinical trial, so I decided to do some investigating – when I was at work, though, with no danger of him overhearing and accusing me of interfering. The sooner he started on the trial, the sooner there was a chance of halting the damage.

It was a beautiful October Monday, sunny, but with a chill bite to the air heralding the changing season. I went and sat on the stone step of the terrace at the back of Fairhurst, glancing behind me up at the house to make sure there were no open windows for my voice to drift through and be overheard. The wintry sun warmed my face as I dialled Mountain Way's number and got through to Deshmukh's secretary.

'I'm sorry,' she said, in a singsongy voice that slightly set my teeth on edge. 'Mr Deshmukh's in with someone at the moment.'

'I wonder if you can help me?' I asked. 'My husband, Ed Naismith, is a patient of his, and he was telling me that a colleague of his, Mr Deshmukh's, I mean, rang him up and invited him to participate in some kind of secret clinical trial. Because of my husband's condition – he's recently been diagnosed with Pick's Disease – he couldn't remember any more details, so I thought I'd try and find out myself. I'd want to know what sort of drugs they were planning to give him, how long for, what it involves, who's running it, et cetera? Ed can't remember the doctor's name. He's waiting for an email but doesn't seem to have had anything yet.'

There was a puzzled silence. 'I don't know anything about that, I'm afraid,' the voice came back, in a less singsongy manner. 'And I'm sure I would do. I've not heard of a clinical trial for Pick's. Let me take your number and I'll call you back when I've had a chance to speak to him.'

I thanked her and terminated the call, turning my face up to the weak, wintry rays. I could hear a woodpecker drilling for insects on one of the bare tree trunks across the lawns, and I wondered if it was the same one I'd heard the day I came for my interview. Could Ed be confused about who had rung him up? Maybe nobody at all had rung, and he'd dreamt it.

The secretary called me back an hour or so later, as I was dusting the music school's Balinese gamelan. As with the purchasing and consuming of alcohol and the regular massaging of my boss's ego, this was not on my job description, but it needed doing, so Alvin had sent me in with a duster and a can of Pledge. The instrument, collectively, was huge, a whole room full of different-sized South-East Asian bells and gongs, and I was the only person in there, so I was able to talk freely.

'It's Becky from Mountain Way,' she announced self-importantly.

'Hi Becky.' I put her on speakerphone and carried on rubbing a rack of cowbell-type things. It was all very dusty – the cleaners had presumably also decided it wasn't in their remit.

'Mr Deshmukh says he doesn't know who rang your husband. He doesn't know anything about a drugs trial for Pick's – and says that to the best of his knowledge, no such trial exists. He hasn't given your number to any of his colleagues – and he wouldn't do, without your permission.'

'Oh. I see. Well, Ed must have been mistaken. I'll ask him about it later. Thanks for getting back to me.'

'No problem!' she sang.

I turned back to the task in hand, feeling miserable. This must be what it felt like for Ed, too, a new and unpleasant world where things didn't quite stack up in the way they ought to. It was disorientating and confusing and my heart went out to him. I wanted to go home, cocoon us both in the safety of our bedroom and not come out again until I knew the pieces would all fit together properly once more.

When I did get home that evening, Ed was lying in the dark on top of our unmade bed, staring at the ceiling, wearing only his dressing gown. The whole room stank of talcum powder, but even that didn't quite mask the musty smell of the towelling gown.

'Hi darling,' I said, noticing as I bent to stroke the hair back from his forehead that my fingernails were filthy from dusting. We made a grubby pair. 'Let me go and wash my hands, I've been cleaning a gamelan today – bet you don't know what that is when it's at home.'

He didn't reply and I sighed inwardly. It was like communicating with a rock, I thought as I walked into our ensuite. A *teenage* rock, I concluded, surveying the bathroom. The bathmat was sopping, the shower curtain had been half ripped off its rail, there was a spilled bottle of bubble bath on the floor, a wet towel in the tub and Ed's large footprints were a dark silhouette in a white settle of talc. It looked as though he'd dumped a whole tub of it over his head. Ed was the only person I knew who still used talc.

'You've had a bath, I see,' I said, raising my voice over the sound of the running taps as I scrubbed at my hands. 'By the way, I called Deshmukh's secretary today to ask about that clinical trial. She said she asked him, but he didn't know anything about it.'

There was a long pause, during which I tidied up the bathroom and went and lay on the bed next to him. The pillows smelled stale too and I realised how long it had been since either of us had changed the sheets.

'I got it wrong. It wasn't him. It was Bill,' Ed eventually announced cryptically.

'Who's Bill?'

'You know, Bill, who I went to junior school with. No, junior doctor school.'

'Medical school?'

'Yes. Medical school. I forgot. It was him who rang me and told me about this trial.'

'How did he know you had Pick's?'

'I emailed him,' Ed said, the 'duh' audible in the statement. 'He's a doctor that does research. What's it called?'

'A medical scientist?' I wasn't sure either.

'Yeah. I knew he does that kind of stuff. I thought he could help me and he says he might be able to if I take these drugs.'

'What's his surname?'

Ed's shoulders moved in a shrug. 'Bill ... Bill ... Can't remember.'

I rolled over onto my right side to look at him. 'You told me it was a colleague of Deshmukh's. I really want to know what drugs he's proposing to put you on. And you'll need to run it past Deshmukh and Dr Lark; it'll need to go on your medical records. I definitely think you should do it, but I'm worried, Ed. You hear some horror stories about side-effects in these trials, things going catastrophically wrong ... We need all the details!'

He rolled towards me, putting his arms round me and pulling me close. He smelled of shower gel and the cloying sweetness of too much talc.

'You worry too much. What have I got to lose?'

'It's just all so vague. I'd be a lot happier if I knew the details.'

He kissed me. 'OK. I'll ask Bill to email you.'

'Please do – but I thought he was going to email *you*? Oh, hello! What's this?'

I grinned, feeling his penis sticking through the open dressing gown and rubbing against my leg, and Ed grinned back. I thought it was the first time he had properly looked at me for days. I manoeuvred myself into a better position and we kissed again, harder.

Two minutes later we were both naked and I forgot about the trial and all my worries. As long as we always had this, we'd be OK. Everything would be OK.

9

'I don't want you to go to work today,' Ed said, looming up behind me in his pyjamas as I put on lipstick in the hall mirror. 'Why are you all tarted up?' He sniffed my neck. 'And why are you going in so early? You're wearing perfume.'

'I always wear perfume!'

I wasn't 'all tarted up,' but I was wearing my interview suit. He was right, though, it was an hour earlier than I usually left. I was surprised – it had been some weeks since he'd had any awareness of what time it was.

'It's open day today,' I added, zipping the lipstick back in my make-up bag. 'Got to go in early to get everything ready. There's a load of sixth-formers coming to look round and a lunchtime Big Band concert to put on.'

'Will *he* be there?' Ed glowered at me in the mirror.

'If you mean Alvin, then yeah, of course. He's the head of depart-ment. Right, got to go, love. If I don't leave now the traffic will be awful. See you later.'

I turned to kiss Ed on the lips but he moved away, tinkering with the old barometer on the wall by the front door. He tapped it, but it hadn't worked for years.

By noon, the open day was in full swing in the recording studio opposite Fairhurst House. Fifty nervous-looking seventeen-year-olds, accompanied by one or both parents, were being given the jovial welcome speech by Alvin. I was hovering by the foyer doors to welcome any latecomers, and the band were all set up and sound-checked for their two o'clock set. Everything was going to plan. One of the other lecturers, Sandy, and I were unwrapping cling film from the sandwiches I'd made first thing and uncorking the wine. More wine. Needless to say, this was Alvin's initiative. I wondered if open days at other unis offered this much free booze?

'Righty-ho,' Sandy said, pouring himself the first plastic cupful as if this was something he'd been looking forward to all day. It probably was, as well. He was a short, stocky man with a faint Scottish accent, bald but with masses of grey body hair crawling out of every shirt opening – collar, neck, sleeves. He always wore the same grey trousers and academic-issue tanktop from circa 1979, and Alvin scornfully referred to him as 'a hopeless lush' – rich, coming from him.

Just as Sandy raised the cup to his lips we heard a faint banging and what sounded like yelling coming from outside.

'What fresh hell is this?' muttered Sandy, scratching his hairy chest. He seemed to be, from my brief acquaintance with him, very much a glass-half-full kind of guy. He reluctantly put down his wine and we went out to investigate.

To my utter, abject horror, the source of the banging noise was my husband, hammering on the huge studio windows, shouting abuse at the top of his voice. As Sandy and I ran out to try and drag him away, I noticed that every single person inside the studio had swivelled in their seats and was staring out at Ed, Alvin's talk forgotten. I couldn't believe it.

'Ed!' I grabbed his arm and pulled, but he was immoveable, a furious light in his eyes, his fists red from banging on the thick glass. 'What are you doing? Stop!'

'You know this man?' Sandy asked, seizing his other arm. Ed tried to shake him off but Sandy's grip was tighter than mine.

'He's my husband,' I confessed through gritted teeth. 'He's not well. I'm so sorry.'

At that point, Alvin burst through the double doors, his face contorted and puce, energy rolling in almost visible waves off him. I imagined I could see both men's rage massing above their heads, like two storm fronts colliding.

'You leave my wife alone, you cheating piece of shit!' Ed yelled in Alvin's face. 'I know what you're fucking up to, behind my back!'

Alvin's fury turned briefly to astonishment. *'What?'*

I tugged his sleeve, puce with mortification. 'This is Ed, Alvin. My Ed. I'm really sorry, this is a nightmare. I had no idea he was coming.'

Or how he got here, I thought. I had the car, so he couldn't have driven. 'Come on, Ed, please. I'll take you home.'

Ed wriggled out of Alvin and Sandy's grips and I lunged for him, grabbing his arm to try and incapacitate him with a taekwondo move – but he lashed out, catching his thumbnail on the side of my face. I felt the blood, hot and thick, begin to slide down under my eye and instinctively bent double, my palm to my cheek.

That was when it all escalated. Alvin tried to grab Ed and force his arm up behind his back, but although Alvin was taller, Ed was a much bigger, stronger man. He punched Alvin hard in the stomach, causing him to stagger and topple like a newborn giraffe, ricocheting off a wooden pillar outside the front doors of the studio. By now the prospective students and their parents had abandoned any pretence at discretion and were crowding up against the windows, as though this was a show put on for their entertainment, one of the official open day activities.

Alvin hit the deck, hard, and I waited for him to jump up – but he didn't. He lay motionless and I realised that he must have hit his head on the pillar. Oh my God, I thought, Ed's killed my boss. In front of an audience.

Thankfully Alvin stirred and moaned, and struggled to a sitting position, dust all over his jacket and his glasses hanging skew-whiff from one ear. He clutched his head but I was the only one bleeding. Ed, admittedly, did look as ashen with shock as the rest of us. Sandy handed me his hankie – of course he was the type to have a pocket handkerchief – and I pressed it against my cheek as I crouched down and touched Alvin's shoulder.

'Are you OK?'

He nodded, anger replacing the shock. 'Are you? You're bleeding.'

'I'm sorry,' Ed said, to the back of Alvin's head. 'I didn't mean to do that.'

Alvin grabbed my arm and hauled himself back up to standing. He jabbed his forefinger into Ed's chest and opened his mouth to speak, when he was interrupted by the shrill bell of the studio fire alarm, shortly joined by the fainter sound of the Fairhurst House alarm from across the car park – the two worked in tandem. The double doors opened and all the guests began to pour out, the sixth-formers looking excited and their parents looking anxious.

'Oh FUCK,' Alvin hissed. 'What idiot set that off? Now we're going to have the fucking fire brigade here on top of everything else!'

I was just relieved that he'd been distracted from another confrontation with Ed, and took a firm hold on Ed's unresisting elbow.

'And the police, I'm afraid,' Sandy added, tapping his mobile screen. He'd obviously dialled 999 when it all kicked off. My heart sank. He slid back towards the studio and for a second I thought he was going to retrieve his wine, but instead he stood by the open studio doors directing the emerging throng: 'This way, please. It's just a drill, no cause for alarm. Please head down to the designated Fire Assembly Point – those two pine trees by the gate. Thank you.'

Margaret appeared from Fairhurst House, her narrow frame swamped by a yellow hi-vis jacket. She looked simultaneously appalled and self-important and held a megaphone in her left hand as she strode down towards the pine trees accompanied by a straggling band of students.

Then with impressive speed two fire engines appeared, drawing up outside the house just as Margaret began to bellow at all our confused guests through the megaphone.

'False alarm, ladies and gentlemen, false alarm! There is no fire. One of the alarms has been mistakenly activated. But please remain at the Fire Assembly Point and await further instructions.'

The fire engines pulled up outside the studio and Sandy went over to speak to the firefighters, which was when more sirens heralded the arrival of a police car with its blues and twos flashing. I groaned.

This was chaos. I was sure I'd be sacked immediately – open days were vitally important in our recruitment drive, and if we didn't recruit the numbers, then we'd all lose our jobs.

'I'll talk to the police,' Alvin said, so grimly that I visualised my P45. I nodded, steering Ed over to a small grassy bank near the Assembly Point. We sat down – or rather, I dragged him down by the hand. My legs were a feeling a bit wobbly but I didn't want to let go of him.

The fight had gone out of him, though. He looked lost and almost close to tears. Not that I could bring myself to feel sympathy for him; not right at that moment. In fact, for the first time ever, I seriously considered divorcing him. I did not sign up for this, I thought. The cut on my cheek was throbbing now, and when I took away the handkerchief I saw that it was ruined, almost completely scarlet.

Ed turned and peered at the cut. 'Tell me I didn't do that,' he said, shamefaced.

'You did.'

'Oh.'

'Yes. What are you doing here, Ed?'

'I don't know. I don't even know how I got here. I just wanted to see you. Then I saw him and felt all upset that you were going to leave me.'

I gave a guilty start that he had articulated the words I'd thought – not that I'd be leaving him for Alvin, of course. I shifted uncomfortably on the cold, damp grass, feeling it safe enough to let go of Ed's hand.

'The police will want to speak to you,' I said. I could see them now, taking notes as Sandy described what had happened, gesticulating towards us. 'You punched my boss. He fell and hit his head – I thought you'd killed him.'

Ed snorted and I glared at him. 'I hope you're not laughing.'

'I'm not,' he said meekly.

'He seems OK now though,' I commented, watching as Alvin began to usher the prospective students and their parents back into the studio. 'Show's over, ladies and gents. A sandwich lunch is served in the studio foyer!'

I could tell he was still livid, though.

'Come on,' I said to Ed. 'Let's go into my office so I can find a plaster.'

It was mercifully quiet back in the main building. The alarms had stopped. The current students had all gone back into their lectures. All members of staff were either teaching or involved in trying to salvage the open day.

'Sit there,' I ordered Ed, pointing at the chair next to my desk while I retrieved the first aid kit and located a plaster large enough to cover the cut.

'Oh shit, Lynn,' he said, sinking his head onto his crossed forearms on my desk. 'I hate this.'

I finished sticking on the plaster, checking its position on my cheek-bone in the mirror over the office fireplace. My face was chalky-white and my blonde hair looked ratty, greyish-green. I appeared to have aged about ten years since the last time I'd looked in a mirror, that morning at home when I put on my lipstick. My eyes had gone from green to grey, a sure sign that I was either tired or distressed.

'I hate it too,' I said, the pity for him finally flooding in. I went over and hugged him, inhaling the scent of spent adrenaline and yesterday's deodorant.

'I'm really sorry. I love you.'

He turned and wrapped his arms around my waist, and it reminded me of coming back from the interview and changing out of my suit – the same suit. I shouldn't have accepted the job. It was wrong and selfish of me.

'I love you too,' I said automatically.

Margaret stormed into the office, face thunderous and her cropped hair in punk spikes from where she'd run her hands through it. She was so angry that she misjudged the distance of the doorframe, and banged her shoulder against the carved wood, almost bouncing off it as she ripped off her hi-vis jacket and threw it onto the floor. For a moment I thought she was going to jump up and down on it, but she just marched over to her desk and slammed the megaphone down.

'Police, ambulances, fire engines. Brawls, concussion!' She was shouting, a weird high-pitched tone of strangled fury. 'On an open day. This is a disaster!' I didn't know if she was aware of the cause of the disaster – but I wasn't about to fill her in. She didn't appear to have noticed Ed, or perhaps she was just ignoring him. She hurled herself into her chair, her long legs splayed out.

'Accident report forms, in triplicate. Security complaining. Students complaining. Parents complaining. Staff complaining. I've had enough!'

I glanced over at Ed and jerked my head to indicate that he should follow me out – I didn't want the police to turn up and start grilling him with Margaret there. When he got up, Margaret narrowed her eyes at him in a way that indicated to me that she had in fact already been fully appraised of who he was.

I suspected I might not be working at Hampton Uni for much longer.

10

'Hello. I'm Martine Knocker from Surrey Police, we met earlier?' said the petite uniformed woman on the doorstep, smiling at us.

I'd known she was coming, of course. She was the policewoman I'd spoken to on campus. As we were leaving Fairhurst House, I'd asked if they could come and take a statement from Ed at home, as a concession to his illness.

'Martine Knockers? Is that a joke? Are you a WPC?' Ed demanded, not even shaking her proffered hand. I'd been the one to open the front door but Ed had loomed up behind me, and I saw a brief look of alarm flit across Martine's face before her smile immediately returned.

After his brief spell of remorse, anything and everything had been getting on Ed's nerves. We'd been home an hour waiting for the ring on the doorbell and on top of his irritation, I felt ashamed and on edge, terrified that Alvin or the university were going to press charges. I'd texted Alvin explaining I was taking Ed home and asking if he was OK. He said yes, but his reply had been curt. I wanted to suggest he went to A&E to make sure he didn't have concussion, but didn't dare.

'We don't use the term WPC anymore,' said Martine calmly, but a nerve ticked in her cheek. 'I'm just a PC.' She was young and slim and sort of attractive, although I realised she was one of those people who smiled constantly, perhaps because someone had once told her she was so much prettier when she smiled and now it was as if she couldn't stop; she'd trained her muscles to have 'smile' as their default. I hoped Surrey police never used her to break the news to families of the death of a loved one.

Ed snorted. 'You're a bit short for a WPC,' was his parting shot before he turned and stalked back into the house, stomping up the stairs. Martine blushed, but continued to smile.

'I'm sorry about my husband,' I said, ushering her in. I lowered my voice. 'As I mentioned on campus, he's not well. He was recently diagnosed with a form of dementia, and it seems to be having an effect on his inhibitions. Not a good effect,' I added miserably. 'He tried to have a pee in the produce section in Tesco's last week too.' Luckily I'd spotted him undoing his flies just in time. 'Thank you for agreeing to come over to us. I'm so sorry this happened.'

Ed's voice bellowed down from the first floor landing. 'Don't you fucking apologise for me!'

I made eye contact with Martine and we both ignored the remark. 'Can I get you a coffee, or tea?'

'Thank you, tea would be lovely. Milk, no sugar ... Sorry to hear about your husband's diagnosis.'

I checked – yes, she was smiling as she said it. Had nobody ever told the woman that it wasn't appropriate to smile *all* the time?

'It's a challenge. Do come through.' I led her into the kitchen and sat her at the table while busying myself with mugs and kettle.

Martine carefully took off her hat – a snazzy-looking bowler-type felt thing – and placed it on the table next to her, before smoothing down her already immaculate dark bob, and I had to take a deep breath and resist a sudden temptation to smash my fist into the hat's crown. It would be no good to anybody if Ed and I were both this irascible and impatient.

When I turned back with the teas, including one for Ed, Martine had taken out a notebook and pencil and was unfolding an A4 sheet. I recognised this as a printout of an online crime reporting form. Had Alvin filled it out, or someone else? Margaret, I suspected.

'Could I ask your husband to join us?' Martine glanced nervously towards the stairs.

As if he'd been listening outside the door, Ed appeared and slid obediently into a chair opposite Martine. He must have sneaked back down the stairs again.

He seemed to be getting good at sneaking around – I kept finding him in unexpected places in the house. Him and the cat. I was half expecting to open the airing-cupboard door and find Ed curled up asleep on the clean towels, or squeezed into the small space between the arm of the sofa and the wall.

I smiled encouragingly at him, placing Martine's tea on a coaster on the coffee table.

'Fortunately, Professor Cornelius has stated that he doesn't wish to press charges,' Martine said. I exhaled, relief pushing out much of my panic in a toxic cloud. Perhaps I wouldn't have to leave after all.

'That's great,' I said. 'Isn't it, Ed?'

He shrugged and turned away. Martine looked sternly – as sternly as she could – at him, her pencil poised over her pad. 'I have a statement from Professor Cornelius and from another witness, Dr Sandy Owden. I will still need to take some details from yourself, though, Mr Naismith, and issue you with a formal warning.'

'*Doctor* Naismith,' he corrected her. 'I'm a doctor too – a proper one, not one of those pony academics.'

'A what academic?' Martine smiled nervously.

'Pony. As in pony and trap; crap. It's cockney rhyming slang. Ed,' I said, in my sternest voice. 'You're very lucky that Alvin's not taking it any further.'

He scowled, but allowed Martine to question him for the next ten minutes: no, he hadn't meant to hurt Alvin, no, he hadn't gone there to confront him, he wanted to see me, yes, he'd got the bus there ... I was impressed that he'd managed that much.

Martine was still smiling away, jotting down notes in her pad, her head bent over it. I noticed that her hair was thinning slightly on top, and felt a pang for the girl. I half expected to see her tongue poking earnestly from a corner of her mouth in concentration, and hoped she had someone at home to look after her. Mum and Dad, probably, I thought, glancing at her bare fingers.

'If no charges are being pressed,' I asked, 'then why do you need to write all this down?'

'Just to have it on record, for the formal warning. I agree, to be honest. So much paperwork! But hey ho! We have to go through the motions.'

'Hey ho,' Ed said, and he and I exchanged glances, sharing a moment's complicit amusement.

Martine glanced up, her smile dropping, just for a moment. 'I have been informed, by the way, of your history,' she commented almost casually.

'Whose history?' I wanted to report this stupid tactless girl.

'Mr Naismith's.'

Ed waved sardonically at her. 'Again, WPC Knockers, I *am* here. And as I just said, it's Doctor Naismith. Would you care to elborate, I mean – elaborate?'

Martine blushed to the roots of her hair. I could actually see her scalp turn pink. 'I'm referring to the disappearance of Mrs Naismith,' she said. 'In 2005, I believe?'

It had to come out some time, I supposed. 'Yes. But this obviously has absolutely nothing to do with that. You presumably also know that a homeless guy, Gavin Garvey, eventually confessed to her murder and was jailed a few years later?'

It felt strange discussing it in front of Ed, like skating on thin ice. Neither of us ever spoke about it and nor, to my knowledge, did Ben. Poor Shelagh had been locked away in a metaphoric box, never to be opened again.

I thought back to my first visit to Ed's house, how there had only been one photograph of Shelagh on display; her, Ed and Ben in a care-fully-posed studio-lit portrait printed onto a canvas block. No other pictures, none of her holding Benjy as a baby, no holiday snaps of the three of them. It couldn't have been healthy for Ben, surely?

He did have a photo of her now in his flat, just a small faded Pola-roid tucked into the corner of a mirror, but only the one. I discreetly studied it whenever I got the chance. Shelagh had her head flung back, laughing at something that an invisible bystander was saying to her. There was a full wine glass in her hand, and her throat was exposed, long, creamy, white, like it was inviting the slash of a knife blade. That was how Garvey claimed he had killed her, but he also claimed that he couldn't 'remember' where her body was, so there had never been any proof of this, or any DNA evidence.

Or perhaps it was just the only photo of her that Ben had left. I suspected that, once enough months had passed to make Ed believe that she wasn't coming back, he'd destroyed most of his pictures of her in a misguided attempt to try and forget her and the pain he was going through. I always wondered if Ben held that against Ed, or if Ed regretted it.

11

Martine Knocker issued Ed with the formal warning – smiling away – and finally left. I escorted her to the front door and hoped that would be the last time we had anyone from Surrey police over the threshold. When I came back into the kitchen, Ed was putting on the coat he'd left hanging on the back of one of the chairs. He was wearing his hiking boots, dropping clots of dried mud from between their treads all over the floor.

'Where are you going?'

'For a walk.'

I was immediately flooded with anxiety. I could practically feel it swirling around my feet and bubbling cold up my legs. 'But ... on your own?'

'I want to clear my head. Stop mothering me, I'll be fine. I'm just going to walk down the toe ... toenail for a couple of miles. I haven't done any exercise for ages. It's not like I can get lost, is it?'

He had a point. But it was the thought of him falling in the river that bothered me most. It was a nice afternoon though, so the chances were that there would be a decent number of dog walkers and cyclists using the towpath, too. And I still felt quietly furious with him, even though I knew it wasn't his fault. It would be nice to have an hour to myself to try and decompress.

'All right,' I said. 'If you're sure. No need to take keys, I'll be here when you get back. Alvin's told me to take the rest of the afternoon off. Is your phone in your pocket? Be back before it gets dark?'

He nodded impatiently and almost pushed past me in his haste to get out, not even a farewell peck on the cheek.

I sat at the kitchen table, my mind racing. I waited ten minutes to be sure he wasn't going to change his mind and come back, then went into his study and sat on his wheely office chair.

I wasn't intending to try and snoop or sleuth, not in the way I had when we first met, but I just wanted to try and find out some more details about this mysterious clinical trial. Perhaps there was an email about it that he'd forgotten. I'd have asked him if I could check, but he'd rushed out so fast I hadn't had the chance to.

Ed's laptop was closed on the desk, buried underneath a sheaf of paper: bills, circulars from local politicians, a postcard from Ben and Jeanine in South Africa, a flyer listing last summer's concerts at Hampton Court Palace.

Wheeling myself gently back and forwards, I switched on the laptop, expecting to get straight in, but in the centre of the screensaver – a photo of Ed dressed as Widow Twanky from a long-ago MADS pantomime, bright-red cheeks, a lopsided wig, flouncy polka dot dress and a wicked expression; that was when Mike first started calling him Edna, if I remembered rightly – I was greeted by a small box requesting a username and password. Ed never used to password-protect his laptop. When had he done that? And why? I racked my brains but couldn't think of the last time I'd even seen him use that computer. I tried various obvious password options under the username EDNAI-SMITH, but nothing worked.

After the fifth failed attempt, I gave up and went to find my own laptop, which was next to the bed from when I'd been watching something on Netflix. I switched it on and waited. It was running ridiculously slowly but eventually I was able to get in. I sat on the bed with the cat, grumbling at him about how much I hated technology. I tried logging into Ed's emails via the Virgin Media website, but that didn't work either as I failed again to guess the password you needed to access them from outside of Outlook. He had such an old mobile phone that he couldn't get emails on there, so that wasn't an option either.

Everything felt frustrating and kind of stale; a niggling unease, like being forced to stay in a windowless room for too long when it was sunny outside. I wondered if Ed felt the same. The horrific event at work, Martine Knocker's visit, a police warning – and I still didn't know if I had a job to go back to. Or if I even should go back.

Sighing, I put away my computer and got off the bed, stripping off my work clothes and getting into sweatpants, Uggs and a long-sleeve t-shirt. Suddenly my unease developed into full-scale paranoia, everything piling up on top of me; him password-protecting his computer, hearing someone on the radio who sounded exactly like him, the memory of someone sneaking around in our house – even his vagueness about the clinical trial. It just felt that there was more to it than the confusion of a man recently diagnosed with dementia.

Was this simply my way of trying to rationalise a situation that defied rationality? Probably. But I *knew* Ed. I knew the sideways tilt of his eyes when he was hiding something. Perhaps the diagnosis had triggered something else in him, something he needed to deal with. I thought of the message I kept getting on my laptop, saying that my start-up disk was nearly full. If Ed's brain was his hard drive, and the Pick's was forcing him to delete data, maybe some kind of pre-deletion memory shuffle had brought something up in him, something he badly wanted to keep hidden?

I hesitated, checking my watch. He had only been gone for twenty-five minutes. I probably had time … and he'd have to ring the doorbell to get back in anyway, as his keys were on the hook by the front door.

I ran downstairs, took a flat-headed screwdriver out of the toolbox we kept under the stairs, then galloped back up to the landing, stopping to pick up the long pole in the corner. I fitted the hooked end of it into the catch of the trap door of the loft, pulling the ladder down in one big, squeaky heft. The metal steps creaked as I climbed up and switched on the light just inside the hatch.

The loft looked untouched – Ed probably hadn't even set foot up here since we moved in, but I hadn't taken any chances. I looked around and found the tiny chalk mark I'd made on the wall above the correct floorboard. It was still there, so faint it was ghostly.

I took the screwdriver out of my pocket and set to work. I'd always known it was risky, bringing the box file with me when we bought the lock-keeper's cottage, but it was my personal proof of his innocence, and important to me because of it.

I wanted to look at it again now to remind myself of this; to remind me that we'd faced other terrible obstacles to our marriage and overcome them, like we would have to overcome this one.

I prised up the floorboard and slid my hand in, closing my fingers immediately on the file and edging it out sideways from where it had been resting on its pillow of yellow loft insulation. It was grey with dust, no other fingerprints visible on its surface, I noted with relief.

I clicked open the folder's hard cover. If Ed had ever seen its contents ... it didn't bear thinking about. It was a betrayal that he would never forgive. There were a few photocopies of newspaper articles about Shelagh's disappearance, and a torn-out feature from a glossy women's magazine that Ed, somewhat ill-advisedly, had agreed to about eighteen months after Shelagh vanished. He was sitting in their front room looking mournful and thinner, but slightly jowly, perched on the padded arm of the sofa in front of the stripped pine door of the first-floor living room.

I read the copy with fresh eyes, and all I could think was how hollow Ed's words were about the bitter loss of his beloved wife, when by then he had already unofficially proposed to me. How, at night, he would slide under the duvet and giggle while he licked me and ran his hands up and down my thighs.

He'd done that on the day of that interview, I remembered.

The article was a weird, crappy mixture of home-improvement porn and heart-wrenching editorial:

'Ed Naismith is a broken man. The only thing that has kept him going – apart from his beloved son Ben, of course – are the renovations on his beautiful Victorian villa in East Molesey, one of Surrey's best-kept secrets; a conservation area within walking distance of Hampton Court Palace. 'It was our dream,' he says, as he shows us around sadly. 'We were always going to do it up together,

so I felt I had to finish it, in Shelagh's memory. It's what she would have wanted.'

And what a renovation! Naismith has clearly channelled all his grief into making every detail perfect. He proudly talks me through everything he's done to fill the lonely months since Shelagh's tragic disappearance, from sanding floors to laying quarry tiles in the re-fitted kitchen. The only thing remaining untouched are the beautiful original pine doors, albeit now adorned with pottery doorknobs sourced from a village in the Atlas Mountains in Morocco...'

Good grief. Who wrote this shite? I tossed it to one side and looked through everything else, things that could either have been romantic keepsakes from the heady early days of our relationship, or painstaking scraps of potential 'evidence' to reassure myself that I wasn't about to marry a murderer.

It all seemed like a lifetime ago now.

Checking my watch again, I decided that I'd seen enough. There was no point in keeping the folder any longer – best that I burned it. It had done its job and convinced me that he really was innocent. Any weird stuff going on now was either in my own imagination, or a consequence of his illness. He wasn't trying to hide anything from me.

Sometimes I felt like I was the one losing the plot. All these crazy paranoid thoughts jumping out at me from behind closed doors, when all Ed needed was my support and love. But would it have been easier, if it hadn't been for all the drama around Shelagh's disappearance? I had no way of knowing.

It was getting to me.

I was about to put everything back in when a faded Polaroid caught my eye, and I picked it up by its thick plastic corner. It was a shot of the interior of Ed and Shelagh's East Molesey house before the renovations, taken from the first-floor landing that led to the living room. I remembered now where I'd found it – in the filing cabinet on a search of Ed's office in the old house. I had only dared steal it at the time because it had fallen out of the 'Home Renovations' hanging file and had been lying on the floor of the metal cabinet drawer; I'd taken it because something bothered me about it, although I hadn't known what.

Then it suddenly came to me – nine years later than it ought to have done. I snatched up the magazine article and re-read the sentence: '*The only thing remaining untouched are the beautiful original pine doors.*' And yet, in the Polaroid in front of me, those same doors, pre-renovation, were thickly painted with white gloss.

I stared and stared at it, gooseflesh sweeping up and down my body. No, I thought. That's ridiculous. I'm adding two plus two and making ten. It doesn't necessarily mean anything. Ed was innocent then, and innocent now.

So why did I feel so uneasy all of a sudden? I'd gone into the loft to reassure myself; thought I'd succeeded – but now I was even more worried.

12

The drilling of the doorbell made me jump so hard that I bit my tongue. I shoved the Polaroid into the back pocket of my sweatpants, slammed the folder shut and shoved it back under the floorboards, my fingers trembling as I wedged the loose board back into place. The bell rang again, more insistently. I grabbed the large blanket storage bag I kept our winter clothes in and hurled it down the ladder before shinning down it and racing to the front door.

'Sorry!' I said as I opened it. 'I was up in the loft getting the jumpers down. How was your walk? You look better for it!'

Ed's cheeks and nose were ruddy and his eyes did look brighter. He even smiled at me as he stepped into the house.

'I'll make us a cup of tea,' he announced, shrugging off his coat and heading for the kettle. 'It's getting parka out there.'

He must have been making a mental association with the coat, which was a fur-hooded parka. I followed him into the kitchen, not bothering to correct him, pausing instead to think about my next words.

'Ed – I just tried to check your emails to see if you'd had any information about that medical trial you mentioned, but I couldn't get into your laptop. Why did you put a password on it?'

Ed tilted his head to one side, considering the question as though it required a tripartite explanation. He surely couldn't have any objection to me looking at his emails. At least he'd never had before.

I was going to say that we had no secrets from each other, but I'd have been lying. I thought of the folder under the loft floor and mentally shuddered.

'I did put a password on it,' he conceded, getting mugs down.

'Yes I know. But why? And what is it?'

I picked cat hair off my sweatpants, affecting nonchalance.

'I don't remember.'

'What – you don't remember why you did it, or what the password is?'

'Either. Someone on the radio said I should. In case it got stolen.'

'Oh.'

So much for that, then. The kettle boiled and he poured water on the teabags. I wondered how long he'd be able to continue making tea, before I was afraid of him scalding himself, or putting a plugged-in kettle into a bowl of dishwater, or any of a million other disastrous things he could do...

'Aren't you going to work today?' he asked.

I sighed. 'I've already been in. You followed me in on the bus and punched Alvin, then the fire brigade and the police came. You've just given a statement to a policewoman who gave you a warning, but Alvin isn't going to press charges.'

He wheeled around, teaspoon in hand. 'Are you serious?'

'Yes.'

'Oh fuck.'

'Don't worry. Could've been worse.'

I remembered those words later that same night, when things got a lot worse.

We went to bed early, exhausted after our long and very awful day. The wind was whisking along the river, stirring the black surface into waves that slapped harshly up against the lock walls. I could hear it as I lay on my left side spooning up to Ed's warm bulk, in a fug of the lavender oil I shook onto my pillow every night to help me sleep. Ed had dropped off immediately, but I couldn't relax.

It was almost midnight, and I was five chapters into an audiobook I was listening to on my phone. Ed had wriggled away from me and turned onto his back but at least he wasn't snoring.

Finally I could feel myself beginning to slide gradually under as I was blearily aware of missing words, then sentences, then paragraphs

– until a sudden roar from Ed shocked me back into immediate wakefulness. Then came a searing, whooshing pain in my right ear as he slammed his hand down on the side of my head.

I leaped out of bed, dancing around and clutching my ear in pain, seeing bright stars dancing with me in the blue-black darkness of the bedroom. 'OW!'

'What?' Ed sat up, disgruntled, as though it was me who had disturbed his slumbers.

'You hit me!'

'Of course I didn't, you silly bitch. I was asleep!' he roared.

Ed had never called me a silly bitch before. It reminded me of the night on the boat when April had got chilli in Mike's eyes and he'd called her something similar. I hadn't realised how hurtful it was.

'Don't you EVER call me that again,' I yelled back. I got back into bed and curled up on the edge of the mattress as far away from him as I could get, waiting for an apologetic hand or word to soothe me. But instead, my side of the mattress suddenly sagged as he rolled back towards me, quick as a flash, and gripped my throat, squeezing hard.

'Ed!' I tried to shriek as he strangled me, but it came out more of a croaky 'Eee'. His mouth was by my ear, his breath hot and stale like a stranger's in an alley. I scissored my legs wildly, flailing to try and get him off me, but he put his full weight on me, incapacitating me, leaning hard on my left shoulder.

'You be very careful, Lynn,' he said, clearly and concisely into my left ear as I choked, not a hint of the hesitation that had characterised his speech patterns for the past few months. 'You know who I am. You know what I'm capable of when I want something. Don't you?'

I moaned. His hair tickled the side of my face and, unbidden and unwelcome, I felt a Pavlovian stab of desire from all the times that his body had been on top of me, whispering in my ear. Then he squeezed harder and all lust vanished, replaced by thousands more twinkling stars behind my closed eyelids. *I'm watching you,'* he whispered, the low timbre of his voice even more sinister than when he'd shouted.

Then as quickly as he'd attacked me, he rolled away again, leaving me coughing and rubbing my throat, stunned, both literally and emotionally.

The narrator of my audiobook droned on as I got unsteadily out of bed and staggered into the spare room, too shocked to cry.

13

We didn't mention it in the morning. Ed was bright and loving, bringing me a cup of tea – tepid, horrible; he clearly hadn't let the kettle boil – and not commenting on the fact that I hadn't slept in bed with him.

I had barely slept, full stop. I had purple bruises around my throat that I managed to hide with a polo-neck black jumper and my head was throbbing. What he had said last night, on top of the thought I'd had on finding the Polaroid, replayed themselves on a loop through my brain. It must have been the disease ... he didn't know what he was saying ... he did know ... he was hiding something from me ... I was in danger ... of course I wasn't in danger, it was Ed ... but which Ed? The Ed I loved and wanted to be with forever, or the Ed who might have killed his first wife? I ought to have gone to the police then, or at least confided in someone to flag up Ed's unusual behaviour ... just in case...

But I couldn't. Because that would open a whole other can of worms.

The same sort of thing happened for the next four nights. Ed drifted straight off to sleep and within minutes came the shout and the attack. If he didn't hit my head, he punched me hard in the shoulder or stomach as if defending himself in a nightclub brawl. I tried putting pillows down at the bottom of the bed and sleeping top-to-toe, but that didn't help either; it was as if he knew. On the fourth night, he kicked me so hard in the hip that I fell out of bed and banged my head on the wooden floor. Building a barricade of pillows down the middle of the mattress made no difference either, he seemed to know where I was and his punches and kicks always found me, until I went to bed every night rigid with tension. Sometimes it happened two or three times in the night until I was unable to even begin to think about falling asleep.

I went back to work, apologetically, sheepishly – but Alvin couldn't have been nicer about it. I offered to resign but he pooh-poohed it immediately, and Sandy and Margaret both went out of their way to be kind to me, so I guess Alvin had filled them in too. Nothing was ever mentioned about it again, at least not in my hearing. But they all looked at me with concern and pity, and I hated it.

At times I felt like I hated Ed, too. He was always so defensive about it at the time, the horrible, dark night-time, although by morning he was tearful and contrite when he noticed my bruises.

On the fifth morning, I was making breakfast in my dressing gown. I caught sight of my reflection in the kettle, the black circles of exhaustion under my eyes matching the black bruise blossoming on my jaw as I moved slowly around the room, as though I was underwater. At least it was the weekend and I didn't have to go to Fairhurst. Toast popped up from the toaster but I was so tired it took me a moment to realise what the sound was. I wondered again if this was how Ed felt.

He wandered in from the front room, where he'd been doing something on his laptop, presumably having remembered his password again. I was too knackered to ask him what it was.

'I'll sleep in the, the, sparse room tonight,' he said, taking the toast out himself and putting it in a bowl, instead of on a plate. 'Of course, I must. I'm so sorry, Lynn, this is awful.'

'You can't sleep in the spare room,' I said, tiredness making it almost equally difficult for me to form the words as he hugged me tightly, making me wince with pain and pull away. I removed the toast from the bowl just before Ed poured milk over it.

'Why not?'

I didn't want to tell him why not. He would only accuse me of babying him again, if I told him that I couldn't let him sleep alone in case he got up at night and wandered; fell into the river or the lock, or lost his way along the towpath and panicked. It was almost November, he could die of exposure in this weather. He could drown so easily, a single slip of the foot down the riverbank, one misjudged step on a moonless night. Just because he hadn't started wandering yet didn't mean it wasn't an imminent development.

'Why not?' he insisted, getting two spoons out of the cutlery drawer and laying them on the table beside the plate of toast. I gritted my teeth and added two knives.

'Because if something happened to you, I'd never forgive myself!'

I can't take this much longer, I thought.

'Nothing will happen to me,' he said, as bemused as if I'd said I was worried about him being abducted by aliens at night. 'I'll only be in the sparse room. What can happen to me in there? Look at you, you're, you're, so teeny. You need some sleep.'

'Tired? Yes. I'm really tired,' I said, slumping into the chair and buttering a piece of toast, which I handed to Ed. I thought he must be tired too. He didn't usually forget this many words.

'Then let me sleep in there. It's got a lock on the door. I'll lock myself in so you'll know that I'm safety. Safe. Safety-safe.' He chuckled, as though he'd said something hilarious.

That wasn't a bad idea – obviously not him locking himself in, but I could lock him in. Could I? I closed my eyes and, almost swooning at the thought, imagined a whole night of uninterrupted lavender-scented sleep on fresh bedlinen, the bed to myself, in the knowledge that Ed was safe. Plus, I had a really busy week at work ahead– we had graduation ceremonies at the Barbican on Wednesday to prepare for, and our student ensembles were providing all the music.

'Promise you won't ever lock yourself in, Ed. What if you couldn't find the key? But, if you agree, maybe I could keep hold of it, lock you in myself? Although – what if you needed a pee in the night?'

Ed shrugged. His pyjama buttons were done up wrong and the fly of his PJ bottoms gaped open. I looked away.

'I won't. When do I ever? And if I did, I can shout you. I think that's a good idea. I don't want to hurt you anymore.'

I didn't correct him. 'I can shout you' sounded better than the correct alternative, somehow. Or perhaps I was just getting used to the new speech patterns. In my imagination, the key to the spare room dangled tantalisingly in front of my eyes.

'No, I guess you don't. Well – perhaps we could try it. Just for a few nights...'

To my surprise, Ed stood up, came around the table and kissed me on the mouth, slipping his arms around my waist and nuzzling his head in the space between my neck and shoulder. 'Lynn ... I do love you, you know,' he murmured, sounding so completely like his old self that tears filled my eyes.

'I know.' I replied, and we stood there a long time, our bare feet cold on the kitchen tiles, warm in the embrace. *I miss you*, I added, into a small silent place in my head.

Then he pulled away. 'Oh, I forgot, I got an email.' He went to his study and came back carrying his open laptop, which he thrust at me. The email was dated the week before.

From: Billyboy8792
Subject: Trial details
Date: 18 October 2016
To: EdNaismith56

Hi mate,
As requested, here's a brief outline of the Phase 3 clinical programme of the drug galdonimene in layman's terms for you to put the good lady wife's mind at rest. Completely understand that it's a decision the two of you should make together and if Lynn would like us all to meet, of course that is fine. I am away though (medical conference in Singapore then holiday) for the next three weeks, which isn't ideal timing because, as you know, I'm keen to get the trial underway ASAP. One of my colleagues can monitor you until I get back, if you decide to go ahead without my initial input. We are thrilled to (probably!) have you on board!
As I explained to you on the phone, the trial is for the pharma

company Biogenetics and you have been approved for the ENGAGE Study (the parallel one being EMERGE). It is split into two phases; a placebo-controlled phase, and an optional long-term extension phase after eighteen months. In the former, you will have a two out of three chance of receiving the investigational medication, and a one in three chance of receiving a placebo. Study medication or placebo will be given in a monthly intravenous infusion to be carried out in my office in Chelsea (contact details below), or, for the examinations, at a local private hospital (depending on their available facilities). You will need to visit once or twice a month and I will arrange transportation there and back for you on each occasion. You are a somewhat unusual case as all the other participants are in the early stages of Alzheimer's rather than Pick's, which makes your cooperation all the more valuable.

The email continued over a couple more pages, detailing how Bill or one of his colleagues would monitor Ed's health for any changes, including interviews, blood and urine tests, ECGs, MRIs, vital signs, and so on, with a few paragraphs detailing how trials of galdonimene on mice had attacked and actually removed the amyloid plaque on their brains and, if it had the same effect on human subjects, would be a huge leap forwards in a successful treatment of dementia.

'You'd have to have MRIs,' was my first comment.

'I know.' Ed looked tense. 'I suppose they can sedate me first.'

'I'll come with you.'

'You'll probably be at work.'

'Can't you do it on one of my days off?'

He shrugged. 'I'd have to do it when he's free I suppose. You can come if you're not working, if you want, but I'd rather do it on my own.'

I flicked to the end of the email to see what Bill's office address was – so far I hadn't even gleaned his surname – but it stopped at the bottom of the third page, mid-sentence.

'Where's the rest?'

Ed looked surprised, so I pointed at the screen. 'Look. It's not signed off at the end. There must be another page with the contact details and so on.'

'Oh yeah. Must have accidentally deleted it.'

I tutted with frustration. 'Why hasn't he written it from his professional email address? This one is clearly his personal one. There isn't even a phone number on here!'

'Email him then.'

'I will,' I said.

It seemed both plausible and simultaneously vague as hell. I scanned through it again. 'But it says there's a risk of brain swelling.'

Ed stroked his stubbly chin contemplatively. 'And if I don't do it, there's a much higher risk of becoming a vegetarian.'

I was momentarily puzzled until he clarified: 'A vegetable.'

'Oh Ed, don't say that. I can't bear it.'

That night I fussed over Ed so much that he snapped at me. But I couldn't help it. The key to the spare room door was burning a hole in my jeans pocket, making me feel so aware of being a jailer that I might as well have had twenty-seven other heavy iron keys on a massive ring chained to my waist.

When I went in to say goodnight he had cheered up again, snuggling down in the spare bed like a child on a sleepover. I kissed him and resisted the temptation to tuck the duvet in around his shoulders as he lay there innocently, his eyes small and helpless without his glasses, but with a smile on his face.

'I think you should do it,' I said quietly.

'Do what?'

'The drugs trial.'

He nodded. 'So do I. It's not like I have anything to lose, is it?'

I went back for another kiss, overcome with pity and affection for him.

'Goodnight then Nurse Ratchet,' he called as I finally headed for the door, and I laughed uncomfortably. 'Don't!'

I turned the key in the lock on the other side, leaning my forehead briefly against the wooden panels of the door.

As I climbed into bed I was assailed by the strangest mixture of emotions – the ever-present guilt, relief at having the bed to myself, excitement at the thought of an uninterrupted night's sleep and the hope that this drug might help him.

14

I felt my phone vibrate just as the coach finally pulled out of Fairhurst's driveway. Slumping back against the grubby velvet headrest, I extracted it from my handbag, feeling exhausted already. It was only 8.20am. Alvin had warned me it would be a long, tiring day, but it wasn't just work affecting me. The stress of Ed's illness was giving me nightmares and what could only be described as lucid dreams.

The night before, I could have sworn I woke up to find a man looming next to my bed, staring at me in the darkness. In my dream I'd seen his silhouetted bulk so clearly that I'd rolled over and buried my head under the pillow in fear. I'd woken up properly with a sudden gasp, feeling like I was suffocating.

And the night before that, I found myself standing by the window, staring out between the curtains at 4am, convinced I'd just seen the glow of a cigarette end by the front gate. In my half-dream state I'd been sure that it was Mike out there, smoking.

This morning I'd unlocked Ed's bedroom door at six, just before I'd left for work. It was the third night he'd spent in the spare room with not a word of complaint. I felt horribly guilty – even with the bad dreams, it was such a relief to be able to sleep without fear of physical attack.

At least work was keeping my mind busy though. Since arriving at Fairhurst House, I'd been helping load timpani, djembe drums, music stands and choir robes into the coach's dark underbelly, then ticking off my list of student performers as they shuffled aboard, looking so peaky and zombified it was hard to imagine that they would be singing and playing to an audience of five thousand parents and relatives at the graduation ceremony at the Barbican in just a few hours' time.

My gut twitched with anxiety as I looked at my phone and saw I had five missed calls from Ed, as well as five voicemails. I couldn't go home now! I imagined having to stop the coach, find a cab, race back, how Alvin would have to shepherd the eighty students on and off stage himself, as well as conducting them. He couldn't – I had to be there, to line them up backstage, check that their concert dress was appropriate, that the choir all had their music in black folders, that the drummers had sticks and the string section had bows…

I clamped the phone to my ear to drown out the coach's engine and the sleepy chatter of the students, and dialled my voicemail. There was a pause before the message began and I braced myself for whatever fresh hell he was about to impart. But he wasn't panicked, shouting about being locked out or injured or confused; he was *singing*. Not an accidental bum-dial where I'd just happened to electronically eaves-drop on him cheerfully singing along to the radio like he used to, but a low, breathy, intentional song. The tone of it made me grip the phone so hard my knuckles turned white and my own breath caught in my throat:

'*Some-body's watching youuuu.*
Some-body's watching youuuu.
Some BODY is WATCHING you.'

Over and over, with such spat emphasis on 'body' that the word felt like a knife through flesh. There was a tune, of sorts, sounding vaguely familiar. It was some song from the eighties, perhaps. Or maybe he'd made it up. His voice was like the middle of a lake at night, so dark and cold that I felt my organs recoil inside my belly.

It went on for several minutes, chilling in its dogged repetition. I wanted to hang up but I couldn't, I was transfixed by the sinister words.

The coach stopped in traffic on the A3 and I saw a woman putting on her bra through a first-floor window in a block of flats. She looked up, locked eyes with me and glared, then smiled flirtatiously without covering her breasts, and for some reason this spooked me even further. I was watching her. She was watching me.

Was Ed watching me? Someone else? What the hell did he mean?

The coach pulled away with a change of engine noise. The woman waved sardonically at me – although then I became aware of snickering from the seats behind me, and realised that it was only my paranoia, thinking she was looking at me. She'd been showing off to the entire coach full of predominantly male students.

This snapped me out of it. Ed was a very sick man. I checked the time of the message – half an hour earlier.

I rang him, needing to hear his voice as it usually was, not as a ghoulish chant.

'Hi Lynn. How's it going?' He sounded utterly normal and my heart slowed down a few beats.

'Fine. We're on the coach, on time to get there by half-nine. Set up and rehearsal, then the ceremony's at one o'clock. What are you up to? Did you sleep OK?'

'Yes, like a – a hog. Just put a wash on. Might go for lunch with Mike.'

'Great ... Ed?'

'Yeah?'

'I just had a really weird message from you.'

'From me?'

'Yes. You were singing down the phone on my voicemail.'

He laughed. 'Singing? Singing what?'

'I don't know. Some creepy song about someone watching me.'

There was a brief pause.

'I don't know what you're talking about. I haven't even rung you today.'

I sighed. What was the point in arguing? He'd forgotten already.

'OK. Well, as long as you're all right. I'd better go. I'll let you know what time I'll be home – make sure you have some lunch, won't you? There's salad stuff in the fridge. Suzan's next door if you need anything.'

I terminated the call and stared out of the window at the exhaust-grimed walls and faded roofs of South London, houses worn down by the ever-passing traffic. I felt pretty eroded myself, and not just by the early start and physical exertion of the day so far. This was only the beginning.

I deleted Ed's message from my voicemail but I couldn't delete the words from my head, where they were repeating in a loop, breathy and threatening: '*Some-body's watching youuuuu…*'

15

The following hours were far too busy to dwell on the sinister voice-mail and what it represented for me, or Ed. I had to assist Alvin at the rehearsal as he worked with the orchestra, chorus and djembe ensembles, practising cues and onstage positioning. The phrase 'herding cats' came to mind several times. The students were giddy with excitement at performing to a huge audience in such an iconic venue and, as Alvin had warned me, there was the usual quota of tears, vomit and lost items. But eventually everything was set up, everyone was at least *meant* to know what they were doing, they'd had their sandwich lunches in the dressing rooms, and the ceremony was about to begin. I finally had a bit of time to myself.

I sat for a moment in the girls' dressing room, surrounded by brown paper bags and detritus from the packed lunches the venue had provided. At one o'clock exactly I heard the opening bars of *Zadok The Priest* strike up through the tinny speaker of the show relay. My phone rang and when I saw it was Ed, I lifted it to my ear with great trepidation.

'Hi darling?'

'Hi Lynn.'

Thank God, he still sounded normal.

'Everything OK?'

'Yes, fine. Just calling to say hello and see how it's going. Are they all behaving themselves?'

'Yes, mostly. One of the sopranos was sick in the corridor but fortunately I didn't have to clear it up myself. The ceremony's just started so I've got a bit of time off now.'

'What are you going to do?'

I looked around the messy, windowless dressing room. 'Not sure. Find a sofa and have a kip, probably.'

He laughed. 'Why don't you go out and get a bit of fresh air? Actually – I meant to say, while you're there could you pick up a, you know, directory of stuff going on in the Barbeque?'

Until that part, Ed had sounded like there was nothing wrong with him at all. I had a pang of yearning for the days when we'd plan theatre and cinema trips to the Barbican, a meal and a film, the last train home, some drunken sex and a tender goodnight kiss ... I missed it.

'OK. You're right, I could do with a change of scene. I'll go and get an event calendar from the foyer.'

Not that there was any point, I thought. By the time I got it home, Ed would doubtless have forgotten not only that he'd asked me to pick one up, but probably also what the Barbican was. And he certainly wouldn't sit through a play anymore.

'You sound a bit...'

'What?' I tried not to be irritated.

'Sad.'

A huge lump stuck in my throat and I tried to swallow it down. 'I'm fine, sweetie. Just tired. It's been a long day and we're only halfway through. It's the thought of folding up fifty music stands and carrying them out to the coach again later ... I'm too old for this!'

'Get them to help you.'

'Yeah. Will do – if I can tear them away from their smartphones long enough. All right – I'm going to go and get a coffee. Thanks for ringing, Ed. It's good to talk to you, honey.'

I made my way through the maze of corridors and staircases out of the backstage area into the main foyer of the Barbican, despair clouding my eyes and making my heart feel weighty as a bowling ball. The future seemed to be simultaneously stuck and unravelling in front of me, a tangled, knotty ball of wool rendered unusable. Like the plaques in Ed's brain. I couldn't remember ever feeling so negative.

The vast foyer had the jittery abandoned feel that a big inside space has when crowds of people have recently vacated it, as if they left their energy behind when they took their seats in the auditorium. It was a relief to be out of the backstage area though. I wandered over to the nearest coffee outlet and was gazing absently at the menu board when I became aware of someone staring at me.

I glanced up and his eyes caught mine. He was a tall, thin man in a grey beany hat and a Gore-Tex anorak thing, open over a suit. He looked familiar and at first I thought he must be an actor, someone off the television. I looked away again quickly, hoping he wouldn't assume that I wanted a selfie or an autograph.

'Waitsey!'

My heart froze then twitched a couple of extra beats, making me feel briefly nauseous.

'It is you, isn't it?' He came over to me and grasped me gently, one hand on each of my upper arms. When I looked at him properly I couldn't believe I hadn't recognised him at first.

'*Adrian*? What are you doing here?'

He didn't answer, just enveloped me in a hug that at first made me stiffen, but then I laughed and hugged him back.

'Have you got time to sit down for a coffee?' he asked, releasing me and scanning my face with a smile so broad I could see a gold filling gleam in one of his back molars. 'I'm supposed to be at my niece's graduation ceremony. But I missed the train and now I'm so late that I think I'll have to catch them afterwards instead. I'll pretend I sneaked in at the back; my sister will never know. The main thing is that I'm here. What about you?'

'Your niece is at Hampton Uni? No way! I work there, in the music department at Fairhurst House – I came up with all the student musicians on a coach this morning. So technically I'm free for the next hour or so ... but hadn't you better go in? It only started about ten minutes ago. You're not that late.'

I stared at him and laughed. It was more than nine years since we'd last seen one another but he looked exactly the same, just a few grey hairs in his stubble, and his teeth were slightly nicotine-stained – this was either a more recent development, or a flaw I'd overlooked back in the days when I used to wear the rose-tinted specs.

'I'd *much* rather catch up with you,' he said, shaking his head in disbelief.

We ordered coffees – that he insisted on paying for – and sat down on leather cubes around a café table. Adrian took off his coat and beany and rubbed his head, which was when I noticed he was no longer wearing a wedding ring. I wasn't sure how this made me feel. Regret, for a second. If I'd known his marriage would eventually break down, perhaps I would never have given up on us. Never met Ed, never agonised over my decision to marry him, never have had to listen to my beloved husband singing threatening songs to me down the phone and punching me in the head ... In another timeline, it might have been Adrian and I arriving together to go to his niece's graduation, sitting in the audience watching Alvin conducting the orchestra and choir singing *Zadok the Priest,* us giggling about what a weird-looking dude he was with his mad hair and pipe-cleaner limbs. We wouldn't have been late, either, because I'd have made sure we didn't miss the train...

But then, to have never met Ed was unthinkable.

'So, Waitsey. Tell me everything.'

I'd forgotten how intense his gaze was. 'I'm not Waitsey anymore, for starters. You almost gave me a heart attack, calling me that! You know I moved up to Hampton?'

Adrian took a sip of his cappuccino. The sight of him licking froth off his top lip made me shiver, although whether with lust, or fear that my old life and my new had collided like this, I wasn't sure. I could almost smell the chlorine from our first encounter. That had involved coffee, too.

'I did *not* know that. You disappeared off the face of the Earth! I wanted to get in touch but couldn't find any trace of you. Which made me proud – you'd obviously done well. So, fill me in...'

His eyes flicked to my wedding ring. 'How long have you been married?'

'Eight years now. And what about you – are you divorced?'

He nodded. 'A few years back. I left the job, too.'

'No! Really? Why? You weren't far off retirement!'

Adrian pursed his mouth, making his chin scrunch into a walnut. I remembered that expression from when something had displeased him. 'Ach, it was a right-old shit-show. Got stitched up by someone who'd been gunning for me from day one.'

'Blimey,' I said. 'I'm so sorry.' Poor Adrian – to be in the job that long and then to have had to leave, presumably without his pension? He'd have been devastated.

'That's life. I'm over it now. What about you, things going well?'

I nodded, then remembered Ed's phone call that morning, and changed the nod to a shake. 'Well. They were. Everything was great, up until a few months ago.' I took a too-big swig of my black coffee and felt the skin on the roof of my mouth shrivel and corrugate. 'Ow, shit.'

'What's the matter? Apart from burning your tongue.'

I sighed. Did I want to get into it? I did, but I was feeling sufficiently tired and fragile that there was a risk I'd start crying – and I definitely didn't want to do *that*. Perhaps I was perimenopausal? Great. Something else to worry about.

'Oh, nothing major. As you say, just life.'

We talked for another ten minutes or so, just chit-chat about his niece, his work as a freelance security consultant, the move he made to Ewell after his divorce. Safe stuff. Adrian didn't push me into talking further about 'life', nor did I quiz him on why he'd undergone those major life changes.

In fact, I didn't ask him anything about his family. I didn't want him to ask me any reciprocal questions; questions which might have led him to work out what I'd done when I left.

Plus, all those years later it still made me feel guilty, that I'd been having sex with him when his wife and son thought he was working late.

Not that I owed her anything, the ex-Mrs McLoughlin – if I'd ever known her first name, I couldn't remember it now – but I prided myself on being a feminist, and doing the dirty with someone else's husband didn't exactly elevate me to the higher echelons of the sisterhood ... I'd never stopped feeling ashamed about that.

Why, then, was I wondering if he was with anyone now?

16
2006

'Your round, Waitsey!'

Weller barged back into the pub, stinking of cigarette smoke. He tousled my hair hard as he pushed past me to his seat, and I had to smooth down the resulting bird's nest. He always did it and it always got on my nerves. He was the sort of guy who would intentionally tilt picture frames crooked just to annoy people. Mussing up my usually dead-straight hair was done on the same principle.

'This smoking ban is doing my fucking head in,' he said, flopping his bulk back on the bench into which we were both squeezed. 'Ridiculous, having to go and stand in the street like a leper every time I want to light up!'

'Give up, then, Wells. It's bad for you. What are you having?' I shouted, draining my pint and getting up to join the crush at the bar. I took off my cardigan and tied it round my waist, something I'd been holding out on doing for as long as possible because I was only wearing a small, tight vest-top underneath, but it was baking hot in there.

'Another pint of Badger, there's a good girl.' Weller, predictably, stared at my chest as he handed me his empty glass.

It was Friday, monthly karaoke night at The Bell, and a tradition with my colleagues from the station. As I stood in a four-deep queue at the bar, I pondered the point that I didn't particularly like any of them all that much – with the exception of my friend Sal, who I adored, and sometimes wished he were single. Sadly, he had a girlfriend so beautiful that my inferiority complex developed its own inferiority complex whenever I saw her. They – my colleagues – were good enough fun to hang out with, but after spending the entire, often stressful, week with them in the office, I wondered why I chose to continue to keep their company on my own time as well.

Although if I didn't, I'd most likely be on my own. Adrian was never available at the weekends – that was strictly family time for him. Which begged the question, if weekends were family time, and weekdays were work time, when was his Waitsey Time?

His expression, not mine.

Waitsey Time, it seemed, was a few snatched hours here and there when he could pretend to be working late and, twice, a blissful naughty night away under the guise of a policing conference in London.

We had our local meet-ups in his recently deceased Mum's terraced cottage, which was actually right across the car park from the pub I was in now. If I turned and looked out of the mullioned-glass windows I would see its little hobbity front door. We had to make sure we never met there on Karaoke Fridays at The Bell. That would give our colleagues something to talk about over their pints. I sometimes woke up in a cold sweat at the thought that Weller could be out on the pavement greedily inhaling his seventeenth Malboro Red of the evening and would spot Adrian – DCI McCloughlin to him, or Cluffers behind his back – unlocking the little wooden front door and crouching down so he didn't bang his head on the lintel as he admitted the pair of us inside for a night of passion on the swirly, dusty carpets amongst his dead mother's horse brasses and sentimental paintings of Victorian children.

Not that Weller would see any of that. He would just see me, lowly PC Waites, being ushered inside for an illicit rogering by the boss. And then he'd spread the word around the station as fast as he possibly could, and my career would be down the pan in minutes. It was an unbearable thought, when being in the police was all I'd ever wanted – but even so, I found it impossible to resist Adrian's advances.

Also, if I didn't join my colleagues on a Friday night, I'd get even more snide comments about my private life. Just because I didn't have a spouse and kids like everyone else did, I had to run the gamut of speculation as to whether I was gay, in a secret relationship (true, but they didn't know that) or just a commitmentphobe. I wasn't a moose – so Weller had magnanimously informed me the other week while staring at my tits again – so there must be some reason I didn't have a bloke, given that I was pushing forty.

'I'm thirty-six. That's not even close to pushing forty,' I'd informed him.

I really, really didn't want anyone to know what the reason actually was.

Truth was, I was ashamed of being a mistress. It went against all my ingrained principles and my mum and dad would have been ashamed of me too, had they been around to find out. I regularly hoped they weren't looking down on me and wondering where it all went wrong.

All these thoughts made me gloomy, and being gloomy made me drink more. When I was finally served, I ordered my own pint first and was three quarters of the way down it before I even carried the drinks precariously back to the others.

'Finally, Waitsey, we're dying of thirst here!' Weller grabbed his Badger off the tray as I was putting it down, and took a long swallow, which he followed up with a large belch.

'You're welcome.' I lifted up my sheet of hair, to try and get some air circulating on the back of my neck. 'It's so bloody hot in here. Are we really staying for the karaoke? I might call it a night actually, I'm knackered.'

'No chance,' said Sal, giving me a side hug and poking his sharp chin into the hollow of my clavicle. 'It's only nine-thirty! You can't leave yet. You promised you'd do *Islands in the Stream* with me and I can't hold a tune in a bucket without you.'

Salim Palekar, thirty-three, eyelashes like a chimney sweep's brush, shiny black hair like a seal's and cute, skinny little legs. He may not have been able to sing in tune, but he was, apparently, an amazing violin player – grade eight, he once told me, which I thought was really cool. Why were the nice ones never single?

A question that answered itself, if you thought about it.

I sighed, pushing him fondly away. 'Where's Gemma tonight? She's got a much better voice than me.'

'Out with the girls. She doesn't like hanging out with us lot of a Friday.'

'Can't say I blame her,' I said, watching Weller screw a forefinger into his ear and then inspect it.

'She likes you, though,' Sal commented, and I wasn't sure whether to be flattered or slightly depressed that Sal's gorgeous girlfriend clearly saw me as no threat whatsoever.

'So, what about it then?' He jerked his head towards the small stage on the other side of the bar, where the barman was setting up an amp and TV screen.

'All right,' I grumbled. 'I'll do it, and then I'm going. Things to do, people to see…'

An appointment with a steaming bath and a good thriller, hopefully. My landlady Nicky was usually out on a Friday night and I hardly ever got to have her house to myself. It was a minuscule two-up two-down with a staircase in the middle so narrow that there wasn't enough room to squeeze past another person on it, and I always felt in the way whenever she was there. When I lay in bed I could reach out and touch both bedroom walls simultaneously. But it was near the station, and Nicky and I got on pretty well.

It was embarrassing to be living in a rented box room at my age. I'd told myself it was only temporary, that I'd find somewhere better – but that had been almost two years ago. If I was honest with myself, I was hoping Adrian would leave his wife and he and I could set up home together, but that was looking less and less likely.

Weller nudged me. 'Check it out – didn't we arrest that little scrote last month?'

He was pointing at a weaselly teenager snogging a girl in a bodycon dress against the pub wall. I shrugged. 'Probably. There have been so many, haven't there, Weller? An endless conveyor belt of losers and druggies. Doesn't it get you down?'

Weller rubbed his hand over his crew cut. He was a big guy, and even his skull seemed to move plumply under his fingers.

'Nah. All part of the job, isn't it?'

The booze was making me philosophical now. 'But it's so boring. All these low-lifes and their petty crime.'

'I love it. I could nick 'em till the cows come home.'

'Yeah, and then I have to interview them. Don't tell me that's not as boring as hell.'

That was my life at the moment, desk-bound, five weeks into a three-month stint of interviewing shoplifters and wife beaters in windowless interview rooms and then spending endless hours writing up the results. It felt like a right anti-climax after what had been such a promising start to the year – I had taken down a robber single-handedly as he fled the minimart whose till he'd just raided, felling him with a well-placed taekwondo kick that sent him flying into a wall. I thought for sure I would get a promotion. But I'd been sent off to write up interviews instead. I was pissed off and impatient, even though I knew that it was an expected part of my career progression, and the promotion had been hinted at as something that I might expect in the future. I couldn't wait.

'I want something to really get my teeth into.'

Weller leaned towards me, a glint in his grey, puffy eyes. 'What – other than the boss, you mean?'

I'd been in the act of draining my pint, and his words made me rear back against the padded bench in shock, the glass knocking against my teeth and the dregs spilling down my top. 'What the fuck do you mean by that?'

I glared at him, my nose so close to his that I could see all his open pores. 'Seriously, Weller, that's bang out of order. You don't know what you're talking about. As if I'd even go there!'

'Steady on, Weller, that's how rumours start,' Sal chipped in, looking nervously at me in a way that made me think, *Shit, they know*.

Surely they couldn't. My face grew hot at the thought. What if everyone knew?

'There's nothing going on between me and Cluffers,' I insisted, using the nickname he hated whilst putting on my best innocent face. 'I don't remotely fancy him, he's far too old! And far too married.'

Weller narrowed his eyes at me. 'We all know he's got a bit of a soft spot for you, though, Waitsey.'

'So? That's hardly the same as me having a rampant bloody affair, is it?!' I injected a laugh into my voice, but sweat was trickling a light finger down my spine. 'Anyway, before you accuse me of shagging the entire station just because I'm not married with two point four kids, I think I shall love you and leave you. Although not in that way, you understand…'

They laughed, but Sal looked uncomfortable. Not half as uncomfortable as I felt, mind you. 'Sorry about *Islands in the Stream*, Sal, maybe next time, eh?'

I hugged him briefly – not Weller, he could go screw himself – and pushed my way out of the crowded pub into the cooler evening air, not bothering to say goodbye to the rest of them on the next table.

Adrian's mum's cottage stood stolidly across the car park, its windows dark, and I felt a pang of sorrow that I couldn't simply stroll over there, unlock the door with my own key, and let myself in to find Adrian waiting for me with that slightly crooked smile I found utterly irresistible.

Instead I walked home through the town centre, out to the ring road, under the pigeon-shit-splattered railway bridge and towards the landmark metal hulk of deserted gasworks, in the shadow of which crouched Nicky's little house.

I sent Adrian a text, to his 'secret' phone, but he didn't reply. Feeling paranoid and unloved, I stripped, hosed the sweat and beer off my body under a cool shower – I couldn't be bothered to have a bath – and climbed into my ridiculously narrow bed, where I lay like a board, hands by my sides, head whirling slightly from one pint too many.

Was this how my life was going to be forever? I checked my phone for a final time – still no reply – then gazed at the framed photo on my bedside table: me saluting the camera on passing-out day, delighted in my pristine new uniform, so many possibilities ahead. It made me smile and, without fail, feel proud.

Fuck Adrian. What was I doing, wasting my life waiting around for him to grant me a few brief moments of pleasure? I was worth more than that. I wanted a husband, kids, people to call my own.

I vowed to end it with him next week. Get a transfer, if necessary. There was so much more I wanted to do, while I waited for my babies. I could apply to join the Armed Response Group. I was fit enough to pass the 'bleep test', the multi-stage fitness test you had to crack before the ARG would consider you. And they had so few female applicants that I was sure I'd stand as good a chance as any.

I fell asleep imagining how great it would be to carry a Glock – but how much greater to sniff the sweet milky scent of my own child's soft baby hair.

17

First thing on Monday morning, I emailed and asked for a meeting with Adrian, but without telling him why. I hadn't seen or heard from him all weekend and with every passing hour of silence my mind became more firmly made up. I was worth more than this.

There were no interviews that morning, and I was up to date with the transcription of the others, so I had nothing to do except drink bad coffee and listen to my colleagues discussing how rubbish and inaccurate the latest police procedural drama on BBC Two was. Adrian emailed me back, very formally, saying I could come to his office at eleven.

At one minute to eleven, I straightened my tunic, smoothed my skirt over my thighs and knocked on his door. 'Come in,' he said gravely and my heart hitched in my chest, much to my irritation.

'Good morning, boss.' I kept my voice as neutral as I could.

'Morning. Have a seat.' He gave me the secret smile he reserved for when nobody else was around.

I sat down, trying not to look at the photo of Adrian, his wife and their son, mouths wide, roaring with white-knuckled delight down a log flume. His son, Kit, was the sort of boy who would probably grow into his looks one day but who at the moment was going through a podgy, unfortunate phase. He clearly took after Adrian, as the wife was – I grudgingly admitted – quite pretty.

I could never quite figure out why I found Adrian so irresistible. Bald and round-faced, if you saw him from the neck up you'd assume that he was overweight, but he was snake-hipped and lean. It was all about the charisma. As soon as he opened his mouth, I felt myself grow tingly with desire. Something about the way he talked made me smile and want to listen to him all day.

Perhaps not this morning, though. He looked rested and relaxed after his two days off whereas I felt achy and sallow, tense with anticipation.

'Good weekend?' I wasn't sure I wanted to know the answer.

He shrugged. 'Not bad. Took Kit swimming. Lunch with the outlaws, that kind of thing.'

That kind of family thing, I thought. The kind I know nothing about. He would have taken Kit to the same municipal pool at which he and I started our relationship eighteen months earlier. I'd already known who he was at work, of course, but seeing him thrashing up and down the fast lane in a pair of budgie smugglers effectively disguised him as well as if he'd been in a hijab. When he stopped at the shallow end to de-mist his goggles, his shoulders heaving, water streaming off his bald head, I thought he looked familiar, but I didn't manage to place him until I bumped into him again in the foyer.

'Oh!' I'd been physically shocked to realise who he was, a sharp electric sizzle to my still-damp skin. 'Hello sir.'

He was sorting out coins for a vending-machine coffee.

'Waitsey.' He nodded and smiled, and I blushed. I hadn't known that he was aware of my existence let alone my nickname. 'Saw you in there. You're a fast swimmer.'

'So are you, boss.'

'You don't need to call me that out of hours. It's Adrian. Would you like a coffee?'

He fed a series of twenty-pence pieces into the slot and pressed the button for cappuccino – presumably for himself – but nothing happened, not even when he pushed the coin return button. I noticed with idle interest the way he pushed it so hard that the tip of his post-swimming, pruney white finger turned bright red. 'Sod's law. Did you say you wanted one?'

I opened my mouth but he continued: 'Tell you what, let's pop into that coffee shop round the corner. The coffee's far superior and you get it in an actual mug rather than a plastic cup that burns your hands.'

That was how it started. Innocuous at first, regular swims followed by a coffee. Then the coffees turned into clandestine pints, and the peck on the cheek into full-blown snogs … and now here we were, eighteen months on, occasional sex on his dead mum's carpet, me in love and feeling lonely as hell. The faintest whiff of chlorine would forever remind me of him.

Back in the office I looked him square in the eye. 'This isn't working for me anymore, sir.'

I didn't usually call him 'sir' unless other people were around.

'What isn't, Waitsey?' His voice was concerned but cagey. We had a tacit agreement not to discuss our relationship in the office.

'I'd like to request a transfer.'

He looked surprised but not hurt or upset. 'To where?'

'I don't have a preference. Somewhere I can have a fresh start. It shouldn't be hard to find another force to take me, should it? I'd like to do ARG training so I'd be happy to go wherever the next course is, outside of Wiltshire of course. I don't have any baggage, no husband or kids, not even a mortgage.'

I didn't mean to sound bitter but it probably came out that way.

'What about your friends?'

I shrugged. 'It's only Sal, really. I'm sure we'll keep in touch.'

Adrian gazed at me and I had to swallow and look away. 'We'd be very sorry to lose you, Waitsey.'

'We?'

He didn't rise to the bait, merely nodding as if he hadn't understood the subtext, and it was at that moment that I realised it really was over, that I had no option now but to see this out. I wouldn't miss Weller and Quint, or my narrow bed at Nicky's. I'd miss her and Sal, and Adrian of course – but I wasn't going to give him the satisfaction of knowing how much.

Adrian weaved a pencil deftly around his fingers.

'How long have you been with us now?'

'Almost three years, sir.'

'Is that all? Seems much longer. You're part of the furniture.'

I gritted my teeth.

'In a good way, I mean. One of the team.'

We sat in silence for a moment, openly gazing at each other. I had to look away first, worried that I was going to cry. What would he do when I'd gone; move straight on to the next gullible PC?

'Actually, there might be something...' he said pensively. 'Not sure it'll be suitable though. Let me look into it and we'll talk again tomorrow.'

At least he sounded reluctant, which made me feel a tiny bit better.

18

'*U*c? I thought I was joining Armed Response!'

I'd never even thought about being an undercover officer before. My mind was reeling. It was only two days since I'd told him that I wanted a transfer, and here we were again in his office, him with a slightly hesitant expression on his face.

'Bloke I know in Surrey Police just happened to mention in passing the other week that they needed someone, so when you said you wanted a change, I gave him a bell and got the intel. They're after a woman about your age, pretty, to chat up this guy they think topped his wife. He can't find anyone in his force to go into deep cover, because they all have families and that. But look – nobody's forcing you. You'd have to have all the training, and it's a major job. I didn't think he'd take you on, as it would be your first assignment, but when I told them how bright you are he sounded keen.'

'A honey-trap? Deep cover? Me? You're kidding.'

'Yeah. They can't find anything on him any other way, but they're sure he's hiding something. Completely hush-hush, obviously, and even if you did uncover something, you'd have to be very smart about how you presented it in court.'

'Sounds a bit dodgy,' I said.

'It is,' he agreed. 'But seriously, no pressure. I can arrange ARG too if you'd rather.'

'But they can't find anyone else to do it?' I supposed I could always do Armed Response at a later date…

'No. His ears pricked right up when I told him about your record, and your discretion.'

I snorted. 'Because I'm having an affair with the boss.'

'No! We don't need to mention *that*.'

I bet we don't, I thought. And yet I felt a thrill of anticipation at the thought of the assignment. This would be a whole lot better than sitting in Salisbury nick writing up interviews. My life was moving up a gear. Sod Adrian and his mum's swirly carpet, sod karaoke night and my cot in the world's smallest bedroom.

'What training will I get?'

'Good girl,' he said, although I hadn't said I'd do it. 'If you're certain. It'll be your basic Level One Surveillance to start with, and then another one straight after that, I imagine. They won't throw you in the deep end, don't worry. I'll put you in touch with DS Metcalfe in Guildford and he'll sort it all out for you.'

As far as I was aware, the Level One undercover course would only teach me to be a test purchaser – in a nutshell, qualify me to pretend to buy drugs as a punter – surely they'd give me a lot more training than that?

As if he'd read my mind, Adrian added, 'Actually, thinking about it, they'll definitely make you do Level Two as well. That'll get you down to brass tacks for the deep cover stuff. A lot of it's just common sense anyway.'

I was so freaking excited I couldn't sit still. 'On it, sir,' I said. 'Thanks for the opportunity.'

'Don't let me down, Waitsey,' he said, and the grin he gave me did make my heart break, just a little bit.

It all happened bewilderingly fast. I gave Nicky notice on the box room that same day, cleared my workplace at the station and entertained fantasies of me becoming a kind of less glamorous Mata Hari. Minus the firing squad though, hopefully.

The worst bit was having to lie to Sal. I wasn't allowed to let anybody know what I'd be doing, of course, so I just told him that I was transferring to another PC role in Surrey and that I'd ring as soon as I was settled. We didn't even get together for a farewell drink. I never saw him again.

I moved up to temporary digs in London to go on the two six-week training courses, which I did back to back, while my new team in Surrey Police sorted out everything else.

By Christmas Eve of 2006 I was sitting on an unfamiliar black pleather sofa in a tiny studio flat in Hampton, wearing a Santa hat and wondering what the hell I was doing, apart from comfort-eating my way through an entire box of mince pies. I knew no one there and no one knew me. It was both terrifying and liberating.

There had been no great emotional farewell with Adrian either. I only saw him one more time after the meeting when he gave me the brief. A few days before Christmas I'd driven back to Wiltshire to pick up the rest of my meagre belongings and we had one last rendezvous.

I had hoped that he might express some kind of regret or apology for messing me around – I was long past the stage of anything more than that, of yearning for the 'I'm leaving my wife because I want to be with you for ever'-type declarations – but it was so far from a great emotional farewell that it was almost laughable. He did allow us to make love between the chilly damp sheets on the spare bed instead of on his dead mother's carpet. Perhaps that was his idea of a romantic goodbye.

It certainly wasn't mine, on a lumpy mattress with such a sag in the middle that we were thrown together on it, flailing like drowning fishermen. I realised I preferred him when he had his uniform on. Naked, he reminded me of something soft and formless, a mollusc without a shell.

It was pretty clear we'd both already moved on.

Afterwards, over a cup of tea in Mrs McCloughlin's formica and lino kitchen, Adrian did say, 'I hope you find what you're looking for, Waitsey.'

'What do you mean?'

'I mean … I hope you meet someone you can settle down with. Have kids and that.'

And what? I thought. I hated it when people said 'and that'. He did it a lot.

'I really do want kids,' I admitted.

'I know you do. I'm sure it'll happen for you. Probably just when you think it's the last thing on your mind, and with the last person you thought it would be, but you'll suddenly realise it was what you were looking for all along.'

This was a very cryptic remark. Adrian wasn't normally given to philosophy – perhaps this was his way of expressing remorse.

'Who knows,' I said, making a face at him as I tucked my shirt back into my jeans. 'Got a job to do first, though.'

Back in my studio flat in Hampton, I reminded myself that it wasn't the first Christmas I'd spent on my own, and I didn't mind anyway, not really. I wasn't sure I could cope with what most people believed to be an ideal family Christmas; overexcited children running around screaming, adults bickering and drinking too much, the problematic relatives you only ever saw once a year and that was too often…

Even when I was a kid, Christmas was just Mum, Dad and me, with the occasional addition of some elderly auntie or another who had usually popped her clogs by the following year. My dearth of relatives never really bothered me until Mum and Dad died, but even then it was more of an embarrassment than a grief. If I was invited to celebrate with friends I normally declined, preferring my own company to the awkward jollity of someone else's distant relatives.

I dropped the empty mince pie box into the bin and decided that I wouldn't crack open the wine until I'd done a few hours' work. Christmas or not, the new job was about to begin, and I had a lot to do.

I hadn't been given all the details of my brief yet, but Metcalfe had provided me with the target's name, Ed Naismith, and that of his missing wife, Shelagh, so I opened my laptop and immersed myself in all the online newspaper articles I could find about her disappearance. Then I searched Facebook – still in its infancy and therefore no help to me at all – obviously this had already been done, but I needed to keep on top of it in case of any new updates. Daylight faded and I imagined the darkness as holly and mulled wine-scented, pressing against the grimy window of my bedsit, everyone else's festive breath fogging it up.

I studied every photograph of Ed Naismith that I could find online, stills from the press conference he'd given, and the photo he'd released of him and Shelagh sitting at a table in the bar of what looked like a country club or tennis club (lots of gilt-inscribed championship tournament boards on the wall behind them), both of them in tennis whites raising a glass to whomever was behind the camera. Shelagh was smiling but I thought there was a tenseness about her eyes – or perhaps I was just imagining it in the light of what was to happen in their lives. I scrutinised Ed's face until I could have erased his features and drawn back in every line and curve.

He was a good-looking man; tall and broad, with a shock of greying, sandy hair and bright-blue eyes. Confident, probably arrogant, looked far younger than his fifty-one years. I suppressed an internal shudder of relief that he was fit; it would make it so much easier to flirt. I wondered how best to engineer a meeting with him. He didn't seem to have a dog, which was a shame. I'd love to have a dog myself, and it would have been the perfect excuse for bumping into him when our dog-walking routes just happened to coincide ... Perhaps I could join whatever sports club that photo was taken in? The trouble was, I was rubbish at tennis and I'd never played golf in my life. Still, where there was a will ... I did a search for local sports and tennis clubs, and found a list that I printed out. I could go and visit them all, check if I recognised the background of that photo. That would be a start.

At that moment a text arrived from Nicky: *HAPPY CHRISTMAS MY LOVE. I HOPE YOU HAVE A GOOD ONE WHEREVER YOU ARE. XXX.* I should have got rid of that phone, but I hadn't. I'd been hoping for more messages, Sal or Weller or Quint even, but the time for that sort of sentimentality was past – although I felt sad that not even Sal had texted.

Christmas was my cut-off period. I replied to Nicky, then I took out the SIM card and snipped it into tiny neat slivers with my nail scissors. I did a factory reset on the phone, deleting all the data remaining, and popped in my new SIM. New number, new life, new goal. The realisation that I myself could be someone new too was thrilling and heady.

19
January 2007

In the end, I didn't need to recce any country clubs or take up tennis lessons. My new boss, DS Metcalfe, had already decided exactly how Ed Naismith and I were going to meet.

'Ever done any acting, Waites?'

I thought that Metcalfe was referring to going undercover – what was that, if not acting? I was about to reassure him of my poker face when he continued, 'Am-dram, I mean. Tits and teeth. The smell of greasepaint, musical theatre, Romeo oh Romeo, is this a dagger I see before me? Et cetera, et cetera.'

'Oh – actual acting, on a stage? Not since I was in school, no.'

Metcalfe laughed. 'Better brush up on your Stanislavsky techniques then. You're going to audition for a play.'

'What?'

It wasn't that I couldn't – or even that I didn't want to – but this was a bit of a curveball. Ed Naismith wasn't, unless I'd missed that part of the briefing, a treader of the boards.

'But he was a GP, not an actor!'

Metcalfe nodded. 'He was. He's also a keen amateur actor and director and, helpfully for you, he's about to direct a play for his local luvvies, the Molesey Amateur Dramatic Group, known locally as MADS. Perfect opportunity for you to get to know him, so it would be ideal if you got a part, don't you think? I suggest you suddenly get very interested indeed in am-dram…'

This conversation was taking place in a small windowless interview room at Woking police station.

'Sounds fun,' I said, doubtfully. I supposed it was preferable to me joining a tennis club when I barely knew which end of the racket to hold.

DS Metcalfe handed me a thick manila folder. 'This is your bible,' he said ponderously, doing a strange sort of fluttery thing with his eyelids that seemed to be his indication of how serious an issue was. He'd done it a lot since I met him an hour ago. 'Notes on Shelagh Naismith's disappearance, transcripts of all the interviews we did with her family and friends. Ed Naismith doesn't have an alibi for the night she disappeared and as you know, we've never found a body.'

'So why do you think he did it then?'

Metcalfe pursed his lips. He was a large man with very fleshy lips, dark and shiny-looking, like offal, and he was balding, a domed head emerging out of the tonsure, just a little island of hair stranded on the top of his head. *You need to shave that right off, mate*, I thought, trying not to stare at it. He was unappealing, physically, but seemed kind and polite. I thought we'd probably get on fine – which was fortunate, because he was going to be my still centre of the new turning world in which I'd found myself. My handler, only contact point, sole confidante.

'Just something about him,' he said. 'Slippery bastard, too smug for his own good. Doesn't seem half as upset as he should about his wife going missing. That, and the fact that her sister's convinced he's done her in. Hysterical, she was. You'll see, it's all in there.' He tapped the folder. 'I'll show you the videos of his interviews, too, see what you think. He fancies himself as an actor and it all just felt very rehearsed. We've got him in three times, searched his house, but we've never had anything we can pin on him. He just keeps insisting that she suffered from depression and might have harmed herself.'

'And did she? Have depression, I mean?'

He nodded. 'GP report's in there.'

'Not a GP from the same practice Naismith was attached to, I take it?'

'No. And her doctor claims not to know him – I know, that's what I thought, too, but it's another dead end. You're our last shot, Waites. If you don't uncover anything, we'll have to write her off as another misper, and leave it at that. Maybe some poor dog-walking bastard will stumble over her body in the woods at some point, then at least we'll be able to figure out what happened, but if not, we're counting on you to see if you can dig up anything we could use to nail him. Any questions?'

'Um … I'd have to get to know him pretty well to get him to open up to me about his marriage. I'm not interested in prostituting myself, you know.'

The little island of hair on Metcalfe's pate shot backwards as his eyebrows jerked upwards. 'As if we would suggest such a thing!'

'So, how exactly am I meant to gain his trust?'

'Men and women can be friends, can't they? I reckon your best bet is to be the new rock in his life. A bit of flirting won't hurt. You can flirt, can't you Waites? You're not unattractive. I'm sure if you put your mind to it…'

'Thank you,' I said, as sarcastically as I dared.

'Search his house again when he's out, in case we missed something. Listen out for clues as to his relationship with Shelagh Naismith. Talk to the boy if you can, without arousing suspicion. Anything that might ultimately give us the evidence we need. DCI McLoughlin speaks very highly of you, and assures me you're up to the task.'

I felt a flicker of something at the mention of Adrian's name. Sadness? Flattery? Loss? I really wasn't sure what it was.

'That's nice, sir.'

'Call me Brian, Waites.'

I laughed at the irony of this, and he joined in – but only after several beats. He was a serious sort of chap.

'So what happens next, Brian?'

He leaned forward, both palms planted on the table. 'We get your life story straight. And before we do that, we pick your new name. That's our goal for this afternoon. In fact, let's go now. We can talk more on the way.'

I was confused. 'Where do we go?' I had a fanciful mental image of some kind of Names Department of Surrey Police where you went to sign yourself out a new one, like the ARG signing guns out for their raids.

'You'll see,' he said, standing up.

Metcalfe and I got the train to the Family Records Centre in Clerkenwell and, five hours later, I had my new name. Cara Lynn Jackson. I chose it myself – or rather, I stole it from a little dead girl. So many dead children, so many names. I had run my eyes down hundreds of columns, searching for a girl born in the same year as I was who had died young. She needed to have had a plain surname – not Smith or Jones, that was too plain – but nothing unusual or easily searched-for online. We needed to share a Christian name: that was trickier, but eventually I found the birth and death certificate of a little girl called Cara Lynn Jackson, born just three months after my real birthday, died aged three of meningitis. Perfect, for my purposes.

Poor little Cara though, I thought, as I'd ordered a copy of her birth certificate. I imagined her as a chubby toddler, one minute running around on chunky legs, gleeful in a sandpit – and then the bewilderment on her feverish face, howls subsiding into ominous silence as her temperature rocketed and her parents – Debbie and Cliff – became more and more frantic as their daughter's life slipped away before their grieving eyes, her identity only to be stolen years later … For some reason I felt more upset thinking about Cara's death than I did about my own parents'.

She had lived her short life in a council flat in Rayleigh, Essex, and later on I visited it, standing outside the address, looking at overflowing bins and flaking pebbledash. Her parents no longer lived there, I'd checked – they divorced a couple of years after Cara's death. Cliff had moved abroad and Debbie remarried, which was useful to me. Made them both very difficult to trace, if someone ever became suspicious.

After going to the flat, I visited Rayleigh cemetery and found Cara's grave. It was in heart-shaped granite with a stone teddy peeping over the top left corner, and the inscription: 'Our Precious Little Girl: We Have You in Our Hearts But Wish We Had You in Our Arms', with her dates underneath.

I made myself put it out of my head; put Cara out of my head. She no longer existed. *I* was Cara Lynn Jackson now; even my new passport said so. But everyone would call me Lynn.

20

Towards the end of January, as instructed, I pitched up at the Molesey Amateur Dramatic Society's open audition. It was for a wartime play about land girls. I was pretty certain I'd never get one of the four parts, having not acted since I was at school, but I figured that there would be loads of other ways I could get involved – I didn't care what I did as long as I got myself in there somehow.

I sidled into the little studio theatre at the designated time and clocked Ed Naismith straightaway, tall and impressive, clad in expensive-looking jeans and a beautifully cut soft leather jacket. He had an amazing shock of sandy hair and his eyes looked even bluer than in the photos I'd studied. As I took a script out of the box, he smiled at me, and suddenly it wasn't difficult to imagine that I really did want a part in the play.

'Isn't he gorgeous?' whispered the woman next to me, a rake-thin forty-something with sparse dark hair scraped into a high ponytail. 'I wouldn't mind being directed to do anything by him!' She chuckled lasciviously under her breath and took a seat in the third row. Grateful for someone to talk to, I slid in next to her and looked around at the couple of dozen women, many of whom seemed to know each other already.

'Marion,' said the woman, holding out a bony hand. When I shook it, I felt the veins on the back of it so thick and prominent that they yielded and squidged under my fingers.

'Lynn,' I said, smiling at her as I flipped through the pages of the script. 'I'm new.'

'Hey, me, too. We should stick together. So – you recognise him, don't you?' my new friend asked confidingly, making sure she wasn't overheard.

I turned and looked at Ed with a casually puzzled expression on my face. 'Him? No – recognise him from where? Is he on telly or something? He looks like he should be.'

Marion smiled, revealing crowded smokers' teeth that ruined her appearance in a flash. 'Not exactly. Don't you remember, he was all over the local news last year? His wife's the woman that went missing.'

I shook my head. 'No ... I've only just moved to Hampton so I wouldn't have seen it unless it was in the national news. Poor bloke! Poor woman, too – what happened to her?'

Marion shrugged, an expression in her eyes that looked to me more like delight than concern. 'She's never been seen again! Just like Richey Manic, you remember, that pop star? She suffered from depression, too, apparently. That's their son over there. Don't know what *he's* doing here. Waiting for a lift, probably.'

'How awful.' I regarded Ed, who was standing on the stage chatting animatedly to the older woman next to him.

His son was a great hulk of a teenager in school uniform, sitting in the raked seating away from everyone else, pecking at a mobile phone and looking disdainful. Even through the greasy blond hair and acne I could see the resemblance between him and Ed. He'd be good-looking, one day, I thought.

The older woman clapped her hands to get everyone's attention. She introduced herself as Sandra, the producer. She was dressed in tight jeans and a clingy, garish top, but her face belied her age. Thick foundation and powder settled in all her many lines and it became obvious, when she adjusted it, that she wore a wig.

She introduced Ed – not mentioning anything of his personal circumstances of course, but talking about his long career within MADS as both actor and director.

'Thank you all for coming,' she concluded. 'It's great to see so many new faces. Right, let's make a start. We're going to call you up in groups of four and get you to read a few lines of the different parts.'

In the first 'round', I read the part of Mabel, a housemaid from Stevenage. Then I read some of Joan, a secretly lesbian farm girl, Millie, the society one, and finally Doris, a seamstress from the East End of London. Ed and Sandra the producer watched impassively, but at one point I saw Ed lean over and whisper something in Sandra's ear whilst gesturing towards me. Sandra nodded briefly. It looked as though it was going well.

Finally we all had to sing a verse of *The White Cliffs of Dover*, four at a time. I was standing next to Marion, but the woman had a voice like nails down a blackboard and it really put me off. I hoped they didn't think it was me.

I went home to my studio that night feeling a sense of achievement, despite being certain I wouldn't be offered a part, but I was even less bothered than I'd been before the audition, because a part would mean performing a quarter of a whole play, in front of whole audiences. Yes, I liked a challenge, but this one was so far out of my comfort zone that it was ridiculous. Surely Metcalfe didn't really expect me to do that?

I'd met Ed, which was my brief. Even if I didn't get a part, they had emphasised what I had thought, that they also wanted costume assistants, ticket-tearers and volunteer bar staff. Plenty of other ways I could get close to him.

So it was with a combination of astonishment, delight and trepidation that I received news the next morning – I'd been offered the part of Mabel. Ed rang me himself. He was completely charming, saying how beautiful my singing voice was, and how well I had read. The first meeting would be in two days' time, for the cast to meet each other and do a read-through. I came off the phone and triumphantly fist-pumped the air. I was in! Metcalfe would be very happy with me. I was pretty happy with myself, too.

21

The first meeting of the cast of *Make Do and Mend* convened at Ed's house a few days after the auditions. I consulted an A-Z and got there on foot, although it turned out to be a lot further from my flat in Hampton than I'd thought. I'd wrapped up warm as it was a frosty day and had ended up taking off winter accessories – hat, gloves, scarf – and stuffing them into my bag at regular intervals along the way. Ed lived somewhere I'd never heard of called East Molesey, which turned out to be a conservation area near Hampton Court Palace. His house was massive, a detached early Victorian villa with gables, stained glass above the door and original wooden shutters at the windows.

I crunched sweatily up the drive and pulled the doorbell – it was one of those horrifically loud jingly-jangly ones that rang on and on for what seemed like an eternity, making it sound like you were a really aggressive visitor when really you'd just intended to announce your arrival with a quick ring. A sulky teenager answered the door, all sallow skin and spots. Ed's son, the one who had been sitting, uninterested, at the audition.

'Who are you?' he demanded, glaring at me.

'I'm Lynn. Is this, er, Ed's house?' I said, although of course I knew full well that it was.

'No, I meant, who are you in the play?' His expression had *duh* written all over it. It had often occurred to me since that Ben had never really stopped looking at me like that.

'Oh! I'm going to be Mabel. The housemaid.'

He gave me a head-to-toe once over and then sniffed. 'Yes,' he said. 'I can see that now.'

I resisted the urge to accidentally-on-purpose elbow him in the face as he reluctantly admitted me into a monochrome-tiled hallway. 'Lovely house,' I said, but he ignored me. 'Da-ad!' he yelled. 'Another one's here!'

Ed's face appeared upside down over the ornate banisters, blood rushing to his already-red cheeks, which were dangling slightly, like a cartoon dog's. At that moment I didn't fancy him at all.

'Lynn! Do come upstairs to the living room,' I wondered if he'd added the last four words in case I thought he was inviting me into his boudoir. 'We're almost all here.'

'Sorry, am I late?' I asked, affecting fluster. His head withdrew and then the whole of him reappeared at the top of the stairs.

'Not at all, not at all. I see you've met Benjy.'

I smiled at Benjy, who did not smile back.

'Dad! I told you, it's Ben now,' he shouted up at his father.

There was a large framed photograph on the wall up the stairs of him, Ed and Shelagh, taken a few years back because Benjy – Ben – was at that stage of childhood where he had enormous tombstone front teeth. Interesting, I thought, trying not to stare at it as I passed. Shelagh was, or had been, exceptionally beautiful, with long auburn hair, green eyes and a delicate smattering of freckles across a tiny little nose.

'Come through,' Ed said expansively, gesturing to the front room. 'Ben's just bringing up some coffee. Aren't you, Benjy?'

There was a growl of 'It's *Ben!*' from downstairs, an extra-enunciated 'n' on the end so it sounded like 'Ben-nuh'.

'This is April, who's playing Doris; and you remember Sandra, our lovely producer?' He put an arm around Sandra, who pretended to shake him off but secretly looked thrilled.

April was a petite blonde with such a pretty face that I couldn't stop glancing at her. Whenever she smiled, the pink of her cheeks deepened into apples and showed off her perfect little white teeth. I felt like a galumphing elephant in comparison, even though actually April and I were a similar size. April's petiteness looked soft and feminine next to my more androgynous body.

Both women said hello to me and April stood up and formally shook my hand.

'You're new to MADS, aren't you?' April asked.

'Yes, I've only just moved to the area.'

April had one of those really intense gazes that you felt slightly trapped by. 'Don't worry, we're all very friendly. A big family, really, aren't we?'

She didn't ask where I had moved from, or what I was doing in the area – which of course was a relief to me, although I had my cover story rehearsed and off pat: I'd split up with my husband and moved here to have a fresh start; I'd always wanted to live round here after fond memories of summers spent with a grandmother who owned a houseboat on the Thames; I was looking for work as a PA.

The others laughed as though she had cracked a hilarious joke when she said they were all a big family.

'April's married to Mike, who'll be our set designer,' Ed said by way of expla- nation, and April thrust the knuckles of her left hand forward to show off an enormous diamond engagement ring with a thick gold band beneath it, as if they had only just got betrothed, even though I later found out they had eleven-year old twin boys. 'And Sandra is Mike's mother.'

'Wow, that's a lovely ring,' I said politely, although it was much more osten- tatious than anything I would ever have chosen. April beamed.

'Isn't this exciting? I just can't wait to get stuck in.' She picked a script up off the sofa and began to read – I noticed she had already highlighted all of her lines in neon yellow – in an OTT Cockney accent, all glottal stop and hammy delivery: '"So I fort I would get off of my fat backside an' get a job on one of them farms. I ain't never been to the cunt'ryside before..."'

'Marvellous, darling,' Ed said. I thought he sounded sarcastic but April gave a little curtsey and looked delighted. Had she only got the part because the producer was her mother-in-law?

'Right, we're just waiting for Robina.' He turned to me. 'She's playing Joan. The fourth member of our cast is Pat, but she can't make it today. You'll meet her at the first rehearsal next week.'

I nodded obediently and sat down on the huge, overstuffed sofa. It was one of those really deep sofas that you had to either perch on the edge of, or sit back so far that your legs stuck straight out in front like a child's.

'Nice house,' I offered, looking around the room at the African artefacts – wooden masks, zebra print cushions – and theatre memorabilia, framed playbills and posters for productions. The whole house looked recently decorated, all the pine interior doors stripped and beautifully waxed, no fingermarks or scuffs on the banisters or walls.

'Thank you. Glad you like it. Ah – refreshments have arrived!'

Ben reluctantly returned, carrying a tray that was almost too wide for him to hold and that wobbled perilously. A pot of coffee and four mugs clinked together, and a plate of Party Rings slid around the tray's slippery surface, almost falling off, as he teetered towards a coffee table. Sandra intercepted it just in time.

The doorbell rang again, but in the way I would have wanted it to when I'd pulled it myself – a brief discreet jangle. Robina had obviously been here before too.

Looking back, I couldn't remember much about Robina at our first meeting. She was lovely – they all were – but it was April's huge blue eyes and china complexion that stuck in my mind. That, and Ed's magnetism.

It was funny, I thought much later, that so many of the people in that theatre group came to play such a huge part in my life in the years to come. Ed, obviously; April and Mike, obnoxious Benjy, my stepson. The costume lady, Maddie, who became my closest friend.

Ed seemed at first to have no interest in me at all, other than as an actor in the play he was directing – but then, why would he? It had only been a year since his wife had vanished. I worried that I was being ridiculously presumptuous to think that I could stroll in and win his confidence, just like that, particularly when the whole thing was a charade.

But then, suddenly, within a few weeks, something began to change.

I started to wonder if I was imagining the new chemistry between us. It just felt too good to be true, both from the perspective of my mission and from a personal point of view. Sometimes it felt so strong, crackling blue and invisible whenever our eyes met, and other times it wasn't there at all. I felt confused, but ever more determined. I had to play it right – too uninterested, and I would never get to know him. Too keen, and I would scare him off.

So for the first few weeks of rehearsals I focussed instead on building my friendships with the three other cast members, as well as with Sandra and Ed. When Ed praised me, I affected nonchalance, while the other three would squeal and blush if he singled them out. I pretended not to notice when he gazed at me and decided that I would only gaze back very occasionally, just enough to make him aware that I might – *might* – be interested. After a couple of weeks I realised it was working – he was definitely beginning to pay me more attention.

22

It took another month of determined but discreet flirting until Ed eventually asked me out, a few weeks before the opening night of *Make Do and Mend*. Naturally I accepted without hesitation.

This was my chance.

'So, tell me about yourself,' Ed said, pouring me another glass of a smooth Malbec. I made a mental note for that to be my last – I needed to stay in control. 'What brought Lynn Jackson to Molesey – or, no, I think you said you live in Hampton?'

We were in a blandly expensive restaurant decorated in shades of cream; carpets and walls and chairs. Ed had already apologised for its boring hotelish appearance but made extravagant claims about the food. He stood out against the neutral decor in a soft cornflower-blue shirt that made the blue of his eyes look ridiculously bright, and I wondered if he had planned his outfit and the restaurant for that very reason. I'd noticed that he was a man very aware of his appearance; never a hair out of place, never without a high shine on his shoes, glancing into every mirror and reflective surface he passed. Every pair of jeans looked brand-new.

I bit my lip, as if his question stirred up painful memories, and stared down at my empty starter plate. 'Hampton Hill, actually.'

Ed raised his eyebrows.

'Nothing exciting,' I continued, trotting out my rehearsed backstory in a suitably glum voice. 'I just wanted a fresh start. Bad break-up, you know? I was married, far too young, army wife, stationed with Dave all over the place. Our last posting together was Cyprus, now he's gone to Afghanistan. I used to come and stay with my granny round here when I was a kid – she had a houseboat somewhere, although I've not managed to find out where – so I know the area a bit, and have happy memories of it. Couldn't afford to live in central London, so this seemed like a good compromise without being too suburban. So, this is the start of my new life. I'm being adventurous and doing all sorts of stuff that I've never done before – like acting.'

He smiled. 'You're not telling me you've never acted before? You're a natural!'

I inclined my head. 'Why, thank you. But actually I haven't, not since I was the Dormouse in *Alice in Wonderland* when I was at school.'

This at least was true.

'I'd never have guessed. And how is the new job going?'

I'd been in my new job for a month or so, office manager in a boring financial advisor's office nearby.

'It's fine, thanks. Easy, you know? Just typing letters and arranging meetings for an accountant called Henry. It's not exactly that taxing, if you'll excuse the pun. Pays the bills, though, and I have my fun outside of work hours at MADS, so it's all good…'

'We could have a lot of fun, you and I,' Ed interrupted with a glint in his eye, reaching out and stroking my finger, the one curled around the stem of my wine glass.

I knew by now that he fancied me, but even so it gave me a shock of anticipation and – I was concerned to discover – arousal.

'I think so too,' I said. 'But—'

At that moment the waiter came to clear away our starter plates. He looked whey-faced, as if he'd been chosen to match the bland decor, concave and hunched. I waited until he had gone.

'But what?' Ed asked. 'But you're still married?'

'I was going to say, but *you're* still married, aren't you?'

It was the first time either of us had acknowledged the missing Shelagh. 'Do you mind me mentioning it?'

My mouth had gone dry so I took another sip of the wine, feeling it soak into my tongue, plumping it up like a sponge in water.

Ed sighed. 'Well, we had to at some point. I assume you know the story, then?'

'Not really,' I said. 'Just a couple of comments people have made, you know, that she's missing and nobody knows where she is.'

'She's dead,' he said bluntly. 'I'm sure she is.' Tears came to his eyes and he blinked them away furiously.

'Oh Ed, I'm sorry. I didn't want to upset you.'

He took my hand then, unfurling my fingers and weaving his in between them. The touch of his flesh on mine gave me a sudden start, a little hourglass of desire tipping over in my belly. Uh-oh, I thought. It was a stark reminder that I'd not had anybody in my life who really cared about me since my parents died.

'You aren't. I am upset, yes, but a year on I'm more upset that she could be so selfish, do that to Benjy, cause this much stress and anxiety to everyone.'

'You think she killed herself?'

'I'm sure she did. She suffered from depression. She used to threaten to do it all the time. We didn't have a good marriage, Lynn. Like you and your husband, we got together far too young and we were so different. She was really shy, crippled by self-doubt. She had all sorts of issues – body dysmorphia, do you know what that is?'

I shook my head – although I did know. I'd seen it in one of the police interviews Shelagh's friends and family had given around her disappearance. In fact, I thought I recalled it had been Ed who had brought it up. I'd had to go away and look it up online.

'It's when you're a normal size but you think you're huge.'

'Like anorexia?'

'Sort of, although Shelagh wasn't anorexic. She was bulimic, and she self-harmed. I think she used to wish she *could* be anorexic and her lack of success at not eating was just something else she used to beat herself up about…'

'But she was so beautiful,' I said. 'That portrait of you all, the one on the stairs at your house – she was gorgeous.' I wondered if he would correct my use of the past tense, but he didn't.

'She really was,' he agreed instead. 'It was tragic that she couldn't see it herself. I tried to get her along to MADS, get her involved in something fun, but she wasn't interested. She hated me going, but she didn't want to join in either.'

'Did she have any hobbies or interests of her own?'

He shrugged. 'Not really. She loved reading, and jogging.'

'Both pretty solitary.'

'I know. She was very close to her sister though, and most evenings they would talk for hours on the phone. Ellen lives outside of Edinburgh so they didn't see each other that often.'

'Must have been really hard for Ellen when Shelagh went missing.'

Ed nodded. 'She lost the plot. Accused me of all sorts. It was a nightmare.'

I sat forward, my eyes wide open with affected shock. 'Shelagh's sister thought you killed her?'

The waiter brought our main courses on enormous cream dinner plates at that moment, putting them down with a weary flourish. Ed squinched his eyebrows between his thumb and middle finger, a gesture of stress. When the waiter had retreated he said, 'No, not that drastic. Just that I had driven her away.'

He snorted, picking up his knife and fork and sawing off a large triangle at the edge of his steak. 'God, if she had any idea how difficult her sister was to live with!'

'Do you miss her; Shelagh, I mean?' I asked, scrutinising my chicken in cream sauce. I appeared to have selected my food to match the walls, the carpet and the waiter. I had a sudden urge for some beetroot or broccoli, something vibrant and colourful.

Or perhaps the urge was for Ed himself, in his cornflower-blue shirt and matching eyes. It was a relief to be discussing Shelagh after so many weeks of her being the elephant in the room. The elephant *not* in the room, or anywhere else, I thought.

'We can change the subject if you like,' I added hastily. 'Wow, this chicken is delicious!'

He smiled briefly at me. 'It's OK, Lynn, really. We had to talk about it at some time. I do miss her sometimes, yes. Mostly I miss her on Benjy's behalf. He adored her. I feel so angry with her that she could do that to him. She didn't even leave a note...'

He stabbed at a chip, his jaw set. 'If she came back now, the truth is I'd divorce her like a shot,' he said. 'The worst part for me is this limbo. I can't move on with my life, not knowing. I just wish they would find her body so we can all have closure.'

'What makes you so sure she's dead?'

The restaurant was filling up around us, and we were both leaning forward and speaking in low, intense voices so nobody could overhear.

'She must be. She would have contacted Ben if she wasn't, I know she would.'

'It's so sad.' I felt genuinely emotional. Poor Ben. It was hard enough being a teenage boy at the best of times, let alone with the sense of abandonment and unresolved grief his mother's disappearance must have engendered. 'I hope he's having some sort of counselling? I lost my parents when I was in my early twenties, so I know how hard it is – and their deaths weren't anything as traumatic as what Ben's been through.'

Ed snorted. 'Counselling? He won't talk at all unless it's to order a pizza over the phone. Everything is communicated via the medium of grunts or text messages.'

'Sounds like fairly standard teenage behaviour to me.'

I wondered if Shelagh had merely decamped to live nearer her sister in Edinburgh, and Ellen's anger towards Ed was some kind of vengeful double bluff? Although it did seem harsh of Shelagh not to have contacted her son in over a year, if that was the case.

'Anyway. Let's talk about more cheerful things. Are you enjoying the rehearsals?'

'I love them! Honestly, Ed, Mondays and Thursdays are the highlights of my week. Everyone's so nice and I don't think I've laughed so much in years.'

This was true. I'd forgotten what it was like to laugh until your sides hurt and your cheeks ached. 'And I love the girls.'

The three other women in the play, April, Robina and Pat, by happy coincidence shared a somewhat dirty sense of humour with me, meaning our repertoire of shared jokes was growing by the week – quite often at the expense of Sandra the producer, who had a tendency to nitpick and criticise.

'I can't believe I didn't do more stuff like this years ago,' I said, scraping up a final forkful of my roasted garlic and Parmesan mashed potato.

'Well, we're loving having you.' Ed gazed at me with an unmistakably lustful expression. Then he leaned forwards. 'Just, er, keep this to yourself though, would you? You know how people talk, and I wouldn't want the others to be jealous…'

I wasn't quite sure if he was joking about the jealous bit or not, but I agreed immediately, feeling a huge rush of adrenaline at it all: my new start, the play, Ed asking me out.

What I wasn't so sure of, however, was my motive for feeling so happy about the progress of my mission with Ed. Was it because Metcalfe would be pleased with me – or because I really did fancy Ed?

'Let's have another glass of wine,' I said impulsively.

23

I came back from a trip to Tesco one afternoon the following week to find Ed waiting for me by the front door looking excited, hovering in the hall in the pitch dark. He looked like a dog waiting for its owner to return and I imagined him having sat on the doormat all day with a resigned expression on his face. He was wearing his coat over the top of his pyjamas, which was his only concession to getting dressed that day.

I dumped five full shopping bags in the hall, switched on the hall light and hung up my jacket. 'Hi sweetie. Were you waiting for me?'

He fished about in his parka pocket, pulled out a folded and creased piece of A4 and handed it to me. 'Look. I printed it when you were out,' he said proudly.

It was another email, dated a week before. I unfolded it curiously. 'So you remembered what your password is then?'

'Yes.'

'So what is it?'

'What's what?'

'Your password!'

'I've forgotten again.'

I narrowed my eyes at him, unable to prevent the thought, *Well, that's convenient,* springing into my mind. 'Next time it comes to you, write it down?'

'OK, bossy boots.'

'Ha ha. Help me with this lot?' I said, gesturing to the bags as I scanned the email and speed-read the contents out loud: *'Dear Dr Nai-smith, my name is Dr Ellie Webster and I am working with our mutual colleague Bill Brown on the Phase 3 trial for aducanumab. I'm sorry to hear of your recent diagnosis of Pick's Disease and appreciate that this must be a difficult time for you and your family. Thank you for volunteering your participation and I would like to invite you to come for the first intravenous infusion on Wednesday, 25th October at 11am. I will send a taxi for you at 10am. I have your address and am looking forward to meeting you.*

I am truly confident that you will see remarkable improvements in a short time from this new drug, specifically in the areas of cognition, memory and behaviour...'

I remembered the sensation of Ed's big hand whacking the side of my head in the night, and winced. Bill Brown. So that was his surname – that was good to know. I hadn't contacted him on his personal email yet because I'd need to get into Ed's laptop to find out what it was. Then I did a doubletake.

'Ed, the 25th was yesterday! You've missed it!'

'Yeah,' said Ed, vaguely, picking up two bags. 'I mean, no, I haven't. I went!'

'*What?* Are you serious?'

'You were at work.'

'Why didn't you tell me?' I wailed, picking up the other three and following him into the kitchen.

He shrugged. 'You were at work,' he repeated.

I sank onto a chair at the kitchen table, my head in my hands. 'But you didn't mention it last night! I asked you what you'd done yesterday and you said "nothing"!'

'I totally forgot. Sorry.'

I noticed that his eyebrows badly needed trimming. Ed had a whole shelf in the bathroom cabinet of grooming devices for the more mature male: nose-hair trimmers, tweezers, nail scissors and so on, but he clearly hadn't gone near any of it in recent months. I remembered how he used to be; sharp haircut, no stray facial hairs, clean-shaven and beautifully dressed in an expensive suit and a well-cut shirt, tall and in control. All those designer jeans and cashmere jumpers in his wardrobe and now he just wore PJs all day. Had he worn his pyjamas to the appointment? In my mind's eye I saw him as how he looked when I first met him, with that particular expression of lazy arrogance in his blue eyes I always found utterly irresistible.

Even when I still thought he could be a murderer.

We all got older, of course ... I certainly didn't look anything like as good as I had done in my thirties – but still ... I'd so have loved to have the old Ed back again.

'Well – how was it?'

'Fine,' he said, putting a bag of frozen spinach into the dishwasher. 'She filled in a long list thing.'

'Form? Don't worry, leave the shopping, sweetheart, I'll put it away.'

'Yeah. Then I got an injection here' – he pointed to the crook of his elbow – 'that took a while. Then I came home. No big deal.'

I had so many questions I didn't know where to start. So many, in fact, that I didn't ask any of them. The mood Ed was in would only yield monosyllables, and if he'd forgotten even going, he was unlikely to be able to give me any satisfactory answers.

'Let's see?' I pushed up his sleeve. One of those tiny round plasters perched on top of a purple vein flowing beneath his skin, but there wasn't any bruising around it. Ed normally had a tendency to bruise after blood tests, but perhaps it was different when stuff was going in instead of blood coming out ... but what did I know?

'Oh my love,' I said impulsively, retrieving the spinach and putting it in the freezer. 'Wouldn't it be incredible if it worked? If it cured you?'

I went over and hugged him, but he backed out of the embrace. 'I wish everyone would stop making such a fuss,' he said. 'It's just a *cold*.'

Later that evening, when Ed had gone to bed, I took out my phone, hesitating before I pressed the name Linda. That was the name I'd saved Adrian's number under, having already concocted a story in my head about Linda being an administrator from a different faculty with whom I'd recently struck up a friendship. Calling 'Linda' was already a regular occurrence – in the ten days since we'd bumped into each other, Adrian and I had talked three times. I felt weird and uncomfortable about it, in as much as I'd never had a friendship with another man, not since my mate Sal in the police, but Adrian had encouraged me to talk, vent, cry – not that I'd do that, not yet. He was appalled to hear my situation, and so deeply sympathetic that I already felt myself looking forward to his counsel. Somehow it was easier to talk to him than to April or Maddie, my friend who'd recently moved to Jersey. Perhaps because he was so neutral?

I knew I had to be careful, not to steer into the choppy waters of 'emotional infidelity' – but he hadn't said or done anything that could be construed as flirtatious, beyond telling me how good I still looked, when we said our goodbyes at the Barbican. He wasn't looking for another relationship, he said, not at the moment.

He was pleased to hear from me, I could hear it in his voice. 'Waits—er, Lynn! How are you? Hold on, I'll just turn down my ratatouille and grab a glass of wine...'

And we talked. I told him about the medical trial, how Ed had gone without me. How I felt about locking him in his room at night. I lightened the tone, made them sound like amusing anecdotes, and Adrian's belly laugh made me laugh too, in a way I hadn't done for ages. When we said goodnight, I went to bed feeling rejuvenated, almost happy, like a woman who was still attractive, listened to, a woman who could make a man laugh.

Nothing more complicated than that.

Well, that was what I told myself, anyway.

24

Two weeks of solo sleeping later, I woke up, stretched and squirmed, toasty-warm and woozy in my bed – how quickly I was thinking of it as 'my' bed. Would I never share a bed with Ed again?

Of course I would, I thought, sliding my legs out and standing up, the joy of awakening unmolested making me feel a renewed optimism about life in general. It had just been a phase he was going through. Perhaps next week we could try co-sleeping again. I had to keep positive, count my blessings, otherwise I'd never stay sane. Work was great, the open day incident seemingly forgotten. I had good friends, a job I loved, my health, Ben and Jeanine were happy and settled ... My phone calls with Adrian were massively helping me process stuff – I kept telling him he should retrain as a therapist. I was sure he was instrumental in me turning a corner in my acceptance of Ed's disease. I could cope with it, I thought, putting on my dressing-gown. I could be positive about anything after a few good nights' sleep.

The only blot on the landscape was my own growing feelings towards him; Adrian. We'd arranged to have lunch later, and I realised I was looking forward to it far more than I should.

My mobile rang and I reached for it, smiling at the thought it was probably Adrian. But the smile soon fell off my face. It was April.

'Mike hasn't come home and he's not answering his phone,' she said. Her voice had an accusatory edge to it that I knew was worry, but that anyone else might have thought was antagonism.

'Oh! Where was he last night?' I squinted at the bedside clock and blinked in shock – it was almost ten-thirty! I never slept that late. Good thing it was my day off. 'I've only just woken up – can you believe it?'

April ignored me. 'He was night fishing. But he's always back really early the next morning, he gets so cold. At this time of year he doesn't even wait for the sun to come up – he says that coming home for a hot breakfast is the best part of it.'

'Can't imagine why he'd want to do it in the first place,' I said, suppressing a yawn and getting back under the duvet to talk to her. 'Sorry, that's not very helpful, is it? Could he have gone to a cafe for breakfast? Phone out of battery?' I glanced at my closed bedroom door and gave an involuntary yelp. 'Oh shit! Sorry April, hang on a minute, don't go anywhere, I just have to go and...'

I couldn't bring myself to say it: *Let Ed out*. As if he was a cat meowing at the back door. I leaped up, chucking the phone onto the bed and racing along the landing to the spare room. What if he'd had an accident? What if he'd been banging and shouting and was really pissed off with me? No – I'd have heard him; or he'd have rung my mobile. I wasn't a heavy sleeper.

I took the key out of my dressing-gown pocket and unlocked the door. Ed was in bed, awake and smiling at me, scrolling through something on his iPhone screen. 'Morning, treasure,' he said. 'Did you sleep well?'

Relief coursed through me. 'Really well! Can you believe the time?' I went over and kissed him, tasting his stale morning breath. 'You only just woke up, too? I'll go and make the tea. I'm on the phone to April, Mike's not come home and she's worried.'

Ed rubbed his head, as he always did first thing in the morning. 'She worries too much. He's only been, um, um, what's the word?' He mimed flicking a fishing rod into water and winding in the reel.

'Fishing! Yes, that's what I thought too. Anyway let me go and finish talking to her.'

I hurried back, the woollen hall rug slipping slightly under my bare feet as I skidded round the corner. 'Hi April, sorry about that, I had to check that Ed was OK. Are you still there?'

I hadn't told anyone that I locked him in at night. It felt too demeaning, for us both.

'Yes,' April said flatly. 'Can you ask Ed if he's heard from him? If not,

I'm going to drive to the lake and check if his car's there. He might have had an accident, or a heart attack, or anything. Probably froze to death, the idiot.'

'Do you know exactly where he was? Hold on, let me ask – Ed!'

I put my hand over the phone and called out to Ed, who was now in the bathroom peeing enthusiastically with the door open. 'Ed, did you speak to Mike last night, or get a text from him? He does sometimes call you when he's fishing and bored, doesn't he?'

'No, nothing,' Ed yelled, louder than necessary.

'No he hasn't, darling, I'm sorry,' I relayed back to April. 'So where did you say Mike was fishing?'

'I didn't say.' April was getting testier by the minute. 'He told me he was going to his usual place, Colly Lake. He's been after this one particular carp for ages and he books a peg near where someone else caught it recently. Will you come with me to see if he's OK, Lynn? You don't work on Fridays, do you?'

I paused, dropping my voice. Ed had flushed the loo so could easily be within earshot. 'I can't. I don't like leaving Ed on his own more often than I have to.'

'Oh for God's sake,' April said, and even under the circumstances I felt slightly hurt at my friend's lack of empathy for our situation. 'Ask your neighbour – that's what you do when you go to work, isn't it?'

'Suzan's away. And I'm already having lunch with ... someone from work.'

'Well, bring him with you then!'

'Um ... all right. We'll need half an hour to get breakfast and so on, we've only just woken up.'

'That's fine,' April said. 'It'll take me that long to get over to you. If he calls in the meantime I'll let you know. I'll leave him a note here in case he comes back while we're out.'

25

April was a terrible driver, her technique not enhanced by her current stress levels. I'd barely closed the rear passenger door before she screeched off, scraping the car's silver flanks along the bare bramble bushes at the side of the lane.

Ed was in the front seat, compliant when I'd clipped in his seatbelt, but looking slightly bemused – as well he might, I thought, he'd been in bed twenty minutes earlier. Breakfast was a piece of toast and Marmite that was still clutched in his fist. From my position behind April, I could see him glance down like he was wondering what to do with it.

April was driving with one hand on the steering wheel and the other running through her hair, making it stand up on end. Seeing her black roots exposed made me feel somehow more protective of her.

'Want me to drive?' I asked, as April veered far too sharply to avoid a pothole in the lane.

'No, I know the way. Easier if I do,' April replied. Her voice softened. 'Thanks for coming with me, guys.'

'Where are we going?' Ed asked. His voice sounded thin and reedy, like a little boy's.

I leaned forward into the gap between the front seats. 'We're going to find Mike, remember? He didn't come home last night.'

Ed laughed. 'Dirty doorstop!'

April didn't smile. 'It's serious, Ed, I'm really worried. He's always home for breakfast after fishing.'

She tailed off, focussing – mercifully – on the T-junction of the busy road at the end of the lane. I swivelled my head left, right and left again, not trusting April to find a suitably large gap in the traffic. 'Now!' I said, and April accelerated out.

Ed chuckled again. 'Back-seat driver,' he chided.

'I don't know why you think it's so funny,' April said, once we were whizzing along the main road. She was setting off all the SLOW DOWN! 30MPH ZONE warnings we passed, their jangling neon seeming to leap out at us.

'He doesn't,' I said.

'Don't speak for me,' Ed snapped.

'Sorry, darling. Look, can we all just relax a bit? I'm sure Mike will be fine, April. If his car's not there then we'll know he hasn't had an accident.'

'Not at the lake, maybe, but what if he's had a crash on the way back?'

April's voice was rising again, so I tried to make mine as soothing as possible. 'He'd have come back on this road so if he'd had a crash, we'd see the police cordon or whatever. If there's no sign of him we'll call the hospitals.'

April's mobile rang in her handbag on the back seat next to me and she actually pressed the brake, in the middle of a busy road, causing us all to shoot forward painfully against our seatbelts.

'April!' we both shouted.

'Sorry. Lynn, get that, will you, it might be him!'

I fished around in the expensive buttery-soft leather bag and found April's iPhone. It was flashing 'Unknown Number'.

'Hello, April Greening's phone. Who is this? No – sorry, she's driving at the moment ... I'm her friend, can I help?'

I listened for a few moments longer, fear and nausea rising in me. April and Ed were silent in the front of the car, April slowing down instinctively, as if she knew, causing a stream of cars behind us to hoot and flash their lights.

'Stop the car,' I said eventually, but April was already pulling over, oblivious to the angry gestures from passing drivers. I could tell from the set of her shoulders that she feared the worst.

'That was the police. They want you to go home, now.'

April moaned. 'Have they found him?'

'I don't know. They wouldn't tell me.'

'Oh God. That means they have and he's dead. If he was safe, they'd have told me, wouldn't they? If he was injured or ill, they'd send us to the hospital. He's dead, Lynn, Mike's dead!' Her voice rose to a wail and Ed patted her shoulder awkwardly.

I got out of the back and opened the driver's door, turning off the engine and pulling out the keys. 'We don't know that. I'm going to drive. You get in the back.'

April snatched them back, her eyes wild, mascara streaked all down her cheeks. 'It'll take forty minutes to get back to my place in this traffic. We're only about a mile from the lake – I'm going there first. If the police are there, then I'll know, sooner.'

'No, April, I don't think that's...' I tried to wrestle the keys out of her hands but April batted me away.

'If you want to come, get back in the car, Lynn, or I swear to God I'm going to drive off and leave you here.'

I didn't want to be abandoned by the side of the road – especially since it would mean that Ed would be on his own in a badly driven car with the distraught April, so I climbed obediently back into the back seat and April pulled out into the traffic with barely a glance in the rearview mirror. 'Just drive carefully, April,' I begged. 'It's not going to help anything if we crash.'

Within minutes April reached the turning for Colly Lake. We drove in silence down the narrow road to the car park but even before we reached the metal height barrier at the car park's entrance, we saw the stark white of police cars and vans through the bare trees surrounding the lake.

I glanced at April. Her hands were clenched on the wheel, and her jaw set.

Crime scene tape fluttered a cordon around the trees nearest the lake and people in white paper suits and plastic overshoes silently milled around. The only non-police vehicles in the car park were Mike's Volvo – and a black private ambulance.

'He's dead,' April whispered. 'I knew it.'

I closed my eyes in horror as a wave of dizziness swept over me.

26

Two detectives came over and officially broke the news to us once we'd got April back to our house.

Someone had slit Mike's throat as he sat night fishing on one of the lakeside docks, and then tipped his body into the lake, where it had been found by a traumatised dog-walker that morning, washed up on the shore. There was no trace of the intruder; and there were no security cameras anywhere around the lake, not even in the car park. Mike had had the misfortune of being there on his own.

Had it been a random dispute with another fisherman, or had it been premeditated, someone who'd followed him out there, lurking behind trees and flexing the wire – for that had been the weapon – between their gloved hands? There were no witnesses, nobody who'd even seen Mike arrive, let alone his assailant.

I texted Adrian with shaking fingers: *SOMETHING'S COME UP, CAN'T DO LUNCH TODAY. WILL CALL WHEN I CAN XX*

Six hours later, the two detectives who had been quizzing us all day finally departed, leaving a vacuum of silence into which we all sank, exhausted and reeling not only from the devastating news but from the barrage of – albeit kindly-put – questions: had Mike had any enemies, could he have gone to meet anyone, who did he usually see when he went fishing? Where had we been last night? On and on. I'd had to admit that Ed had been locked in, but I was glad, even when the detectives looked askance at me.

'It's to stop him wandering,' I said, not wanting to admit anything about the nocturnal violence. April had given the detectives the name of one of Mike's business associates, an ex-partner in his firm who been ousted in a boardroom coup before the company was sold, and had apparently had a serious grudge ever since but, other than that, none of us had been able to provide any useful information.

Ed was devastated. We all were. He'd never been one to cry in front of people, but his eyes were red-rimmed and swollen and I guessed that he'd been weeping in the bathroom. I was almost as concerned about him as I was about April – he was taking it so badly that I was scared that it was causing his condition to deteriorate. He suddenly seemed a lot weaker – I'd just had to open a jar of coffee for him. He'd been wrestling with it for minutes but when he eventually shoved it at me and demanded that I did it, the lid twisted off in one easy turn in my hand. He had no energy, and seemed to be exhausted after walking even a few paces. Mr Deshmukh had warned us that this was a symptom, too – but of course it might have just been the shock of the news.

April howled most of the day, curled into a ball on the sofa surrounded by crumpled tissues. I didn't leave her side, apart from to check on Ed and talk to those who needed to know. I wasn't sure how good I was for her though. I couldn't stop crying either. My recent flare of optimism seemed long forgotten. Now it felt as if everything was falling apart and I was back in the shadowy land of full-on paranoia. Mike had been murdered, as had Shelagh, all those years before. How could two people so close to Ed lose their lives? What were the chances? And what with Ed's illness, it felt like we were being stalked by tragedy. In this grim frame of mind, I couldn't stop my thoughts turning once again to all those worrying incidents: people creeping around our house. Someone standing smoking outside at 4am. Ed's increasingly strange behaviour...

I shook myself. I'd dreamt those things, hadn't I? And if Ed was behaving oddly, it was just because of his illness. It was the shock of Mike's death getting to me and making me irrational. I was seeing ghosts and demons where there were none...

The dark day dragged on into darker evening and eventually petered out altogether into an exhausted silence. I was desperate to speak to Adrian, but didn't want to leave Ed or April on their own. I thought it inadvisable to turn on the TV, since the brief snippet of local radio news bulletins I'd heard had contained newsflashes of Mike's murder. Watching anything else – a comedy, or a movie – seemed inappropriate and none of us could concentrate anyway.

The phone finally stopped ringing – once the police left, I'd been making and fielding calls all afternoon to and from stunned friends, including Maddie and Naveeta, both in floods of tears. Even though I lit a roaring fire, the house still felt chilly and silent. I rang Ben and broke the news to him and we decided it would be best under the circumstances if he didn't, as planned, bring Jeanine over for dinner. It had been her twenty-sixth birthday the previous week and this was meant to be a belated celebration.

Ben sounded shocked, of course, but not as upset as I feared. Mike had known Ben since Ben was in nappies, but they hadn't had any more connection than Mike having been a friend of the family. He had been more concerned about Ed; how he was in general, and how he was coping with the news of Mike's death.

Before he hung up he said, 'Now probably isn't the time to mention it but – I assume you didn't know how much you and Dad gave Jeanine for her birthday?'

'Yeah I do. Thirty quid, wasn't it?' I had got her a card last week and asked Ed to go to the local Marks and Spencer to buy her a thirty-pound gift voucher, which I had tucked inside the envelope after we'd both signed it.

He laughed hollowly. 'It was three hundred, Lynn. We thought it was a mistake. Don't worry, she's not going to spend it. Take it back when you get a chance.'

I groaned. Ed's inability to remember the value of money seemed to be the latest development in the unpleasant, downward-hurtling roller coaster of dementia – it wasn't the first time something like this had happened. He insisted on trying to pay for a twenty-six-pound Chinese takeaway we got a few days before with a ten-pound note, and almost got into a fight with the delivery man over it. Then, last week I'd found myself locked out of our joint bank account when I'd tried to pay a bill online. At first I thought Ed had done something – tried the wrong password too many times – but when I asked him he shook his head, a blank look on his face. The next day, when I tried again, I managed to access the account fine, so it was probably just a software error, but now this £300 gift to Jeanine. I sighed into the phone. Ben was right, we had more important things to worry about at the moment, but it only added to my sense of unease. I chewed at the inside of my cheek, and I decided I'd check our other bank accounts as soon as I could face doing any of that admin-type stuff. Ed had obviously managed to get back into his computer so God forbid he might be rootling around causing havoc in them. Three hundred quid! Perhaps I should change the passwords and keep them from him from now on.

Although the thought of his reaction if I did that and he realised made me blanch.

'Thanks Ben,' I said, tears welling again. He was such a good person really. He and Jeanine both – it would have been easy as anything to say nothing and spend the voucher.

April had taken a tranquilliser and was now curled up in the corner of the sofa in a glassy-eyed catatonia. Ed wasn't much better, sitting across the room from her in the Pembroke chair, his arms hanging uselessly at his sides. He'd been uncharacteristically quiet for the past few hours although his face was still pink with distress. I'd hoped the dementia might shield him a little; act as an anaesthetic on his emotions in the same way that April's Temazepam was doing, but he seemed to know what had happened.

'I've changed the sheets on the bed in the front spare room.'

I laid my hand on April's forearm as she sat gazing into space. It was only 8pm, but frankly, I thought, the day couldn't end soon enough. I saw myself that day as if in a speeded-up film, running around after the two of them as they sat in grief-stricken – or dementia-confused – silence.

'Thanks,' April said without looking up.

It was the room Ed had been sleeping in, the one with the lock on the door, but I decided that I couldn't make April sleep in the smaller of our two spare rooms. That one only had a single bed so narrow that it was like a child's bed, and it was as hard as rocks. Every time I looked at it, it reminded me of the tiny box room in Salisbury – and then, of Adrian. Ed and I had been meaning to get rid of that bed for ever but it was used so seldom, since Ben always slept in the double if he stayed over.

So I would have to take my chances sleeping with Ed tonight. I wondered if I could persuade him to take a Temazepam too, or even slip one in his drink – and then had a word with myself. I couldn't drug my husband ... Could I?

'Let's all go to bed,' I said. 'I think we've all had enough of today, haven't we? Ed, will you make us some hot milk?'

Ed lumbered obediently out into the kitchen. He still seemed OK to use the cooker and had only left the gas on once, but I would follow him in in a minute and check on him.

April turned her head slowly, like a tortoise, and peered up at me. For the first time ever I thought that she looked all of her forty-five years.

'You're right,' April said. 'I've had enough of today. But do you know what? Mike won't be back tomorrow, so that won't be any better. Or the next day, or the day after that, or any day, ever again...' Her face crumpled up again and her voice rose to a howl. 'Because some bastard ... *cunt* ... has killed him ... Oh Lynn, I'm never going to see him again. I can't bear it!'

She had barely finished speaking before she dissolved again into heaving sobs that vibrated through her chair and into the floorboards, making me feel as though my own heart was rattling in my rib cage. I hugged her tight, crying myself again at the loss of vibrant, stroppy, larger-than-life Mike, who'd been a part of Ed's life for so many years. It seemed unthinkable that he was no more.

I half-carried April up the stairs and into the spare room, helping her get undressed as if she was a child, tenderly pulling her sweater and t-shirt over her head and feeding her arms into the sleeves of a pair of Ed's old pyjamas. I had already left a hot-water bottle in the bed, and

April wordlessly clutched it to her belly as soon as I pulled back the covers and lifted her legs into bed. 'The pill will make you sleep,' I said, kissing her forehead.

I wanted to add something else, like *Tomorrow's another day*, or *You'll feel better in the morning*, but realised that neither of these platitudes was remotely helpful. Instead I closed the door quietly and went back down to check that all was in order before we turned in, that Ed hadn't left any milk boiling over, that the doors and windows were locked, the cat in and the cat flap secured for the night. I felt like a zombie, staggering round the kitchen, deadened with shock and stress.

By the time I came up for bed five minutes later, Ed was already lying there with the duvet drawn up to his chin. A single tear rolled down his cheek.

'I know,' I said. 'I know.'

When I got into bed with him, I realised he was still fully dressed, minus his shoes. I was about to get out and help him into his pyjamas but was suddenly overcome with a wave of exhaustion so debilitating that all I could do was sink into the mattress and close my eyes. Before I could even articulate the thought, *So what if he wears his clothes in bed for one night?* I was already asleep.

I woke up some time later and squinted through the dark at the digital clock. 3am. I reached out for Ed – but his side of the bed was cold and empty. Alarmed, I sat bolt upright and switched on the bedside light. The door to our ensuite bathroom was open and he wasn't in there, but the main bedroom door was shut. Then I remembered he'd gone to sleep fully dressed, and felt even more concerned. What if he thought it was daytime and had left the house?

I jumped out of bed and slid my feet into the tatty Uggs I wore around the house. The heating had gone off and the air was chilly and still. I dragged on my dressing gown and opened the door quietly, not wanting to disturb April, but my heart was pounding so hard that I thought the ducks on the river could probably hear it. I was halfway down the stairs, treading silently, when I heard voices. I stopped, one foot in mid-air. Definitely voices, not the radio, a low rumble coming from the kitchen. I listened harder. Silence, then a higher reply.

Relief flooded over me. Ed wasn't AWOL, he was talking to April in the kitchen. How the hell had I not heard either of them get up? I was sleeping so heavily these days. Perhaps it was my hormones.

I carried on down into the hallway, no longer trying to be quiet. The kitchen door was closed and I hesitated outside it – I didn't want to barge in on April if she was finding it easier to grieve with Ed, as Mike's oldest friend. Or perhaps April was counselling Ed? That thought caused a small sour churning in my belly. I loved April, but *I* wanted to be the one that Ed confided in, not April.

When I pushed open the door, they both looked up. Each was clutching a tumbler of Scotch, with the open bottle of Glenfiddich on the pine table next to them. Ed was doodling on the corner of the local free newspaper. Every single kitchen drawer was pulled out and all the cupboard doors were swinging; a regular occurrence as Ed could never find what he was looking for, or remember what he wanted to find in the first place.

'Hi,' I said, going round and automatically closing everything again. 'Neither of you able to sleep? I can't believe I did – I went out like a light.' I frowned at April's glass. 'Not sure you should have that, not with the Temazepam.'

April just shrugged.

I got another glass down from the dresser and held out my hand for the Scotch bottle. 'Give me some. What were you talking about?'

April stared down at the table. 'Nothing much,' she said. Her eyes were pink and so puffy that she looked as if someone had punched her.

Ed's mouth was set in a small cross line, probably because he'd been woken up and was disorientated, I thought. He never liked his sleep being disturbed. I went across and kissed the top of his tousled head.

'Are you OK, darling?'

He stood up, frowsy in his crumpled clothes, a single sock on his left foot, the other one bare, one point of his shirt collar sticking skywards. 'Fine. Going back to bed.'

'Your PJs are under the pillow,' I said pointedly. 'I won't be long.'

Ed traipsed back up the stairs, his shoulders slumped and his head bowed. All he needed to complete the picture was a blankie trailing from one hand and a teddy pincered by the ear from the other.

'Not like Ed to wake up in the middle of the night,' I said when he'd gone, sipping my Scotch.

April's elbows were on the table and her chin rested heavily in her palms. Fresh tears came to her eyes.

'He just came on to me,' she said bluntly. 'I'm sorry, Lynn.'

'What?' I was so taken aback that I choked on the whisky, coughing and spluttering as it burned my windpipe. April got up and filled me a glass of water, with infuriating slowness, as I made *hurry up I'm dying* gestures with my hands. Gulping at the water with streaming eyes, I gradually got my breath back.

I'd always known that Ed, on an aesthetic level, fancied April – who wouldn't? She was gorgeous. But he'd always complained about how high maintenance she was. He used to come back from pints at the pub with Mike, marvelling indiscreetly at Mike's latest story of April's demands and quirks, her knack for spending his money, her hairdressing bills. 'Couldn't be doing with all that nonsense,' he used to say. 'Silly vain cow.'

I remembered chiding him for those sorts of comments. 'She's our friend!'

He'd grin. 'I know. But I'm glad I'm married to you.'

I remembered the warm glow of those words.

'What happened?' I asked, not sure if I wanted to know.

April ran her finger around the top of her glass as if she wanted to play a tune on it. 'I couldn't sleep, not even with the pill. Well, I dozed off for a bit but woke up again about an hour ago. Then I heard a noise, Ed on the stairs, and came out to check he was OK. When I got down here he was just standing in the middle of the kitchen looking a bit ... lost. I wasn't sure he even knew where he was at first, or who I was. I said, Ed, it's me, April, shall we have a cup of tea? I put the kettle on and next thing I knew he had his arms round my waist and was sort of nuzzling my neck. At first I thought he'd remembered about Mike and was just giving me a cuddle – or maybe that he was upset about him and needed a cuddle himself, I don't know – so I turned round and hugged him back, but then he ... he...'

Tears filled April's eyes. I put my hand on top of hers.

'It's a symptom, you know that, don't you? Inappropriate behaviour, loss of inhibitions. The consultant warned us it was likely to happen. He's so fond of you, he probably just got mixed up.' I paused. 'I sort of don't want to know, but at the same time I do – what did he do then?'

April bit her lip. 'He, um, pressed himself against me and tried to snog me. I pushed him away and he seemed to get it, that it was the wrong thing. I'm sorry, Lynn. But I want you to know that I didn't do anything to encourage him.'

I came round the table and hugged her. 'Of course I know you didn't. Forget about it. He tried to kiss a Jehovah's Witness who came to the front door last month. It's just part of the disease.'

April gave a watery smile. 'Poor bastard,' she commented, and it was my turn to fill up – again.

'I know.'

'At least Mike's ordeal was over in seconds,' she said. This was perhaps more blunt than I could usually have tolerated; a reminder of the long years of suffering that lay ahead. But if it made April's loss feel in any way less devastating, even for a moment, I supposed I could let her say it. I poured us both another whisky and took a deep swallow, feeling it spin filmy cobwebs in my brain, temporarily muting the pain.

'Will he remember he did it, in the morning?' April asked softly. 'I don't want it to affect our friendship. And I don't want him to feel awkward.'

I smiled ruefully at her. 'I don't think he will, or at least, if he does, he won't see it as anything to be embarrassed about. It's so weird, this loss of inhibition. I really hope it's just a phase in the illness and won't stick around for long.'

I had a flash of a memory: 'Did I ever tell you about his dad, when he was in a nursing home? He used to say the most outrageous, inappropriate things to this black male carer who worked there. I never witnessed it – I only met him a few times – but Ed said it was horrendous. Whenever the guy came near Victor would shout out things like "Let me suck your huge black cock!" Even though he'd been completely PC and heterosexual when he'd still had all his marbles. Awful.'

We pondered this for a moment and both managed to giggle, briefly, even while tears still pricked in our eyes.

'God,' said April. 'Can you imagine?' But then her face settled back into lines of devastation again. 'I think Mike once told me that story, about Ed's dad.'

I sighed. 'Well, anyway, please don't worry about what Ed tried to do. Hopefully he won't do it again, and if he does, just be firm and tell him it's not appropriate.'

'Bonk him on the nose with a rolled-up newspaper,' said April, but she wasn't smiling. She drained her glass. 'I'm going back to bed, too. Hopefully I'll sleep a bit now. Got so much to do tomorrow, all of it horrible. The police want to talk to me again. I have to register Mike's death and find out when they're likely to release his body. Funeral arrangements, notice in *The Times*, the boys are coming down...'

'That'll be nice for you though, won't it?'

I didn't tell her that it might be months before they released Mike's body for a funeral. They'd almost certainly want to do a second autopsy when and if they charged someone with his murder. It was so hard on the families, not being able to have the closure of a funeral. I made a mental note to suggest a memorial service if nothing had happened within a couple of months.

April shook her head, then nodded, her voice trembling. 'No. Yes. I suppose so. But they're so destroyed and I'll have to be strong for them when I just feel like curling up in a ball and crying...'

'I know,' I said. 'Let me know if there's anything I can do, you promise? We're here for you, any time, day or night.'

27

'I love my husband,' I said, running my hand slowly over Adrian's bare chest. We were lying naked on the bed in his flat – the blandest rental property I'd ever set foot in, everything in shades of magnolia and beige, no pictures on the walls or photos on the shelves. Nothing *major* had happened between us ... yet – just a bit of 'fiddling and interfering', as my girlfriends and I always referred to it – but then, I hadn't ever thought things would go this far.

It was my day off, two weeks after Mike had been killed. Ben was with Ed; April was with her boys. I'd told them I was going for a spa day with a friend from work – 'Linda'. Adrian and I had gone out to lunch near his place in Ewell, and I'd badgered him to see his apartment. I'd only had two glasses of wine but then we'd kissed for the first time in ten years and, in what seemed like two minutes flat, we were sliding around naked on his beige sateen bedspread. I'd called a brief halt to try and process it all.

'I know. It's OK.'

'Well, it's not really, is it?'

'Don't think about it. And don't feel bad about it. You need an outlet. The pressure you're under ... it's massive.'

I wasn't convinced. That sounded like a cheater's justification. I wondered how many times he cheated on his wife, when they were married. I didn't ask, as I suspected there might have been quite a few.

I couldn't shake an intuition that his premature departure from the police may have had something to do with a woman, but he wouldn't be drawn whenever I tried to quiz him about it. I wondered if he'd shagged the wrong colleague's wife, or some such transgression.

'I'm worried about you, Waitsey,' he continued. 'You don't look well. Gorgeous, obviously – but not well. Are you coping OK?'

I rolled onto my back and thought about it. Was I?

'I don't know. Most of the time, yes. But I just feel so uneasy about Mike's murder. I mean, of course I would do – an old friend's been murdered. But I can't get rid of the thought that Ed...'

I couldn't say it.

Adrian looked shocked. 'You think Ed killed him?'

'No! No. Of course not. Ed would never do something like that. And, anyway, he was definitely home with me. It's just ... Might he have said something to someone – something ill-judged about Mike, and they didn't realise Ed's sick and can't know what he's saying? Or worse, he's got in with some people and because of his dementia he wasn't able to judge that they were using him – I don't know, for information about Mike's finances or something. I can't even articulate it; it's just a feeling. I told you about seeing someone outside our front gate in the middle of the night a couple of months ago, didn't I? And that other time – I think it was the day of Ed's diagnosis – I heard someone creeping about. Footsteps on the gravel. Weird stuff ... At the time I just assumed I was imagining things and having vivid dreams – because of all the stress, you know? But now...'

Adrian propped himself up on an elbow and reached for his e-cig, a concession to my hatred of smoking. 'Don't you think you should tell the police?' He exhaled a huge cloud of vapour out of the side of his mouth.

I sat up, grimacing at the thought. 'Sometimes I think I probably should. But then I think, I can't, not with the state he's in. I can't imagine what it would do to him, having the police poking around again, asking more questions. It was bad enough after Mike was killed, and the open day debacle.'

I was going to say 'it was bad enough after Shelagh was killed', but I didn't want Adrian to know about that, in case he worked out that Ed was the guy I'd been sent in to investigate. He had asked me about my undercover assignment and how it had gone, of course, and I'd told him briefly that I hadn't found anything to suggest that 'my target' was guilty of anything, and indeed that someone else had later confessed. And then I'd changed the subject. I really didn't want him to know. If I was honest, it hurt a little that he *didn't* know, hadn't bothered to find out what situation I was being transferred into. Still, that was all in the past.

'Would he even understand?'

'Probably not. Give us a puff?'

Adrian handed me his vape. Whilst I loathed actual smoking, I quite liked the pretence of vaping, the satisfaction of an exhalation. I only ever did it with him. Having said that, I was feeling so wrung out these days, so harried by the wreck my life had become, if he'd had a pack of real cigs on him I'd probably have chain-smoked them.

'So you don't really think he was involved in Mike's death, do you?'

I shook my head. 'No, I really don't. It's impossible. Mike was a very rich man, and pissed off a lot of people when he sold his business. I'm sure it's to do with that. The most obvious explanation is the most likely – we both know that...' I knew I sounded unconvincing; I wasn't convinced myself.

We sat in silence for a few minutes, passing the e-cig between us like a bong. I still couldn't relax though.

'I've never been unfaithful to him before,' I blurted.

Adrian put his arm around me. 'Do you remember when we used to shag on my mum's carpet?'

I managed a laugh. 'Of course! You took me to all the best places...'

I had a mental image of that dingy cold cottage, with the crooked horse-brasses and spider webs in every corner, a dead woman's house, with her imprint still in the sofa cushions. But at least it took my mind off Ed for a moment.

'I'm sorry,' he said, cupping my breast and stroking my nipple with his thumb. 'It was pretty crap of me, thinking back on it. I was trying to be practical – her place was nearby, and free. But I never spoilt you nearly as often as I'd have liked to.'

'You did take me to a hotel. Twice.'

'I did.'

He gazed down at me, still caressing me. I put my arms around his back, grateful for his attempts to cheer me up. He felt so different to Ed; lean, smooth and silky where Ed was much hairier and muscled.

'Did you miss me when I left?' I wasn't fishing for compliments, I was genuinely curious.

'Yes. Quite a bit, as it goes. But I also felt a sense of ... relief. That I could work on my ... other relationships.'

Was he being coy about mentioning his wife, or did he actually mean 'work on his other affairs'? I didn't know, and didn't want to.

'I can't leave him, ever. And this is not going to become a regular occurrence, OK? We're friends, that's all.'

'Understood, Mrs Naismith.'

He put down the vape and kissed me with growing intensity, rolling onto me so I could feel him hard against me. Lust and guilt fought a brief battle – it wasn't too late to say no – but I couldn't. I didn't want to.

'Friends with benefits,' Adrian murmured, sliding a finger inside me, making me moan.

28
April 2017

Life eventually settled back into a routine. As I suspected, there could be no burial for Mike since his killer still hadn't been found, but a couple of weeks before there had been a moving memorial service, at which we'd all cried buckets.

Ed and I both saw as much as we could of April, who was slowly recovering from her grief, although she was still quiet and withdrawn, not a patch on her former extrovert self. I saw as little as I could of Adrian, but we talked at least once a week, and met up once a month. He wanted to see me more frequently but, although his kind and calm presence massively helped me decompress, I felt so guilty about being unfaithful to Ed that I wouldn't agree to it. I loved our conversations and meetings though, even more than the occasional sex. As gratifying as the sex was – particularly since Ed no longer showed any interest in me physically, and rebuffed my advances if I made them – it was always too fraught with guilt and remorse for me to properly enjoy it.

Ed's condition had also seemed to stabilise over these few months – or perhaps I was just getting used to the new reality of having a partner with dementia. He really did seem better, though. He wasn't getting nearly so many words wrong, and I was finding fewer misplaced items around the house. We'd also been back sleeping together in our bed for a few months now – no sex, but no violence either. He was still in the clinical trial but had consistently refused to tell me when he was going for his appointments, shouting at me so loudly not to 'fuss' or 'nag' whenever I asked him that eventually I stopped asking and let him get on with it. They always sent a taxi for him, so it wasn't as if he could come to any harm en route. I was still unsure why he was so reluctant for me to accompany him to any of these appointments, though. Maybe he felt embarrassed and humiliated by the whole thing. Or maybe he genuinely did keep forgetting the dates, only to remember when the taxi driver knocked at our door. I'd searched thoroughly for the email with Bill's details on it, but try as I might, I couldn't find it – nor the one from Bill's colleague that Ed had printed out. I suspected Ed had thrown it away. I comforted myself by observing the gradual but clear improvement in his condition. Never look a gift horse, and all that, I told myself.

One Thursday morning, though, after months of me asking, suddenly Ed said, 'I've got an appointment at ten-thirty. Want to come with me?'

He was dressed and clean-shaven, whereas I was still in my pyjamas and Uggs, reading the paper and drinking my morning coffee, enjoying the fact I didn't have to go to work that day.

'Eh? What appointment? Where?'

'Bill wants to discuss the results of my scan. Will you come? He said he thought it was a good idea if you did. He's sending a, a, camel.'

'Ed! Yes of course! But – you had a scan? When? Were you OK? I must go and get dressed!'

'Can't remember exactly. It was all right though. I didn't freak out. I was a brave boy.' He made a winsome face at me and I laughed, although my mind was racing.

'Does that mean you think you might be able to fly again soon? We could go on holiday somewhere hot this summer!'

He grinned. 'Maybe. Not sure though. A ten-minute scan is one thing ... a long, er, plane ride is another.'

Sure enough, at nine-thirty on the dot a minicab – not a camel, but I'd deduced as much – pulled up on the track outside the house and beeped its horn. I'd just had time to dress in jeans and yesterday's shirt, tie my hair up and swipe some mascara on my lashes so that I didn't look too ghostlike. Ed was calm and lucid, almost like his old self. He was even in a pair of new jeans, so stiff that he walked like a soldier on parade.

'What's the address of where we're going?' I asked the cabbie, a small North African man with a sparse beard and moustache.

'Chelsea Clinic,' he replied, meeting my eyes in the rearview mirror.

'Have you driven Ed there before?' I enquired, but Ed's expression darkened.

'Lynn! Don't be nosy. No he hasn't. It's someone different every time ... I think,' he added uncertainly.

'Our firm does a lot of work for the clinic,' the driver said, and we drove over Hampton Court Bridge in silence.

Forty minutes later we arrived at our destination, a very modern chrome-and-glass building overlooking the Thames.

'Nice,' I said. 'Is this where you always come?'

Ed nodded. I brushed a speck of dandruff from the shoulder of his lime-green cashmere pullover and smiled affectionately at him. It was so lovely when he had a good day – and there seemed to be more good days than bad at the moment. Long may it last, I thought.

Automatic tinted-glass doors slid silently back to admit us into a large, cool lobby. I looked around and headed for the reception desk when a small, rotund man intercepted us, grabbing Ed's hand and pumping it enthusiastically before turning to me.

'And you must be Lynn! I can't believe we've never met before. Bill Brown. A pleasure to meet you.'

'Hello,' I said, before submitting to a similarly vigorous greeting. 'I know, me neither – you and Ed have been friends since medical school?'

'We have,' he agreed, beaming like a Cheshire Cat, 'but there was a hiatus in the middle of at least, what, twenty-five years. Lost touch after we graduated and I lived abroad for a long time. Good old internet, hey? Where would we be without LinkedIn?'

'Where indeed,' I murmured, scrutinising him. He must have been Ed's age but looked younger, with a smooth, round, bald head and tauter skin on his face.

'Come on round,' he said, ushering us into a corridor off reception. 'Sorry if I seem a little manic, but I am in a state of – well, close to euphoria!'

'Really?' Ed and I exchanged glances and Ed grinned at me. I reached for his hand and squeezed it.

Bill showed us into a consulting room, framed certificates bearing his name on the walls, a huge vase of tropical-looking flowers and floor-to-ceiling windows overlooking the river. 'Wow!' I said. 'Impressive.'

'Sit down, please,' he said, gesturing to two leather chairs across the desk from him. He was almost fidgeting with excitement as he picked up the huge brown envelope that was lying on his leather-topped desk, next to a photo of him with his arm around an attractive freckly girl. I was idly hoping that this was his daughter rather than his wife when he tipped up the envelope and some scans fell out. He unfolded and donned the glasses that had been sticking out of his shirt pocket, clipped the top scan up on a wall-mounted light box, and switched it on.

'These are Ed's scans from just over seven months ago, in which you can clearly see the start of some considerable amyloid plaque build-up on these areas of the brain; here, and here.' He pointed with a small neat finger.

I was confused. 'But Ed didn't have scans seven months ago. He refused. I was there. We were in Mr Deshmukh's office.'

'I did, honey,' Ed said, looking me in the eye. 'Next time I went in. He went on about it so much that I gave up ... no, *in*. I gave in. I didn't tell you because it was too depressing. Then I forgot. It was all right though.'

'Anyway!' Bill chirped. 'That was then. As you know, Lynn, Ed's been in a trial for this new drug galdonimene that we're all getting very excited about. I've been assessing his cognition and general condition with questionnaires and interviews since, in tandem with ECGs, blood tests and so on, and...'

He paused, suddenly serious again, turning to Ed: 'You did explain, Ed, that I shouldn't be doing this?'

'Doing what?' I was alarmed.

Ed frowned. 'Um. I'm not sure. Did I, darling?'

'You just said Bill had asked me to come with you this time, to discuss how the trial was going.'

'Oh. I guess I forgot. Sorry, Bill.'

Bill took a deep breath. 'As a medical professional, I've wrestled with the ethics of this, but I'm afraid in this instance my personal loyalty to Ed has won out over the rules of the trial – which are that no results are to be disclosed until at least the end of this eighteen-month phase. But as I said, I've been assessing his condition and I could see some remarkable improvements in cognition and vocabulary – surely you have noticed it too, Lynn?'

'Yes ... I have. I wasn't sure if it was just that I was getting used to him having Pick's, but I was thinking he seemed better. So...?'

My heart was beating faster and my head started to swim, as if I knew my name was about to be announced to a stadium full of people. The air in the office felt charged with anticipation.

With a flourish, Bill took out a different scan and pinned it up next to the first one. 'This is Ed's brain now. Well, as of two weeks ago.' He pointed at the same areas and even I could see that they looked different, the newer one more plumped up. 'There are clearly defined areas of actual improvement.'

He beamed at us.

'I'm thrilled to tell you – in the strictest confidence, you understand – that in just seven and a half months, the plaques have melted away from Ed's neurons, leaving them free to regenerate instead of killing them off. The drug has worked *spectacularly* well on him! And there is no reason not to believe that it will continue to do so, with no side-effects at all – we were a little worried that it may cause swelling to the brain as it did in some of the lab trials on mice – but no, absolutely not. If it carries on working as well, I'm confident that Ed's brain will be as good as it was five years ago! It's nothing short of a miracle, and the breakthrough we have all been waiting for.'

Tears came to his eyes and he wiped them away with a handkerchief he whipped out of his trouser pocket. His voice quaking with emotion, he continued: 'As I'm sure you realise, this will have profound positive implications for the treatment and cure of dementia of all types. Profound! This is game-changing, folks. I'm just so happy that it's happened to you, my friend...'

He rushed across to Ed and dragged him out of his seat to hug him, pressing his face against Ed's cashmere chest. I could see the pink tips of his ears throbbing as Ed embraced him back, laughing and crying at the same time.

I was speechless. So many emotions whirled through me that I couldn't take it in. Ed had been *cured*? Surely the first person ever to be cured of dementia ... Ed was going to be better!

'Can we tell Ben?' I managed, through the tears now streaming down my own face.

Bill broke away from the embrace and gripped my forearm. 'No – I'm sorry, Lynn, but you must promise not to tell anybody at all. Nobody! If anyone notices the improvements in Ed's condition, you can say he's on this trial and it seems to be working, but you won't know for sure until the eighteen months is up. Please, please, promise me you won't! I would lose my job. I'm only seeing you both now because Ed's a friend and I know you'd want to know.'

I wiped my eyes too, staring at Ed as if seeing him for the first time. 'This is ... this is ... incredible. Are you sure it's not just a blip? Could the scans be wrong – I mean, are you sure they're both Ed's?'

Bill laughed. 'I know it seems unbelievable.' He pointed out Ed's name and the date on both scans, the diseased one from last September, the new one from two weeks ago. 'But it's not a blip. It's true. We need to celebrate! Lunch tomorrow, Ed, my friend, on me?'

Ed grinned and nodded, then grabbed me out of my seat. My legs were shaky as he and Bill both took my hands and gleefully whirled me round right there in his office, until we collided in a disbelieving, joyful huddle.

29

Muzzy-headed from the champagne Ed and I had consumed the night before, I went into work a couple of hours late the next morning, first dropping Ed off at the station to catch a train into London for his celebratory meal with Bill. I'd like to have gone with them, but Ed didn't offer and I supposed that they just wanted to have a boys' lunch together. I had quite a lot of work to do, anyway.

Not that I could concentrate after Bill Brown's momentous news. My relief and delight was tempered with confusion – and, I had to admit, a tiny dose of scepticism. I kept thinking that there must be some kind of mistake. Bill had mixed up Ed's scans with someone else's. Nobody had ever been *cured* of dementia before! It was too good to be true. But then that was the point of medical trials for new drugs, wasn't it? Hoping for breakthroughs like this. I chastised myself. I ought to have been bursting with pride, knowing that Ed would go down in medical history. And the relief *was* overwhelming, there was no doubt about it. So why did I feel so unsettled?

Perhaps it was because I'd finally got used to the reality of Ed's illness, only to be suddenly liberated from it. Now we had a future again – hope, freedom. I felt like a calf who'd escaped from an abbatoir and was cautiously frolicking in the sunlight, not quite knowing what to do with itself in the fresh vastness of liberty.

The students were all away for the Easter break and Fairhurst House seemed echoing with emptiness, silence bouncing off the dado rails and the high ceilings of the common room. Margaret was on leave, and the teaching staff didn't bother to come in either once lectures had finished. 'Working from home' seemed to be a euphemism for 'getting on a plane and going somewhere hot for Easter.'

I tentatively allowed myself to wonder if, now that Ed was better, he might be up for doing what most of the staff had done, and going on holiday too. I'd have given a small body part to go and lie on a tropical beach.

I rang Adrian, needing to voice my confusion. 'Something incredible's happened,' I said. I was standing at the photocopier copying the Fauré *Requiem* for next term's Chamber Choir.

'Oh?'

'That clinical trial Ed's been on? Apparently it's worked. Completely worked! It's already reversed the dementia. We're over the moon.' There was silence on the line. 'Ade?'

'Still here,' he said, and coughed. 'But ... *really*? I thought it was an eighteen-month trial?'

'It is – but the results so far have been so dramatic. He had another set of scans.'

'I thought you said he wouldn't have them before?'

I paused. 'Yes – that's what I thought, too. Turns out he did have some at the beginning, he'd just forgotten. It is weird though, that I didn't know about *either* set ... don't you think?'

'Hmm,' said Adrian contemplatively. 'Yes and no. Entirely possible that he meant to tell you but his short-term memory was too fucked. But – wow. Will he be all over the papers?'

'Not yet. There are huge improvements, and the doctor said his scans look almost completely clear – although yesterday he told me he was getting a camel instead of a cab, so he's obviously not a hundred percent yet – he'll stay on the trial till the end, make sure it's not an aberration. He's told us not to tell anyone.'

'Well, that's brilliant,' he said, but his voice sounded flat. 'I suppose that means that we won't be able to meet up anymore, I mean, if you've got your husband back...'

It was my turn to pause. I felt terribly ashamed of myself. It was the exact same feeling I'd had before, the turning point that made me request a transfer; a sudden point of no return – or, perhaps more accurately, a return to lost senses.

'I hadn't thought that ... but now you mention it ... I'm sorry, Adrian. I like you so much. Please could we still be friends? But I can't sleep with you again. Not least because if Ed's got his faculties back, he's far more likely to find out.'

'Right,' said Adrian sulkily. 'So it was fine for you to cheat when you were less likely to be found out...'

I was silent. That was pretty much the size of it. 'I'm sorry,' I repeated. I felt slightly irritated with Adrian, though – I'd made it clear from the start that nothing could come of it. 'Perhaps one day we'll both be single at the same time, and then we can give things a proper go.'

'Perhaps.'

I eventually terminated the call, my toes curling so much that I almost got cramp in my feet. But I was relieved at my impromptu decision. I had Ed back, and now it seemed like we had things to look forward to once more. And if, God forbid, it turned out to be a blip, then all the more reason we should make the most of any quality time we had left together.

I couldn't wait to get back to my newly cured husband to discuss possible holiday plans. I left work an hour early and drove home, thinking about where we could go.

As I parked the car behind the house and walked round to the front door, I was imagining the zing of a Dark and Stormy cocktail on my tastebuds. I could hear the mushy swoosh of crushed ice as I stirred it with a straw, the shock of the cold glass on my bare belly as I lay on a day bed on a hot, empty beach...

Our house was quiet and chilly so I switched on the central heating and made tea, saying a mental farewell to my vision of baking sun and cool turquoise waters and wondering instead, as I waited for the kettle to boil, how Ed had got on in London. He hadn't replied to my earlier text but maybe he'd still been with Bill. Surely even a late lunch would be winding up by now? I'd got so used to Ed always being home, and to the daily feeling of trepidation about what I'd be coming back to, being without it felt like something was missing, like the realisation that you'd left a full bag of groceries in the supermarket car park. Even now I knew he was so much better, that sense hadn't dissipated at all.

I called him, but his mobile went straight to voicemail.

'Hi sweetie. How did it go? Just wondering which train you're getting, so I can come and pick you up from Hampton Court. Let me know! Dying to hear how you got on! Call me! Love you.'

I suppressed a slight feeling of annoyance that he hadn't rung me when his lunch finished. Then I had the other, worse, niggle of worry I got every time I didn't know where he was. What if the recovery had only been temporary and the Pick's had returned? Or Bill was wrong? Imagine going through all this, for Ed to be back on his slow decline to insanity, hope cruelly wrenched away from us just as we were getting used to having him better again...

My phone bleeped – but it wasn't Ed. It was a text from April: *Hello darling, just to say, check your emails – I've just sent you one Xxxx*

I opened the lid of my laptop and went to Outlook Express, where one message in bold waited for me, entitled 'Guess What?!?' It was nice to see April being excited about something after being so grief-stricken for the past six months. I clicked on it and read, with raised eyebrows:

Darling Lynn,

Please don't be cross with me but I've done something a bit impulsive. I'm sorry I didn't tell you, or say goodbye, but if I had, I might not have been able to go through with it.

I've gone to Australia!! I only decided a few days ago, after the memorial – which, as you probably saw, was so unbearably painful that I want to put as many miles between Mike's death and me as I can. Of course I know that I won't ever be able to travel far enough to forget him, not even if I flew to the moon. I'll never forget what we had and the life we made together. He was my soul mate and I haven't even begun to get used to life without him.

Don't worry, I'm not going to do anything stupid. I've got the boys to think of – even if they are all grown up. I want to be a granny (a glamorous one, of course!). Maybe one day I'll meet someone else and get married again although I can't imagine that right now.

You've always been such a good friend to me, Lynn. I do love you, you know, and I'm sorry. For leaving without saying goodbye, I mean. Although of course I will be back! Not sure when, probably in a few months. Do you remember that book we read in book club last year, Wild? About that woman whose mum died and she ended up walking a thousand miles down the Pacific coast, up and down mountains, on her own? At the time I thought she must be mad, but now I can really see why she wanted to do it. To remove yourself physically to try and heal yourself emotionally.

As soon as I get there (I'm on a layover in Singapore at the moment, typing this on one of the airport computers) I'll Skype you – assuming there's internet of course. Apparently it can be very unreliable.

I'm going to a sort of yoga commune – no, that sounds too hippie – more like a retreat place, run by this guy Doug, an old school friend of Mike's. He heard the news about his death and messaged me on LinkedIn. It's on a sheep farm in the outback. Can you imagine? He offered me a free place for as long as I want, to get my head together. Meditation and massages and – best of all – a complete change of scenery.

Again, I'm really sorry I didn't say goodbye in person but you know me, I hate goodbyes, and I think you've seen enough of me sobbing all over you to last a lifetime, so I just decided to take off. Also I was a bit worried you might try and talk sense into me and I'd end up not going ... I hope I'm not making a horrible mistake. I wish you could have come with me but I know you can't leave Ed.'

'Well, you could've asked,' I said out loud when I got to that bit, blinking. 'Bit sudden, isn't it?' I was hurt that April thought I'd try and talk her out of it – why would I do that? Travel was an excellent idea.

It's the only thing I think might take my mind off poor Mike, just a little bit. I still can't believe he's gone and my heart breaks into more bits every morning I wake up without him. We always wanted to go to Ayers Rock together and never got round to it, so I guess I will just have to go for both of us, now the memorial's finally over...'

I sighed. It was tough for her all right.

The boys have been supportive. They're so busy with work that they said they were glad I was going to get a break, and that they felt guilty that they only see me once every couple of weeks. I do hate the idea of being a burden on them, so it's best all round if I take off for a bit. As I said, I'm not sure when I'll be back – got an open return.

Love you, sweetie. Hugs to you both, A XXX

I wasn't sure what to think. I was happy for April, that she was escaping and doing something proactive to take away the dull ache of mourning – but it was so sudden! Who went to Australia on a whim like that? I hoped she wouldn't regret it. And I would miss her.

I wanted to tell Ed, which reminded me about his radio silence, so I texted him again: *GETTING WORRIED HONEY, PLEASE CALL? XXX PS. GUESS WHAT, APRIL'S GONE TO AUSTRALIA!!!*

I rang several more times, but each time the phone went straight to voicemail as if it was switched off or, more likely, had run out of battery. Ed's phone had a notoriously short battery life.

I ran upstairs to check by his side of the bed and was impressed to see that the phone charger was missing. Good. Hopefully he'd be able to plug in his phone on the train home. Lots of train carriages had sockets these days.

I lit a fire, made myself an omelette, fed the cat, had a glass of wine – but just one, assuming I'd be driving to the station later on.

Eight o'clock came and went, then nine, then ten. Perhaps he'd lost his phone altogether, and he never could remember my mobile number to borrow someone else's phone and call me.

He knew the home phone number though, and he hadn't called that...

I Googled the Chelsea Clinic on my phone and left a voicemail on their answering machine asking for Bill to call me urgently – but it was a Friday, so he might not get it until Monday. Then I tried 'Dr Bill Brown at the Chelsea Clinic', but that yielded only the same switchboard numbers.

Then I went into our office, noting that Ed had taken his laptop with him. That wasn't so unusual. He'd always liked watching movies on the train into town. Maybe his old habits were really returning, I thought.

But then some impulse – some residual suspicion; some part of my police training that I would never lose – made me slide open the drawer in his office that housed all our important documents. I hadn't looked in it for ages. There was a hanging file for birth and exam certificates, mortgage stuff and one for passports and driving licences. There was my familiar green leather passport cover, the one that used to belong to my mother that I appropriated when she died.

Ed's passport was missing.

I lay awake till dawn, experiencing Ed's absence more keenly than at any other time we'd ever been apart. With each dark hour that ticked slowly past, I felt more guilty for the days during his illness that I'd relished being alone in the big double bed, with him locked in the spare room. When I eventually drifted off, I woke myself up half an hour later out of the recurring nightmare I hadn't had for several years. I used to get it regularly and I always woke with tears on my face: I was out in the garden practising my taekwondo kicks and punches, but in the dream I was always eight months pregnant. I kicked so hard that the foetus inside me just fell out and got swept away on a great bubbling river of thick blood, waving its little arms and calling to me as it vanished, the blood-river flowing into the Thames and tinting it dark pink, the baby gone for ever.

And now it looked as if Ed was gone too. How cruel would it be, that after the unspeakable relief of his cure, he'd just got up and left me?

Unless he'd had an accident? The missing passport wasn't necessarily significant – in fact, I convinced myself that it wasn't at all. Ed hadn't used his passport for years, since his fear of flying precluded us from going outside of the UK on holiday. It had probably just got mislaid, or was still in a bag from the last time we went abroad, whenever that had been.

I racked my brains, trying to chase the nightmare out of my mind. Spain, in 2009? No, the villa holiday in 2011 with Mike and April, that had been the last time.

I decided that if he hadn't returned by 6am I would start calling around our friends to—

I suddenly sat bolt upright in bed and moaned out loud in horror at the thought that I should have had hours ago. A memory that either through subconscious fear or negligence I hadn't entertained: a memory of April, just a few months ago, ringing me to ask if Ed and I had seen Mike, because he hadn't come home from his fishing trip.

Mike hadn't come home, and was found the next morning with his throat cut.

Ed hadn't come home and wasn't contactable...

I snatched up the home phone next to the bed and dialled three digits with shaking fingers, my diamond engagement ring sparkling in the weak morning light coming through the curtains.

'Police, please.'

30

My heart sank when I saw that it was the same rictus-smile police officer who'd attended after Ed punched Alvin; PC 'call me Martine' Knocker. I was staring out of my bedroom window at the river when she and another man walked up the garden path. The other man was a burly guy with a bright-red face and really long legs and Martine had to scuttle to keep up with him. I noticed she was looking worried while simultaneously smiling – which didn't inspire a lot of confidence in me.

I looked down and realised vaguely I was still in my fleecy pink onesie. I didn't want them to have to inform me that my husband was dead while I resembled an overgrown toddler. I stripped it off, ducking out of sight behind the window. What *did* you wear to be told your husband had been murdered? Jeans? A dress?

They didn't tell me anything straightaway. Martine Knocker made me a cup of disgustingly sweet tea and put it on the table without using a coaster. Ed would be mad when he saw that. If he saw it.

'We have no reason to believe that any harm has come to your husband,' said the red-faced policeman, Constable Laurie, in between sneezes. He'd started sneezing as soon as he got in the front room. 'Sorry. Cat allergy,' he added.

Relief flooded over me. Ed wasn't dead ... at least as far as they knew.

Martine handed her colleague a tissue out of a packet she took from her tunic pocket and he mopped his eyes and blew his nose, as if I was the one breaking bad news to him. I lifted a protesting Timmy up under his armpits and shut him out of the room, then sat down on the sofa, automatically curling my legs under me and cradling my mug like I was about to watch TV.

'So, Mrs Naismith,' said Laurie, taking out a notebook. 'Let's get some information, if we may. When did you last see your husband?'

'Yesterday morning, about eleven-thirty. I took him to Hampton Court station to get a train into central London. He had a lunch appointment with an old medical school friend of his called Bill.'

'Is it safe for him to travel on his own?' Martine looked disapproving through her smile. At least she had remembered something from our last encounter, although I didn't appreciate her censorious tone.

'As a matter of fact, he started on a clinical trial eight months ago that's having astonishing results.' I hesitated. I wasn't supposed to discuss the trial. But surely the police didn't count? 'It's strictly confidential – but because Bill is the doctor who's running the trial, and he's an old friend, he told us off the record: Ed's condition really has improved dramatically. Of course I wouldn't have dreamt of letting him travel alone, not until recently. It's like a miracle. But as I said, we can't talk about it publicly because we signed a confidentiality agreement. He's like a different person already. That's what they were meeting to celebrate.'

'Goodness!' Martine said. 'That's great news. Perhaps there's hope for us all!'

I glared at her. She sounded so bloody flippant.

'What restaurant were they going to?' Laurie asked.

'I don't know,' I confessed. 'He didn't tell me.'

'I see. Well, where is this trial held, and what's this Bill's surname?'

'I don't know if it's the same for the other people on the trial, but Ed was being treated at the Chelsea Clinic. Dr Bill Brown.'

'What time did he say he was coming back? Did you try and get hold of him?'

'Yes, of course. But I just assumed his phone had run out of battery. He'd taken his charger with him so I thought he might plug his phone in on the train home. He hadn't told me what time he'd be back but if he ever goes up to London – I mean, when he used to, before he got ill – he would usually get a train back about eight o'clock. He likes to wait until the worst of the rush hour is over.'

'That's a long lunch,' Martine commented. More tacit disapproval. I wanted to slap her.

'He probably went to a gallery or something afterwards. He sometimes does.'

'Can you give me any more details about Dr Brown?'

'I can't, I'm afraid. That's all I know really. I met him for the first time on Thursday in his consulting rooms but Ed's been having monthly appointments with him or one of his colleagues since October last year ... I've left a message at the clinic as I don't have a number for Bill, but it's closed at weekends.'

'We'll contact them as well, of course. Does Ed go up London a lot?' Laurie asked.

Up London. Ed hated it when people said that. I gritted my teeth.

'Obviously, like I said, he didn't go at all when he was ill. Before then he used to go up to spend the day with his son sometimes – or we both would, make a day of it and visit museums or galleries, maybe meet up with friends.'

'And you weren't tempted to go with him to this lunch?'

I pulled at a loose thread in the sofa cushion. 'I had to work.' For some reason I didn't want to admit I hadn't been invited.

'What do you do, Mrs Naismith?' asked Laurie.

'It's Lynn, please. I'm the music administrator at Hampton University, organising concerts. But I think you already knew that, from when Constable Knocker here had to come round before, when Ed was ill.'

Stress was making me scratchy.

'Apologies,' he said, scribbling hard. 'And when did you start getting worried about Ed?'

I thought I heard a trace of censure in his voice too – sort of, *Why didn't you call us last night?* But I couldn't blame him. That's what I would have thought when I was a PC.

'I was a bit worried when I didn't hear from him yesterday evening, but I thought they'd probably just gone somewhere to carry on drinking after lunch, or to an exhibition. Lost his phone, didn't think to ring me when he was with Bill, missed the last train back ... It was only this morning when I woke up about five and he still hadn't called – and that was when I remembered what happened to...'

Suddenly I found I couldn't say it. 'To...'

The officers were leaning forward with pained, expectant expressions.

'To his friend Mike Greening?' Martine supplied, and I nodded.

'I don't know why it didn't occur to me before. I feel terrible! Mike's not even been dead six months but it just seems so far from reality, that someone could have done that to him. But nobody would hurt Ed, nobody!'

I shut my eyes, no longer angry but close to tears.

'I sincerely hope not, Lynn, but we have to look at the coincidence of your husband knowing Mike Greening...'

'I know.'

Just because I couldn't imagine that anyone would hurt Ed didn't mean that nobody would.

'Let's be positive for a moment?'

Let's, I thought.

'We checked before we came and there have been no reports round here involving a man meeting your husband's description. I would assume that someone would have found him by now, had there been an accident or incident. We'll check the hospitals, and speak to the Met to make sure no one's called anything in up London. If it weren't for Mike Greening's murder I would say it's actually too early to be worried at all.'

'I'm sorry to have bothered you,' I said. 'You're right. He'll probably show up at any minute...'

I stared out at the towpath, willing Ed to materialise. Should I mention his absent passport? They hadn't asked. And if I did mention it, they'd immediately assume that it was an option that he could have run away and therefore wouldn't take it so seriously.

Constable Laurie's thoughts seemed to be heading in the same direction: 'What did your husband take with him yesterday? I mean, are any of his things missing?'

I shook my head so violently that I felt the ends of my ponytail whip against my cheeks. 'Nothing. Apart from his phone and charger, and his laptop. He definitely didn't take any kind of suitcase, just a canvas bag, because I gave him a lift to the station. He hasn't *voluntarily* gone missing.'

I paused, then decided I should tell them: 'And I can't find his passport.'

There was another pause. I saw a split-second exchange of glances between them.

'But then, I haven't seen it for years,' I hurried to say. 'We haven't been abroad since 2011. So that doesn't mean he took it with him. He easily could have moved it somewhere stupid – when he was ill ... you know...'

Laurie took a slurp of his tea. The man's big, sausagey fingers were as red as his face. He cleared his throat with surprising delicacy. 'And, er, can you describe what his state of mind was when you left him?'

'He was happy,' I said, annoyed that I couldn't keep the tremor out of my voice. 'Really happy. Back to his old self, excited about how much his memory has improved. So grateful to be feeling well again. He said he feels like he's had a reprieve. The only awful thing is how much he still misses Mike. They ... were good friends...'

I was going to say 'used to be best friends', but for some reason I didn't.

'Why would he take his laptop with him, if he was just meeting a friend for lunch?'

'He always used to take it when he went into town. He prefers going online on it, says his phone screen's too small to be able to see stuff properly. And he likes watching movies on the train. I didn't think anything of it, except taking it as another sign of his recovery – he hadn't been interested in doing that for a while.'

Laurie had filled up several pages of his small notebook. There was silence while he scratched away, broken by a startled yelp from Martine when Timmy suddenly leaped up onto the windowsill and mewed outside the window, outraged at his expulsion.

'Sorry,' Martine and I said simultaneously.

'So you think he might have his passport with him?' Laurie asked.

I stood up so quickly that the blood drained from my head. 'No! That's not what I said. I said I couldn't find it. He could've put it somewhere daft. And anyway, he definitely wouldn't have gone abroad – he's terrified of flying.'

Martine put a reassuring hand on my arm and I had to resist the impulse to shake it off.

'I know, I know,' she soothed. 'It's so difficult. But we have to ask these questions, you understand?'

I sat back down again. 'Yes. I know. I'm sorry.'

'So he's likely still in the country.' Laurie looked as uncomfortable as I felt.

'I'm sure he is. But you can check that, can't you.'

Laurie jotted something down. 'We can, yes. One last question and we'll leave you in peace: Has Edward's behaviour or personality changed at all, since his miracle cure?'

These two were hopeless cops. It would have driven me mad to be in a team with them. 'It's Ed, not Edward. Well, yes, obviously it has – last year he had dementia and now he doesn't!'

'Sorry. That's not what I meant. Is Ed's personality different now to how it was *before* he was diagnosed with dementia?'

I thought about it, picturing Ed how he was then. Funny, sarcastic, irascible, affectionate. 'No,' I said, deciding there was no point in mentioning his phase of violence and occasional threatening messages. 'I'd say on balance it's about the same.'

After Laurie and Martine had finally gone, with their list of what Ed was wearing – overcoat, new jeans, brogues, green cashmere jumper – and photographs of him that they borrowed from off the top of the mantelpiece and which I instantly missed terribly, the house felt yawningly empty and still.

I drifted from room to room, unable to settle at anything. I called April's mobile and left a voicemail, but didn't say why I was asking her to ring me back – I didn't want to upset her when she was so far away.

For something to do, I painted my fingernails a metallic silver colour. Then I started to empty the dishwasher without waiting for them to dry properly, and three nails smudged immediately.

'Fuck,' I said, out loud, hurling the empty plastic cutlery-holder across the kitchen, where it crashed into Timmy's bowl and sent cat crunchies skittering over the floor. 'Fuck, fuck, fuck!'

I'd never felt this alone, even when Ed was ill. What was wrong with me? *Waitsey* wouldn't have been this pathetic. How had I changed so much, become so dependent?

In that moment I saw my life for what I feared I'd become; at best a doormat, at worst, a pawn in something bigger than I had allowed myself to think about in years.

31

I rang Maddie in Jersey.

'Mads,' I said when she picked up, hearing the faint sound of waves crashing on the beach in the background. 'Ed's gone missing.'

I heard a little gasp.

'He didn't come home last night,' I rushed on before she could reply. 'Something really weird is going on. The police have been round, and I'm going to wait a while to see if he turns up, but I ... I just have this feeling that he won't.'

It gave me a shock, saying it out loud for the first time.

'Oh,' said Maddie, speaking at last. 'What do you mean, you don't think he'll turn up? So sorry, darling. How stressful, after Mike. Are you all right, Lynn? You don't sound like yourself ... you sound different.'

'I *feel* different. I'm going out of my mind. If he doesn't come back today I'm going to bloody well go and look for him.'

'Has he been wandering then?'

'No, it's not that. I know this sounds weird, but ... but something's telling me it's nothing to do with his illness.'

Maddie, of course, didn't know that he'd been cured; that the trial had worked. We'd only had the news for a day.

'Really? He's a vulnerable person – so if the police are involved, I'm sure they will mount a huge investigation. Has anyone tweeted an appeal yet? They'll find him, don't worry.'

She thought I was just in shock, I could tell from her purposefully calm tone.

The cat jumped into my lap and I stroked him automatically as he settled down, kneading my legs with his sharp claws and shedding ginger fur on my black jeans. The needling pain kept me focussed.

I shouldn't have told the police about Ed's miracle recovery. I felt like I'd sealed his death warrant. They wouldn't look for him nearly so hard if they thought he'd merely absconded for his own reasons – they'd already told me his case was 'low to medium risk'. Why hadn't I kept my mouth shut?

'Oh Maddie. It's complicated – I'm not supposed to tell anyone because it's confidential to the trial, but I told the police and now I wish I hadn't...'

'Told them *what*?' She sounded alarmed. 'What's confidential to the trial...?'

I took a deep breath. 'Well. It's brilliant – at least, it was. Now I'm worried that there's more to it.'

'Spit it out, Lynn, you're not making sense.'

So I told her about the visit to the Chelsea Clinic, the scans, Bill Brown's tears of joy, our champagne celebration. Maddie listened in stunned silence – not speaking for so long, I had to ask her if she was still there.

'Yes ... my God, Lynn, this is ... incredible! I really didn't hold out much hope that the trial would work!'

'No, me neither. It's incredible, and I can't tell you how relieved we are – were – but now, one day later, he's vanished. What am I meant to make of that, after all the other weird stuff that's gone on? Mike's murder, Ed's behaviour – you know, sometimes he said and did stuff that I didn't think was anything to do with his Pick's.'

'Hard to tell though, surely?'

She wasn't necessarily doubting me, I knew that. It was a genuine question and one that I'd asked myself enough times. I took a breath. I couldn't keep my fears to myself.

'His passport's missing.'

She gasped again.

'But then, I hadn't seen it for years. It might just be somewhere else in the house.' I was offering Maddie the same kind of justification as I had given to the police. It sounded just as brittle the second time.

'You don't think he's run away?'

'I don't know!' I wailed, my voice abruptly loud. 'I don't fucking know anything, except that something's off about this whole thing.' I hesitated. 'And now April's gone to Australia.'

'*Has* she? What, on holiday? She didn't tell me! I spoke to Naveeta last night and she didn't mention it either – you know she would've done if she knew.'

It was true: Naveeta loved to gossip.

'I got this long email from her – April, I mean – saying she was already halfway there, it was a spur of the moment thing, she said. She's going on a yoga retreat, for a couple of months at least.'

'You're not...' Maddie stopped. I could almost hear her measuring her words. 'You're not suggesting that Ed's done a runner with her, are you?'

I was silent. The night of Mike's death came back to me; the two of them tête-à-tête in the kitchen. April claiming Ed had come on to her. It was as if the memory had been waiting behind a closed door in my mind.

'I've never had any reason to think she had her eye on him. She's our friend. She wouldn't! If anyone did, I'd have thought it would be Naveeta, you know how flirty she is around him. But what if April's grief made her act out of character?'

Maddie sighed. 'Oh Lynn. No. She's a flirt too – but you're right; she wouldn't. Did she even know he'd been "cured"?'

I noted the way she said "cured", and imagined her wiggling speech-marks with the two forefingers of each hand. It made me angry. Ed *had* been cured!

'No. Well, not unless Ed told her himself.'

'Well then. They'd hardly have planned a joint escape to Australia within twenty-four hours of getting the news that he was better!'

She was right. I didn't know why I'd even thought it. 'I'm losing the plot, Mads. I've been feeling so paranoid and ... well, scared. Spooked, I suppose. For months now, if I'm honest. For ages I really felt like something bad was going to happen. Then Mike was killed, and now Ed's disappeared. What if they're linked? If the same person who murdered Mike has come after Ed?'

Maddie's voice was sober. 'I know how worried you've been, but I thought it was all to do with Ed's illness. Do the police think there might be a link?'

I shrugged, as if she could see me. 'They haven't a clue. They still have no idea who killed Mike, and no leads, so they don't have anything to go on.'

'This is awful,' Maddie said. 'I wish I was there to help. Please come and stay if – if...'

'– if I need to,' I finished flatly, neither of us capable of articulating the unthinkable. 'Thanks Mads. I will. Listen, I'm going to go now. The police are looking at all our accounts, and I need to as well. I don't want any more nasty surprises.'

'OK darling. Promise you'll let me know if there's anything at all I can do. Hopefully he'll come strolling home any minute now. Maybe he just went on some sort of massive post-illness bender – to celebrate, you know. I would if I were him.'

'Maybe,' I said. Then again, more quietly, with diminishing confidence: 'Maybe.'

32

After a weekend of doing almost nothing but fretting, waiting, and arguing with myself – wandering the house and garden, and searching every nook and cranny for the missing passport, on the Monday morning I finally received a piece of news.

Martine – Constable Knocker – rang to say that they had spoken to the Chelsea Clinic.

There was no Dr Bill Brown renting premises there, nor had there ever been.

I couldn't make my voice work for a moment.

There were several William Browns on the GMC's register, she told me, hurriedly. The police would be contacting them all to check. She paused before continuing. None of the ones listed had a dementia specialism, though, so it was highly unlikely that any would turn out to be Ed's Bill.

I still couldn't speak. My mind was working too fast. Could Bill really have been a fake? If so, who was he? None of this made sense. And if he was a fake, then that meant the entire medical trial must have been a sham. Either Ed himself had been used as some kind of pawn – or, worse, he'd known about it all along, perhaps even set it up himself.

In which case, the whole purpose of it had been to fool me. There had been no real diagnosis, no scans, no Pick's. Just lies. Months, years, of lies.

I thought about Ed's vagueness, the forgotten passwords, the lost emails, the appointments he only told me about afterward. The scans he wouldn't have, then did have. The missing passport, the miraculous results I had to keep a secret. The night he grabbed my throat and threatened me. The many nights he hit me. Real symptoms of a real illness – or faked symptoms of a faked one?

What the fuck was going on? He wouldn't do that to me. He couldn't.

I grimly agreed to send her over all the scant correspondence I did have about the trial – which was hardly any, given Ed's myriad excuses, from refusal to let me go with him to his appointments, to his claims of forgotten passwords. Martine said they would also obtain Ed's medical records from Mr Deshmukh, and from his GP.

Then she told me they had checked flight manifests, and Ed hadn't left the country – not by plane, at least. But perhaps he was just holed up in a hotel somewhere, I thought. Or had sneaked out by car or coach, which would be easier to do undetected. I suggested this, which merely made Martine comment that there wasn't a lot they could do if he'd simply decided to do a bunk. 'If no crime has been committed,' she concluded.

'No crime? What about impersonating a medical consultant? Hiring consulting rooms under false pretences?'

'That's a different matter, and of course is a criminal offence. I'm referring to your husband, Mrs Naismith.'

'But, don't you see? If Bill Brown is a fake, then Ed hasn't really been cured. And if Ed hasn't been cured, that means he's either still ill – or he never *was* ill in the first place!'

'Yes ... it's a bit of a mystery really, isn't it? But he must have been ill. I remember when I met him after the incident at Hampton University. He was not a well man.'

'Exactly!' I cried. 'So could you please raise the risk level at least to medium? I wish I'd never told you he'd been cured!'

Martine promised that she was doing what she could, and that if Ed was intercepted leaving the country, his name would be flagged up on the system and the police informed.

'Would they detain him?'

'If it was felt he was a risk to himself or others, then yes, most likely.'

Martine ended the call by saying she'd check back in tomorrow, and

I told her I was going to stay with friends but that I'd have my mobile with me at all times.

I put the phone down, frustration overwhelming me. It was as if I was going round in circles, my mind so dizzy I was staggering to keep upright.

I hadn't intended to talk to Adrian at all since I broke up with him – but I needed to now. I needed to hear his calm, reassuring voice. I left him a message before I changed my mind, trying to keep the hysteria out of my own voice. 'It's me. I hope you don't think I'm using you, and don't call back if you don't want to – but Ed's gone missing. There's no way he could've found out about us, is there? He just vanished, three days ago. There's something fishy going on. Oh, Ade, I'm worried that this whole thing's been a set-up from the start, that he was never even ill ... I think I've—'

I almost forgot myself and said, 'fucked up'; I almost told Adrian that maybe I'd been too hasty in concluding that Ed was innocent of any involvement in Shelagh's disappearance.

I was losing the plot.

I ended the call then sat at the kitchen table, my laptop open in front of me. With a well opening up in my stomach, I logged into our savings account online.

Last time I'd looked, it had contained nigh on ninety thousand pounds, intended as our emergency funds, strictly ring-fenced for any future unforeseen circumstances. When Ed had sold his big house in Molesey, the year after we got together, he'd been able to buy the much smaller lock-keeper's cottage outright, with about seventy grand profit left over. My name was not on the deeds of the cottage, because I hadn't contributed anything towards it, and we'd not been married then, anyway. It had all made sense back then. As had putting my own savings into the same account. Over the years I'd carefully put aside monthly contributions from my old job in the financial advisor's office and then from Hampton Uni. It was nothing like as much as Ed had saved, of course, but a tidy sum nevertheless. Over the past few months

I'd come to accept that we'd most likely have to use all this cash to pay for Ed's residential care one day. But now ... now I had a very bad feeling about what I was about to discover. As soon as the screen displayed BALANCE, my fears were confirmed. The savings account now contained just three pounds and forty-two pence.

He'd transferred the rest out yesterday and left me with nothing.

'You BASTARD', I screamed, picking up my laptop and only just preventing myself dashing it onto the tiled kitchen floor.

Maybe someone, murderer of Mike, perhaps, had held a gun to Ed's head and forced him to withdraw the entire amount – but it seemed unlikely. My rage coagulated into a cold, hard lozenge of bitterness that stuck in my chest and made my breathing shallow.

I sat back in my chair, panting with shock.

There was no way I was putting up with this without a fight.

It was some time later, when I'd spent many long minutes outside, staring into the river and visualising the remnants of my life with Ed flowing away on the current, that I made a decision. I realised with a sinking heart that there was nothing for it: I would have to revisit my original investigation into Shelagh's disappearance. It had always been a Pandora's Box I'd never wanted to open, in case I discovered I'd somehow made a terrible mistake. But now I knew I had to. I had no choice.

I needed to talk to Shelagh's sister – if I could find her. I remembered we still had Shelagh's old address book, useful for Christmas cards to Ed's distant relatives, so I hurried back into the house, retrieved it from the study and searched through from the As, since I couldn't remember Ellen's last name.

I didn't have to go very far, just to the Bs, and found Ellen Brigstock Lamb. That was definitely her – Brigstock was Shelagh's maiden name. But it was an address in Scotland, written in Shelagh's small, careful handwriting. Damn – Ed had told me a few years ago that she'd moved. Where, though? I couldn't remember. All I recalled was Ed saying 'good riddance to that evil cow', when he'd mentioned it – so it must have been a fair distance. He only knew because Ben told him he'd had a birthday card from her. Ben couldn't stand her either, so it was highly unlikely he'd have kept her change of address.

Still, at least I now had her surname.

Where *had* she moved to? I racked my brains so hard it almost hurt. I had a feeling it was to an island off the British coast somewhere. Isle of Man? Orkney? Jersey? How could I find out?

I dashed back to my laptop and opened up Facebook. I'd never had my own account – it was frowned on in the police as being a security risk, more so back in the early days when it was a new invention and seemed mostly to consist of poking people and buying cartoon farm animals. Since then I couldn't take the chance of any of my old police colleagues stumbling across me, even under a different name. Now though, needs must.

I set up an account with a random fake name – Christine Ellingham – and did a search for Ellen Brigstock Lamb. I found a listing for her immediately. In Alderney. Bingo! I'd known it was an island. I felt the familiar thrill of discovering something new, as if my old police skills were beginning to wake up again.

There were no contact details though, and the profile didn't yield much other information. Her profile pic was an empty beach at sunset. I clicked on Message and a dialogue box appeared. Was it that easy to contact someone, even if you weren't friends with them on the site? It seemed it was.

I hesitated, fingers poised over the keyboard, wondering how to word it. Eventually I typed:

Dear Ellen, I hope you read this. You'll see this message coming from someone called Christine. But my real name is Lynn and as you may be aware I married Ed Naismith after your sister was declared officially dead. I'm sorry to intrude but I'd really like to speak to you about him. He's now vanished, too, after some pretty weird incidents, and it occurred to me that you might possibly be able to shed some light on the situation. I'd be most grateful if you

would meet me – I can come to you in Alderney. Thank you. I very
much hope to hear from you, either by writing back on here, or on
my mobile.

I put in my mobile number and signed off the message, wondering
how Ellen would feel when – if – she received it. She'd been the one
who badgered the police to investigate Ed in the first place, so she obviously hadn't had a good relationship with him.

I couldn't sit around waiting for a reply so I simultaneously began
defrosting the freezer – long overdue, the door barely closed – packing
a suitcase and Googling the best way to get to Alderney. There were
direct flights from Southampton, but I wanted to fly from Gatwick,
which meant I'd have to go via Guernsey. That decided me: I'd stop
over at Maddie and Geoff's in Jersey too. Might as well. It would be
so good to see them; grounding. I needed that bit of stability right
now.

I booked air tickets departing the following morning, paying with
my credit card, then called Naveeta and asked her to have the cat for
me, telling her I'd explain when I brought him over.

Before I'd even finished packing, I discovered several more things
regarding Ed's disappearance, all of them fuelling my rage and suspicion. It wasn't just his passport and the savings that had gone – his
favourite pair of deck shoes was missing, as well as his birth certificate
and a boar's head family crest signet ring that used to belong to his dad.
He'd hardly have randomly taken all *those* items to lunch with Bill.

You bastard, became my constant chant as I whirled about the
house. 'You bastard,' as I aimed my hairdryer at the ice on the inside of
the freezer, until I was able to break off chunks of it to lob hard into
the sink. 'You *bastard*,' as I futilely rang his mobile for the thirtieth time
and emailed him for the twentieth.

Yet, at the same time and despite evidence to the contrary, I wasn't
able to stop entertaining the belief that I could be wrong. He might
well be lying dead somewhere, murdered by the same person who gar-
rotted Mike. I veered back and forth between fear for his life and a

sixth sense that he'd been fooling me for years; see-sawing up and down on a pivot of heartbreak.

Or maybe he'd discovered I'd slept with someone else and had left me?

The house was completely silent, apart from the sound of the last pieces of melting ice from the freezer drip-drip-dripping into the tray on the kitchen floor. My phone rang into the silence and I lunged for it, praying it was Ed.

But it was Adrian, returning my call. It was so good to hear his voice again, as reassuring and calm as I'd hoped.

'I really don't think he could have faked it, do you?' he said almost immediately. 'They'd never have accepted him in a medical trial if he was faking it, they'd have rumbled him in a heartbeat. And anyway, he couldn't possibly have faked brain scans. You're bound to be stressed and panicked because he's missing, but don't fear the worst.'

But his calm voice wasn't having the desired effect – and I realised I was snarling my reply. 'He's emptied the savings account. His passport's missing! If he's done the dirty on me, I'm going to fucking find out, and I'm going to kill him.'

'Woah, woah, hold on. You're putting two and two together and getting four hundred. One thing at a time, eh? He might have been under duress when he took the money out, maybe he got into some kind of debt when he was ill? Perhaps he took the passport with him to withdraw the money?'

'He transferred it online, into an account I didn't recognise. I think he set up a new one.'

'OK, so maybe the passport's just got lost – you said he hasn't been abroad for years.'

I sighed and took several deep breaths. 'It's possible, I suppose.'

'All I'm saying, gorgeous, is don't complicate things. "Sufficient unto the day is the evil thereof", as my dear old mum used to say. Just sit tight, don't go haring off. He'll need you to be at home for when he gets back.'

'*If* he does.'

'Happy to meet up, if that'll help? How about a massage and a hot bath – strictly platonic, of course?'

I huffed, but managed a smile. 'Platonic. Yeah, if you say so...'

'It would be!' he protested. 'If you wanted it to.'

'Thanks for the offer, Ade, really. And the advice. You're probably right, I'm getting ahead of myself. But I've already booked flights to the Channel Islands. I'm going to Jersey to see Maddie. I'll go crazy if I sit here on my own waiting – and anyway I don't think it's wise to hang out with you right now, tempting as it is.'

'Very tempting,' he agreed. 'Well, do what you need to. And remember I'm here if you need me. Just don't overthink things, not yet.'

We hung up, but I didn't feel at all placated. Usually I'd trust Adrian's counsel implicitly, but I could tell he thought it ludicrous – the idea that Ed had been faking and that it was all a massive lie. He was probably right.

By the evening, the freezer was clean and as empty as our savings account. I crammed a reluctant Timmy into his cat carrier and called in next door to see Suzan. She stood wringing her hands in the doorway as I explained the situation as concisely as I could, without actually telling her my suspicions.

'I'm so sorry,' she said. 'Are you sure you don't want to leave him here, and I'll just pop in and feed him twice a day? Won't it be stressful for him to be relocated, if you're not going for long?'

She gestured towards Timmy, who was mewing at my feet. A small cloud of cat hair floated out of the basket's wire sides, a sure sign that he was indeed stressed.

'Thanks ... but I don't know how long I'll be away, and he tends to wander off if there's no one in the house to entertain him. I don't want to have to worry about him going AWOL too!'

'I wish I could have him for you, but, you know...'

I couldn't tell if her eyes were watering from the proximity to the cat hair, or out of concern for Ed. Timmy was a particularly allergenic feline, it seemed.

'I know. I wouldn't expect you to, don't worry about it. But please keep an eye on the house, and if you see Ed, call me straightaway, day or night?'

She hugged me, sneezing into my shoulder. 'Of course. I'll keep my eyes peeled, I promise. And my ears, if you can peel ears.'

I drove away with Timmy in his basket on the passenger seat, watching my house recede in the rearview mirror, feeling slightly comforted by having Suzan as my own personal neighbourhood watch.

Next stop Naveeta's. I hadn't intended to tell her about anything other than the fact that there was still no news regarding Ed's whereabouts – but I'd forgotten Naveeta's ability to worm gossip out of a stone.

'Are you all right, darling?' she asked, when I arrived, her smooth, long-nailed hand on my forearm, her nine-year-old twin girls lurking around her knees, hiding behind her skirt like much younger children would. They had all rushed out onto the driveway to meet me. 'What's going on? You look terrible. Come in, come in! Are there any updates?'

She arranged her features into a pouty, concerned expression that suddenly irritated me so wildly that I wondered again if I was menopausal. These mood swings were exhausting – but, I supposed, I didn't know how you were meant to feel when your husband had probably done a runner with your life's savings...

'No news,' I said, biting down a sarcastic apology for not looking my best. 'Listen, thanks for taking Timmy.'

I allowed myself to be ushered into the hall, where the twins pounced on Timmy's cat carrier and were trying to undo it and extract him. 'Girls, best if you shut him in a spare room with a litter tray for a couple of days – don't let him out here otherwise he'll try and make a run for it.'

'We don't want to lock him in the spare room!' wailed Bina. 'That will be horrible for him!'

I had a flashback to all the nights I locked Ed in the spare room. 'He'll be fine,' I said, swallowing the lump in my throat. *You bastard!*

I forced myself to think instead. If he had really done this, he was a shit and I wished I'd bloody well locked him in and thrown away the key.

'They prefer small spaces when they're in an unfamiliar place, I promise you. Once he feels at home there, you can let him roam a bit more.' I turned to Naveeta. 'Don't let him out of the house for at least three weeks though, will you?'

Naveeta looked alarmed. 'Three *weeks*? How long are you going to be gone?'

'I don't know,' I said. 'I'm going to visit Ben this evening. Then I'm going and stay with Maddie if there's still no news. I can't sit in that house on my own waiting to see if he comes back; I just can't.'

I certainly wasn't going to tell her about visiting Ellen.

'Where do you think Ed is, darling?' Naveeta asked, as though Ed was a lost wallet. I half expected her to say, 'And when did you last have him?'

Good question though. Had I ever really had him?

'I don't know. Perhaps he's run off to Australia with April. You heard that she's gone to some kind of commune over there?'

'I know!' Naveeta, seeming to forget the gravity of the situation, looked like she was settling in for a gossip and then realised what I had actually said. 'No, of course he hasn't! Why would you say that?'

'I don't know,' I said, 'I don't really think they have. But it's a bit of a coincidence that they've both disappeared at the same time.'

'April hasn't disappeared, she's gone on holiday to try and get over her husband's death!'

I sighed. 'Yeah. I know. It's just weird. First Mike, then Ed's miracle recovery, then April taking off, and him not coming home...'

I had already said more than I'd intended. Naveeta had this annoying way of making me do that. Sure enough, she was all over it: 'What miracle recovery? What do you mean?'

I supposed, if the whole trial had been faked, then there was no need for secrecy about it anymore. In which case, I ought to tell the police my suspicions – but I couldn't do that. Not until I was sure. My undercover debacle could not come out. It just couldn't. Because if Ed had faked his illness, what else had he managed to fool me about?

'He's been in a medical trial,' I said reluctantly. 'This new drug has reversed his symptoms.'

Allegedly.

'You know, I *thought* he seemed better!' Naveeta shrieked. 'Oh my god, Lynn, that fantastic!'

'Great – for him,' I said sourly. 'Not so great for me, if he's been cured and immediately done a runner.'

'He wouldn't! Why would he? And surely you don't really think it's all connected to Mike's murder, and April?'

I pulled myself together.

'No, you just get mad thoughts. It's just panic, that something awful's happened to him. Please, Nav, please don't say anything to anyone. Promise?'

She crossed her heart with a flourish and nodded vigorously. I didn't believe for a minute that she meant it.

'Anyway,' I said. 'I'd better get going. The girls are dying to get Timmy settled in, I can see.'

The twins giggled, jostling over the handle of the cat carrier as they manhandled it upstairs, with Timmy yowling in protest. I had to look away, suddenly emotional as he disappeared around the top of the stairs. It felt like I was losing everyone all at once.

'But surely you'll stay for a cup of tea or a glass of wine at least?'

Naveeta tried to drag me through to the kitchen but I resisted, taking my car keys out of my bag and turning for the door. 'No, honestly, thanks, but I'm going to Kingston to stay with Ben and Jeanine.'

I intentionally made it sound as though I'd be staying at Ben's for some time. I didn't want Naveeta to know how soon I was leaving for the Channel Islands, because I didn't want her to pick up on my fear that Ed wasn't ever coming back.

33

I pressed the buzzer at the entrance to Ben's building. When he answered, I could hear the frantic tone even in his disembodied and crackly voice. 'Lynn! Any news?'

He buzzed me in at the same time, so I concluded he didn't really want me to update him over the intercom. As I climbed the stairs I saw his large outline fill the open doorway of his first-floor flat, bouncing anxiously on the balls of his feet. He rushed out and gave me a more effusive hug than he had in years.

Poor Ben. He looked so pale. He wasn't my favourite person, but he didn't deserve this, especially so hard on the heels of his elation at his dad's supposed miracle cure – we'd told him, of course. He smelled of aftershave and fabric softener, with a top note of garlic and I briefly clung to him, thinking that he was the closest thing to Ed that I might ever see again.

'Come in,' he said. 'Jeanine's out at Zumba. I'm just cooking risotto so we can all eat together when she gets in.'

'It smells great.' I was starving. It was only a fifteen-minute drive from Naveeta's house to his flat, but I felt exhausted.

'So, is there?' Ben asked, pouring me a glass of white wine without asking if I wanted one. 'Any news, I mean? I guess not, otherwise you wouldn't be here.'

He froze in the act of handing me the wine, holding the glass tantalisingly just out of my reach: 'You haven't come in person to tell me something terrible, have you?'

'No, please don't worry. At least, don't worry any more than you already are. I haven't heard anything at all.'

'Well, no news is good news … maybe. Stay and talk to me while I stir, otherwise my rice'll stick.'

I leaned against the fridge, trying not to be in the way.

He poured stock into the large frying pan, frowning in concentration, looking in profile so like Ed that I had to grit my teeth. He was even wearing an apron similar to the one Ed wore in the kitchen. The rice sizzled and roiled as he stirred it.

'I'm going to stay with Maddie in Jersey for a while,' I said cautiously.

'When?'

'I'm flying from Gatwick tomorrow – I'll get the train to the airport. I wondered if I could leave the car here. You and Jeanine are welcome to use it, of course.'

'Tomorrow?' He rested the wooden spoon on a chopping board and turned to look at me. 'But what if Dad comes back and you're not there?'

I sighed, regretting bringing it up so soon.

'Ben ... Can we talk about it after dinner, when Jeanine's here too?'

He switched off the gas ring under the pan with an aggressive flick. 'No. If there's something you aren't telling me, I want to know now. Where is he, Lynn?'

'I don't know! Of course I don't know. I'd never put you through what I'm going through. If I knew, I'd tell you.'

He softened a little. 'Sorry. I'm just so worried about him.'

'Me too.' I put a hand on his arm and he gave me a tight-lipped smile.

'That's done, I think,' he said, putting a lid on the rice. 'Let's sit soft.'

Ed hated that expression almost as much as he hated 'up London' and 'at the end of the day.' Ben obviously remembered this at the same time and half laughed, half sobbed.

I smiled, too. 'I won't tell him you said that.'

We went through to the living room and sat at either end of Ben's enormous grey L-shaped sofa. It was dark outside but the curtains were open and the lights from the cranes on the nearby building site were almost pretty.

'I can't believe you're going away when he's still missing,' Ben repeated, but in a less confrontational tone.

'It would do my head in, sitting in that empty house day after day wondering if he's going to come wandering down the towpath at any point,' I said. 'Whether he's safe, or if the dementia's back, or if he's just done a runner ... I've given the police Maddie's address. I'll have my mobile with me. But I need to be with a close friend, Ben. April's gone to Australia, to some commune or spa or something, and doesn't even have proper internet, so she's not available. Maddie's my other best friend and I know it'll be easier for me to cope if I'm with her. I'll come straight back if he turns up, I promise.'

'Why would he do a runner?' Ben asked, in a small voice.

I paused. I wasn't sure how much to tell him. Ed was his dad, after all. 'I don't know. But there have been so many strange things going on. The miraculous recovery, for one...'

'Yes,' he said. 'That clinical trial. Was it kosher?'

Our eyes met. 'If it wasn't kosher, Ben, then you know what that means...'

Ben's mouth tightened into a furious line and he was silent for a moment. 'That he faked the whole thing.'

'Yes. Or he was conned into it somehow.'

'Do you think he was?'

I thought of the savings account. Bill was in all probability a fake. Surely *he* was the villain of the piece? Perhaps he'd persuaded Ed that the trial wasn't free, that it cost ninety grand, and Ed didn't want to admit to me that he'd spent all that money without consulting me, so he'd run away? That seemed like a plausible explanation.

Except – the trial *had* worked. Which implied that, if Bill was a fake, Ed had never been ill to start with.

The police were aware that Bill was probably a fake. I decided I'd tell them about the missing money too, so they could trace the account that Ed had transferred it into. Then I'd know.

'I have no idea. Maybe. At the moment I think both are equally likely.'

Then I saw Ben's face and backtracked.

'No. No, I can't believe that. He was so ... lost, when he was ill. And

I don't believe he'd ever be so cruel as to make us all think he had what Pops had! I know that him faking it is the obvious conclusion, but do you really think he could have kept up an act like that for all these months? He's a good actor but he's not *that* good. I've seen his brain scans, Ben, the old diseased ones and then the recent ones with the damage reversed. There's no logical explanation other than the drug really did work…'

I was confusing myself again.

Ben jumped up and paced around the room, ducking his head to avoid the dangly chandelier. 'But … but … I'm sorry, I don't buy it. I sort of get that we're all sworn to secrecy about the trial, if it's still got another year to run – but why isn't there a national appeal for Dad's safety? The police must think that he still has dementia, that he's vulnerable!'

'I told the police about the trial, and his cure. I had to.'

'Oh. Perhaps it would've been better if you hadn't. Then they might be taking it more seriously.'

Ben topped up our wine glasses but the wine was going to my head so I left mine untouched on the coffee table. I needed to stay in control. 'Got any salty snacks, Ben?'

Salty snacks – that was one of Ed's expressions.

'Sorry.' He jumped up again and dashed back to the kitchen. It was funny, seeing him as he was now, when he'd been such a sulky, pudding-faced teenager. I couldn't blame him for that though – back then, he was a boy who'd just lost his mother.

When he came back with a bowl of crisps, I impulsively reached for his free hand and gave it a squeeze. 'Thank you.'

'For the salty snacks?'

I laughed. 'No. For turning out so well. For being kind to me and so close to your dad. You were having such a tough time when I first met you. It's a miracle you ever accepted me.'

His eyes filled with tears and he batted at his face like a small boy would. 'I didn't think I ever would,' he said. 'I couldn't believe Dad just moved you in so soon … but I suppose, you can get used to anything eventually and you were all right, I guess. Perhaps it was for the best, because it forced me to move on and to accept that Mum had really gone for good.'

'Do you remember much about that time?' I asked, leaning back against the sofa and eating the crisps, thinking how much he would hate me if he knew the truth of why I came into their lives.

'Of course. I remember it all. I was thirteen when she went missing, not three. It was fucking horrible. Excuse my French.'

'It must have been. Particularly when the police thought your dad was a suspect.'

'I was terrified they were going to take him away and lock him up and then I'd have lost them both.'

I almost asked him if he thought Ed had had any involvement with Shelagh's disappearance, then bit my lip. I couldn't ask him that, not now. *I'd* been utterly convinced of Ed's innocence. 'He didn't have anything to do with it,' I said instead.

'I know. But Auntie Ellen kept banging on about it, evil witch. That's the only reason the police kept sniffing around.'

It gave me a start, him bringing her up like that.

'Do you ever speak to her?'

He snorted. 'Auntie Ellen? Are you kidding? She accused Dad of being a murderer!'

'She was upset. She probably feels bad about it now. She'd probably be really pleased to hear from you.'

'I am never speaking to that woman again. I don't give a shit that she's my only family outside of Dad … and you, of course,' he added.

'Do you have her new address?' I asked casually.

'No. She's still in the Channel Islands somewhere with her chinless husband as far as I know. Maybe you'll bump into her when you go to Jersey. Please don't send her my regards if you do.'

'When did she move there?'

Ben shrugged. 'Five years ago? You aren't going to try and contact her, are you? She'll only give you a load of shite about how Dad killed her sister.'

'I was considering it,' I said neutrally. 'You never know, she might have some information about your dad that could be helpful. Maybe a place he loves that we don't know about?'

'She won't. She's mental. And she hates Dad.'

At that moment we heard the click of the front door and the thump of a sports bag being dropped.

'I'm back! That was really knackering!' called Jeanine, sticking her head around the living room door, her face a dull beetroot colour and her hair escaping in damp rats' tails from a ponytail. 'I'm – oh hello Lynn, Ben said you might be coming. Are you staying?'

'Just for tonight – if that's OK?' I got up to hug her.

'Ooh, don't hug me, I'm really sweaty. It's fine! Ben, did you make up the spare bed?'

'I don't care if you're sweaty,' I said, wrapping my arms around her as Ben rolled his eyes again, having clearly not made up any beds. 'It's good to see you. Give me the sheets and I'll do it.'

'Good to see you, too. So sorry to hear about Ed. Is there any news?'

'No,' Ben interrupted. 'And Lynn's about to bugger off on holiday.'

I frowned, breaking off the hug. 'It's not a holiday, Ben. It's an escape, a break. Do you really expect me to sit around on my own all day waiting for the phone to ring?'

Jeanine looked upset. 'Oh, please don't argue! It's so tough for you both. Let me have a quick shower and then we can eat – is it ready, Ben? It smells lovely.'

'It's ready,' Ben said, not meeting my eyes.

'I'll lay the table,' I offered.

34

Over dinner, Jeanine continued to look anxiously between us, as if a fight was about to break out at any minute. It was odd seeing them both without Ed there.

I filled them in with more of what the police had said, omitting the fact that there was no record of a Bill ever being at the Chelsea Clinic. Surely Adrian was right – you couldn't fake brain scans. Could you? I didn't want to worry Ben any more than he was already worried.

'My concern is that the improvement in his behaviour was some kind of ... aberration – maybe he'd had a bang on the head that made it look like it had gone – and the dementia suddenly came back. Maybe he's forgotten where he lives, or something.'

'But you said that the police had checked the CCTV at the stations and on the trains?' Jeanine poured iced water from a jug into all our glasses.

I nodded. 'He did get the train to Waterloo, but they don't know where he went after that. They've checked the flight manifests though, and he hasn't flown anywhere. Yet.'

'Why did you tell the police he'd been cured?' Ben turned to Jeanine. 'I told her she shouldn't have done that. I'm sure they'd make more of an effort to find him if they believed he was still ill.'

'I thought it was for the best,' I said. 'Maybe you're right. Maybe he wasn't cured at all.'

'But the scans? You said they showed his brain had repaired itself. I'm sorry, Lynn, but the more I think about it, the more I just don't buy this whole clinical trial healing thing.'

'Why not? They only trial drugs that they think have a good chance of working, don't they – I mean, why else would they bother? I think we have to take it at face value. Because otherwise it means your dad was lying through his teeth the whole time he was pretending to be ill.'

'Does it, though? Could the scans have been mixed up, or wrong?'

'I asked that, at our appointment,' I said. 'Bill said not, but I suppose it's possible. It wouldn't reflect very well on him, though, would it?'

I sighed, feeling very alone all of a sudden. 'I wish my mum was still alive,' I blurted.

I could go for months without thinking of my folks, but when I did miss them, like now, it was with an intensity that surprised me.

'When did you lose her?' Jeanine asked sympathetically. 'I've never heard you speak about your family.'

'I don't have any. Dad died of cancer when I was eighteen, and Mum followed him about a year later. Car crash. No brothers or sisters. So it was lovely to meet Ed so soon after I arrived in Hampton – even though it was a nightmare time for him and you, of course.' I gestured to Ben.

'Why did you move to this area, again? I've forgotten,' Ben asked. Was it my imagination, or did he have a combative glint in his eyes?

'I'd just split up from my husband and I wanted a fresh start.'

'Oh, that's right. The army bloke. But didn't you say he was overseas?'

'Yes, he was.'

'So why would you need to move towns then?'

I shrugged. 'I fancied a change. Too many bad memories.'

'Seems odd, to move somewhere where you don't know anybody at all. Wouldn't it have made more sense to go somewhere where at least you had a couple of mates? I mean, you're always going on about how you want to move to Jersey because Maddie and Geoff have gone there.'

I laughed, without humour. 'What is this, an interrogation? I don't know. I suppose I didn't really have any good friends after being stationed abroad with Dave for so long. Army life's like that. I'd let all my school and college friendships lapse.'

'Do you ever hear from Dave these days?' Ben asked. Again I thought it odd that he was so interested all of a sudden.

'Never. Once we got divorced I never clapped eyes on him again. Horrible man. Biggest mistake I ever made.'

Time to get off the subject. In a long-distant echo from down the years, I heard my mum's voice: 'Oh what a tangled web we weave, when first we practise to deceive.' Shakespeare – or perhaps Walter Scott, I couldn't remember, but it made me miss her even more.

My mum felt like someone in a storybook now, or a dream; a distant memory of woodsmoke-scented woollen jumpers, tweed skirts and headscarves. If my parents were still alive, I'd never have started any of this. I'd never have been able to keep up the deception for as long, if the pull of family ties had remained.

'Anyway,' I said wearily, standing up to clear the plates. 'That was delicious, Ben, thank you. Shall I put the kettle on?'

I made a pot of coffee and brought it back in with three mugs threaded through the fingers of my other hand. Ben was tapping away on his phone and Jeanine had disappeared into the bedroom, where the roar of a hairdryer confirmed what she was doing. Ben looked up and opened his mouth to speak. I braced myself for more difficult questions, but thankfully he seemed to have moved on from the subject of my cloudy past.

'What about this Bill person? Did Dad actually meet him for lunch?'

'Who knows?' I poured us both a coffee. 'He said he was going to. I don't know where they went, though, and I don't have any contact details for Bill. The police are looking into it. I should have taken his mobile number when I met him, I don't know why I didn't. Ed printed off an email from him once, but when I looked for it later I couldn't find it.'

'Can't you access Dad's emails?'

I paused. 'That's one of the weird things, Ben. Your dad had a password on his computer when we first met, but then he went for years without one. And now he's got one again, which he changed recently. Why do you think that is?'

'Why indeed,' said Ben, slightly pompously, as he topped up his glass again. 'His illness, probably. Dementia makes people paranoid.'

'Could be,' I said, putting my hand over my glass so he couldn't top me up too. 'Anyway, he's got his laptop with him. He always takes it on the train.'

'Do you know his Apple ID password? If you did you could log in as him and use Find My iPhone to locate him.'

I shook my head. It was a good idea though. The scaffolding of a headache built up inside my temples and I checked my watch: nine-forty. Too early to go to bed – and besides, this might be the last chance in a while I got to pump Ben for information. He was a little bit drunk, which was good.

'I suppose people only password-protect their computers when they have something to hide. Like an affair...' I pretended that this thought had only just occurred to me. 'No ... Ed wasn't having an affair, I'm certain of it. I'd have known if he was.'

I watched Ben like a hawk as I said it, checking for the slightest aversion of his eyes or tiny complicit twitch indicating he might know something that I didn't – but there was nothing. I meant it – I didn't believe Ed was seeing anyone else. His behaviour hadn't changed at all from the time I met him until the start of the illness – I was pretty sure I would have spotted the signs if he'd met someone.

I felt a shudder of guilt about Adrian. I was glad I hadn't seen him before I left. I definitely wouldn't have sex with him again...

Unless of course Ed really had done the dirty on me. In that case – all bets off. I had a brief image of Adrian and I settling down together in the countryside; Agas, open fires, a puppy and long brisk walks together. But somehow I couldn't see it, and the image dissolved like a swirl of instant coffee in boiling water.

Ben didn't show any signs of keeping anything from me either. He merely remarked, 'Dad was ill for most of the last year. I doubt any sane woman would fancy a guy who tries to take a piss in the vegetable aisle of Tesco Metro.'

I winced, wishing I'd never told him about that particular incident. Poor Ed.

And yet – who would even try and pee in Tesco if they weren't really mentally ill? If Ed had wanted to steal all the money from our joint account he could have just withdrawn it all and buggered off.

Which made me think there must be more to it.

I felt again the sting of such a betrayal, pricking all over my body like a thousand razor cuts. Had he really been so unhappy that the moment he recovered his faculties, he couldn't wait to disappear with our savings? If he had, he'd hidden it well.

'Ben,' I said carefully. 'If your dad was going to have a rush of blood to the head and decide he wanted to get away for a bit, do you have any idea where he might go? I honestly think that's what he might have done. Maybe as a reaction to getting his health back; maybe as part of some kind of bigger picture. Maybe being cured blew his mind and he's had a breakdown and that's why he didn't think to let us know he was going. He was ill when Mike died – he hasn't had a chance to come to terms with that, either. Grief does strange things to people.'

Ben pursed his lips. 'He'd go and lie on a beach somewhere, I reckon; you know how much he loves to get a tan. I don't think there's anywhere here with any great sentimental value for him. The house he grew up in got knocked down years ago – I think it's a Kwik-Fit or something hideous now.'

'His passport is missing. And he's taken quite a lot of our savings with him, so he could afford to go anywhere he fancied.' I stopped myself saying 'all our savings' – I was trying to be gentle.

'Really?'

I touched his forearm. 'But, I've got to say, it's been so long since he used the passport that I honestly don't know if it went missing recently or ages ago. He wouldn't fly anywhere while he was ill, nor for a couple of years before that. Do you remember you invited us to share a villa in Tuscany that time and we couldn't come, because Ed wouldn't get on a plane?'

'Mmm. But if he's better now...?'

'I hate the thought of him going off somewhere without me,' I blurted. 'We've barely been apart since we met.'

'It's a better option than him lying in a ditch somewhere,' Ben said. 'Poor you, though, Lynn, it's a bit of a lose-lose situation, isn't it…?'

I blew my nose on my paper napkin. 'I just don't understand why he hasn't been in touch, if he's just gone away.'

But I intended to find out.

35
2007

Three weeks after Ed and I starting dating, I let myself into his house with the keys I'd had cut the day before, hanging the spares back on their hooks by the coat rack without him noticing. Ed and Ben had left for a parent-teacher meeting at Ben's school and I sneaked in through the back gate and unlocked the kitchen door.

I'd officially been to the house plenty of times by then. I knew the layout of all the rooms. I knew where he kept the Hoover, which bin the junk mail went into, where the drawer with the stamps was – and his computer password.

I slipped into the kitchen and stood still. The smell of bacon fat lingered in the air and, beneath that, a whiff of the contents of the kitchen bin. The house was definitely lacking a woman's touch, I thought, observing a sticky patch on the floorboards near the fridge, and a solitary furry lemon in the fruit bowl.

Tiptoeing into the hall, I was about to climb the stairs up to Ed's office when the letterbox banged loudly on its springy hinge, and a load of envelopes clattered to the black-and-white pottery-tiled floor. I almost jumped out of my skin and then froze, in case the postman could make out my shape through the stained glass panels of the front door. His red jacket loomed close and for a horrible moment I thought he was about to press his nose against the glass, but then he retreated into a blur again and I exhaled.

I crept up the stairs, keeping as close to the wall as I could, my fingertips in their numbing vinyl gloves tracing the smooth emulsioned panels. I even knew that this wall used to be papered in that bubbly Anaglypta wallpaper so popular in the seventies – I'd overheard Ed telling someone that he only got rid of it recently.

Reaching the first-floor landing, I didn't go into the sitting room at the front of the house in case anyone saw me from outside, but turned right into the small, untidy room that Ed used as his study. I hadn't yet had the chance for a good snoop around it.

I started by rifling through the clutter on his desk but there was nothing of interest, just a couple of mail-order catalogues, take-away menus, bills – paid and unpaid – some sheets of A4 covered in Ben's scrawl; an English essay on *An Inspector Calls* that Ed had bossily annotated in the margins and a couple of scripts of *Make Do and Mend*.

I slid open the filing cabinet to the right of his desk. It contained captioned hanging files with titles like 'MADS – Subs', 'MADS – programmes', 'MADS – AGM', and, further back, 'Payslips', 'House Renovations', 'Old Chequebooks', 'Benjy Reports'. At the very back of the drawer were a few unidentified files so I pulled out a bulging one to find it full of newspaper clippings and online printouts about Shelagh's disappearance. The photo used was in most cases the same one, a snapshot of her sitting astride a stile wearing green wellies and a Barbour jacket, pointing a finger at the photographer, her head thrown back in laughter. She certainly didn't look depressed.

I wondered if it was normal for a bereaved husband to collate the newspaper articles on his wife's disappearance. I wasn't sure that I would, if my partner went missing. What would be the point? I skim-read them all, although of course I knew the story intimately. The short pieces did not tell me anything I hadn't already gone over numerous times. The same words jumped out at me in all of them: 'out of character', 'please contact', 'badly missed by her husband and fourteen-year old son'. Nowhere did it say that police were concerned for her mental health, or that she had a history of depression, or was in any way as unstable as Ed made out.

I arranged the files back into the drawer in the same order, instinctively deciding to check underneath them before I closed it. I shoved them all hard to the front of the drawer – nothing hidden at the back – and then did the same the other way, feeling around underneath with my fingers. All that was down there was a faded Polaroid, which I pulled out and examined. It was of the interior of the house, taken from right outside the door of the room I was crouching in now, looking towards the living room. The walls were indeed still papered with the Anaglypta wallpaper, which had then been painted a very unappealing mustard colour. There were beige carpets on the floor instead of the polished floorboards and the two visible open doors were glossy white, instead of the stripped pine that they now were.

The photograph might have slipped out of the House Renovations folder – unless Ed was hiding it at the bottom of the cabinet? I couldn't put my finger on why he would, but I put the photo in my jacket pocket anyway, and arranged the hanging files to cover the space in the drawer.

I glanced at my watch. I probably had at least another forty minutes before Ed would be back – Ben's school was a good half-hour's drive away – but I didn't want to cut it too fine. I searched through and behind all the books on the wobbly black metal bookshelf beside the desk, hoping for a journal written by Shelagh, although naturally that would be far too easy … I had a brief mental daydream of finding one, filled with examples of Ed's violence towards her and her desperation to get away before he killed her… As if! I'd be lucky. The police would have found it anyway, ages ago.

The shelves were groaning with play scripts, volumes of poetry, dramaturgy, old yellowing copies of *TMJ* from Ed's former years as a GP and some thick medical tomes that I accidentally knocked sideways and they went down like oversized dominos in a cloud of dust. Nothing of interest.

I booted up Ed's desktop computer and it came to life with the loud boom of Windows announcing its awakening, which made me wince. I entered his password and scrolled through as many files as I could whilst waiting for all Ed's data to transfer onto the memory stick I had plugged in to the side of his console. Ed didn't strike me as the kind to keep a diary, but you never knew. It was easy to hide a personal document in amongst everything else – but that part of it wasn't my job. Someone with far more time on his hands would be tasked with searching through every single document with the digital equivalent of a nit comb. The data finally finished downloading and I removed the memory stick, zipped it into my jacket pocket with the Polaroid and checked around that I had left everything exactly as it was.

Time to go.

I could get used to this, I thought, taking another bow. The dust motes spar-kling all around me were whipped into a frenzied cloud by the audience applause, lit by the footlights. Perhaps if I chucked in the police to marry Ed, I would become an actress instead. It was amazing to look up and see the first few rows of audience, so many supportive faces beaming with enjoyment as they clapped.

It was the first time I'd had that thought – leaving the police, not becoming an actress – and it shocked me. Up until that point, I had been able to objectify my time in Molesey as nothing more than an assignment, albeit with someone I really was attracted to, knowing that at some point in the next few months it would all be over and I'd be back on patrol, or in the office, or perhaps on the Armed Response training course I'd initially wanted to do. I quashed the thought immediately, although not without regret that I would soon have to say goodbye to Ed and become Waitsey again.

I saw him up in the lighting box applauding too, smiling that smile right at me as we took our final curtain call of the run, in front of the authentic 1940s tractor that was as much a part of the play as we were.

It was a heady rush of mixed emotions, realising that for the two hours of the six performances over the past week, I hadn't had to stop to consider the impact on *me*, beyond my assignment, of what I'd be losing when it was over; the bonding cemented by the hundreds of lines we'd learned and the hours of rehearsals we'd spent together – particularly April and me. I'd never had such a close girlfriend before. As if she'd read my mind, she squeezed my hand and beamed at me as we bowed for the third time. I'd miss it so much. I totally understood why people claimed that the buzz of performing was addictive.

I couldn't believe I'd even had the thought that I might resign to be with

Ed. Being in the police was all I'd ever wanted – until I met him, at least. I'd be branded a failure, a waste of space and taxpayers' money. It was unthinkable, shameful.

But I'd have Ed, and it was beginning to feel intolerable to go back to a life without him. Waitsey was already feeling like a distant memory, someone I used to know. Within the space of five months as Lynn Jackson, I had stepped so far out of my comfort zone that it felt like a different country. I'd been sent in to investigate Ed and I had done so to the best of my abilities – but it had been life-changing for me. I had my own place (admittedly courtesy of Surrey Police, and I'd have to either leave it or take over the lease), new friends – April and Maddie especially – and a new-found confidence from actually pulling off acting in a play.

As we stood on stage for the final time on the last night, sweaty and elated in our land-girl costumes – me and Pat in beige dungarees and khaki shirts, Robina and April in jodhpurs and bottle-green pullovers – I had the words 'be a leaf on a tree' chasing themselves around my brain, like a plastic bag circling in a gusty little cyclone. I'd read those words recently in a book on how to find happiness and they resonated deeply. The book had been on Ed's bookcase, dusty and tatty. It must have been Shelagh's – she'd read a lot of self-help, self-improvement manuals; not that they'd done her any good. It meant: be part of a community of like-minded people who you feel comfortable with, and that was exactly what I was doing.

Before we'd even skipped off stage to begin the last-night party, I was back to feeling guilty that I was using my work to further my own personal development; that my current happiness was predicated upon Ed and Ben's misery and loss. It was, at best, extremely unprofessional and, at worst, immoral of me. I thought about those male undercover agents who somehow managed to suppress similar thoughts and went on to have long-term relationships and children as their UC aliases. They got away with it. Why couldn't I? I seemed to be finding the inevitable schizophrenic aspect of the job more problematic than some of my male predecessors had.

In the last couple of months Ed and I had got closer and closer. When I went home to my bedsit at night I relived the feel of his hand in mind, the texture of the soft skin inside his elbow and the smell of his neck; aftershave and his own irresistible scent. I lay in bed getting turned on at the memory of his kisses and the sensation of his fingers stroking the hollow in the small of my back. Perhaps it was because we still hadn't 'gone all the way' that it was so unbelievably potent. I'd thought Adrian and I had that naughty frisson of forbidden attraction permeating all our liaisons, but what I felt for Ed completely swamped that.

And yet I had investigated him. I had snooped and spied, foraged and reported everything back to DS Metcalfe. There were no red flags, nothing that sounded odd about Ed and Ben's accounts of what happened. Nothing to prove or even indicate that Ed had any involvement in Shelagh's disappearance.

If he ever found out, it would all be over between us.

Everyone in MADS was gossiping about us, so April informed me in one of the now-regular coffee meets I had with her and Maddie. I'd initially felt uncomfortable discussing it with her, because she and Mike were such good friends of Ed's and, I'd assumed, Shelagh's – but she confessed to me that they had never got on with Shelagh all that well. They had both found her cold and distant. From a work perspective though, for me, April's intel was very useful. An inherent lover of a spot of tittle-tattle, she never held back on her theory that Shelagh had taken her own life.

When I discreetly enquired whether Shelagh and Ed had a tempestuous relationship, April just laughed and shook her head. 'I don't think either of them could summon up the energy to argue,' she said. 'Shelagh was a miserable cow.' Then she'd looked guilty and apologised, although whether that was to me or to Shelagh's spirit, I didn't know.

'Go for it,' she urged me at the last-night party, back at her and Mike's house, her eyes glittering with some emotion I couldn't read. 'It's just so lovely to see him so happy again.'

As the director, Ed had wanted to have the party at his place, but April wouldn't hear of it. I wasn't sure whether this was because she thought it was inappropriate given Ed's situation, or because she wanted to show off her own house, which was predictably perfect. It was a 1920s gabled mock-Tudor affair just outside Esher, interior-designed to within an inch of its life, scented with lily of the valley and Pledge. The downstairs loo had a shelf of the fluffiest, softest towels I'd ever seen, making me think ruefully of the two threadbare, faded excuses for towels in my tiny bathroom.

In fact you could have fitted my entire studio flat into her kitchen three times over – but I didn't feel envy at her life, just a guilty gratitude that I was part of it. I'd been on stage with her without her knowing that Lynn Jackson was also a part I was playing. I felt like a Russian doll, Waitsey inside Lynn Jackson inside Mabel the landgirl.

The party was hot and boisterous, fuelled with relief at a successful run and the unlimited champagne that Mike had laid on for everyone in MADS. After an hour or so we were all dancing in the cavernous kitchen, Ed trying to do Ceroc moves with me when everyone else was pretending they were at a rave in the nineties, which for some reason made me laugh uncontrollably. He spun me around and from one side to the other until I was dizzy, while next to us April did the 'big fish little fish, big box little box' move to the Rolling Stones *Goin' To a Go-Go*. The two elderly front-of-house volunteers were in a huddle in a corner gossiping and Keith, the stage manager, was lumbering awkwardly from side to side completely out of time with the music.

'He needs to consult the manual,' Maddie whispered in my ear when I stopped for breath, which made me laugh harder – Keith had, on the second night, referred to the script as 'the manual', much to the hilarity of the rest of us.

'I can't believe it's all over,' I said to Ed a bit later.

'What's all over?' Ed pulled me closer as the opening bars of *I Heard It through the Grapevine* started up, his brushed-cotton shirt soft against my cheek. Maddie and Geoff slow-danced next to us, beckoning April and Mike to join in, but they were busy topping up glasses and opening more champagne, whooping as the cork shot up to the ceiling.

'The play, idiot! This is the most fun I've ever had in my whole life.'

'It doesn't all have to be over,' he said, grinning at me. 'You could always audition for the next one. We're doing *Don't Get Your Vicars in a Twist*.'

I thought about how I would soon be somewhere else – I didn't even know where – and at once I felt sad and lost all over again, ripped up by the roots, my task completed. I had my exit strategy already planned out, a sudden phone call from my supposed ex-husband begging me to give our marriage another chance. An imminent posting to Cyprus. A few days pretending to agonise about it, then the rueful decision to try again. Then I'd be gone, no trace left except the eight-by-ten photos of me and the other cast members that had been pinned to the theatre foyer walls but which would now be languishing in a folder marked 'Productions – 2007'.

But now I didn't want go. I didn't want to leave Ed, or April and Mike and the rest of MADS, or even my little bedsit.

'I don't think bedroom farces are really my sort of thing,' was all I said.

As the party wore on and more champagne was consumed, I had to press my lips together in an effort to stop myself demanding sex from Ed. I wanted to grab his hand and drag him out of the party and back to my bedsit. Or even down to the river. It was a hot night, we could have found a secluded spot of parkland where he could take me up against a tree or bent over a park bench … I felt wild with desire as I imagined him flipping up my short skirt, pulling down my pants and entering me from behind. Every time we hugged I could feel his thick erection pressing into my leg or my crotch, to the point I worried the other party guests would notice it through his baggy chinos.

I never imagined I could ever fancy someone who wore chinos, but I did, even with the fourteen-year age gap. I fancied Ed with every nerve ending, every sinew and fibre. I was sure it was because we had denied ourselves for so many months. Possibly, for Ed, also because he hadn't had sex for a very long time – since at least a year before Shelagh vanished, according to him.

But the thought of DS Metcalfe's censure prevented me. That, and word getting back to Adrian McLoughlin, or being on my police record till the end of time … I could not be that unprofessional, I just couldn't.

At least that's what I thought until the sixth glass of champagne … or was it the seventh? By then they had all vanished from my mind, Adrian, Metcalfe, my UC course trainer, all the colleagues I'd ever had. I was drunk and high on happiness, professionalism discarded along with my land-girl dungarees on the dressing room floor. It was a hot night, I was playing my part brilliantly and I was, against my better judgement, hopelessly in love.

So when Ed steered me out into the garden and said, his hand on my breast, 'Let's get out of here, shall we? We can walk along the river,' I didn't make an excuse about being tired or feeling unwell, or that it was 'too soon'. I simply nodded, immediately flashing back to my earlier fantasy, and let him walk me right out of there without saying goodbye to anybody.

If I could have changed anything, it would have been that decision.

On that hot night down by the river, to a soundtrack of the delicate splash of minnows and the distant crying of a fox, Ed made love to me in a way so perfect that I thought I could die with happiness – until I sobered up, and it started to become apparent just what a complete fuck-up I'd made of everything.

It got a hell of a lot more apparent three weeks later, when I found out that I was pregnant.

I was an idiot. What the hell was I going to do now?

I was six weeks gone before I made up my mind, living with morning sickness and indecision that made my stomach churn constantly. I became intimately acquainted with the porcelain interior of my bedsit's toilet.

Naturally I didn't tell Metcalfe at any of our fortnightly meetings. I was mortified and ashamed of myself, wracked with confusion and rigid with panic, veering between making appointments for a termination on three separate occasions, only to cancel them on the day, and fantasising about the sheer joy of having a child.

Immediately after the event – and before I discovered I'd conceived – I told Ed that the sex had been a drunken mistake, that I was sorry but however incredible it had been, it couldn't happen again. I told him that I'd heard from my army-officer ex-husband Dave, and he was putting pressure on me to meet up, talk about what had gone wrong for us.

Ed seemed genuinely upset by this and I felt terrible, but I had to say something. I felt a fingernail's distance from it all getting completely out of control.

We continued to see each other once a week or so now that the play was over, but emotionally I retreated, making haughty small talk and teasingly rebuffing his advances just enough that he didn't give up altogether, rewarding him with little smiles and the occasional Jane Austenesque eyelash flutter that I hadn't even been aware I knew how to do. I was amazed he didn't tell me to bugger off.

All the while I was aching for him inside, clueless as to how I was going to be able to extricate myself from the situation without leaving my heart in a dozen pieces.

If I kept the baby, I lost my career and possibly Ed too – although he'd told me several times he'd love more children, being faced with the imminent reality could have been a very different matter.

If I had an abortion I wasn't sure I'd ever be able to live with myself. I was thirty-seven – the clock was ticking and it might be my only chance … How could I just get rid of something I yearned for?

I kept up appearances as best I could. I carried on pumping Ed for information as often as possible, while simultaneously trying to avoid telling him much about myself, and certainly not my latest news.

He knew that my parents were dead, I was an only child, I was separated from Dave and I had no children and no other relatives. I was born in Rayleigh, Essex, had studied English at Leicester Polytechnic before it became a university, I had a scar on my leg where I'd fallen off a horse aged nine and my shin bone had snapped in half and broken through the skin, sticking out in front of me like a turkey wishbone. It was like being on that TV show *Would I Lie To You?* Sometimes I had trouble remembering which facts were true and which made up – except the fact of the tumbling ball of cells in my belly that was growing bigger by the day and which would, soon enough, no longer be able to be kept secret.

I made it my business to know as much about Ed as my memory could retain; more, after we slept together, as if it would somehow counterbalance my extreme unprofessionalism. I lay awake at night making mental notes:

Sent to boarding school in England aged eight, parents lived in Kuala Lumpur.

Scar above lip from having cancerous growth removed ten years ago.

Met Shelagh when she was a dental nurse and he was having a wisdom tooth out.

Proposed to Shelagh on a fairground Big Wheel – she turned him down for the first three revolutions and agreed to marry him on the fourth. Was a GP for twenty-four years, dreaded patients with foot or crotch ailments as fungus of any sort makes him gag.

Good at DIY, cooking and dancing, a terrible singer.

Fuck, I'm pregnant.

Fuck.

I even started wishing I *could* find some evidence that he'd killed Shelagh, for then surely my mind would be made up about what to do about our relationship.

On a hike in the Surrey Hills one day about six weeks after the closing night of *Make Do*, I asked casually, stopping to tie my jumper round my already-swelling waist: 'So – what's the worst thing you've ever done?'

As far as discreet intel-gathering went, I was pretty sure that this wasn't in any *Bumper Book of Undercover Investigating*, but I was desperate.

He stopped with me, looking surprised. 'Worst in what sense?'

He was used to me bombarding him with questions.

'Um … I don't know, just worst. Like, the thing you feel most bad about.'

He thought about it, wiping his forehead with his forearm. It was a very steep hill, and a hot day.

'I snogged Mandy Jennings when I was going steady with Susie Holliday. We were seventeen.'

I laughed. 'Oh come on! That's the worst thing you've ever done?'

'What about you? What's yours, then?'

'I asked first.'

'And I told you,' he said, grabbing me from behind and trying to tickle me. I giggled and twisted away, still looking expectant.

'Are you serious? You want more than that?'

I pretended to look stern. Obviously I didn't think he was going to say, 'Er, let me think – yes – I murdered my wife', but I scanned his face for any change of expression. 'I need to know what sort of man I might, at some point in the future, be committing to…'

He brightened and I couldn't prevent my heart giving a little jump. 'Really? You want to commit to me?'

I shrugged. 'Well, it's been – how long now? Four months, since our first date?'

'Four months, two weeks and four days,' he said, taking my hand. 'When we slept together, I thought that was it, that we'd be a couple. You've backed away so much.'

'I told you why that is,' I said, shamefacedly. 'I'm really sorry, Ed. You know it's not because I don't like you or don't want to be with you, but…'

'I know,' he said impatiently. *You so don't*, I thought. 'But why would you even think about going back to someone who's cheated on you and messed you around for years?'

That was what I'd told him, that 'Dave' had had an affair with one of his subalterns. I imagined her to be as busty as I was flat, with full, cherry-red lips and curly dark-brown hair, curvaceous and vivacious, flirting with him until he couldn't resist. Their affair had been going on for years but he swore it was over now and that she – Sinead, I christened her – was getting married to someone else.

I sat down abruptly under a tree, its twisty roots providing a natural seat, and patted the root next to me. Ed flopped down, fresh sweat glistening on his forehead and blooming under his arms, and I handed him a bottle of water.

'We've only slept together once.' I watched him deftly uncap and swig at it.

'Tell me about it,' he replied, with feeling. 'You aren't half giving out mixed messages, you know.'

'I wasn't ready. It was only because I was drunk,' I said primly.

He stared challengingly at me, lifting up his Ray-Bans so that I could look into his piercing blue eyes. 'And do you think you might be ready again any time soon? I don't want to lose out to *Dave*.' He said the name like it was a bad smell.

Actually I'm so ready, I thought, fortunately managing to stop myself saying it out loud and adding to the arsenal of mixed messages. Poor Ed. But I wanted him so much. It gave me a faint shock. I wriggled closer to him, drinking in the smell of his warm sweaty body. Even his sweat turned me on.

This was another fact I was not prepared to share with Brian Metcalfe in our fortnightly debriefings.

'The thing is, Ed,' I arranged my expression into something close to tearful. 'I do want to. It was fantastic when we did – well, what I remember about it, of course. I really, really want to be with you, but…'

'But what?' His voice was teasing, with an edge of frustration. He pushed my damp fringe out of my eyes.

I looked away, at a nearby crow pecking something on the grass. 'Dave aside, what if…?'

'What if what?'

I could tell he was trying not to get impatient with me. Play it cool, I told myself.

'What if we were to start getting serious and then suddenly Shelagh comes home? What then?'

He slumped back against the tree, sighing heavily. 'So that's it.'

'Well, it's certainly not because I don't fancy you,' I said with feeling. 'And it bothers me more than a few pleading emails from Dave, who's probably just feeling lonely and horny. I love my life here. I don't want to leave.'

This at least was true.

There was silence for a few minutes.

'Look,' he said eventually. 'I can't tell you for certain that Shelagh won't come back, because I don't know where she is. As I've told you from the start, my instinct is that she's committed suicide because I don't believe she would abandon Benjy like she seems to have done. She didn't leave a note – which I suppose could mean that she isn't dead – but that's not very helpful to you, is it?'

He leaned in close to me again and touched the side of my arm, sending goosebumps skittering up and down my skin in a small Mexican wave of desire.

'All I can say, Lynn, is that I really, really like you. I can see us having a future together, I honestly can. And I've said this to you before too, but if Shelagh walked in through the door tonight, I'd still want to be with you. I'd be happy she was back, of course I would, because Ben would have a mother again – if he ever forgave her, that is – but as far as her and me continuing to be married? No chance. I wish you could divorce a missing person, but you can't. I can't have her declared legally dead for seven years, but as soon as I do, I hope that you and I are the ones getting married.'

He kissed me, long and slow and hot.

'Does that help? I want to marry you, Lynn. I love you.'

That was the clincher.

'We're having a baby,' I blurted, bursting into tears. He reared back in shock and my heart sank – but then his face lit up and an enormous beam spread across it, tears springing to his own eyes as he hugged me tightly and almost yelped in my ear:

'Oh my God! Really? Are you serious? Oh Lynn, that's … wow … that's … When? A baby! I can't WAIT!'

I would always remember that moment as the happiest I had ever been. Ever.

'Y ou're really quitting? Why?'

This was the question I'd been dreading for weeks.

I didn't want to tell Superintendent Nicholls the real reason I was leaving the police force but I knew I had to bite the bullet. Off the record, I'd already informed Brian Metcalfe, and his disgusted reaction had made me cringe. I'd told him that I felt out of my depth, that I'd not had enough training to merit being sent straight into deep cover without experience of some less stressful deployments first, but my voice sounded whiny and plaintive, even though it was true. Telling *his* boss, a man I'd never even met before, was even harder, but I was pretty confident that Nicholls would have to accept my resignation, for fear of being sued.

'I'm sorry, sir, but this was my first UC job and it was too much for me. It would have been, even if Ed Naismith and I hadn't fallen in love. We're engaged and I want to be with him. I'm having his baby. I'll keep my new identity and there's nothing tying me to the past. No one will ever know. He has no idea. Nobody does.'

'Good *God*.'

I did not believe it was possible for anybody to look more disapproving. He took off his cap and ran a hand wearily through his thinning brown hair.

It was odd to be back in the building where I'd done my training. It felt as though as I was being fired – which in fairness I would have been, had I not got in there first. My Level One and Two undercover courses and sub-sequent assignment had been a complete failure and a waste of taxpayers' money, because I hadn't managed to find a shred of evidence that Ed had killed Shelagh.

And now nobody would even believe I'd tried very hard.

Superintendent Nicholls shook his head. 'Well. I wasn't expecting that. I have to ask you, Waites, are you absolutely, one hundred percent sure that Naismith's not manipulating you for his own ends; playing us at our own game?'

'Absolutely not, sir. I did the best I could, despite my inexperience. I have witnessed his utter incomprehension and sorrow at his wife's disappearance. I've searched his house with a fine-tooth comb, and Brian and I are agreed that there isn't a trace of intel to suggest he had anything to do with it. Shelagh Naismith was suffering from mental-health problems and was on prescription medication for depression. Here's my full report.'

I laid the folder on his desk and he lifted his chin slightly in acknowledgement as I doggedly carried on:

'His interactions with others – not at all suspicious. His house – clean, nothing incriminating. His repeated concerns about her mental health, backed up as I said by her medical records, and by verbal evidence from their son Ben, who recalls overhearing her on more than one occasion saying she wanted to kill herself and if it wasn't for him, she would.'

'*If it wasn't for him,*' repeated the superintendent with heavy emphasis. 'So why should we believe she did?'

'With respect, sir, I really can't see why we should believe she didn't, apart from her sister's assertions. Which, from the interviews with Ellen Brigstock that I've read, are based on nothing more than her own concern for her sister and her confessed dislike of Ed Naismith. Besides,' I added, knowing that this was the rub, 'there's nothing that would stand up in court. Nothing at all. She wouldn't have wanted to leave her son, but if she was mentally ill, she would have convinced herself that he would genuinely be better off without her in his life.'

'Then how do we explain the lack of a body?'

'It happens, sir. I'm convinced her remains will be found at some point. Ed is certain she'd have taken herself off somewhere very remote.'

'And you are seriously planning to marry the man?' he asked, staring at the discreet diamond ring on my left hand.

'Yes, sir, at some point, once Shelagh Naismith has been officially declared dead. We're aware that we might have to wait the full seven years for that.' I stood up a little straighter, gazing defensively at a point past his right ear.

He'd missed a bit shaving and a small square of stubble on his cheek briefly snagged my attention.

'You know you can't legally get married with a false name?'

'I am aware, sir. I told him I was going away for a couple of weeks to finalise my divorce and sort out the necessary paperwork. During this time I am in fact going to change my name to Jackson by deed poll. I'd already led him to believe that Jackson was my maiden name, that I ceased using my married name when my imaginary husband and I split up.'

Nicholls groaned, without bothering to hide it. 'So you will be Lynn Jackson permanently.'

'Just until we get married, sir, then I have decided I will take his name. I'm confident that I'm untraceable as Lynn Waites. I was never on any social media. I have no family and I've cut all ties with friends I had before moving to Hampton. Nobody knows that I am – was – in the police, and Waites is not a particularly unusual name. I have gone to great lengths to leave no traces of my investigation.'

I thought apprehensively of the box file in which I'd kept any potential evidence. It was very well hidden, but I'd need to dispose of it as soon as I got back to Molesey. We were moving to a new house by the river soon, downsizing from Ed's Victorian villa, as much for a fresh start in our own place as for any financial reasons. I couldn't wait for my new life with Ed to begin properly, without the guilty shadow of duplicity hanging over me.

I didn't mind legally changing my name. It was no big deal. I'd be doing it again one day anyway, at the registry office with Ed. Lynn Jackson was a good enough name for me in the meantime.

To try and take my mind off the harsh words and disgusted reactions from my police colleagues as my career limped to its inglorious end, I hugged myself with pleasure at the thought that Ed and I would one day be married. I thought then that it would be with our child proudly standing between us as a beribboned bridesmaid or a sailor-suited little ring bearer.

But that part of it was not to be.

I lost the baby, a month after quitting the police. Just like that. Ed and I had gone to bed, made love, he'd kissed my stomach and then we'd gone to sleep – to wake up to a horror movie in the dark, small hours; our baby, my precious beloved child, a mere tiny clot in the sea of metallic-smelling blood on the mattress, me not even realising that the howling sound I heard was coming from my own throat. I was screaming, *'Don't leave me! Don't leave me!'* but I didn't know if I was talking to Ed or the baby.

'We'll try again!' Ed had pleaded, covered in my blood, desperation in his voice. 'We'll have more, I promise. Two – three – as many as you want, my darling. I'll *never* leave you. Just don't leave me, please?'

Of course I didn't leave him. I loved him, even though his promise never came true.

In the end we didn't have to wait seven years to get married. It was only a year later that we got the call saying that Gavin Garvey had confessed to Shelagh's murder. Garvey refused to say what he'd done with the body, but her necklace was found in his pocket on the night he was arrested.

There was a trial, from which I stayed completely away, claiming it was too upsetting, but really in case anybody who knew me as Waitsey happened to spot me in the papers, or in the couple of brief local news items that ran on TV. I thought Ed would have a big problem with me not accompanying him to court, but to my surprise he didn't seem to mind at all.

Despite the lack of a body, Garvey was convicted and jailed for fifteen years, and Shelagh was finally declared officially dead.

A month later, in a registry office in Weybridge in front of a select group of witnesses comprising April and Mike, Maddie and Geoff, and Mike's mum, Sandra (our producer on *Make Do*), plus a few others from MADS, Ed and I became Mr and Mrs Naismith.

There was no beaming flower girl or ring bearer standing between us as we made our vows, but Ed's jubilance helped make up for the permanently aching hole in my belly and my heart. It was a strange feeling, celebrating and mourning simultaneously.

But I had Ed, and I told myself that that was the most important thing of all.

Maddie greeted me with open arms in the arrivals hall at Jersey airport.

'It's so good to see you, Lynn. I'm really sorry about Ed, but he'll turn up, I'm sure he will.'

'Ben thinks I'm a terrible human being for going away while he's still missing.' I returned the hug, inhaling her familiar lavender scent. She was as solid and reassuring as ever, taut and muscled from all the yoga she did, my favourite person to hug. Her clothes were always loose and soft, layers of cotton and linen in muted earth-mother tones. I didn't want to let her go.

'Oh, sod what he thinks. He'd probably prefer you to be holding a twenty-four-hour candlelit vigil seven days a week while he carries on with his life exactly as normal, but that's hardly reasonable, is it!'

I grinned and fished for a tissue in my pocket. 'You should be available on the NHS,' I said, blowing my nose. 'And anyway, I'm not just going to sit around while I'm here. I didn't tell you on the phone, but I've tracked down Shelagh's sister. She lives on Alderney now. I'm going to go and visit her. I sent her a message on Facebook asking if I could – but to be honest, even if she says no, I'll go and find her anyway. I need to talk to her.'

'*Shelagh*-Shelagh? Ed's other wife?' Maddie had taken the handle of my suitcase and started wheeling it towards the car park, but stopped abruptly, almost causing a small pile-up behind her with a couple with a toddler in a buggy. 'Why do you want to see *her*?'

'I'll tell you over lunch. Can we go to that place I like in the port?'

'Already booked,' Maddie said.

Within forty minutes of the plane bumping onto the tarmac, we were sitting underneath a heater at an outside table overlooking St Aubin's harbour, huge menus in our hands and wine glasses being filled by a handsome young waiter. Sun dazzled on the water and I squinted at the yachts' masts swaying by the harbour wall.

'I want to get my hair cut while I'm here,' I announced, taking a big mouthful of the cold white wine. 'Can we go this afternoon?'

'Sure. I'll take you to my place. Gino's great, if he's got a free appointment. A trim?' Maddie reached out and lifted one of the ends of my long blonde bob. 'It looks OK to me.'

'Nope, all of it. As short as yours is.'

'Why? Bit drastic, perhaps? And I thought Ed liked your hair long.'

'He does. Did. But fuck him. I reckon he's been faking the dementia and now he's done a runner.'

'*What?*' Maddie said, so loudly that the women on the next table all looked over. 'No way, Lynn! He'd never do that.'

She had been leaning her chin on her hand and my words made her so flustered that she dug her nails into her cheek, leaving three crescent-shaped marks.

'But he didn't want me to come into London with him on the day he disappeared. His passport's missing – and so is all the money from our savings account.'

'Oh my God.'

Maddie filled our glasses, dripping icy water from the wine cooler across the table. Her hand was shaking. 'Hang on, though. I don't see how that equates to him faking being ill for the best part of a year?'

'I think he was planning his getaway and pretended to have dementia as a diversion, so he knew nobody would suspect he was up to anything. I certainly didn't.'

'That's because he probably wasn't!' Maddie was getting more distressed. 'Lynn, think about it. I know you're hurt and desperate and perhaps he has done a runner, but it doesn't add up! Why would he lie to us all for so long first? Have you looked at all the other possibilities? He might have got mugged in London, forced at gunpoint to withdraw all the money from your account, and then lost his memory, or had an accident?'

'Our savings account doesn't have a cashpoint card,' I said. 'He transferred the money online into a different account. And the police checked around all the hospitals for anyone matching his description brought in on that day. I know I sound paranoid, but – don't you think it's odd that he seems to have been completely healed after just a few months on some clinical trial that even I was hardly allowed to know anything about?'

'I admit, that did seem to happen very fast,' Maddie conceded. 'But, regarding his passport, you told me on the phone that you hadn't seen it for years anyway, so you can't be certain he took it. And you said Ben confirmed that it's a real trial. Are you sure you're not adding two and two and making five?'

For the first time ever, I felt annoyed with Maddie, not least because she was saying exactly what Adrian had said. 'Give me some credit. What do you think I am, some hysterical irrational woman making up conspiracy theories? It might have been a real trial, but the doctor was fake! I wouldn't say this lightly.'

'I know you wouldn't,' Maddie soothed.

She picked at a slice of fresh baguette. 'Also – just suppose he was in with the doctor and *had* been faking it, wouldn't it have made more sense for him to disappear with people thinking he did have dementia than after he'd been supposedly cured? They'd assume he'd wandered off and fallen into the canal or something.'

'Yes, but, if he was faking, he'd have known that a missing person with dementia would be searched for much harder than someone in good health who'd just chosen to up sticks and go. Perhaps that's why he pretended to be cured. Or perhaps he just got bored of pretending to be losing his marbles.'

'Then why pretend in the first place? It doesn't sound like it's been a barrel of laughs for him either.'

That was the question I didn't want to answer. Fortunately Maddie amended it to an easier one: 'How had things been, between you?'

Our dressed crabs and chips arrived and I paused until the waiter had topped up my water glass.

'That's another thing – we had almost no sex at all, all the months he was ill. Our relationship changed completely. You know how he always had to be in charge of everything before: the car, the holidays, running the house? Well, obviously he couldn't – or didn't – do any of that. I took over everything, and just sort of completely mothered him, I suppose. I've heard of couples who have loads more sex once the husband gets Alzheimer's or whatever, but it didn't happen with us. We've only shagged a couple of times since his diagnosis, and we used to be at it like rabbits...'

Maddie looked horrified. She and Geoff had a very active sex life, apparently, and I knew she couldn't countenance the idea of a sexless existence. I couldn't bring myself to tell her the truth, though, that I'd supplanted my dearth of action with Ed with a few clandestine shags with Adrian.

'In fact, he slept in the spare room for a few weeks, because he started getting night terrors and punching me when we were asleep. It was awful. That was around the time that Mike was murdered.'

'Oh, come on, Lynn, how extreme would that be, for him to have faked all that?' Maddie said. 'Surely he wouldn't go to all that trouble – and why, anyway? And he had a professional diagnosis, didn't he – he couldn't have fabricated that.'

'Well, that's all weird, too. When I went to the consultant with him for the diagnosis, Ed refused to have a brain scan because of his claustrophobia—'

'He never used to have claustrophobia.'

Maddie had known Ed for longer than I had – she'd been doing costumes for the drama group for years before *Make Do and Mend*. Mads from MADS, that was how she was first introduced to me.

'Exactly,' I said. 'He apparently developed it before he got ill. That, and a fear of flying. The doctor said it could be a symptom – but it could also be very convenient ... But then, get this, the day we went up to London for the appointment with Bill – he's the guy allegedly running the trial – Bill produced some scans dated just after Ed's diagnosis showing that his brain was damaged. Ed claimed he hadn't remembered having them done but that he'd obviously been persuaded. So that's on my list of things to do: check with Mr Deshmukh, the original consultant, about that. He'd have been the one who convinced Ed to have them – but how come I didn't take him to the hospital? And if I didn't, who did?'

'Could it have been April? Maybe she took him to her hospital and did them there.'

I paused, a forkful of crab halfway to my mouth. 'April...'

April had been a radiologist in a private hospital about five miles outside Guildford, but she'd left a few years before when Mike made his millions. She'd never really spoken much about her job, to the point that I had forgotten she ever did it.

'You know, I never thought of that. But why wouldn't she have told me? And could she, anyway? She left that job years ago, surely you can't just wander in and start giving MRI scans to your mates!'

'She might not have told you – she might have thought you'd be upset he agreed to go with her and not you...?'

I made a face. 'Really? As if! I'll email her and ask her – have you contacted her yet?'

'Yes, I sent her a message the other day after you told me she'd gone. She hasn't replied though. I still think it's all a bit sudden, isn't it? I wondered if that was part of the reason you wanted to come over, because she wasn't around either. But now you say it's because you're visiting Shelagh's sister...'

'I wanted to come anyway, silly. I knew you'd make me feel better. In fact, I'm glad April's gone away, because I'd have felt guilty about leaving her if she was still at home.'

'Well, I'm very glad you're here. Let's get the bill and go and see if you can have your hair cut.'

My phone buzzed with a notification and I smiled at Maddie as I picked it up to check. Then the smile fell off my face. 'Ellen's replied to my Facebook message,' I said.

Later that evening, freshly-shorn and seated in front of a roaring fire, I re-read Ellen's message out loud to Geoff, having filled him in on the whole situation:

"*Dear Lynn, I'm here if you wish to come and see me. You will find me in the flat above the HSBC Bank in Victoria Street, the main street in St Anne (the only town on Alderney). I would offer to pick you up from the airport but I have a broken leg so I'm afraid I can't drive. Let me know which flight you're coming on and I'll book Max the Cab for you. I warn you, though, I have plenty to say about Ed Naismith and none of it good.*"

Maddie was on the window seat hemming a skirt, a pool of white light from an anglepoise lamp illuminating her fingers as the needle flashed in and out of the material. She looked up.

'She really doesn't like him, does she? Do you want me to come with you?'

Her voice had a distinct note of hesitation to it, and I guessed from this and from the look Geoff shot his wife that spending a couple of hundred quid on travel and hotels was probably not what they wanted to do just for a day or two.

'No, thanks for offering, Mads, but it's fine.'

They both looked relieved.

'You're not worried, are you, about what she'll say when you meet her? You're sure Ed had nothing to do with it.'

'It' being Shelagh's disappearance, a question disguised as a statement, and clearly one that Maddie found hard to articulate.

I stared out of the window as I tried to think how to reply. It was almost completely dark outside, the sky already dotted with the stars that would later multiply and fill the velvety blackness.

'I'm not saying that I do think Ed was involved – but I want to try to rule it out for my own peace of mind. It won't be anything she hasn't already told the police though, of course. They got a confession from that man Gavin Garvey a couple of years later, didn't they? But he was homeless and admitted that he'd rather be in jail where it's warm and he gets three meals a day. There was no DNA evidence and he couldn't say what he'd done with Shelagh's body. I always thought it was a bit iffy, but he had her necklace in his pocket so it probably was him.'

Maddie had no idea how hard I'd looked for evidence last time. But maybe there had been something I'd missed – or even, shamefully, glossed over, once my endorphins were in overdrive and I thought about Ed a hundred times a day, his engagement ring on my finger, his baby in my belly...

Could Ed have known Gavin Garvey? Paid him, even? There had never been any evidence of this, but still ... it didn't mean it couldn't be so.

Please, God, no. That would be a catastrophe on every single level: personal, professional, ethical. At least Ed had never known I was undercover, so whatever machinations he may or may not have engineered regarding our relationship hadn't been motivated by deception.

Geoff saw my stricken face and patted my knee with his big calloused hand. He was not a handsome man – he had an unfortunate squarish head, emphasised by his male-pattern baldness, and a jutting chin. But he and Maddie were made for one another; they were aging comfortably together, gently moaning about the indignities of it all – stiff knees and complicated digestions, failing eyesight and everything heading south.

'I hope you're not opening some sort of can of worms by going.'

'So do I, Geoff,' I said fervently. 'So do I.'

40

It was unseasonably chilly in Guernsey. As soon as I got off the plane from Jersey the next morning – so many planes to go such short distances, why wasn't it possible to fly straight from Jersey to Alderney? – I started to shiver in my thin jacket. I thought enviously of April doing sun salutations on a verandah overlooking the outback, the object of her yogic attentions shining down on her lithe, bronzed body. I imagined the pleasure of sunshine soaking into my own bone marrow and pinkening my cheeks.

I rubbed the back of my goosepimpled neck. I liked my new haircut, though, despite the draught. Ed had always loved my hair long and never wanted me to cut more than a couple of inches off. This radical chop was an act of rebellion, trying to tempt fate perhaps. Let him come back and be pissed off when he saw it.

I had an hour to wait, so to pass the time I logged onto the airport's wifi and checked my emails. To my surprise, there was one from Alvin; from his personal email account rather than the university's. I'd emailed him to apologise and to ask for a month's unpaid leave because of Ed going missing – but I was still barely able to believe that he hadn't fired me. I was relieved he hadn't – if Ed really had gone, I would need an income.

Hi Lynn, I've alerted HR and they are in agreement with me that we can extend your leave of absence in these unusual circumstances. Tell me to mind my own business but I am curious, having known Ed and Mike a little, many years ago at MADS. I'm aware that I wasn't Ed's favourite person but I'm guessing that you don't know the real reason for that. Probably nothing to do with anything but if you want to chat you know where I am, and my mobile number's at the bottom of this email. I do hope he turns up safe. Alvin x

I sat up straight in the uncomfortable moulded plastic airport chair, suddenly oblivious to the sounds around me, the tannoy and the rumble of suitcase wheels. What the hell did *that* mean? I would have to call him, but I didn't have time – my flight was about to board.

I tapped out a hasty reply: *Thanks for being so supportive, Alvin, I will definitely give you a ring when I get the chance. Lynn.* I hesitated then decided against adding a kiss.

There was nothing from April, so I quickly sent her another message, bland and brief, not mentioning anything about Ed's disappearance:

Hi darling, dying to hear how it's going. Nice people? How was the journey? I miss you so much. WRITE SOON and send pics. Love you, Lynn xxxx PS. Long shot I know, but did you ever take Ed to hospital for some scans?

I closed my laptop, drained my coffee and headed for the gate. Suddenly I felt exhausted and that all I wanted was to be back in the cottage, back in time, Ed pottering around nearby, Pick's Disease and murdered friends not existing in our lives. All the adrenaline that had rocketed to my head like cocaine over the past few days subsided, leaving me deflated like a limp balloon.

The second flight was quick and painless, and within half an hour, my bag was rolling down the single conveyor belt into the small prefab cabin that constituted Alderney airport's arrivals. As good as her word, Ellen had sent a cab for me – the driver was waiting for me by the door.

Once in the car, I reached for my seatbelt but there wasn't one, and the cabbie didn't have one either. He drove down narrow country lanes for mere minutes until the sea suddenly appeared, flanking a long, curved white-sand beach. Two minutes later, we were driving up a narrow cobbled street with brightly coloured Victorian shops and cottages on either side, linked by cheerful streams of bunting. My first thought was that it was almost deserted, and my second, that I could easily have walked.

'This is the main street.'

'Why's it so quiet?'

The driver pulled over and parked on the pavement. 'It's lunchtime,' he explained, which didn't really clarify things. He got out, lifted my backpack off the rear seat and pointed me towards a small Georgian house. The front door, under a sign for HSBC Bank, was open. It was disconcerting to have gone from being in the clouds to arriving at your destination all within the space of ten minutes, I thought, as I paid him the paltry sum he requested.

'Just go through that door and straight up the stairs.'

I thanked him and knocked at the door marked Private in the bank's tiny lobby. There was no reply so I tried the handle and it opened.

'Hello?' I called up the stairs. Huge, bold oil paintings lined the walls all the way up, most of them hung crookedly and I had to resist the urge to straighten them as I passed. There was another door at the top – again, open.

'Ellen? It's me, Lynn Naismith. Are you there?'

A voice called back from the depths of the flat: 'Come in.'

I hesitated before stepping inside, in the nervous knowledge that I was about to meet someone who really, really hated my husband.

41

I perched on the end of a sofa covered in a wrinkled Indian throw, between two malevolent-looking cats that flanked me like bodyguards. Ellen was hopping around the adjacent kitchenette on crutches, throwing teabags into mugs and boiling the kettle, wheezing audibly. I had already offered to help twice but had been turned down. Surely the woman would let me carry the tea in, though?

The flat smelled of patchouli, cat, cigarettes and old food. Perhaps it was because Ellen was currently too incapacitated to clean, but I suspected it always smelled like this. There were tacky china cats and dogs of different sizes on every available surface, most of them covered with a thick layer of dust. Several lay on the carpet, having presumably been batted off by a bored cat. I itched to pick them up.

'So your husband's away? Must be hard to cope on crutches without him to help.'

Ellen wasn't especially fat but she had an absolutely massive bottom that swayed and banged into cupboard doors, as if her hips had been modelled on the wide bolsters on the dresses of Queen Elizabeth I's time.

'I'm getting used to it,' she said in a high, slightly winsome voice, propping one crutch against the kitchen counter to reach for a plate and a packet of biscuits. 'He'll be back in a couple of days.'

She coughed and the crutch promptly slid sideways and clattered to the floor. I jumped up to retrieve it. Ellen hadn't volunteered any information as to where he was or what he was doing. I'd already gathered that this was not going to be a relaxing chat.

'How did you hurt your leg?' I asked, eyeing the bright-blue plaster encasing Ellen's lower left leg.

'Slipped on the cobbles outside, nothing dramatic. Broke my ankle.' She had some kind of regional accent, pronouncing 'nothing' as 'nuffink,' although I couldn't work out which part of the country. Possibly estuary mixed with West Country, I concluded.

'Ouch. Shall I take those?' I gestured at the two mugs of tea and plate of biscuits, and Ellen nodded, her cloud of frizzy iron-grey hair gently undulating.

There was a long wiry hair attached to the inside of one of the mugs, so when I returned to sit down I passed that tea along the coffee table towards Ellen's end of the sofa. Ellen heaved herself down and propped her foot on the end of the low table. Her toes were long and unpleasant, yellowing nails and sprouting black hairs, like something intimate that oughtn't be on display.

Ellen coughed again. There was an inhaler lying on the sideboard across the room and I caught her glance at it.

'Here, let me.' I leaped up again and fetched it, and Ellen took a long puff.

'Breathing problems AND a broken ankle. I'm a wreck.'

I laughed, thinking she was joking, but then realised she wasn't. *Breeving problems.* Estuary; yes, that was it. In a weird sort of way, Ellen was family. Had been Ed's family. He'd never really spoken about her, but I could immediately tell how much he would have disliked her – even before she started accusing him of being a murderer. He had no time for whingers, smokers – with the exception of Mike – or winsomeness and my first impression of Ellen was that she well and truly ticked all those boxes.

I briefly tried and failed to imagine a family Christmas, Ellen and Ed facing off over the turkey, Ellen with fag in mouth, Ed with carving knife in hand...

'So,' Ellen said, regarding me with small round eyes, once her breathing had returned to normal. 'Ed Naismith. You know he killed my sister?'

That's my husband you're talking about. 'I don't believe he did,' I said evenly. 'He was devastated when Shelagh disappeared.'

Ellen snorted. 'Yeah, right. Devastated. Mr Am-dram himself. He put on a good performance, sure. Bet he practised it for hours in front of a mirror before he spoke to the press.'

'The police thoroughly investigated him on the basis of your claims.'

'He had no alibi!'

'He did. He was at home with Ben that night. And more importantly, Gavin Garvey confessed. What makes you think Ed killed her?'

'He was having an affair. Shelagh found out. Then she vanished.'

I half-reared up out of my seat. 'No, he wasn't!'

'How would you know?'

I thought of the case notes and police interviews I had spent hours and hours reading, the illicit searches of Ed's house I had conducted, the discreet pillow talk I'd initiated, the frantic forays into his mobile phone every time he was out of the room, my heart thumping through fear of discovery and my lust for him.

'I just would. I would have known.'

There had never been any indication of an affair, never. Ed and I had locked eyes and known pretty much from that moment that the other was the The One. Unless the affair had been and gone by then?

'Who was this so-called affair meant to have been with?'

There was a large mirror hanging on the wall opposite where we sat, tilted downwards slightly so that I could see us both reflected in it. Next to Ellen I looked tiny, as if someone had taken a laser and shrunk me to fifty percent of Ellen's size. *Honey, I shrunk the wife,* I thought.

I missed Ed, suddenly and fiercely.

Ellen shrugged and stuffed a whole shortbread biscuit into her mouth. 'Some slapper,' she said through a mouthful of crumbs.

'You're wrong,' I said. 'He and I got together a few months after Shelagh went – and before you think it, no, I had never met him before, I'd only just moved to the area. We fell in love pretty fast. We were inseparable.'

There were some framed photos on the mantelpiece, dusty and faded-looking; one of Shelagh and Ellen in their teens or twenties, sitting on a picnic rug on a windswept beach. Although I couldn't see any resemblance now, I would have known from that picture they were related. They had the same dimples and the same-shaped chin. Ellen had obviously drawn the short straw in the familial looks department, though.

There was a photo of Ben, too, when he was a boy of five or six, in a wetsuit on a beach. A tubby little boy in an identical wetsuit stood next to him, one arm draped casually around his shoulders. He looked slightly familiar. Ben had been fifteen when I met him, and I didn't recall that any of his friends had been in his life since primary school. And yet there was something about the large mole on the boy's chubby cheek that definitely rang some kind of a bell in my memory. I was about to comment on it when Ellen delivered a vicious verbal parry:

'Inseparable? Don't you think that's a bit weird, for a man who was allegedly "devastated" that his wife had gone missing? If he was all that devastated, he'd never have fallen for someone else straightaway.'

I felt breathless, winded, like someone had swung a wrecking ball into my belly. Of course this had occurred to me at the time, how could it not? But our feelings for each other had developed so fast – helped by the tiny ball of cells in my womb rolling and growing – and the more time had gone on, the more I had rationalised it to myself as True Love. But stated so bluntly like that, it sounded utterly damning. Damning of Ed, of our relationship, of me.

'He said that he was devastated,' I eventually managed, in a voice that didn't sound anything like my normal one. 'But lots of men who lose a partner just want to find someone else as soon as they can. It's not unusual, it happens all the time. Besides, he told me privately that he and Shelagh had lots of problems. They weren't happy together. Obviously he was really worried,' I emphasised hastily, 'that something might have happened to her, and upset because Benjy had lost his mum, but Ed told me that their marriage was on the rocks and had been for ages before Shelagh left. He's sure she killed herself.'

I was explaining far too much, far too frantically.

Ellen rolled her eyes as if I was a particularly stupid small child – and at that moment, this was exactly what I felt like. 'Well, then, it was entirely likely that he would have been having an affair.'

'He wasn't!' I repeated, feeling uncharacteristically like bursting into tears. 'But if Shelagh thought he was, then doesn't that make it more likely that she did commit suicide, given that she had a history of mental instability?'

Now Ellen glared at me with open hostility. 'She did not have a history of mental instability.'

I was dying to tell her that I'd seen Shelagh's medical notes and that the woman had been on all sorts of anti-depressants. Ellen's nostrils were flaring with either rage or misery and she had begun to wheeze again as she spoke:

'Why are you defending him, anyway? He's clearly done the dirty on you as well. Don't you want to catch him and get him put away?'

The 'trying to keep calm' thing wasn't working – even if what she said was exactly what I did want, if it turned out he'd 'done the dirty' on me. But I wasn't going to admit that to Ellen.

'He's my husband. I love him and, I have to say, I resent you hurling accusations in his direction when he's not even here to defend himself. You were the one who put him through hell the first time round, insisting that he'd harmed Shelagh, sending the police to investigate him even after they'd already been convinced he had nothing to do with it!'

I had to make a massive effort to keep my voice from rising, to keep it together.

Ellen, meanwhile, had picked up her crutch and was pointing the end of it at me, as if she wanted to machine-gun me down.

'You're still *with* him?' she said, disgust imprinted on her features. 'In that case, I want you to leave my flat. Now. I thought you wanted help bringing him to justice, not help in letting him off the hook for whatever crimes he's committed since! I heard that his mate Mike had met a sticky end and you know what my first thought was? Ed. Who else? He's done it once, why wouldn't he do it again? What you need to work out is why. And I'd watch my back if I was you. He cottons that you're onto him and you'll be next.'

I stood up, blood roaring around my head and my heart pounding painfully in my chest. I wanted to grab the end of the crutch and jam it right back into Ellen's pasty face.

How fucking dare you, you pathetic, mean-spirited old witch! I shouted at top volume inside my head. Externally, I managed a strangled, 'Don't worry, I wouldn't stay here listening to this bullshit if you paid me. He's a sick man, and he's gone missing. I thought you might be able to help me, but I was clearly wrong.'

I hefted my backpack onto my shoulder and headed for the stairs. Ellen's voice followed me, suddenly strident enough that anyone in the bank downstairs would have heard every word: 'Shelagh was terrified of him. She told me numerous times that she was scared he was going to kill her. And he did! He did.'

I stumbled out of the flat, down the stairs and past a small, curious-looking queue of customers stretching out of the open door of the bank.

42

I was shaking so much I marched straight into the pub next door and ordered a double brandy, downing it at the bar in one huge gulp, much to the curiosity of the barman. I shuddered as it burned and shocked my gullet.

'Are you OK?' he asked. He was old and grizzled, tired-looking with a red nose and rheumy eyes. A once-white apron was wrapped around his thin midriff, finger-shaped coal stains over where each of his hip-bones was.

I nodded. 'Fine. Thanks. Can you tell me where Blacks Hotel is?'

''Bout four doors that way, across the road,' he said, jerking a thumb out of the door. My heart sank. I'd only booked myself into a hotel practically opposite Ellen's flat. Great.

It wasn't Ellen's fault that she'd lost her sister, nor broken her leg. OK, so the woman wasn't the most pleasant person I'd ever met, but I supposed that I too would end up fairly bitter if I suspected my only sister's husband had killed her and nobody would listen to my suspicions about it.

Except the police *had* listened. They'd taken Ellen's accusations seriously enough to send me in to investigate, spending thousands on an undercover operation lasting over a year.

I had been utterly convinced that Ed was innocent.

Or rather ... I had convinced myself that I was convinced Ed was innocent.

Not the same thing at all.

And that was before Ed had been ill for a year, then miraculously got well again – then vanished. That was before he threatened me in the throes – or under the guise – of some kind of dementia psychosis, before Mike was murdered, before April suddenly disappeared.

I left the pub and walked slightly unsteadily along the road, hoping Ellen wasn't looking out of her front windows. Why the hell had I bothered with the expense of a hotel? My business in Alderney had been concluded in less than half an hour, I could've been back at Maddie's in time for dinner.

Blacks Hotel did not look like a hotel. A discreet sign was all that identified it from the outside as anything other than a large stone townhouse. I pushed open the door and was greeted by a rotund lady of indeterminate age in a tweed skirt. There was no reception desk, just a tiny front room with an honesty bar, two armchairs and a tea tray.

'Lynn Naismith, I'm guessing?' the lady asked, smiling, her eyes disappearing into ruffles of wrinkles. 'You're in Hibernian.'

I hoped I wasn't emitting brandy fumes when I opened my mouth to confirm my identity. The lady showed me up a very narrow winding staircase, which made me glad I didn't have my big suitcase with me.

'Here we are!' she said, opening wide another low door and gesturing for me to go in first. The room was small and cosy – tartan wallpaper, a matching tartan rug on the bed, and a large painting of a thistle on the wall.

'Very Scottish,' I said. 'Oh – I get it – Hibernian.'

The woman laughed as though I had made a hysterical joke and I suddenly felt very tired again.

As soon as I was alone, I flopped down on my back, sinking into the mattress and trying to gather my thoughts about the disastrous meeting with Ellen.

What had I hoped to get out of it? I suspected the reason I'd felt so angry was because I'd hoped that, in the intervening years, Ellen had come to regret her misjudged vigilantism towards Ed. But if anything, she was even more bitter. And in accusing Ed of having something to do with Mike's murder, too, she'd tapped straight into my own worst fears. The woman was either insane, or horribly prescient.

I pulled my mobile out of the back pocket of my jeans and found the email from Alvin, with a hyperlink to his phone number. I pressed it and heard it ring.

'Professor Alvin Cornelius.'

It always amused me how he insisted on his full title. He loved people to know that he was a Prof. 'Hi, Alvin. It's Lynn. Naismith.'

'Lynn, hello! How are you?' There were faint traffic sounds in the background.

'I'm all right, thanks. I'm in Alderney, at the moment, in the Channel Islands.'

'Oh! Holiday?'

'Um, no. Not exactly. Although I did come over to Jersey to spend a few days with my best friend.'

'Any word from Ed?'

'Nothing, thanks for asking. I got your email. Is now a good time to chat?'

'Sure. Give me a second, I'm driving. Let me put you on speaker...'

His voice faded out and then returned, sounding more echoey. 'Can you hear me?'

'Yes, that's fine. It's so weird you knew Ed all those years ago. I hope this isn't too personal, but I was wondering – what was he like, when he was married to his first wife?'

There was a brief silence and I thought I'd been cut off, but then heard a distant siren.

'Well. Put it like this, when you got the job at Hampton and I realised that you and he were married, I was surprised. You asked me if I remembered him, when you told me about his dementia, and I kind of swerved the question because I did.'

I had so many more questions, even though he hadn't answered my first one yet. 'Why were you surprised?'

'You just seemed like such a...'

Perhaps he was going to say 'mismatched couple' or something, but he stopped abruptly and instead said '...so different.'

'Really? In what way?'

I hadn't ever really thought about it, although I supposed from the outside we did seem quite different. But Alvin had never seen us together, bar that disastrous open day punch-up, so it felt like an odd thing for him to say.

He sighed. 'I don't want to talk out of turn, Lynn, but since you're asking – well, you're so nice. So kind and attentive and interested in everyone. To be honest, the Ed Naismith that I knew was a bit of a ... knob. No offence.'

I couldn't help smiling. Ed could definitely be an acquired taste. 'None taken. Did you ever see him with Shelagh?'

'I wasn't at MADS for that long. I did one show with them – an Ayckbourn, I think, in the late nineties, maybe 2000. Ed was in it, too. He was a superb actor, really natural, but I didn't warm to him as a person. Or as a director, in my brief experience of that. I only saw him with his wife – first wife – once, when she came to the show. We were all in the bar afterwards; she tried to say something and he just talked over her in a really condescending way. I recall feeling sorry for her.'

'Weren't you in *Death of a Salesman,* the one he directed? I'm sure I remember him saying something about that, when I mentioned your name.'

Alvin gave a small laugh. 'I wasn't. I auditioned and didn't get it, but by then I'd realised I really didn't like Ed, so I wouldn't have taken it even if he'd offered it to me.'

I hesitated. 'This is slightly awkward, but I'll come clean: what he actually said about it was that you had a bit of an, um, diva hissy fit in the audition? Chucked your script on the floor and stormed out, argued with him and Mike?'

He laughed again, much more heartily. 'Absolutely not! Lynn, you know me pretty well by now. Can you see me doing that? I'm not averse to yelling at a student with the musical ability of yeast, but I'm not one for throwing my toys out of the pram.'

'No,' I agreed. 'I always thought it sounded odd, when Ed told me. I can't imagine anyone less likely to have a tantrum than you. I assumed he'd just mis-remembered.'

'I'm not surprised that he came up with a story like that, though, to cover up what I saw...'

I wondered if I had heard correctly. 'Saw?'

'Lynn, I don't want to sound like I'm gossiping and, like I said in my email it might have been nothing, but...'

'What?'

The sky outside was darkening. A wind had whipped up and from my bed I could see the bunting strung to and fro across the main street flapping wildly in the twilight.

I realized I was holding my breath.

'It was the day of the *Death of a Salesman* auditions. I was a bit early, came straight from work and parked in the car park round the back, you know, there are a few spaces at the back of the theatre?'

I nodded, as if he could see me.

'When I drove round, I saw a couple jumping apart. They'd been kissing in the fire escape doorway. It was Ed and another woman, but I didn't see who she was, other than she had blonde hair in a ponytail. They shot inside and he couldn't meet my eyes during the audition. There was no sign of the woman.'

'Not his wife, then,' I stated flatly. Shelagh's hair had been dark auburn.

But Ed had always been so strident about infidelity, always said how shocking and unforgivable it was! Who had this woman been? If that had happened in 2000, it was years before I had been sent to Surrey.

After the call concluded, with me promising to keep Alvin updated with any developments, I lay back on the bed and closed my eyes, falling almost immediately into a deep dreamless sleep, as if my system had abruptly crashed and shut down.

I woke with a start two hours later, April's face looming unbidden into my mind.

43

I lay staring at the ceiling, my imagination running riot as though my thoughts were chasing each other around the room, squawking and bouncing off the walls. Snatches of recent conversations kept repeating on me like a hot curry, Ellen's vitriolic voice saying 'Mr Am-dram himself'; Alvin commenting 'He was a superb actor, really natural'.

An ex-GP who was good at acting could definitely have pulled off feigning dementia. Particularly when he'd had plenty of first-hand experience of knowing how to behave, having watched his own father go through it. It was the ultimate in method acting. Ed always had loved a challenge and I knew he would have seen it like that, throwing himself into the role, giving himself months to prepare and execute the biggest part he'd ever played.

For what, though? To escape with our pension pot? Another woman? To kill Mike, or have him killed, for some reason? Just for the hell of it?

Rage rose in me, and then was gone in a flash. There was no way he'd faked it. I sat up, determined to stop torturing myself like this. Why would he spend months creating an elaborate pretence, only to knock it on the head? The dirty clothes, the lack of grooming and bathing – whatever the reason, I just couldn't believe Ed would put himself – and Ben – through that voluntarily. This was a man who could feel queasy at the smell of a cheesy sock. Ed loved his clothes! He'd always taken such pride in his appearance.

An affair seemed the most likely reason for it all, though.

I thought again about April, analysing my friendship with her and how she was when she was around Ed. I was sure I had never spotted any telling little lingering glances between them, or illicit embraces. I remembered that night on the boat when Mike had screamed at her for getting chilli in his eye, and Ed and I had later talked about how temperamental their marriage was. Ed always claimed that while April was really pretty, he'd hate to be married to her because Mike moaned so often about how high-maintenance she was.

An elaborate double bluff?

Again, no way. If April had been the girl Alvin caught Ed snogging in a doorway, and Ed was still seeing her, that would mean they'd been having an affair for well over ten years!

Ed loved *me*. I was sure of it.

Unless Ed and April had been on and off over the years, and the shock of Mike's death and then the joy of Ed's recovery had made them suddenly re-evaluate their lives and decide they wanted to be together...?

I remembered coming downstairs the night after Mike's death, finding the two of them with their heads together at my kitchen table. My husband and my best friend – well, second-best friend, after Maddie.

I got off the bed and went to the window. If I craned my neck, I could see Ellen's flat. It was eight o'clock and getting dark now, a few people sauntering up and down the street, presumably heading out to restaurants or pubs.

There was a butcher's shop opposite, whose window was empty of everything except some springs of parsley and a few packs of sausages. My stomach growled at the thought of sausage and mash, and I realised I hadn't eaten anything since the croissant that morning at Guernsey airport. I turned on the overhead light, pulled down the blind, then took out my laptop. A couple of emails and then I'd go in search of food.

I wrote to Maddie first:

I'm here and have seen Ellen. What a piece of work! I mean, I knew she wasn't a fan of Ed's but she was bang out of order. She thinks Ed was having an affair and insists he killed S. She even

implied he'd murdered Mike as well!! I stormed out. Tell you the
rest tomorrow. Xxx

There was still nothing from April, which gave me a twist of unease
in the pit of my belly – although it was plausible that she just didn't
have any internet in the outback.

Bit of a coincidence that she upped sticks the same day that Ed
went missing though, I thought again. Yet, I rationalised, if they *had*
planned it, they would surely have staggered their disappearances. Far
too obvious for them both to take off on the same day, surely? And the
police had confirmed that Ed hadn't flown anywhere.

I went on to Facebook, opened up my fake profile and did a search
for April Greening.

April's page came up immediately, her profile picture a lovely shot of
her and Mike on the boat – taken by me a couple of years ago, I realised
with a faint start. They looked happy and relaxed. There were no other
photographs showing, but being inexperienced in Facebookese, I
didn't know if this was because there weren't any, or because April's
privacy settings hid them from all but her friends.

I clicked 'add friend' and wrote a brief accompanying message:

Hi April! Great to find you on here. I'm new to all this stuff
– what a dinosaur, eh?! Can't even figure out how to add
a photograph. I'll get my hubby to help. Anyway I hope you
remember me from school. We were in awful Sister Margaret's
class together. I was the one who totally had a girl-crush on you
– you were by far the prettiest of us all. I see from your profile pic
that you still are. I'll stick up some photos of those days as soon as I
work it all out. Do write and tell me what you're up to. I'm living
in Windsor with my husband. No kids but two black Labs! Bye
for now! Christine xxx

April had often talked about Awful Sister Margaret, who had been
the bane of her life at the convent school. She'd never mentioned

anyone called Christine, as far as I remembered, but she was hopeless with names and a sucker for a compliment, so I thought this could work.

I paused. I could have just joined Facebook as Lynn Naismith and added April that way – April was always on at me to join. But I wanted to see if April would respond to a fake request, thus proving she *did* have internet access, when she had ignored my emails.

I clicked on Monty Greening and his twin Caspar. Neither of them had any sort of privacy settings in place, and I scrolled through thousands of photographs of them both in a variety of exotic locations, sometimes with April and Mike, mostly with a succession of beautiful girls in tow and similarly bronzed and fit men of their age in bars, up mountains and on beaches. There were a few comments further down Caspar's page under a photograph of Mike that he'd posted: *'So sorry to hear about your dad, dude,'* and *'Hope the memorial went well, sorry we couldn't make it. Our thoughts are with you and Monts.'*

Nothing from April; nothing public, at any rate. Looking through Caspar's 'About' section, I found an email address that I copied down. I typed a quick email:

> *Dear Caspar, just wondered if you could give me your mum's postal address in Australia? I want to post her something for her birthday and I know it can take weeks to get anything out there. How's she getting on? She hasn't replied to my emails – have you heard from her? Dying to know what she's up to. If she's sent you any photos will you forward them? And if you Skype her, please ask her to contact me urgently, there's something I need to speak to her about (tell her not to worry though!). All the best to you and Monty, love, Lynn xxx*

Pressing 'send', I thought about trying to write to April again, but my stomach began to rumble so loudly that I felt sick and faint. Food, I thought, closing the laptop lid. Now.

An hour later, full of fish pie and red wine from a quirky family restaurant right next door – no sign of Ellen, thankfully, just lots of comedy condiment sets on the tables, Rodney and Del-Boy in pottery salt and pepper incarnations – I climbed the narrow stairs back up to my little tartan hotel room. The first thing I did once inside was check my emails again. My laptop creaked into action and I noticed again how slowly it was running. Annoying, since it was only a couple of years old.

My emails eventually loaded. There was still nothing from April, but a new message from Caspar:

Hi Lynn, hope you're OK. No, sorry, I don't have an address for Mum! All I know is that it's a sheep station where they do yoga and stuff – sounds crazy, doesn't it? She said she'd be in touch via Skype and FaceTime, but we've not heard from her yet apart from an email when she arrived with a photo, which I'm forwarding. She said the guy who runs it is called Douglas and the yoga was nice, but not much else.

April had been in touch with the twins, so she must have had some internet connection at some point. Interesting, I thought. I clicked on the attachment and a photograph of a scrubby view under a vast cerulean-blue sky slowly appeared, pixel by pixel, a rusty-brown painted verandah rail in the foreground. It could have been anywhere.

It took a matter of seconds for me to copy the image into a Reverse Image search on Google, where the same image immediately appeared as part of someone's collection of photographs of Australia on Flickr. Someone who wasn't April, and the photo had been taken back in 2012.

Not April's photo, then.

I exhaled. It wasn't *definitive* proof that April wasn't there, but it was fairly damning. Why else would she nick someone else's photograph and pass it off as her own? And why would she lie to her sons about where she was?

'Where are you really, you husband-stealing bitch?' I said out loud, hearing my voice crack. If April had betrayed me too, I thought my heart would break into pieces. The only thing that would be worse would be to find that Maddie was in on it and had helped stitch me up.

I logged into LinkedIn and went to April's account to check through her contacts, which was allegedly how she had ended up getting the invitation to Australia. But there was nobody there called Douglas or Doug, and nobody based in Australia, either.

Think, Waitsey, think. Where would they go, if they had gone somewhere together?

Waitsey. I hadn't thought of myself as Waitsey for years.

Somewhere hot, that's where.

I sat up straight and rubbed my lower back, which was beginning to ache from being hunched over the laptop. I imagined I was back in the police station incident room and there was a pristine whiteboard ready to write out all our theories and leads.

Say Ed had been planning it for years. It would have to be for something really major. Money, probably.

How would faking illness then running away bring him tons of money? *April,* was the obvious answer. She was rich ... really rich. She'd be inheriting all Mike's Internet of Things wealth, plus a hefty life insurance policy payout.

Ed would have known that – but not three years ago, which was when he started claiming he was too afraid to fly anywhere.

I couldn't help dwelling on the thought that Ellen had planted more firmly in my mind: *Unless he killed Mike himself.* Had been planning it all that time.

No, it was impossible. Ed had had a rock-solid alibi in me – I'd personally locked him into the spare room that night. It was far more likely that it was someone with a grudge against Mike; a sacked board member, perhaps. He'd made some enemies in his time, he said.

But ... but ... if Ed had been faking the Pick's Disease, he could have done it for the sole purpose of exactly that: to get me to unwittingly give him an alibi. He could so easily have got himself a duplicate key to the spare-room lock, or hired a hitman. I'd been sleeping so heavily that he probably could have held a rave downstairs without me waking up, so it would have been simple to sneak out, lock the door behind him, and go and murder his best friend so that he could run off with his lover, April, and live off her wealth somewhere sunny.

I remembered the day of his diagnosis, the noises I thought I'd heard outside on the gravel. It could have been him, sneaking over to the studio to ring April when he saw I'd nodded off in the conservatory, then jumping back into bed and pretending to be asleep when I'd gone up to check on him. If I'd caught him, it would just look like he'd been wandering or sleepwalking, his mobile slipped into his dressing-gown before I could spot it, April still on the other end of the line, knowing she had to keep silent...

'My friend April,' I said, to the painting of the thistle. 'My *friend*.'

I forced myself to sit back down on the bed. I might be putting two and two together and coming up with eight. I could be doing them both the most massive disservice. Ed might be lying dead in a ditch somewhere, and April really was on her sheep farm in the lotus position with a slice of cucumber on each eyelid.

But – and here was something else I'd never thought about before – I never used to be a heavy sleeper, not until a few days before I started locking him in the spare room to stop him hitting me in his sleep. Now that I thought back, it was *Ed* who had put the idea into my mind by suggesting he locked himself in. He'd have known I'd never let him do that – but he'd made it look like it was my idea. And I'd slept like a baby for those weeks, despite the guilt, waking feeling groggy every morning but relieved to have slept so well.

The bastard had been putting something in my Ovaltine to make me sleep!

I groaned out loud, not least because it seemed that I owed Ellen Brigstock Lamb an apology. Ed could well have killed her sister.

44

I did not return to see Ellen again before I left the next morning, even though I knew I'd been rude to her. Let's just see if she was right first, I thought, and then I'd apologise for storming out.

My eyes were sticky with fatigue and sleeplessness as I sat in the same taxi back to the airport, all five minutes of the drive, with the cabbie chatting away about the weather; fog and sea mists and cold fronts. 'Anyway, here we are again,' he said, pulling up to the door of the tiny terminal.

By the time I finally stepped out of Jersey airport, I was wearing an uncharacteristically foul mood like an overcoat. Even the sight of Maddie waving at me from her car didn't raise my spirits.

'Hi.'

'Oh dear,' she said, getting out and hugging me. 'You look exhausted. It didn't go well then?'

'That was a lot of flights in a very short time. I need to talk to you both. Is Geoff home?'

'Yes. Oh Lynn, are you OK?'

'No.'

'We'll look after you,' she said, and I felt very slightly better.

Not for long, though. Like the sun, my momentary optimism had vanished again by the time we got back to Maddie and Geoff's. We were ensconced in their conservatory overlooking the garden, a streak of choppy grey ocean behind it. Tiny sparrows pecked at something on the lawn, until a large ginger cat stalked across the grass and they all took flight.

'That bloody cat! I'll wring its neck if I can get close enough to it. It keeps pissing on my hydrangeas.'

Geoff came in with a tray of tea and homemade banana cake, which he plonked hastily on the coffee table so that he could rush over and bang on the patio door to scare off the cat, which gave him a look of disdain, lifted its tail and unleashed a thin stream of pee on the holly bush nearby, shuddering theatrically.

'I swear it does that on purpose,' Geoff said, and glumly handed me a plate with a fat slice of cake on it.

I couldn't even pick at the cake. I felt flimsier than the sparrows and more vulnerable. I wasn't able to speak for a while, knowing how it was going to sound when I did.

'Talk to us, come on, spit it out, sweetie,' Maddie encouraged. 'What happened? Does she still think Ed killed Shelagh?'

'Yes. But it's not so much what she said,' I said, eventually. 'More what's been happening for the last decade.'

I caught the glance that shot between Geoff and Maddie.

'Go on.'

I opened my mouth and began to tell them all my fears, omitting the part about why I'd come to Molesey in the first place, of course; beginning instead with what Alvin had said on the phone about Ed snogging someone at MADS and how that could have been April. How April hadn't replied to any of my emails and had sent Caspar a fake photo of the alleged holistic sheep farm.

'I mean – a holistic sheep farm? How unlikely does *that* sound?'

Maddie didn't even crack a smile, trying to take it in.

'So you're now sure Ed's gone off somewhere with April?'

'Not just that, Mads. I have a horrible feeling that he's been planning this for years. That he faked the whole dementia thing to give him an alibi for killing Mike. That, like Ellen thinks, he killed Shelagh too, all to be with April.'

Maddie's face drained of colour and Geoff was motionless. Then she stood up and began pacing around the room.

'Lynn, I ... I don't know what to say. But you can't believe that, surely! You love Ed! Ed *adores* you! He's your husband! He's not having an affair with April. We'd know! We'd have been able to tell...'

I gritted my teeth hard to try and stop tears springing into my eyes. I'd thought Ed adored me, too. He was the love of *my* life, without a doubt.

'I'm not saying they've been having an affair the whole time. Maybe it's been on and off. But you've got to admit it's the most likely explanation. Oh – and I just remembered, right after his supposed diagnosis, I was convinced there was someone sneaking around in the house when I thought he was asleep. I bet it was him! And other strange things happened, you know, blinds down when I knew I'd left them up, that sort of thing.'

They looked unconvinced, so I ploughed on. 'And what about the money? The money's gone, all our savings.'

'*All* your savings?' Geoff asked, grim-faced.

I nodded. 'Everything. Our retirement money.'

Maddie was still not prepared to accept it. 'But even if he did, it doesn't mean he planned it all along. Like you said, what if that was just a leftover symptom of his illness? It could've changed his character, his personality ... dementia does that. Robs them of who they were.'

'But he's "better" now,' I said, with heavy ironic emphasis. 'Funny that, isn't it?'

'What proof is there of the recovery? Apart from his behaviour and his language improving? He must really have been part of that trial, surely. Didn't you see an email about it?'

I sighed. 'There are the brain scans that show his brain as normal again, and the first lot I told you about, the ones I didn't know he'd had when he was first diagnosed, that show it as damaged.'

'Which hospital?' Geoff asked, delicately picking walnuts out of his cake and leaving them on the side of his plate.

'I don't know but after Maddie suggested it, I'm guessing it *was* that hospital where April used to work. It would've easy enough for her to call in a few favours, steal or borrow someone else's diseased brain scans and put Ed's name and the wrong date on them. Probably would only have taken a few minutes at a computer. So when he was "cured" and re-scanned, it would look as though his brain had been restored.'

Maddie leaned her forehead against the conservatory door and stared out at the sea. 'I still don't believe it. I'm sorry, Lynn, I know you're desperate for answers but – not April. Are you saying that she and Ed plotted to kill Mike? She just wouldn't! And I don't believe that Ed would be enough of a bastard to put you through eight months of hell, believing he had Pick's Disease! Why would he do that?'

'I told you. Because he wanted an alibi for Mike's murder. Around the time that Mike was killed, Ed started punching me in his sleep – at least that's what I thought – so he suggested I lock him in the spare room at night so I could get a good night's sleep, and not be worried that he'd wander. Well, actually, he suggested he locked *himself* in, but he'd have known I wouldn't let him do that, and he could have been planting the idea for *me* to suggest. Which I did. So then, when the police interviewed us, I could – and did – confirm that Ed was ill, and locked in a bedroom that night for his own safety and mine. He could easily have had a spare key. And, you know what else? I think he was putting something in my tea to make me sleep.'

I was unable to keep a tremor out of my voice but I forced myself to stay calm. 'He loved Mike – although they definitely weren't as close in the last few years as they used to be. I put that down to the illness too but just say, hypothetically, that it was April all along he really loved and wanted to be with. Then perhaps they did split up for the first few years that I was with Ed, and perhaps he was in love with me enough then to want to give things a go...'

Maddie held up a hand like she was stopping traffic. 'No, no, no, that doesn't make sense! Why would he kill Shelagh to be with April, only to break up with her and marry you instead?'

I shrugged miserably. 'Why would he do any of it? Logically though, just say he's completely innocent – then where is he? If he'd been in an accident, I'd know by now. His passport and our money are gone. April's gone. Mike's dead. What am I supposed to think?'

'It does seem weird,' Geoff agreed. 'You need to find them, and if they're not together that'll put your mind at rest.'

'I set up a fake Facebook profile and sent her a friend request, pretending to be an old schoolfriend. April's so rubbish with names she probably won't smell a rat. I thought if she replied, then I'd know she can get internet wherever she is, and that she's ignoring me.'

'And has she?' Geoff asked.

'I don't know, I haven't checked. I'll look now.' I pulled out my laptop from its grubby, stripy zip-up case – grubby, because it had been Timmy's favourite place to sit. The ginger cat outside reminded me of Timmy and I wondered how he was getting on with Naveeta and the girls.

I switched it on and waited. 'It's been so slow recently. I don't understand why – I mean, I've not got much on it, and it's only two years old.'

Geoff tipped his head to one side and his jowly neck settled into a different and lopsided concertina of folds. 'How long has it been running slow?'

'A few months now.'

'Can I have a look at it?'

Geoff's job back in Surrey had been in IT.

'You can if you want,' I said, handing it over, 'but to be honest, a slow laptop is the least of my problems.'

His hands were big and solid, comforting, with startlingly white moons on his fingernails. 'It's not that...' he said, 'I just want to check something.'

He keyed in some commands while Maddie perched on the arm of the sofa and rubbed his greying hair affectionately. She was still gazing out to sea with a troubled expression in her huge green eyes.

'I'm not making it all up,' I said, and she turned sharply.

'Oh, Lynn, of course you aren't! I wouldn't think that of you, not for a second. It's just ... such a huge accusation, of both of them.'

'Shit,' Geoff said, his fingers frozen over the keyboard.

'What?' Maddie and I said in tandem.

'Just been going through the processes. I'm really sorry, Lynn, but someone's installed spyware on here.'

Maddie's hands flew to her mouth.

'Three guesses who that would be, then,' I forced myself to say. 'Is that why it's been running so slowly?'

'Almost certainly. Can you pinpoint exactly when it started its go-slow?'

I groaned. 'Around the time of his diagnosis. I remember moaning to Ed about it and it was as if he didn't understand what I was talking about. But – if it was Ed, which it must have been – that means he was definitely faking the Pick's.'

'And I'm afraid it also means that he can see whatever you've done online ever since then,' Geoff said apologetically.

Maddie jumped up off the arm of the sofa and faced us, her hands bunched into fists at her sides. Tears began to stream over her round cheeks, so fast that she looked like a crying cartoon of herself.

'How can you both be so calm?' she shrieked. 'Ed ... our friend Ed, your husband Ed ... *faked* all that? He's a bastard who's lied and cheated and spied on you, possibly murdered either his first wife or his best friend – or both – and you're just – sitting there? I want to fucking *kill* him!'

Maddie, who wouldn't kill a wasp that had stung her.

'I'm not calm, Mads, I'm not. But don't forget I've had longer to think about it. I've had my suspicions about him for ages – I'd have to be a completely gullible idiot not to. April, however – she's another matter. It never crossed my mind that she and Ed might have been...'

I stopped. Was this true? I thought of April fluttering her eyelashes at Ed, putting her hand over his at dinner, flattering and complimenting him, shrieking and splashing him flirtatiously in the sea on our joint holidays. I'd always thought that was just her manner – but she'd never done that with *Geoff*, for example. She was equally affectionate to Mike, but not as flirty as she'd been with Ed, I realised in technicolour hindsight.

'Well,' I conceded. 'We all knew what a flirt April was, but I didn't think for a second they had any history.'

'Me neither,' Maddie sniffed. 'Like we said on the phone, if it was anyone, I'd have thought it would be Naveeta, she's always been all over him.'

Geoff put my laptop to one side and wrapped his arms around me. 'We're so sorry, Lynn. You don't deserve this.'

I remembered the glib excitement with which I had undertaken my original mission, just to escape the affair with Adrian Sodding McCloughlin, and then, how easily I'd let myself be lured back into bed with him again, while my husband was – or wasn't –battling a terminal illness...

Whatever 'it' was, I probably did deserve it.

45

I linked my fingers at the back of my neck, massaging the knobbles of my vertebrae.

'So the question is – where are they, and how do I find them?'

'You said the police had confirmed he hadn't left the country?' Maddie said, wiping her eyes on the napkin Geoff had supplied under the banana cake.

'He might have done by now. He's not a high-risk missing person, which means that even if his name was flagged up at airports, it would be up to the discretion of the airline staff as to whether they detained him or not.'

'How about asking them to check if there's a record of him and April having gone somewhere together? Tell them what you think he's done.' A cake crumb stuck to Maddie's cheek.

'Yeah. Maybe.'

I imagined the humiliation of confessing my fears that Ed could have been instrumental in Mike's murder, and therefore possibly Shelagh's too. Being interviewed by Superintendent Nicholls or Brian Metcalfe and having to admit that, ten years after the event, I'd spectacularly miscalculated: cost the taxpayer thousands of pounds to let a guilty man go scot-free, just because he had wooed, flattered, impregnated and pretended he couldn't live without me.

Rage rose up in my gullet like sick, reeking green and toxic. All the sympathy I'd had for Ed, and for poor widowed April. All the tears I'd shed for their plights, while all the time they were scheming and lying. Using me. I imagined those tears as acid, burning where they fell. Scarring Ed's smug features and marring April's peachy bloom. I changed my mind.

'Nope,' I said firmly, reaching forward and gently flicking away the crumb, trying to stop my fingers shaking. 'Not telling them. Not until I know for sure.'

'Lynn – I think you must. He's spying on you!'

I'd never seen Maddie look so troubled.

I snorted. 'Spying is the least of it, if he killed his first wife and his best mate. But back to the spyware, Geoff, for a minute – what does that consist of, exactly? Does it mean he can see everything I've done on my laptop in the last few months, or just some stuff? Emails?'

Geoff was looking a bit emotional, too. The tip of his nose had turned pink. 'It depends if it was spyware that harvested your passwords – in which case it would probably just be emails he could read – or a key-tracker that follows everything.'

'So would he – *they,* assuming April's with him – have seen that I was the one who sent her that Facebook request?'

'I'll need to check. Give me another hour and I should be able to find out.'

I thought of the email I'd sent Maddie yesterday, expressing my suspicions about April's disappearance and Ed's being on the same day. At least I'd never mentioned Waitsey in any correspondence to anybody, and Adrian and I had never emailed each other. That was something.

'Dammit. He'll know that I suspect him. I emailed you about the meeting with Ellen. And I emailed Caspar asking for April's postal address – oh, and I told April she needed to contact me urgently, that I was worried...'

'So will he know for sure that you've figured out that he was faking it, and that he's done a runner with April?'

'Not for sure, I don't think. But he must know I'm very suspicious if he knows I went to visit Ellen.'

Maddie sat down on the floor in the lotus position, inhaling deeply through her nose as she tried to gather herself.

'God,' she said. 'He had us all fooled. What you must have gone through...' She looked up. 'Do you think *April* knew he wasn't really ill?'

'She must have done, if she did the fake scans for him. But if she didn't, then maybe he fooled her, too. I still can't believe that she would have agreed to him murdering Mike. She might be a vain, shallow cheating bitch but she's not a psycho. She and Mike had their issues and rows and he could be horrible, but they were married for so long ... Why would she have wanted him dead? She could just have divorced him if she didn't love him anymore.'

'Mike had money, didn't he? I'd say that would be a good enough excuse, if I was Ed,' Geoff said, looking up from the laptop. 'April and Mike and Ed were all good at acting. They might all have been pretending the whole time. It's *despicable*.'

He gnawed at the tuft of hair growing under his bottom lip, his teeth worrying at it. 'I'm sorry, Lynn. Now I'm the one who's jumping to conclusions. I know it's not looking good, but as you rightly said, we don't have any actual proof. April might still Skype you tonight and show you round her sheep farm with her iPad, and then you'll feel bad you ever doubted her.'

'I think it's unlikely,' I said.

Suddenly all three of us burst out laughing; a tired hysterical laughter borne out of stress and disbelief. I had a mental picture of April, with her three-hundred-pound highlights and top-of-the-range Sweaty Betty yoga pants, earnestly panning her iPad around pens of sheep dip, treading daintily to avoid piles of sheep shit, mystified, bronzed outback farm workers wondering what the hell she was doing there.

'Why are we laughing? This is horrific!' Maddie croaked.

'That bastard, pretending to have a life-threatening illness!' I roared – but then Maddie stopped.

'That really isn't funny, Lynn,' she said, sober again.

I stopped laughing, too. 'I know. But if I don't laugh, I'll ... well, I don't know what I'll do but it won't be good. I just want to get some proof. Confront them. Unless I have firm evidence, he'll wriggle out of it again. So – let's think: if Ed and April were to run away together, where would they go?'

'Somewhere hot,' Maddie and Geoff said in tandem.

'Exactly. That's what Ben said – about Ed, anyway. The Caribbean, I reckon. Every time I ever talked about moving to Jersey to be nearer you guys, all Ed would say was that it wasn't hot enough. Jokey stuff about how you couldn't get Banks beer or Dark and Stormy cocktails in Jersey.'

'Banks beer is from Barbados, right?'

'Yes, but you can get it all over the Caribbean,' Geoff said, still busy on my laptop. He was a guitar player and kept the nails on his right hand long, so he sounded like a secretary with a manicure as he clicked away at the keys.

'Would he go somewhere that you and he had gone before?' Maddie asked.

'I doubt it. If he's planned it that far in advance, I reckon he'd pick somewhere that doesn't have any connection with me. If he's with April, they might be on a boat, or with access to one. They're both such good sailors.'

'Did he leave a computer we could hack into? His search history might make interesting reading.'

'No, he took it with him when he went into town that day. I thought it was so he could watch iPlayer on the train.' I snorted with fresh derision at my gullibility.

'Hmm,' Geoff said. 'That's too bad. Maddie, while I'm still on Lynn's laptop, will you get the iPad please? You can log her in to check Facebook, see if she's had any bites from April.'

Maddie retrieved an iPad from the drawer of the mahogany writing desk in their living room, powered it up and handed it to me. I took it, frowning as I tried to remember the login details that accompanied my fake profile. 'OK ... here we go ... no, nothing. That's disappointing.'

'Perhaps she smelled a rat because you – your alter-ego – doesn't have any other Facebook friends,' Geoff said. 'Why don't you get a few more then try her again? Do you know the name of anyone she genuinely did go to school with?'

'There was a girl called Sally she used to talk about,' I said, thinking hard. I imagined April and this Sally, as giggly schoolgirls, radiant with teenage beauty, blithely setting off on a lifetime path of using their allure to manipulate and acquire.

'She's got one friend called Sally in her friend list.' Maddie pointed at the screen. 'Looks about the right age.'

Sally Prentiss was mid-gallop on a horse in her profile pic so it was hard to tell much about her other than she rode. But that fitted in with what I knew about April's boarding-school-privileged upbringing.

'Don't forget,' said Geoff, 'they might not have any wifi or internet access, especially if they're on some remote island somewhere. Or on a boat.'

'Good point. But I know them well enough to be certain that they'd make sure they could check in every couple of days at least, even if they were at sea.'

I scrolled through Sally Prentiss' pictures, hoping vainly for a scan of an old school photo or something, but there were only a few, mostly of horses.

'I'm not sure this is the way to go. I think it's a waste of time. Even if April responded to my friend request, she's unlikely to announce to me, as "Christine", that she's run away with her husband's best friend to a specific place in the Seychelles or the Caribbean, is she? All it would prove is that she's online and ignoring my emails.'

'Phone records?' Geoff suggested. 'Are the bills in both your names?'

It started to rain, fat droplets splattering with loud plops against the conservatory roof and windows.

'Good idea,' I said after a while. 'He's obviously ditched his mobile and got another one – but the bills for his old one are in his name so I don't think I'd be able to access them.'

'The police could do it in a moment!' Maddie wailed. 'I think you're insane not to ask them, Lynn, honestly.'

I grabbed her hand. 'I know it doesn't make sense, but promise me you won't call them? Promise? It's really important. I can't tell you why, not yet, but I need to find out for myself before I get them more involved than they already are. I mean, they do know about the missing money and passport, and they are looking into it. I just don't want to bring up the stuff about Shelagh and April until I've got a bit more information.'

Maddie sighed, following my gaze to watch the rain sliding down the glass. Then she glared at me. 'All right. But if you go haring off after them, I need to know you aren't in danger, and if you think you are, you need to swear to me that you will call the police then. And if you don't, I will. Do you understand me?'

'We'll come with you,' Geoff said.

'Don't be daft!' I shot back. 'Not unless you fancy spending thousands of pounds on flights and hotels for what'll probably be the most unrelaxing holiday you'll ever have. Seriously, I can handle myself. I just need to see them together and confront them.'

Geoff stood up, groaning slightly with effort. 'Sun's over the yardarm. Who wants a glass of wine?'

'Just a small one for me, thanks,' I said absently. 'Maddie, pass that back over, would you?' I gestured at the iPad. 'Our home phone bills will be online, although Ed handled all that sort of thing...' How pathetic that made me sound! How unreconstructed, Fifties housewife. Waitsey would have sneered.

'I mean, he liked to. It was a control thing.'

I typed Ed's email address into Virgin Media, my fingers hovering over the empty password box.

'Was he imaginative about passwords?' Geoff asked, handing me a half-full glass of red. I resisted the urge to throw it down in one gulp.

'Not really. He wasn't one of those people who has different passwords for everything and makes them up out of a string of numbers and letters...'

'...so that you have no possible chance of remembering them when you need them,' Maddie grumbled in Geoff's direction and he smiled at her, tapping his forehead.

'Better safe than sorry,' he said. 'So Ed's would likely be a person, then, or a significant date. Or a pet? A sports personality?'

I tried as many as I could think of but nothing came up. 'This is hopeless.'

'Ring them, and tell them that your husband's run off and closed your joint account and you need access to the bills to be able to pay them. It can't be the first time they've heard something like that.' Maddie handed me the phone.

'Worth a shot.' I dialled the number, eventually got through to a lady in a call centre and I explained I'd forgotten the password to the online account. I didn't even need to give the sob story. All I had to do was to give Ed's name, date of birth, our address and the first and third letters of the 'security code' for the account.

'F and I,' I said, punching the air in triumph. 'Great. Yes, please, if you could send the temporary password to Maddie dot Morley at gmail.com.'

When I hung up, Maddie shook my arm. 'What was it?'

I laughed. 'It just came to me. We always used *Fringilla* as our code word, you know, the name of April's boat. Ed changed all the passwords for everything, I bet, but he forgot that they ask for an additional security word when you phone up. Result!'

The email pinged into Maddie's inbox and from there it was matter of moments to change the password on the Virgin Media account and access all our home phone bills from the past year as PDFs.

'I'm only going to look at the calls he's made since his supposed diagnosis. And he won't know, because I'm on your iPad!'

'You're amazing, Lynn,' Maddie remarked. 'Seriously. If I found out that Geoff had done all this to me, I'd be a gibbering wreck.'

'You wouldn't be.' I scanned through the lists of phone numbers.

Geoff cleared his throat. 'I think what you mean is, "Geoff would never do that to you."'

'Yeah, well, that goes without saying. Wait – I don't recognise that one.' It was an area code I couldn't place. 'Oh, no, it's nothing. It's my Auntie Daphne in the Cotswolds, my annual phone call to her on her birthday.'

Most of the other numbers were local, or 0345. There weren't too many to sift through, as neither Ed nor I used the home phone all that much.

'How do you know that Ed wouldn't have used his mobile to make all the arrangements?' Geoff asked.

I snorted. 'Because it's Ed – he's far too tight to call a different continent on his mobile. I bet you anything.'

I called up the bill from October, seven months ago, and Maddie tapped the screen. 'That one's overseas, look.'

I zoomed in closer. 'A twenty-minute call, at 4.20am. Think we might have something here ... area code 001 – that's America, isn't it? Ed doesn't know anyone in the US, as far as I'm aware ... So what state is 784?'

I switched to a new tab and Googled it, slapping the arm of the sofa when the result sprang up: 'It's not a state, it's in the Caribbean! It's St Vincent and the Grenadines – I knew it! Ed's such a cliché. He thinks he's been so clever, and we've tracked him down first go.'

'Ring the number,' Maddie said, her eyes wide.

'OK. They're only four or five hours behind us, aren't they?'

I put it on speakerphone and the faint transatlantic burr of dialling tone crackled around the room, then an answering machine clicked on. The three of us sat stock-still and listened to the American female voice:

'Hello. You have reached the offices of The Mustique Holiday Company. All our operatives are currently busy but please leave us a message and we'll be sure to return your call. For villa rentals press one, for all other enquiries press two...'

'Mustique! That completely makes sense,' I said bitterly, hanging up. 'Trust Ed to go to one of the most expensive, exclusive islands in the whole of the bloody Caribbean.'

Ed had never taken *me* to Mustique, or anywhere in the Caribbean, despite his professed love for it. Not even for our honeymoon, which had been in southern Spain. A few years after that, he had begun saying he was claustrophobic and afraid of flying.

Had he really been planning it for that long?

Geoff was already looking up the website for the Mustique Holiday Company. 'Wow. You're right. It ain't cheap. There's only about a hundred villas on the whole island and they start at nine thousand dollars a week, off-season. Look, that one's forty-five thousand to rent – a *week*!'

'Isn't Mustique where Princess Margaret and David Bowie had houses?' Maddie asked, looking over her husband's shoulder.

It was getting cold in the room, and she moved into the living room to light the fire, half-laid in the grate. 'It looks like a stunning place,' she commented.

'Of course it does,' I said. 'Ed and April wouldn't have gone to all these lengths to run away to anywhere less, I'm sure.' My stomach was roiling with acid fury and heartbreak. 'Well, they're in for a surprise, aren't they, when I turn up to wreck their little clandestine buzz.'

'You aren't really?' Maddie called back through the archway. She was kneeling by the fireplace twisting old newspapers into kindling.

'Of course I am. I told you I wanted to talk to them.'

Maddie stopped, brandishing a newspaper stick. 'But what's the point? Surely you can just confirm they're there, somehow, and then tell the police? And anyway, you don't know for sure that's where they are.'

'I can't report him to the police for running off with another woman. I'm going to get evidence of what he's done, and *then* report him. Plus I want to make April squirm, that treacherous, cheating...'

My voice trailed off. Was I being ridiculous? What if Maddie was right; I chased them all the way over to Mustique and they'd gone somewhere else, or never even been there? Perhaps Ed had just enquired and found it too expensive. Maybe they were in a caravan park on Canvey Island.

Ha, I thought. Fat chance.

It was a start though, proof that instead of being locked in his bedroom Ed had been downstairs at night making phone calls to the Caribbean. Proof that he probably never had Pick's at all.

'Anyway.' I forced levity into my voice. 'They'll be a whole lot easier to find on an island that tiny than if they'd gone to Barbados. Even if I've missed them, someone must know where they were planning to go after that. I'll take photos of them with me; show everyone, in case they're using false names. Expensive villas will have housekeepers; butlers probably. Pool guys. The person Ed spoke to about renting the place. Someone will know.'

'I'd never have thought of any of that,' said Maddie. 'You're the one who should be a detective!'

I turned away so that she couldn't see my face.

'Bingo!' Geoff said. 'I've traced the spyware and it's only on your emails. So that means he won't be able to see anything else, like flights you've booked.'

'That's good. Thanks Geoff. Can you take the spyware off? No – wait, don't do that, because then Ed will know I'm on to him for sure. Might even send a few red herring emails, make him think I'm doing something different.'

Maddie touched a match to the laid fire and it flared up immediately, crackling as the twigs caught.

I delved into my handbag and extracted my credit card.

'How much do you think a flight to Mustique will cost? I'm going to go home tomorrow, pack my bikini, and get over there. He's there, I know it.'

46

The taxi dropped me off at the end of the lane and I stood for a moment watching the river flow silent and almost black past me. It felt as though the current was sweeping away my old life on its sinister swirls, and I wondered if I would ever get it back.

I dragged my suitcase over the gravel part of the driveway and up the front doorstep, relieved that I'd not seen anyone I knew on the train back from the airport.

The case was heavy, full of far more clothes than I had actually needed for the unpredictable weather of the Channel Islands, but I hadn't known how long I would be away. Now that I was going to Mustique, I'd be packing a different kind of wardrobe altogether.

It was still and very cold inside. Ed's wellies were in the hall, there was a circle of cat hair on the armchair, and I felt the absence of both other occupants of the house. I had half wondered if Ed would be sitting in the front room watching TV when I got back, his illness real and returned, but the house was exactly as I'd left it the week before.

I thought about ringing Ben but decided not to, because then I'd have to tell him that I was about to fly to the Caribbean. I would rather be certain of Ed's whereabouts before whipping everyone up into a frenzy of anticipation – and I definitely wasn't ready to share my growing suspicions about his treachery. My car was still outside Ben's flat, but it would just have to stay there.

I also wanted to ask him about the photo on Ellen's mantelpiece, about who that tubby little boy next to him had been. How come I had such a strong feeling that I recognised him, when I hadn't known any of Ben's childhood friends? It was still nagging at the back of my mind and I couldn't think why – but I couldn't do that either, without admitting I'd been to see Ellen. Ben would go nuts if he knew I'd gone to quiz his auntie.

It was probably nothing, anyway, just some kid he'd met on the beach.

Once I'd switched on the heating, opened the post and drunk a cup of tea – herbal, since I forgot to buy milk – I went up to the spare room and tugged out the vacuum-packed bag of my summer clothes from under the bed, along with my bigger suitcase. I picked out all the things I'd usually wear on a summer holiday and rolled them up, slotting them neatly into the case. It felt weird, on such a grim mission.

There was another reason I'd wanted to come home before flying out again, apart from to pack. I sat down at the kitchen table with my laptop and downloaded a free 'make your will' template. I spent the next hour updating it, omitting Ed completely and making Maddie the executor instead, then printed it out. My old will had left everything to Ed, and there was no way I was going to keep it that way. Not that I had a lot to call my own, since our joint savings had gone.

I also cancelled the life insurance policy I'd had for years, with Ed as beneficiary. Finally, I wrote a long letter 'to who it may concern', explaining as best I could my thoughts and fears, and giving directions to the box under the floorboards in the attic. I sealed it into an envelope and took it, and the will, next door to Suzan.

'I'm re-doing my will!' I said as chirpily as I could when she opened the door. 'I've just survived several terrifying flights in tiny planes and it reminded me that I've been meaning to do it for ages – will you witness it for me please?'

'Of course. Come in. My friend Minty is here at the moment. Any news on Ed?'

I shook my head. I'd supposed we'd have to accost someone on the towpath to get them to act as the second witness, so Minty's presence was a stroke of luck. She was a lady of around Suzan's vintage, far less well preserved but very courteous and kind. All I could remember about her afterwards was the one very long wiry hair protruding from her doughy cheek.

They read through my efforts with an embarrassed reserve – 'Goodness,' said Minty, 'it feels a bit like rifling through someone's knicker drawer!'

Suzan obviously spotted the omission of any mention of Ed, but she just raised her eyebrows at me. 'Are you sure?'

'Absolutely,' I said. 'Maddie will make sure Ed's looked after. I trust her implicitly.'

Suzan didn't yet know that Ed had been 'cured', and that worked to my advantage. It would have been weird to entrust all my worldly goods to someone who was fast losing mental capacity.

They both watched as I signed and dated, and did the same. 'Thanks,' I said. 'Much appreciated. I'm going away again tonight – and in my current pessimistic mood, I've written a 'to whom it may concern' letter in case I get eaten by a shark –' *or bumped off by my treacherous husband*, I thought '– or run over by a bus. Could you keep it here please? And, er, if Ed comes back, please let me know before you let him read it? I don't want to freak him out.'

'Is everything all right, Lynn?'

I shrugged. 'Well. As all right as everything can be, when Ed's missing. But I'm going to find him. I'll let you know as soon as I do, and hopefully we'll be back home again pretty soon...'

Suzan narrowed her eyes at me but, perhaps because Minty was hovering, she didn't push me further. I could tell she thought I was being paranoid; probably had been thinking it for months. I remembered her face, the day I asked her if it could have been Ed on the radio phone-in – which, it only just occurred to me, almost certainly *had* been him.

'I hope so,' was all she said, giving me a hug. 'Stay safe.'

'I'll do my best,' I said.

47

The Barbados-bound jumbo jet was a behemoth in comparison with the tiny Channel Islands planes, as if it had eaten them as casual snacks. It seemed impossible to believe that it would ever achieve enough velocity to heave itself into the air.

Once on board, squashed in the middle seat of three, I stared through the porthole window at the drizzly runway as the captain began his spiel. The man in the window seat wore a baseball cap backward over a grey ponytail, and might have been attractive were it not for the thin crop of black bristles marching down the bridge of his nose towards its tip, like mini porcupine quills.

'Holiday?' chirped the lady on the other side of me, a matronly sixty-something with such thick foundation on her face that I could smell it, cloying and chemical.

'Yes,' I lied, smiling at her and hoping she wasn't going to ask me any more questions.

'Whereabouts are you staying in Barbados?'

'I'm flying on from there straight to Mustique. My brother's rented a villa there with his, er, partner. It's his sixtieth birthday so I've come out to surprise him.'

This was partly true. I'd rung the property company back again and spoken to a cheery West Indian lady called Connie, trying to 'check' that 'my brother, Ed Naismith' was renting a villa on the island. I pretended I was planning a very secret visit to surprise him on his birthday, which really was next week, and was making sure that he'd still be there.

Connie had been annoyingly discreet. She kept saying, 'I'm afraid I'm not at liberty to divulge that information, ma'am,' in a whiny voice at the end of each of my questions about how long Ed was planning to stay and if he was there with anyone.

'But I'm his sister!' I'd protested. 'He'll be there with his wife – April.'

I tried to sound as matter-of-fact as possible. 'April Greening,' I confirmed, swallowing hard. 'She goes by her maiden name.'

'I'm afraid I'm not at liberty to divulge any details about our guests,' Connie had stubbornly insisted. 'Not without their prior permission.'

'Oh, please don't tell him I'm coming!' I managed to inject a laugh into my voice. 'That would spoil the surprise!'

'I sure won't, ma'am.'

'So you can confirm they're there?'

'Forgive me, ma'am, but if you're his sister, wouldn't he have told you himself where he was going?'

I was prepared for that question. 'He just emailed us that he was flying to Barbados and then they were getting a smaller plane on to Paradise. I guessed it was Mustique because he's always wanted to go there. But anyhow, I don't want him to know I'm planning to come out.'

'Couldn't you have confided in his wife, ma'am, if she's travelled with him?'

I gave the fake laugh again, although my heart was breaking. It sounded very much as if Connie knew full well April was there, too. 'Oh no! She's hopeless at keeping a secret. I so want to surprise them both!'

In the end, Connie hadn't given me any specific information, but when I'd begged her to confirm if Ed *wasn't* there, so that I could continue investigating other luxury islands in the area, I'd heard a brief reluctant smile in Connie's voice and she had said, 'Well, ma'am, I'm afraid I cannot confirm that either.'

'Thank you, Connie, you've been very helpful. I'm going to book my ticket now.'

Ed was in Mustique, I was certain. And I was ready to confront him.

The 747 lumbered along the runway at Gatwick and into the sky as I clutched my left armrest – the matronly lady had commandeered the other one, resting a plump liver-spotted hand on it. She wore the biggest diamond engagement ring I'd ever seen and I took my mind off the plane's shuddering ascent by staring transfixed at its winking facets.

Perhaps that had been another sign I should've heeded. I had seen Shelagh's engagement ring, immortalised in the studio portrait hanging in the hall of Ed's old house, and that ring had been enormous and ostentatious. I glanced down at my own and, not for the first time, found it lacking. Ed wasn't short of money but he had bought me a ring with just about the smallest diamond I'd ever seen.

I twisted it contemplatively around my finger. At the time I had just assumed it was a reaction to losing Shelagh; Ed's decision to pare down his life and perhaps an unspoken guilty relief at not needing to pander to her complicated needs any longer. But now I thought it was more likely that Ed couldn't be arsed to buy another expensive ring; that he didn't love me enough to want to anyway. He just wanted to replace Shelagh as soon as he could, maybe even as a smokescreen for his affair with April...

The lady was banging on about visiting her son and his family in Barbados, although I hadn't asked. Two stewards and a drinks trolley were fast approaching, so surely the monologue wouldn't continue for much longer. I tuned out and thought back to my visit to Maddie and Geoff, and the horrible but necessary encounter with Ellen in Alderney.

Before I'd even been given a drink, I was overwhelmed by tiredness, a soul-deep fatigue that crashed over me like a dull, salty wave. In the battle of exhaustion versus adrenaline, the former was winning, helped by the droning lady next to me. I muttered an apology, closed my eyes and slept for the next few hours solid, not even properly waking when the man in the window seat squeezed past me to go to the loo.

48

The view over the Grenadine Archipelago was stunning. As the Twin Otter – the latest in my recent assortment of planes – flew lower and lower in the clear blue sky I could see bobbing fishing boats and, on the island, the shimmering private pools of huge villas studding the greenery like sapphires.

It was late afternoon, local time, when the little plane finally touched down on the tiny landing strip in Mustique. I disembarked, the heat hitting me hard, burning the crown of my head and making me squint even behind my shades. It was even hotter than it had been in Barbados airport, which had been a humid jumble of long queues of sunburned tourists and bored-looking uniformed officials.

Another day, another island – but what an island! Mustique looked about the same size as Alderney but that was as far as the comparison went. I felt a stab of rage at the thought of April and Ed lying on a double sunbed with cocktails in their hands, soaking up the sun that ought to have been mine.

Mustique's air felt purer and less humid than Barbados. Was it always this hot here in May? I felt disorientated; exhaustion and jet lag giving me a sudden longing for my wood-burning stove, or for the office, to have a poster to design at my desk in Fairhurst. I wondered how the temp was getting on. Not so well that Alvin wouldn't want me to come back, I hoped, although I couldn't blame him if he kept her on. I'd been nothing but trouble for him since I started.

While I waited for my suitcase I told myself to get it together, to think of this as an adventure, a holiday, of sorts, rather than the likely end of my marriage, or worse – I hadn't thought as far as what would happen if, after questioning him, I still believed Ed really had killed Shelagh and/or Mike.

I was glad I'd redone my will, though, and written that letter.

As for my possible revelation about the Polaroid of the stripped pine doors, I decided to try and put that to the back of my mind for now, shelve it until I could be absolutely certain – which wouldn't be until I got back to the UK again.

I shuddered, and the man next to me, a snappily-dressed colonial type complete with straw Panama hat, three-piece cream linen suit and bulbous alcoholic's nose, asked me if I was all right.

'Fine,' I said, unable to summon a smile. 'Thank you.'

This was no holiday.

Realising that I couldn't just pitch up on a private island without proof of address for the stay, I had booked the cheapest place on the island, but it was still six hundred dollars a night for a garden cottage in the island's only hotel.

A busty hotel rep at the wheel of a small buggy met me once I was out of the tiny airport. I climbed into the back, sweating profusely and thanking the driver.

'You're welcome, ma'am, and please do enjoy your stay here with us. My name is Sunny.' She tapped the name tag on the beige waistcoat that strained across her ample bosom.

As with the man in the Panama hat, I found I couldn't be bothered to make small talk. The gravity of my mission had drained it all out of me like I had a plug in my heel. With every rotation of the buggy's wheels along the narrow lane, my focus sharpened. I felt like a sportswoman mentally preparing for the biggest challenge of her career. It was a strange disjointed sensation, this fierce fight-or-flight focus among the vivid colours of sea and flowers and lush green of the undulating mountains.

The air smelled of frangipani and salt, but I had nothing but dark thoughts in my head. When I took my mobile out of my bag, switched it on and heard the voicemail that Martine Knocker had left me just after I turned off my phone on the runway at Gatwick, the dark thoughts swelled and expanded.

'Hi, Lynn. I have an update for you. I'm afraid that Ed's name popped

up as having taken a flight from Heathrow to Barbados two days ago. He was interviewed at the airport and ... I'm sorry, but perhaps you could give me a call when you get the chance, and I'll talk you through what he said. So that's where he is. The official was satisfied that he was in sound mind and not a danger to himself or anybody, and let him board the plane. I hope that this at least puts your mind at rest that he is alive and safe, although I appreciate that this is not ideal news for you...'

I knew it.

I gritted my teeth. This did put my mind at rest. But not in the way Martine meant. I now was almost certain I wasn't on a wild-goose chase. My only unverified assumption was that Ed had taken another flight on to Mustique from Barbados. It would be exceptionally annoying if he was still in Barbados and I had missed him. But my intuition, and the phone call he'd made to the Mustique Holiday Company, told me I wasn't wrong. Unless he'd subsequently changed his mind about travelling on, he was here. I was certain of it. He had probably not bought a through ticket from London intentionally – as a smoke-screen, knowing that if his departure was discovered, it would be much easier to track him down in Mustique than Barbados. Barbados being a far bigger and more populated island, he would want us all to think he was there, not Mustique. He was good, I had to give him that...

I had no intention of ringing Martine back, at least not while I was here. I didn't want her to know I'd flown out in pursuit of him – the action of a deranged, vengeful person. I sent her a text in reply instead:

'Thanks Martine. Looks like he faked the whole dementia thing so he could leave me. He's cleared out our joint savings account too. I'm still away staying with friends but I'll call when I get home again. Too upset to talk about it at the moment. Lynn N'

I hoped that would keep her at bay.

After a few minutes we arrived at the hotel, a beautiful low-slung colonial-style affair. The sun was setting behind it and the sky had begun lighting up peach and apricot as Sunny checked me in and showed me to a tiny cottage – more of a luxury shed, really – in the gardens. It had a little verandah and painted pink shutters. I looked longingly at the pool as we passed it, but decided I would keep a low profile for now. It was too late to go in search of Ed tonight, and I didn't want to risk going for a swim and have him spot me, on the off-chance he was on the premises – he might even be staying in this hotel. Everything seemed to be run by the same company.

I'd rather confront him in daylight.

49

After a fitful night of jetlagged sleep dreaming of Ed and April – they were on Alderney not Mustique, doing yoga on a sheep farm; April turned to me and said, smugly, 'See? I told you I was here' – I awoke to sunlight streaming in shafts through the half-closed shutters and decided that I was categorically, whatever happened, no longer Lynn Naismith nor, as my passport still said, Cara Lynn Jackson.

From now on I would be Lynn Waites again. Fuck Ed Naismith.

I took off my engagement and wedding rings and put them in the room safe with all the happy memories of me and Ed, my passport and the return ticket.

I had a week to find him, then my credit card would be at its limit. Oh, so what? I thought. If he didn't come back, I'd sell the house anyway, pay off my debts, buy a little flat somewhere.

I put on dark glasses, a straw hat, flip-flops, bikini, and tied a floaty sarong around my breasts, the uniform of the middle-aged lady on holiday somewhere hot. With my newly shorn hair, I didn't think that Ed would notice me from a distance, if he was here. He wouldn't be expecting to see me, and I was planning to have my eyes on stalks making sure he didn't bump into me up close.

I sidled into the restaurant for breakfast on the outside stone terrace, too paranoid about running into him, with or without April, that at first I didn't stop to appreciate the view, the faint hot honey-suckle scent of the bougainvillea in pots, the drooping blue jacaranda trees around me.

The hotel didn't seem very full. There were only four other occupied tables, and Ed very definitely wasn't there. When a young waiter came over to pour my coffee, I took out my phone and showed him the most recent photo I had of Ed. He was grinning wickedly and raising a glass of red wine to his lips. I maximised the photo with two fingers as far as it went and Ed's face filled the little screen.

'Can you tell me if you've seen this man here recently? He's my brother and I think he's staying somewhere nearby.'

Unlike Connie on reservations, the boy did not question why, if Ed was my brother, I didn't just contact him myself. He squinted carefully at the photo. His skin was soft and smooth and his shirt beautifully ironed, and when he leaned down to look more closely I smelled soap and deodorant. I had to suppress a sudden urge to give him a maternal cuddle, but it would have creased his shirt. His name badge said 'Winston.'

'I bet your mum's really proud of you,' I blurted. Why did I say that? Poor boy, he looked as mortified as I felt.

If I hadn't lost my baby, I'd have had an eight-year-old now. Before I had the miscarriage, Ed said several times he wanted more kids, but it never happened, and he refused to go and have fertility tests. I'd gone on my own and been told all was fine, so I knew it wasn't me.

'Thank you ma'am,' Winston said shyly, then gestured to the photo. 'I'm sorry, no, I have not seen your brother.'

'OK. Thanks, Winston. Do you happen to know where the office for the Mustique Holiday Company is, who books out all the villas?'

'If you ask at reception, they can put you in touch. I hope you find him, ma'am.'

After breakfast I wandered over to reception and repeated my request. My phone screen was covered with sweaty fingerprints after it had been passed around amongst the staff, who, it appeared, also handled the admin on the villa rentals for the island – I'd thought it was a separate company but it seemed not. None of the three ladies behind the counter was called Connie, I was relieved to see.

They looked at one another, then back at me.

'I'm sorry, ma'am, but we aren't able to give out clients' details,' the oldest of the three said.

Which surely meant he must be here. My heart jumped painfully in my chest.

'I've come a really long way just to see him,' I said. It wasn't too difficult to make tears spring to my eyes. I lowered my voice.

'The thing is, we fell out about a year ago. It was my fault. He's been trying to make up with me since, and I wasn't having any of it, and now *he* won't talk to *me*. It's a big mess. Anyway, he's here, and it's his sixtieth birthday today and I really, really want to turn up at his villa with a bottle of champagne and an apology; surprise him. I'm worried that if you let him know I'm here, he might decide he doesn't want to see me and then I'll have had a wasted trip...'

I made my eyes as teary and puppy-dog as I could. Today really was Ed's birthday, which they'd be able to verify if they checked his booking or his passport.

I felt a genuine pang of loss, remembering numerous other birthdays together, dining out somewhere decadent, or dinner parties at home with April and Mike and Maddie and Geoff.

'Please?' I croaked. 'It means the world to me. I—'

I gave a sob, and one of the ladies handed me a tissue. They moved away and went into a small huddle to discuss my case, then the senior lady returned – Yvette, her name badge said. Plump and motherly, with a tight grey perm. She ushered me to the seating area in the lobby and we sat on opposite rattan sofas under a ceiling fan, a glass-topped table between us, like a job interview. She was going to tell me, I was sure.

'I'm truly sorry, Mrs Jackson. We do really sympathise but we have a very strict privacy policy here on Mustique. I hope you understand. We have so many celebrity guests and many of them come specifically for the discretion we offer. I simply cannot tell you where your brother is staying. All I can do is to inform him you are here and ask his permission to divulge his address. Or tell him yours.'

Damn, damn, damn. 'Oh. That's so disappointing. But of course, I understand.'

'Are you sure I can't contact him for you?' she asked gently, but with a slight edge to her expression, sort of, *It's weird if you don't let me*. 'I'm sure if you've come all this way he would be delighted to know you're here?'

I shook my head. 'No. Please don't tell him. It's really important that you don't.'

I didn't care if it made me look a bit deranged. I'd find him some other way. It was a tiny island. I would dredge up all the basic surveillance techniques I'd learned from the first time I had to spy on him.

'Very well. May I do anything else to assist you, Mrs Jackson?'

'Yes please – I'd like to hire one of those little golf jeeps, the – what are they called?'

'Kawasaki Mules, ma'am. Certainly. Please follow me.'

50

Three days later I still hadn't laid eyes on Ed. I forced myself to stay calm, but felt edgy and panicked, seeing him in the face of every middle-aged white man on the island as I hung around all the public places I could find – not many, on a private island – in my little rented Mule. I went to the jet-ski hire shack, the tennis courts, staked out the three restaurants and as many of the beaches and bays as I could, a constant recce which gave me a painful crick in my neck and a low-level feeling of nausea that compounded my jet lag.

Sometimes I almost – almost – forgot why I was there, as I lay on mostly empty beaches, lulled by gentle waves dissolving onto white sand, the sun fierce on my cheeks, my Kindle loose in my hand as I drifted off into yet another catnap, my skin tone two shades darker with every passing day.

I didn't show Ed's photo around anymore because I didn't want word to get back to him, but by noon on the third day I was beginning to think I'd have to soon, otherwise my week would be up. Or perhaps I was destined to wander Mustique forever, like a sunburned and peeling ghost.

In the end I got my breakthrough in the swimwear shop, one of Mustique's handful of chichi little stores, with their Hansel and Gretel carved decorations and pastel colours. I was browsing the bikinis – in the knowledge that if April was on the island, she would definitely pay a visit here at some point – when an English couple came in. The woman looked like a lollipop; massive head on a frame so spindly that it seemed it would never support her, teetering in on kitten-heel slides in transparent lime-green plastic, the sort of shoes a five-year-old girl would love if they had Disney princesses on each foot, but which probably cost about four hundred quid.

Her husband was podgy, wearing shorts that were three inches too short and too tight for his chubby legs. They were representative of most non-native people I'd seen on the island and, as I rotated a rack of very expensive sunglasses, I was so busy trying to eavesdrop on their conversation that I almost missed Ed walking past the window.

I made an involuntary sound in my throat that made lollipop-lady break off her conversation – something about the rainforest shower not working properly – and stare at me.

I rushed past her, accidentally banging her bony shoulder in my haste. 'Sorry!'

I opened the door just enough to peer out. It was Ed. I'd know that familiar, slightly rolling gait anywhere. His legs were tanned a deep mahogany brown, he was wearing a floppy pink cotton hat and long Hawaiian-patterned swim shorts, carrying a bottle of sun cream.

I swallowed hard, sweat breaking out on my forehead. My pulse thumped so hard in my ears that the speckled marble floor of the store momentarily shifted under my feet and I had to take a few deep breaths to steady myself.

He was here. I knew it!

But at least he was on his own.

'Are you OK?' the man in tight shorts asked me. It was a good thing I wasn't undercover any more. People had been asking me that all week. I may have remembered the surveillance techniques but not, it seemed, how to carry them out unnoticed. I nodded, apologising again, before sliding out of the shop and following Ed. He was about twenty feet ahead of me, striding purposefully towards a line of buggies. My own Mule was parked in the opposite direction on the roadside – damn, I thought, making a 180-degree turn and breaking into a run towards it, my flip-flops slapping on the boardwalk, my hand clutching the knot of my sarong between my breasts to stop it falling off.

I looked back to see Ed climb into his Mule and drive in my direction as I got into mine. I ducked down, pretending to scrabble around on the buggy floor to pick something up so that he wouldn't see my face and then, once he'd passed, I set off after him at a discreet distance. I realised I was clenching my teeth so hard that my jaw ached.

He was heading for Macaroni Beach, on the east side of the island. I knew that the road would soon peter out so I parked up and walked the rest of the way. It was breezier on this side, and I could hear the waves rolling in. The sound helped calm the pulse that was still hammering its panicked tattoo inside my head as I crept along the path leading to the sea.

The long white beach was almost empty, bar a couple of body-boarders in the water and a family punching a beach ball at one another at the far end.

I saw Ed immediately, sitting on a huge, square patterned beach towel. He'd stripped off his t-shirt and was squeezing sunscreen into his hands. I watched from behind a tree as he rubbed it into his shoulders and chest, cupping his palms and applying it to his face vigorously, like he was exfoliating.

Even with my suspicions as fierce as they were, I wanted to stroll over and massage the excess into the little tuft of hair near the base of his spine and the parts of his mid-back he couldn't reach, just as I'd done for years on all our shared holidays. So many beaches, so much sand between our toes.

But why would he choose to do this without me? I felt damp with self-pity as I watched him frame his eyes and gaze out to sea.

He took off his shades, lay down on his front and buried his face in the crook of his arms, and I wanted nothing more than to join him on the towel, feeling the hot skin of his back under my hand, inhaling the scent of his sun cream and salty sweat.

Then I thought of the emptied bank account. The spyware on my laptop. The missing passport. Shelagh's mysterious disappearance, Mike's death, 'Bill', who didn't exist...

And then, like a conjured-up personification of my doubts, some-thing in the sea caught my attention. A woman, swimming steadily towards the shore until the water became a lighter shade of turquoise and she could wade back through the waves. She strode up the beach towards Ed, posture-perfect in a tiny blue string bikini, the muscles moving in her lean legs as the sand shifted beneath her.

The breath stopped in my throat as I watched her approach the towel, giggling as she deliberately squeezed her wet hair over Ed, who roared and rolled over. Then she flung herself down next to him, put her hands on his chest and kissed his shoulder, and I watched as my husband grabbed her and pulled her on top of him, hugging her effusively with both arms around her slim waist. If they'd been in the sea instead of higher up the beach, they'd have looked like Burt Lancaster and Deborah Kerr in *From Here to Eternity*. My stomach turned sour with jealousy and shock – but not surprise.

It was April. Of course it was.

51

I lurched backwards on my arse into the scrubby bushes. Before I was even able to scramble up, I was vomiting over the ants scurrying about in the dirt, just managing to avoid puking all down myself. Heaving and gasping, I leaned on a tree trunk as white stars popped in my vision and tears and snot ran down my face.

It took me a few minutes, most of a bottle of water and several wet-wipes to regain some kind of shaky composure, so many bitter thoughts running through my head that I felt I would never be at peace again. Gone were all the notions of this being some kind of mental aberration on Ed's part, or a return of the disease, or anything other than outright betrayal.

I wanted to kill them both. For a few minutes, I seriously considered it. I would follow them back to wherever they were staying, and stab them in their bed. At least Martine Knocker didn't know I was here. If only I hadn't had that conversation with the hotel staff, telling them I was looking for Ed … Then I calmed down some more, enough to try and figure out a more sensible plan of action.

I moved along the beach, to the shelter of a shack with a palm-leaf roof where I was fairly sure neither of them could spot me, and waited. They finally stopped snogging and both seemed to fall asleep, motion-less apart from a sea breeze ruffling their hair. I watched, emotions rolling through me in great tidal surges of misery and rage.

I wasn't sure what to do, how to confront them, but as the minutes passed I realised that I wanted to get Ed on his own. I couldn't bear the thought of April's tearful apologies and pathetic excuses. But I couldn't think how to go about it, without trying to kidnap April and lock her in a cellar somewhere.

Then an opportunity presented itself: Ed woke up and got to his feet. He'd always had far too short an attention span to enjoy lying on a beach for long. He looked out to sea for a moment, then down at April, and then set off, walking towards my end of the beach. I could almost hear his thoughts: *Quick walk, stretch the legs, build up a proper sweat, then I'll have a dip.*

It was too good a chance to miss. My heart thumping in my throat, I dashed behind the shelter, out to the bushes and trees that formed the barrier between beach and land, and along the narrow dirt path as far as I could go. Then I doubled back down onto the sand, walking straight towards Ed, waiting for him to clock me. My legs shook uncontrollably as I tried not to stumble.

We approached one another. Thirty feet ... twenty ... ten ... he glanced up and saw me, a polite 'fellow-tourist' smile on his face – and then he recognised me and stopped in his tracks, the smile frozen as he did an exaggerated double-take.

'Hello, Ed.'

I was not going to shout and scream. I was going to play him at his own game.

He looked so floored that for a moment I almost felt sorry for him. He glanced behind him, presumably to check that April was still asleep then, consummate actor that he thought he was, recovered himself and flung his arms wide.

'*Lynn*? Is it really you? My darling heart – but what are you doing here? This is incredible!'

He enveloped me in a sweaty bear hug and for a split second I wanted nothing more than to return it, to fit my head into that familiar groove between his collarbone and his hot neck ... until I realised that all he was trying to do was to edge me around so that he completely blocked my view of April.

'Looking for you,' I said, my voice muffled against his chest. 'Darling.'

'Wow. I don't know how you did it, but you found me. And spoilt the surprise!' He rubbed the back of my skull. 'You've cut all your hair off! It looks ... it's very short ... but it suits you. I think.'

I knew he'd hate it. This was good; two fingers up at him. Thankfully I managed to resist his embrace.

'What surprise?' I wriggled free and pushed him away, my forefinger pressing his chest until he was at arm's length.

He grabbed my hand, a hurt expression on his face. 'You aren't wearing your rings!'

I almost laughed. 'Ed ... that's the least of your problems right now. We need to talk, don't we? And – what surprise?'

'Well, that's one of the things we'll talk about! I can't believe you're here! Have you just arrived? Let's go and get some lunch, shall we?'

I wanted to say yes, just to see how he'd manage to negotiate leaving April asleep on a towel without telling her where he was going, but decided against it. I was going to play this my way.

'Tell you what,' I said instead, 'I'm not feeling great at the moment. Bit of a dodgy stomach. Something I ate, probably. I was about to go back to sleep it off. So how about an early dinner tonight, at your villa? You could cook something for me, or get some room service in.'

'It's hardly a villa. Little cottage, more like.' He hesitated, scratched his salty hair.

'What's the matter, don't you want to? Are you here with someone, is that it?'

Would he really pretend he wasn't? If I shouted April's name, she'd hear me. My stomach constricted like an egg timer being flipped.

'What?' He shaded his eyes from the sun. 'With someone? A *woman,* do you mean?' He shook his head slightly and I was almost impressed – he seemed genuinely puzzled, as if unaware his mistress – my friend – was lying asleep on a towel a hundred feet away from us.

Then he took my little finger gently, the way he used to. 'Lynn – you're right, we do need to talk. There's so much I need to explain...'

'You're not kidding.'

'But it's incredible that you're here! I'm so happy. It's so weird, you know. I might as well tell you now – the surprise was that I was going to ring you tomorrow and get you over. I was actually planning to buy you a plane ticket later today!'

'Really.'

'Yes! Look, Lynn – I know I owe you a massive apology for not being in touch, but I can explain, if you'll let me. I wanted to get everything ready for you, then give you a holiday of a lifetime out here, you know, after all you've been through in the last year, having to look after me and then deal with me vanishing like that ... you deserve so much better.'

I made a sardonic grunting sound and Ed looked desolate.

'So that's what you concluded – that I was having some mad affair with another woman and we'd run off together?'

The fucking brass neck of him. 'Well, that's part of it.'

'Oh, Lynn ... As if! I love *you*. Always have. You're my girl.' He went to hug me again and this time I let him, standing on a white beach on a tiny little island thousands of miles from home, the sun beating down on us, soaking his lies into the hot skin of my shoulders.

'So – tonight?'

'OK,' he said. 'But let me come to you.'

No chance. I pretended to think about it for a moment.

'No – kind of you to offer, but my room's tiny so we'd have to have dinner in the restaurant, and we need to talk in private. I want you all to myself. Where are you staying?'

Once he realised I was adamant, he gave me his address on the island without batting an eyelid, even going so far as to grab my hand and tell me he wasn't sure if he could wait that long. I was so tempted to say, 'Great. Just let me go and say hi to April first,' but I managed not to. String him along as long as possible, I thought.

'See you at five then. Let's make it early, I've still got jetlag.' I turned to go but he grabbed my wrist and gave me a Judas kiss on the cheek that almost made my eyes fill. I walked back to my Mule having to curse him with the worst swearwords I could think of, in rhythm with my footsteps. I was pretty sure that rage and adrenaline would be the only fuels keeping me going from that point on.

52

I thought about the satisfaction to be gained from showing up early, just to see the look on their faces, but instead I was bang on time, parking my Mule on the mountaintop road by a turning with a hand-painted sign saying 'Surf View'. The lane led to a small villa discreetly screened from the road by beautifully manicured hibiscus bushes.

The vista opened up ahead, a stunning backdrop of azure sea and turquoise sky spread far below me, beyond a riot of flowering plants marking the divide between cliff and cottage garden: spiky birds of paradise, delicate jasmine blooms, orchids of different colours. I smelled barbecue and the ever-present frangipani. A small plunge pool adjoined the marble verandah, water trickling down an artfully placed pile of stones to imitate a natural waterfall.

Ed must have been looking out for me, as he flung open the front door when I approached. 'Ta da!' he said, spreading his arms wide. 'Do you like it?'

'It's gorgeous. Really pretty. Will you show me round?' I handed him the bottle of wine I'd bought that afternoon.

'Sure. How did you get up here?'

He opened the front door into a cool, spacious living area, deco-rated in neutral shades of grey, sand and white.

'Cab,' I lied. I wanted him to think I was going to drink as much as I intended to get him to.

'You look beautiful,' he said. 'Your hair is growing on me.'

I didn't bother to make the obvious pun.

Predictably, there was no sign of April, nothing out of place except Ed's swim shorts left on the coffee table and an open copy of a book about how to improve your golf. I almost smirked at the thought of how they must have been running around like headless chickens trying to get all her stuff hidden. Where was she? Biting her nails in a bar somewhere, hopefully, the treacherous bitch.

'Golf?' I picked up the book and glanced at it.

'There's an amazing course on Canouan, the next island over. Going to play golf by boat, how cool is that? Even I can't go diving *every* day. Hey, the diving here is incredible. I can't wait to take you. I thought we'd go next week when I was planning for you to arrive, but now you're already here, maybe we could go out tomorrow? You could take your PADI qualification! Do you remember, you were going to do it in Greece that time but you got a tummy bug and couldn't. How is your tummy, by the way? Are you feeling better?'

'I'm fine now.' I replaced the book on the table, trying to quash the sense of desolation I felt on hearing him use the word 'tummy'. He'd always done it and I'd always found it massively endearing. 'Let's not get ahead of ourselves. We've got a lot of things to sort out first.'

'Ah. Yes. Sort out. Of course. How did you know I was here, by the way?' His voice very much had the tone of someone who was forcing himself to sound casual.

'The phone bill, basically, from when you booked. That, and some educated guesses. Got any beer?' I wandered into the kitchen and opened the fridge, which contained four bottles of Banks wine – Ed's favourite – and a couple of mangos. I took out two beers and uncapped them on the edge of the kitchen counter. Ed laughed again. 'I've really missed seeing you do that,' he said, accepting his and knocking back most of it in a couple of gulps. 'Cheers, Liz. *So* good to have you here. Let's go and admire the view.'

Who the hell was Liz?

'Who's *Liz*?'

'What?'

'You just called me Liz!'

He looked confused. 'No, I didn't.'

'You did. I thought we'd put all that nonsense behind us now?' No need to be sympathetic, not any more.

He opened his mouth as if to speak and then changed his mind, looking genuinely shocked.

'You were going to show me around?' I put the cold bottle against my hot cheeks in turn, deciding not to press the point yet, not until I'd heard what he had to say.

'There's not much else to see. Bathroom.' He flung open a door to reveal a large and luxurious wet room. One toothbrush by the basin, one wash bag.

'And bedroom.' He ushered me through to the final room, smaller than the living room but spacious and light, perfectly tidy, the white bedspread smooth and scattered with pink petals, five white pillows of different sizes arranged with mathematical neatness.

There was an unfamiliar red suitcase on the floor by the wardrobe.

'Whose is that?'

'Mine.' He had the grace to look sheepish. 'I, er, bought it at the airport. The whole thing was very spur of the moment.'

'I see.' *Lying arsehole.* 'So, are we eating then? I'm starving.'

I wasn't remotely hungry.

'Yes – it's outside.'

I followed him out onto the verandah to a small, white wrought-iron table, an ostentatious-looking seafood salad in a bowl between two place settings. We sat down and he served me a portion, dropping fat prawns and cherry tomatoes through the gaps in the lattice table-top. His hand was shaking slightly and I was glad to see it – he wasn't as in control as he wanted me to think.

The only sound was the water bubbling into the plunge pool and the tweeting of invisible birds in the trees above. Bright flowers in pots decorated the patio and an ammonite embedded in a great lump of rock sat by the doors.

'That looks delicious. Did you make it?'

He shook his head. 'I'd say yes, but I'd be lying. I ordered it.'

Ed, lying? Surely not.

I took a forkful to show willing. 'It's good. So...'

'So,' he echoed.

'Want to talk me through why you decided to leave the country without telling me, emptying our joint savings account at the same time?'

He sighed. 'I'm so sorry. I really am. I had my lunch that day with Bill – we went to a little Lebanese place near his clinic – and he warned me that the Pick's might come back, that it was brilliant that it appeared I'd been cured, but it could have been some sort of anomaly that they'd have to keep a very close eye on, and he wanted me to take part in tons more studies and suddenly I felt myself getting panicky and depressed, and we got quite pissed—'

'Bill, who I'd never heard of before and who the police could find no trace of when they tried to get hold of him? Bill, who there was no record of at the clinic?'

Ed shrugged, peeling the label off his already-empty bottle of beer. 'He exists. You met him! That was only his temporary office, he told me, while his regular one was being decorated. Anyway, we talked about me having been ill, and how extraordinary it was that the trial worked so incredibly quickly and so well, and how hard it had been on me and you when I was ill, thinking I was going the way Dad went and, I don't know, the depression got worse and worse. I felt suicidal, Lynn, perhaps it was delayed shock, I don't know. I stood on the platform at Waterloo after lunch and I couldn't shake the sense that the Pick's would come back for me, that I couldn't possibly have been healed for good, it was some sort of temporary blip...'

His eyes were full of tears and he scrubbed his arm across his face. God, he was good.

'What about the money? Why did you take it all out? There was ninety grand in that account!'

He leaned forward and grabbed my hand, holding it tight in his sweaty palm. 'I wasn't thinking straight, Lynn. I just had this mad idea that I wanted to get away, on my own for a bit and then send for you. I didn't want to tell you because you'd have been upset at the idea of me going without you...'

'Not as upset as Ben and I were at the thought of you lying in a mortuary drawer somewhere,' I interrupted, but I let him continue to hold my hand. He had the grace to look ashamed.

'I transferred the money into a new account online. I thought I'd need your signature but it turns out I didn't. I was hoping you wouldn't notice. It's still our money though. I hadn't actually intended to transfer the whole amount, I was only going to take nine grand for our holiday, but I was drunk when I did it, and only realised later that I'd accidentally added an extra zero. Obviously I'll put the rest of it back!'

I rolled my eyes. 'But, Ed, you took your passport with you. That means that you must have planned it.'

'I didn't plan it!' he retorted hotly, as if he was outraged I'd think such a thing. 'I'd taken that canvas bag with me, remember, just for my laptop and headphones and stuff, and found my passport in the side pocket when I was on the train on the way up to town! I didn't know it was in there; I haven't used it for years. It was what gave me the idea. As soon as I saw it, I wanted to run away, just for a little while. I thought, I've got my passport and I could get money – originally I thought I might head over to Spain then I decided to come out here, have a week of fishing and relaxing and getting my head together, then bring you out to join me. It's been so many years since I could face getting on a plane, and it felt so liberating. Rush of blood to the head, you could say. I stayed a couple of nights in a hotel at Heathrow first but I was still on too much of a bender to bring myself to call you. I sobered up halfway across the Atlantic wondering what the fuck I was doing, but it was too late by then.'

His lies were almost entertaining. Almost.

'You told me that morning that even though you'd managed to have scans, you were still afraid of flying. And you can't have been that drunk at Heathrow – the police just told me that you were interviewed at the airport. You were convincing enough that they let you fly.'

Even he couldn't answer that. We sat in silence and I watched a tiny iridescent hummingbird hover next to a hibiscus bloom, before darting away into the bushes.

Ed was gazing at me now with what looked like such love that even though he didn't have a good answer, even though I'd seen April with my own eyes, I still thought I must surely be mistaken.

I wanted so much to be mistaken.

I suddenly felt twice as hot as before, as if sweat was popping out of every single one of the pores on my body, and felt an urge to jump into the pool.

'I'm going to open that wine.'

I headed back inside to the air-conditioned coolness of the kitchen, found the glasses and uncorked the white wine. I poured him an enormous glass and myself a much smaller one that I topped up with water from a jug on the counter, making sure that Ed hadn't seen me do it. He was still outside, gazing at a piece of squid on his fork. My phone was in the pocket of my dress, so I took it out and surreptitiously switched on the voice recorder app before replacing it. I didn't think that he was likely to confess to any crimes more serious than an affair with April, and I knew that even if he did, it was unlikely anything I captured would be admissible in court, but it was worth a try.

'I'm glad you're safe,' I blurted when I returned, the bottle tucked under my arm and the phone recording in my pocket. I handed him his glass and forced myself not to reach out and touch his face. His cheek looked hot and bristly, wonderfully familiar. The marionette lines either side of his mouth seemed to have deepened since I last saw him, and the creases on his forehead, but I wanted him. To my fury, I wanted to rip off his clothes right there, and not just to force a confession out of him. We hadn't had sex for months – but he'd been ill (hadn't he?) and anyway, surely even the most passionate couple didn't carry on swinging from the chandeliers after almost a decade together. He was sixty, after all. Sixty today.

I wasn't ready to wish him happy birthday though.

'I know you and April had an affair,' I said, making it easy for him. I held my breath and waited for his expression to change.

But he merely rubbed his hand through his sandy hair, making it stand on end.

'Of course we didn't,' he said mildly. 'I would never cheat on you. I love you, Lynn.'

'And you honestly didn't plan this trip in advance? Just … took off?'

He swigged his wine, as I knew he would. He always drank when he felt pressured. I topped up his glass.

'That's about the size of it.'

'I see.'

'Don't you believe me?' He sounded hurt.

'Well,' I said, in the same tone as if I'd asked him to pass the salt, 'it's all a bit of stretch, don't you think? What with the savings going missing and all.'

'I told you, that was an accident. I only meant to borrow some of them. They're still our savings, darling. And I did it all for you.'

I clenched my teeth, forced myself to smile and raised my glass, clinking it against his. 'That's a relief. I would hate to lose you.'

'And I you. I really do love you, Lynn.'

I decided to continue to play along, although what I felt for him at that moment was very far from love. 'I love you too. Cheers.'

I clinked glasses with him and took a gulp of my watery wine. 'So now I'm here, let's start our holiday, shall we?'

He grinned with relief, believing he was at least temporarily off the hook. 'Cheers to that.'

I don't know how I managed it, but for the next half-hour my acting skills matched Ed's. I was determine to lull him into a false sense of security to see what I could get out of him once his guard was down and his alcohol levels up. To any casual observer we would have appeared as a normal married couple on holiday. We chatted; about Ben, about Ed's 'illness'. The cat. Suzan. Naveeta's love life, April's holistic sheep farm. Memories of our lives together, plans for the future. He fetched another bottle of wine from the kitchen and I drank as little of it as I could while ensuring he drank as much, until I noticed his speech beginning to slur slightly.

I also noticed that he changed the subject when I mentioned Mike's name.

How cocky he was, to think he could get drunk and not slip up.

Our heads were edging closer together, our eyes locked. Chemistry fizzed and crackled between us and, perhaps because I knew it would be the last time we would ever be that close, I encouraged it. I forced myself to pretend it was real, that we were fine.

It was dark by the time our lips touched, the black shapes of bats flitting around us, zoomorphic winged fibs. We kissed harder. I put my hand in his lap and felt him hard under my fingers.

'I've missed you so much,' he said.

'I've missed you too.'

'I want you, Lynn.'

We stood up, Ed so fast that his metal chair clanged to the ground. I took his hand to steady him and we clung to one another. He pushed me up against the wall of the villa and stuck his hand up inside my sundress, saying my name over and over again, suddenly as soft and damply vulnerable as a newly hatched baby bird, as if all the strength in his body had diverted itself to his hard dick.

I couldn't risk my phone falling out of my pocket and him seeing that it was recording – and besides, I suddenly felt a wave of revulsion for him as I mentally recalled the sight of him and April on that beach towel earlier.

'No,' I said forcefully, shoving him away. 'No.'

Time to go in for the kill.

53

'What's the matter?' he asked, alarmed, but trying to hide the traces of anger settling in the creases by his eyes.

I took a deep breath and squared up to him, every muscle in my body tensed for flight. I kept my voice level, though:

'Can we just stop this ... this ... *charade*? Right now. You need to start giving me some credit, Ed! I've thought about nothing else since you vanished. I hoped that by tracking you down I'd be able to put my mind at rest – but you've confirmed all my worst suspicions.'

His body jerked, once, and he stalled for time. I couldn't read his expression any more.

'What?'

'I know April's here, for fuck's sake. I saw her on the beach with you earlier! But what doesn't make sense is for you to fake Pick's for all those months, just to be with her. You wouldn't be that cruel to Ben, not unless there was more to it.'

He was rigid now. I felt behind me on the table for the empty wine bottle, just in case.

This was it. No going back.

'Bill was a fake, there was no medical trial. Your illness was faked and I bet those scans were, too. April helped you. You did it so you had an alibi for killing Mike – but why would you need to kill Mike? You and April only needed to get divorces if you wanted to be together, so there's more to it. This is all about you having killed Shelagh, isn't it, Ed? And I tell you something else, just from a Polaroid photo I found of your old house, I've worked out what you did with her body.'

With one powerful movement he sprang at me and grabbed my throat with both hands, choking me. Shit. He'd been too fast for me.

I tried to swing at him with the bottle but he released one hand and easily disarmed me.

'Oh dear,' he hissed in my ear, my husband gone and replaced in a flash with this murderous stranger. 'I'd really hoped it wouldn't come to this. Let's hear it then, Miss Marple – how exactly do you think I killed Shelagh? Like *this*?'

He squeezed harder.

'Turns out you *are* smarter than I gave you credit for,' he said, squeezing so hard that black spots danced before my eyes and my feet went numb. 'I didn't think you'd work it out. I wish you hadn't, though, because obviously I'm not going to be able to let you go home now.'

Of course it had occurred to me that I'd be in danger by confronting Ed, and Maddie's warning rang in my ears, about calling the police if I needed to. I'd re-written my will, for God's sake! Yet now it was happening, I felt nothing but surprise and shock.

I could feel myself losing consciousness, but at the last minute he loosened his grip and pincered my forearms instead, pulling me up and frogmarching me over to the same wall we'd just kissed against. There was no passion in the way he shoved me against it this time.

I'd researched the emergency number, 8111, but how could I call it? And anyway, he'd have killed me long before anyone showed up ... I heaved air into my lungs, coughing and gagging. 'Let me go, Ed, unless you want me to be sick in your face.'

He let go of one arm, enough to allow me to twist round. I retched and pretended to vomit – it wasn't difficult, my stomach really was contracting – and he released the pressure on my upper arm enough for me to double over. I gathered all my strength, tensed my muscles then jabbed my free elbow into his groin, with as much weight behind it as I could.

He groaned and let go of me, cupping his hands instinctively over his crotch. I leaned sideways and karate-kicked him in the face, although the impact knocked me over, too. He was winded, which gave me time enough to scramble to my feet and grab the stone fossil by the door – it was so heavy that I felt my arms almost pull out of their sockets but I managed to heft it as if it weighed nothing. I jumped onto his chest, pinning his arms down with my knees and holding the fossil above his face. It was the size and girth of a beach ball and would shatter his head like an egg if I dropped it.

'You bitch,' he managed, blood pouring out of his nose and mouth.

'You strangled Shelagh, didn't you, then you dumped her body in an acid bath at one of those door-stripping places and destroyed the evidence.'

He froze. My arms ached and shook from holding the stone and my throat throbbed, but I gritted my teeth and blocked out the pain. *Please still be recording,* I silently beseeched my iPhone.

'And now, unless you want me to drop this on your face, I want to hear you say that you killed Mike, too. You faked Pick's for almost a year for the sole purpose of getting me to lock you in a bedroom at nights so you'd have an alibi for his murder. Correct?'

Ed didn't answer, but I knew I was right.

'Why, Ed? Money? Did someone pay you to do it? Did he find out you'd killed Shelagh, is that it?'

He didn't reply, not even struggling any more. I felt the flex of his biceps pinned beneath my knees and the warmth of his prone body under my thighs.

My husband.

The man who knew that spicy food and hot soup gave me hiccups, that I was prone to blisters, that I hated anchovies and cooked celery. The man who brought me soup in bed when I was recovering from flu, feeding it to me in tender spoonfuls. The man who knew everything about me.

Almost everything. There was one thing he didn't know; how and why we originally met.

That's what I'd always believed, anyway.

Without warning, he bucked hard enough to knock one of my legs off his right arm, giving him the velocity to roll sideways, jerking his head out of the way within millimetres of the ammonite as I dropped it. It smashed on the ground next to him and shattered into pieces.

Within an instant our roles were reversed and he had my arm

twisted up behind my back again and my face pressed painfully into the shards of stone.

What he said next shook every happy memory of our years together straight out of my head, forever.

'So, *PC* Waites, not as good a cop as you think, are you? You thought you were so clever but you know what? I've known what you were since before I proposed to you; why the hell else do you think I'd have married you? I used to follow you when you went off to meet your, what did you call him? Your handler. Metcalfe, wasn't it? God, how it made me laugh. Yes, I killed Shelagh, but it was an accident, and yes I killed Mike because the fucker has been blackmailing me for the last three years, he found out about me and April, and he already had a good idea about Shelagh, but you can't prove it, and you won't live to. Interesting, though, how *you* can accuse *me* of lying – our whole fucking relationship has been a lie.'

He yanked me to my knees and before I could wriggle out of his grip, he had lifted me round my waist like a sack of coal. I screamed as loudly as I could but with bewildering speed he lugged me to the edge of the plunge pool and dropped me in.

Goodbye, iPhone voice recording.

The cold water closed over my head and as I tried to right myself I felt Ed's big hands pressing me down, holding me under.

Goodbye, Waitsey...

No no no no, I'd got this far, it couldn't end this way. It couldn't ... My chest compressed and contorted and I felt pressure build behind my eyes. I thrashed about, trying to shake him off, my arm agony where he'd twisted it but he had his fingers entwined in my hair and it was impossible to get out of his grip. Kaleidoscopic colours danced and swirled behind my eyelids and I felt my movements grow weaker. I couldn't fight him. I couldn't breathe.

This was really it, and it was so sudden and brutal.

I prayed and struggled to the best of my muddled abilities and then my thoughts simply began to dissolve in the stilling water, no longer fizzing like aspirin but just slowly melting away into nothingness.

54

Then, through the dark water, the distorted sound of another voice screaming. I felt the pressure on the crown of my head replaced by the cloying Mustique night air.

Arms dragged me to safety, yanking and rolling me awkwardly onto the ground, choking and coughing again to get the water out of my lungs. Where was Ed? I opened my eyes slowly to see a silhouetted figure crouching down in front of where I lay spluttering and panting on my side.

'Oh my God, Lynn, I'm so sorry, you have to believe me, I didn't know he'd killed anyone, let alone Mike. He killed my husband...?'

'April,' I croaked. 'Where's Ed?'

April sobbed. She was deathly grey-white beneath a suntan, tears and mascara all over her face, her hair matted and her body shaking with emotion.

'He's here ... I think he's dead.'

She moved away from me and, through my double vision I saw two Aprils pick up two limp hands and feel for a pulse. Then the two Aprils began to attempt CPR, pounding on Ed's chest and wailing. I crawled over to them and tried to push her away.

'Get off him.'

She shook me off. 'But he's not breathing!'

'Good. Leave him, April, or I swear to God I'll kill you.'

I couldn't have killed her if I'd tried, though. I had no strength in me at all, but she sat back on her haunches and stared at me, wild-eyed.

'What happened?' I asked, my voice rasping and unfamiliar.

She nudged her chin towards the heavy iron chair, now lying by the pool with a dark stain on it. 'I ... I ... hit him with the back of that,' she whispered.

Because he was drowning me, or because she heard him admit to killing Mike? At that moment I didn't even care. I was just glad that my husband was dead and I was alive.

'Have you been here all along?'

April nodded. The tears pouring down her face kept my own eyes resolutely dry. 'I was in the bushes with my suitcase. He thought I'd gone out but I wanted to hear what he said to you. I heard everything. I didn't know, Lynn, I swear. I didn't know he'd killed my Mike. I thought he'd been murdered 'cos one of his dodgy business deals went wrong, that he'd pissed the wrong person off. I didn't know Mike was blackmailing him. I never thought it could be Ed ... I'd never have ... I wouldn't...'

She tailed off. I felt a swirl of dizziness but forced myself to focus, getting onto my hands and knees like a dog to drop my head as the blood returned. My face throbbed.

'Can you get me some painkillers? We need to work out what we're going to do.'

April obeyed, staggering into the villa and returning with a glass of water, a roll of kitchen paper and a box of paracetamol. I took four tablets, thinking that I should probably drink the rest of the water, but finding that I couldn't. There was so much water in me already that I felt like frogspawn, gelid, drowning from the inside.

About ten minutes later my double vision had gone and I could breathe properly again. We were both sitting on loungers on either side of Ed's blood-soaked body. April had put down kitchen roll around his head, to try and stem the slow thick spread of blood across the marble verandah.

'Why would Mike blackmail Ed?' I asked. 'It's not like you guys needed the money.'

April gave a sob. 'The thing is, we did need it. Everyone thinks we were so loaded but we weren't! Mike did sell the company for a shit-load of money, but he spent and owed most of it, then lost the rest on the stock market and wouldn't admit it to anyone. All of it, Lynn!'

She sounded almost accusing, as if Mike's profligacy and bad financial planning was my fault.

'But where did Ed get the money to pay him? Our savings were all still there till a few days ago.'

April shrugged. 'He must have had a secret account. He did once tell me that he got seventy grand more for his and Shelagh's house than he told you. I remember that we laughed about you not knowing.'

I wanted to kill her, and it helped me stay calm. Hate was a more empowering emotion than betrayal.

'Then there was Shelagh's life insurance,' she mused, almost as if she was talking to herself. 'That was a *hell* of a lot more than he told you it would be.'

'Right. So it all ended up in yours and Mike's accounts then? Nice to know that we've been bankrolling you for the past few years. My *God*. And I had to go out and get a job because we didn't have enough income. How the hell did you have the brass neck to pretend to be my friend all this time?'

I didn't think I had ever been so disgusted in my entire life.

'I didn't know he was blackmailing Ed,' she insisted, doe-eyed. 'I think that's terrible.'

'Right. So it's fine that you were sleeping with my husband, but you think it's unforgiveable that Mike was extorting money from Ed. You know what? I bet Ed was only shagging you to get his own back on Mike.'

It was a chicken-and-egg situation, a circle of hate and vengeance; was Mike blackmailing Ed because Ed was sleeping with April, or was Ed sleeping with April because Mike was blackmailing him about Shelagh? I supposed I'd never know. Something else occurred to me: 'You *must* have known that Ed killed him, if you knew that he faked having Pick's. You helped him, didn't you? You faked those first scans.'

She couldn't meet my eyes. 'Yes ... I put his name on the films of someone else's diseased brain and printed them out. But he told me he was doing it so that we could run away together. I never would have done it if I'd had any idea he was going to kill Mike ... I didn't want to be with Mike anymore but I'd never, ever have wanted him *dead...*' She tailed off, sobbing again.

'Did you know that Ed killed Shelagh, too?' My head was still pounding but I felt an icy calm settle on me. I was alive. Ed was dead. Ed was a murderer.

She shook her head violently.

I eased myself back on the lounger with difficulty, letting the warm night air soak like dark sunshine into my aching bones.

'So you've been having an affair with my husband since before he and I got together. You let me and Ben go all those months, thinking we were losing him. Top friend you were, April.'

She blustered through her heaving sobs. 'Come on, Lynn, don't play the innocent – let's not forget how you and Ed met. You were trying to get him sent to prison!'

I groaned. So she'd known that all along, too? So many secrets, so many hollow friendships. 'Only at first. Then I stupidly believed he was innocent, and quit the police. Why did you befriend me in the first place then, if you were shagging Ed, and I took him off you?'

She laughed mirthlessly, a kind of huffing sound. 'Because you marrying Ed and me befriending you was the only way I'd get to keep him. If he hadn't seduced you, you'd have had him arrested and locked up. He only did it to stop you investigating him.'

'Ed loved me,' I said hotly, trying not to look at his bleeding body. 'I don't care what you think, or what was going on between you two, but he loved me as well. He wasn't faking it, not all the time anyway. He couldn't have managed that. It was so ... *real...*'

April nodded. 'He did. He loved both of us, he used to tell me so. It kind of made me feel better about it all, in a way. Better about what I was doing to you. But I never believed he'd killed Shelagh. Never!'

I made a scornful noise in my throat that she ignored, continuing: 'At least, I wouldn't let myself believe it. He said he was innocent, that he couldn't face being arrested for something he didn't do, and going through a trial, risking imprisonment ... he said if he married you, then we could just carry on having an affair until he could divorce you and then we could be together. Then you got pregnant and, let's face it, Ed was delighted – for all the wrong reasons.'

That was such a low blow that I felt like crawling right back into that cold pool and letting the water swallow me up for ever this time. Our baby, my only chance at being a mother, and Ed used it to his own ends. Thinking he'd got me properly onside – that he was free and clear. He was probably thrilled when I had a miscarriage.

'He got a vasectomy after that,' April added spitefully. 'That's why you never conceived a second time.'

I vomited again, not caring that it splattered over my feet and legs and the sun lounger I was sitting on, retching and retching until it felt like my insides were being pulled out of me and there was nothing left except foul strings of saliva. The number of times he'd soothed me by saying we'd have another baby, lots of babies, when all along he knew it would never happen ... No wonder he'd refused to go for fertility tests. Right then, if I'd had the energy, I'd have got up and danced on his dead body.

When I finally stopped I wiped my arm over my mouth and turned on April, bunching my hands into fists to stop myself slapping her.

'Could you have *been* any more naive?'

'*Me?*' She shot straight back. 'What about *you*? I believed him, the same way he fooled you! And I wanted to be with him ... I told you, I didn't know Mike was blackmailing him until just now. I was so shocked.'

Even though she seemed to know more about the state of Ed's finances than I did, I realised that I believed her.

'Did Mike find out that Ed killed Shelagh, then? Or was it about you and him? But Mike wouldn't have stayed with you if he'd known, surely.'

'I have no idea. I think he must have found out something – some evidence. I bet he also knew that Ed and I had been lovers; I bet he was doing it to punish him. That's the sort of thing he'd do. Not the other way round – not what you just said: that Ed was only sleeping with me to get at Mike.'

'Whatever. What evidence, though?' I thought of the months I'd spent searching for evidence against Ed, and somehow *Mike* had managed to unearth it? 'And why did they – how could they – carry on being friends under those circumstances? No wonder they didn't want to see so much of each other. That's insane.'

'I have no idea what evidence he got. Maybe he saw something that he didn't realise the significance of till later, like, I don't know, Ed taking her body somewhere at night. Or Ed talking to that homeless guy, the one who confessed. I don't suppose we'll ever know for sure now.'

I suddenly remembered that night when I'd woken from a drugged sleep, sure that I'd seen Mike smoking by the front gate in the early hours. It *had* to have been him. Presumably he'd have wanted cash from Ed, so it wouldn't show up in any bank accounts, and had come to collect. I suspected April was right; Ed must have had an account I didn't know about – possibly the same one he'd just transferred our savings into.

The *last* of our savings, as I now realised.

I looked over at Ed's body again, and then at April, who suddenly resembled a very old lady. I felt the same, like we were two residents propped in wingback armchairs in a swirly carpeted old folks' home, gazing vacantly at a too-loud television – instead of at the dead body of my husband with his skull staved in.

'We need to get rid of him,' I said bluntly.

She lifted her head slowly, like a tortoise. 'What? You aren't going to call Security?'

'I could do. But do you really want Caspar and Monty to find out the truth? How do you think Ben will feel, to learn that his dad killed his mum? That Ed faked the illness and you helped him do it? How could you live with yourself?'

In the light from the kitchen window I could see the white marks on her face in the shape of her sunglasses, the freckles on her nose that I knew only popped out in the sunshine and the slightly wrinkled skin on her cleavage as she processed this. She was utterly familiar and yet suddenly a complete stranger.

'You're just saying that because you don't want it to come out that you were an undercover cop who totally fucked up.'

Had she always been this much of a manipulative bitch? Temper flared in me, mostly because she'd put her finger on exactly what I thought.

I denied it anyway.

'Well, *that's* bullshit. I didn't fuck up – I found no evidence, then I fell in love! But OK, then, have it your way. Let's call security now, tell them everything. I'll be happy to explain that you killed my husband, that you're a liar and a narcissist, not to mention the shittiest, most disloyal friend in the entire history of friendship. You're probably an accessory to the crime of Mike's murder, even if you didn't know it – because you knew all along that Ed was faking Pick's. You'd been cheating on Mike with Ed for years. You benefitted from all the money that Mike blackmailed out of him, while shagging Ed behind our backs. Your children will never speak to you again. You'll go to prison.'

Bitterness like battery acid ate away at me as I visualised April's designer wardrobe and their luxury holidays, funded by my retirement pot.

'Maybe you're right,' she conceded, trying to hide her relief. 'But what do we do with his body?'

I'd been thinking about this. 'We're on top of a cliff, aren't we?' I said slowly. 'We tip him over and hope he gets eaten by sharks. You report him missing tomorrow. I'm going to pretend I was never here at all – at this villa, I mean. People know I was here on the island looking for Ed, but if I'm asked I'll just say I never found him. I'll say I was worried for his mental health, that he was afraid the drugs trial hadn't worked ... The police think he's in Barbados.'

I remembered Ed's face earlier when he'd called me Liz, the genuine shock on it. 'Speaking of the drugs trial, who *was* that Bill guy then? He clearly wasn't a real doctor.'

April looked at the ground. Ants were scurrying around, perhaps attracted by Ed's blood, and she deliberately lifted one foot and began crushing them one by one under her designer flip-flop.

'Stop that,' I snapped and she drew her knees up, wrapping her arms around them and rocking back and fro.

'He was just a petty criminal who could act,' she confessed. 'Ed paid him to pretend he was an old friend and rent that consultancy room, for the one day, just for you to see it and think the whole thing was kosher. He faked the certificates, the lot. I don't know where Ed found him.'

I shook my head. 'He used you, just as much as he used me,' I said. 'You thought he was doing it so you two could play happy families together. But he was only doing it so that I'd give him an alibi for the night he killed Mike, to get him off his back.'

'I can't believe it,' April whispered, crying again. 'I'm sorry.'

I ignored her. 'We're going to have to get rid of all this blood before the cleaners come tomorrow.'

'Thank you, Lynn. Really.' April reached for my hand but I moved away.

'I'm not doing this for *you*. I'd happily see you rot in jail. I just want to keep the kids and, frankly, me, out of it. Come on, we've got to move him.'

I stood up. 'We'll put a bin liner over his head to stop him bleeding through the garden. Can you go and get some?'

April didn't move. She just stared at me, her lip wobbling like a child's. I wanted to slap her.

'I am really, really sorry, Lynn. For all of it. Please forgive me, I know I've been a terrible friend. I did – do – really love you, you know. I always hated myself for being so two-faced, but Ed … was just Ed.'

'He was,' I agreed, 'Thank you for the apology – which you've clearly only made because you've been busted. Now go and get bin liners, and find bleach and mops for later.'

'So do you? Forgive me?'

'No chance,' I said, hobbling towards Ed's body.

The shadowy bats continued to whisk out of the eaves, swooping across to the trees and back as the frogs and cicadas switched up the volume on their night-time serenade.

'And if we do make it back to England without being arrested,' I continued, 'I never, ever want to see you or hear from you again.'

She turned and went inside, leaving me alone on the terrace with Ed's face-down body among the smashed shards of the ammonite.

55

The rest of that night was a blur of heat and trauma. Dragging Ed's corpse through the bushes to the precipice, I forced myself to try and dissociate completely; to turn myself into an automaton with no remorse, no regrets, no emotion. Not then, anyway. Time for that later when this was all over. The bin liner over his head stopped him trailing blood from his skull through the garden, but I was more glad of it because it meant I didn't have to look at his face.

Ripping off the bin liner and rolling him over the edge of the cliff without a word, the sound of his body crashing and bouncing off the rocks on the way down, audible above April's sobs, the tiny splash as he vanished under the surface. It was so, so risky, but we had no other choice.

I thought about forging a suicide note, but decided against it. We'd stick to our story, if questioned: he and April had a row during which he said he was going to top himself, but she didn't believe him as he'd said this before. She would say he stormed out and didn't come back that night. She would then report him missing in the morning, claiming he thought the Pick's was back and couldn't handle it.

If asked, I would maintain I never clapped eyes on either of them while I was in Mustique.

'But I'm bound to be a suspect, if I've got no alibi!' April moaned, as we scrubbed and scrubbed at the marble verandah until all traces of his blood were gone – at least all traces visible to the human eye. If CSI ever showed up in their paper suits and overshoes, we were doomed.

'Your problem,' I said, shortly. 'You killed him. And if you tell the police I was here, we're both screwed. I'll spill the whole story and you'll be in it up to your neck.'

When it began to get light, fluffing up the branches of the bushes, trying to hide the crushed path Ed's body had created. Checking that anything with Ed's blood on it was securely wrapped up, for me to dump in a trash can on my way back to my room. Fishing my dead mobile out of the pond, where it had fallen out of my dress pocket. We worked in silence, nothing left to say, the horror filling any spaces where words might have been.

I was back in my bed by six in the morning. Unless I'd been really unlucky, nobody had seen me.

56

April reported Ed missing later that day. She must have given a very convincing rendition of 'distraught mistress', because when the coastguard found his body two days later, the police from St Vincent and the Grenadines immediately accepted her insistence that he'd been in a suicidal frame of mind when he stormed off.

I had only been home for a day when I received a third visit from Martine and Constable Laurie, who took off their hats and informed me of the sad news that Ed Naismith's body had been recovered from the sea off Mustique where he had been on holiday with his lover. He must have flown on from Barbados to Mustique to meet her. I acted my socks off: the betrayed, bereaved wife, finding out that not only was her husband dead, but that he'd cheated on her with her best friend...

'Was it a sailing accident?' I whispered tearfully, noticing through the open living room door that my suitcase was still in the hallway. Luckily I'd removed the luggage tags.

'Apparently his dementia had returned, or perhaps the trial had showed incorrect results. But he allegedly said he didn't want to live with the illness, and jumped off a cliff.'

For once, Martine was not smiling.

'Oh my God.' I rocked and keened and wailed. Ed would've been proud. 'I thought April was in Australia! How could she do this to me?'

We were all good actors it seemed, when push came to shove.

April and I never did speak again. She didn't pitch up at Ed's funeral, as I'd feared she might, which was a relief because I'd only have had to throw her out. My friends turned out in force to support Ben and me, though: Maddie and Geoff, Suzan, Naveeta, a load of people from MADS and Ed's former GP practice and – to my surprise and gratitude – Alvin and his wife, Sheryl, who I'd never met before. She was lovely, as pretty as her photograph in Alvin's office, but about four foot eleven. She only came up to his chest and must have had a permanent crick in her neck from gazing adoringly up at him. They were both really kind to me, and Alvin begged me to come back to work as soon as I was ready.

'I can't stand the temp,' he said to me mournfully, at the post-service reception back in my house. 'She just doesn't stop *talking!* It's driving me insane. She and Margaret get on like a house on fire. There is no work whatsoever getting done in that office.'

I couldn't help thinking of the lengthy pub lunches we'd enjoyed when I was in the job before.

'I'll come back on Monday,' I announced. 'I need to keep busy ... well, busyish...'

He grinned at me. 'Attagirl. If you're sure. The Big Band tour to Germany is looming early next semester, and you can't miss that.'

When Sheryl turned round to get a sausage roll from the buffet he leaned in and whispered in my ear, 'And I've got no one to have lunch with! The landlord at The Feathers thinks I've been dumped!'

Everyone – apart from Alvin, who kept judiciously quiet – reminisced about Ed for several hours, until eventually they all trickled home again, red-eyed and tipsy. Ben and I slumped on the sofa while Jeanine cleared up around us. My smart black shoes were killing me, so I propped my feet on the coffee table.

'Leave it, darling, I'll do it,' I said wearily.

'It's no problem.'

'Thank you.' I smiled at her. All day I'd been feeling hollow, dry-eyed and businesslike, holding it all together as I played the part of the grieving widow who'd lost her beloved husband to infidelity and suicide, when inside I was full of rage and sorrow. I wanted to stand up during Ben's eulogy and shout that our entire marriage had been a sham. It was only out of affection for Ben – and fear of the consequences – that I didn't.

Only a few of my friends knew that April had been with him on Mustique – the fewer the better, as far as I was concerned. At the wake, a couple of people asked where she was and I just said that as far as I knew she was still in Australia.

But then, after it was all over and there was only me, Ben and Jeanine left, the anger began to seep away for the first time in the couple of weeks since my return from Mustique.

Ed's armchair was empty, its seat cushion still pushed into a hollow by the shape of his bum. His books were still on the shelf, many with pages dog-eared by his fingers. When I took one down and flicked through it, I found what looked like one of his nose hairs stuck to the flyleaf. Ben was there, looking just like him. It was as if Ed was just in the kitchen chopping onions, or over at the lock studio doing whatever it was he used to do over there, and I couldn't believe that he wouldn't come in at any minute.

Then it occurred to me that mostly what he would have been doing over at the studio was planning this elaborate charade to get Mike off his back, to stop the blackmail...

I wish he could have told me. But of course he couldn't, for to do that would have meant confessing that he really did kill Shelagh – or at least opening up that particular Pandora's Box again, and he'd known all along I'd been in the police. I wondered how – and what – Mike had found out. I agonised for ages about whether to tell Metcalfe, to make amends for the hopeless job I'd done first time around. The boys were all adults. They'd just have to cope with it.

But I didn't. It was too risky. I was relieved that Gavin Garvey had taken his own life, because I couldn't have lived with myself knowing that an innocent man was in jail. I wondered what Ed had done to Garvey to make him confess ... perhaps that was what Mike had discovered. I would probably never know.

'Lynn? Are you OK?'

Ben crossed the room and knelt down in front of me, looking into my face and touching my knee. The unexpected affection from him finished me off and I crumpled. I couldn't tell the police.

'I miss him!' I wailed, burying my head in my hands and sobbing properly, for the first time since Ed's death.

'So do I,' said Ben, crying again, too. 'I can't believe he was cheating on you. I'm so sorry, Lynn.' He came and sat on one side of me and Jeanine squeezed onto the sofa on my other side. All three of us stayed there for a long time, holding on to one another.

'It must have been his illness. At least we won't have to watch him suffer,' I said eventually.

Ironically, the autopsy had concluded that he did have signs of early dementia after all. I wasn't sure if this made me feel better or worse.

That night, after Ben and Jeanine finally left and I was alone, I took a big roll of black bin liners and started getting rid of Ed's stuff. All the books, designer jeans and cashmere jumpers in the garage in one pile for charity – I'd let Ben have a sift through them first in case he wanted anything – photographs and toiletries in another to be dumped, and then lastly, the box folder from under the floorboards in the loft. The one that he'd apparently known about since before I even put it up there. I took it out into the garden and burned it on the bonfire that Ed had started building just a few weeks earlier.

I went back to work the following week, immediately knowing I'd done the right thing, even though Fairhurst House was very quiet and the place seemed dead without the students. The academic year had finished a month ago and there was very little to do, apart from administering a few commercial bookings in the recording studio next door, and finalising the plans for the Big Band concert tour. Alvin was around a fair bit, as he was composing a new symphony up in his office, and a few of the lecturers and support staff were in and out, but Margaret and I mostly had the place to ourselves.

Then she went on holiday for a week – hiring a narrowboat in France with her partner, she informed me – at the same time that Alvin and Sheryl went away for a couple of days, and I found myself completely alone in Fairhurst. Both Alvin and Margaret had fussed over me, worried about leaving me on my own, but I brushed it off:

'I've got loads to do. I'm going to reorganise the music library, it'll take me all week.'

'Well, call me if you need me,' said Alvin. 'I'm only at the in-laws. Probably be glad of an excuse to attend to an emergency at work.'

'Want me to flood one of the bathrooms for you?'

He laughed. 'No need to go that far, although it's a tempting offer. Look after yourself, OK?' He paused. 'And it doesn't have to be an emergency, Lynn – even if you just need to chat to someone, I'm at the end of a phone.'

'Thank you,' I said, giving his knobbly, angular torso a brief hug.

The next day, four hours spent alphabetising dusty sheet music in a cupboard focussed my mind enough to make a decision: it was time to make the call I'd been thinking about since I got home.

I was going to get in touch with Adrian. I needed to see him – and now I was single again, there was no reason not to.

I washed my grubby hands and called his number, leaving him a voicemail whilst wondering if he was screening my call, or really not available.

'Hi. It's me. I know I said I wouldn't contact you again – but things have changed. Drastically. Give me a ring, I'll fill you in. I'd love to see you again.' I hesitated. 'I've really missed you, Adrian.'

I winced, remembering howling the same words to Ben after the funeral, about Ed. Although hadn't Ed's own actions proved it was possible to love more than one person? April had insisted he loved us both.

I decided not to feel guilty about Adrian any more.

He rang me back later that evening as I was sitting in the studio across at the lock, Ed's yellow oilskin coat still hanging behind the door, a huge glass of red wine in my hand. We talked for a few minutes, but I refused to tell him on the phone what had happened. 'Can I tell you in person?' I asked, turning my back to the oilskin and watching the evening light on the river as it flowed steadily past, wishing the water could take all my bad memories away with it. I found myself doing the same thing most evenings.

'Lunch tomorrow?' he asked. Hearing his voice gave me a pang of comfort and I wished I'd told him more, earlier. Perhaps there was something he could have done.

'I'll be at work – but it's dead up there at the moment. You could come and meet me and we'll go to the pub.'

'Sure. Text me the address then, and I'll see you at one. Oh, and Waitsey?'

He wasn't supposed to call me that. Not that it mattered anymore. 'Yes?'

'I've missed you, too.'

I spent the next morning at Fairhurst in a lather of anticipation, occupying myself by tidying up the instrument store. I moved various discarded parts of the gamelan, put guitar cases into neatly stacked rows and dusted the ancient old double bass that leaned against the wall by the door, looking at my watch every five minutes.

At 12.30 I washed my hands and face, combed my hair and put on some bright red lipstick, wondering as I gazed in the mirror if Adrian would think I'd aged, after all this stress. I felt like I had.

At 12.50, the buzzer on the front door sounded and I jumped. Through the security camera I saw Adrian's tall, stooped figure looming in grainy monochrome. Wiping my sweaty palms on my jeans, I went out and opened the door myself, rather than buzzing him in.

Then we were face to face. For a moment we just stood there and then he beamed, spreading his arms wide. 'Waitsey – sorry, Lynn. Good to see you, girl.'

'Hi,' I said, as coolly as I could, grinning back at him. 'Come on in.'

I kissed him on both cheeks and ushered him inside. Strangely, I didn't get the frisson of lust I usually did, not straightaway. If I was honest, he looked a bit ... seedy. He had far too much aftershave on, clearly an expensive one, but ridiculously overpowering, and a brown leather jacket I disliked.

'Cool place to work,' he commented, taking in the honeycomb-panelled ceiling of the hallway, the wooden bishop on the newel post and the elaborately carved door of the admin office.

'It's been like the *Marie Celeste* today – literally, we are the only people in the entire building. Coffee? Or do you want to go straight out for lunch?'

'Lunch, I think! I'm starving. We can do coffee after.'

We drove in my car to The Feathers, the same pub that Alvin and I frequented for our lunches. I installed Adrian at a table under a large faded green parasol in the small walled garden, while I went in to order sandwiches and a bottle of wine.

I was fizzing with the unfamiliar sensation of anticipation as I carried the tray back out, warm sun beating down on the crown of my head.

He watched me approach, his gaze appraising and appreciative as he lit up a cigarette, turning his head away to exhale two streams of smoke through his nostrils.

'You've started smoking proper fags again?'

The garden was filling up around us, office workers mostly, plus a rowdy table full of builders drinking Cokes and playing a game to see who could flip the most beermats off the edge of the table. I poured us both a glass of wine.

'It's the stress. Been worried about you, Waitsey,' he said, making a silly face. 'So, come on, spit it out – where had your other half gone, and did he come back?'

It was still hard to say out loud. I took a gulp of wine and looked away, at a sparrow fluffing its feathers on the pub's wall.

'He's dead. He took all our savings and ran off with one of my best friends. April, not Maddie,' I clarified. I'd talked about both of them to him.

'Shit. I'm so sorry, Lynn. What happened?'

'He took her on a swanky holiday to Mustique, they had a row, he jumped over a cliff. They found his body a couple of days later. I'd sort of suspected it but it was still a shock.'

'So did he really have Pick's?'

Adrian squeezed my leg. I let him.

'Yeah. Perhaps that was why he jumped; couldn't handle the fact that he wasn't really cured. Or maybe he felt guilty. Or maybe he was just pissed and fell. I'll never know.'

We sat drinking in silence for a few minutes. I took off my thin cardigan and tied it round my waist.

'Every time I see someone do that, it reminds me of you,' he said, still caressing my leg. Part of me thought this was insensitive and rather inappropriate, given what I'd just told him, but another part of me disagreed and didn't want him to stop. Even his aftershave was growing on me.

'Really?' I hadn't been aware that I did it all that often. I looked at my watch. 'Wow, it's two o'clock already. I'd better get back.'

'Thought you said that no one's around?'

'They aren't. But I don't want to take the piss.' I leaned slightly toward him. 'Want to come back for coffee?'

'Great,' he said, as I picked up the empty bottle and stuck it upside-down in the ice-bucket.

'Come on then.'

I drove carefully back to Fairhurst, my heart pounding, the scent of Adrian's aftershave filling my car.

I swiped us into the still-empty building and headed along the corridor to the kitchenette, outside the instrument store. He followed me and stood watching as I filled the kettle and took a teaspoon out of the drawer. Sexual energy crackled between us like static.

I made two coffees and handed him one, just as his phone rang.

Funny thing about Adrian and his phone. He never usually had it with him when we used to meet, to the point that the sound of its ring startled me. He never took any photos of us together, or showed me any of his. I'd never asked to see any, because I didn't want to be reminded of his family, the little family that I might have been instrumental in splitting up. He always claimed that I was the only one he'd ever had an affair with – but he was very vague about the reasons he left the police, and my instinct told me it had something to do with another woman. I wished he had told me, if there had been other women. It would have made me feel less guilty about our liaisons in his dead mum's cottage all those years ago. But all he would ever say about the reason he left in disgrace was that a colleague had 'stitched him up'; he refused to go into details.

He put his coffee down next to mine on the draining board and delved into an inside pocket of his jacket. Extracting the phone, he squinted at the screen and killed the call. 'Well, they can wait,' he said, about to put it back in his pocket. I caught a glance of the phone's wallpaper, a photo of a handsome, dark-haired young man leaning against a souped-up red sports car.

'Hold on a sec, that's never your Kit? How old is he now?' I reached out to grab the phone, but to my surprise he snatched it away.

'What? Let's see.'

Adrian scowled at me. 'You've never shown any interest in him before. Why are you so interested now?'

'I – wow. Sorry. I didn't realise it was an issue. It's not that I'm not interested in him ... I just ... still feel guilty that you and I were sneaking around together when he was just a little boy. Come on, let's see? What does he do now?'

I knew that Adrian met up with him occasionally, that he was about Ben's age, but little more than that. Shit, I thought. I'd obviously hit a nerve. But if he'd wanted me to show more interest, why hadn't he talked about him more? I'd assumed he didn't want to.

I supposed, looking back, that the conversations during our recent liaisons had been very dominated by Ed's supposed illness and strange behaviour.

'I'm really sorry,' I repeated, grasping his wrist. 'I've been so self-obsessed. Show me. I want to see.'

Something weird was going on. The sexual tension was gone and the silence in the empty house seemed heavy with resonance all of a sudden, perhaps it was the mulish expression on Adrian's face, a kind of suppressed anxiety as he reluctantly lifted out his phone again. I'd never seen him look anxious before. Why did he not want me to see a photo of Kit?

The moment I saw the picture of the young man with a mole on his cheek, I realised why. In a revelation that made the floor blur and swirl, it all clicked into place. How had I not figured it out before, even when it had been right under my nose – or, more accurately, on Ellen's mantelpiece in Alderney?

Shit.

Adrian's son Kit and my stepson Ben had once surfed together on a British beach, pudgy in wetsuits. On holiday together.

Kit was the other little boy in the photograph. I'd subconsciously remembered him from another photograph, the one Adrian used to keep on his desk in his office, of him and his wife and Kit going down a log flume, screams ripping from their open mouths, the mole clearly visible on Kit's cheek.

Kit and Ben knew each other – or had done, once, even if Ben didn't remember it.

Which meant that Adrian and Ed had definitely known each other, too, from way before I'd even met Adrian.

I handed the phone slowly back to him. A failing fluorescent tube flickered above his head, as if transmitting my panic. I could feel the colour drain from my face and began to back away from him, my legs shaking so much that I could barely stand. We didn't speak, he just nodded.

'I'm sorry, Waitsey. I didn't want you to find out.'

For a second Adrian looked regretful, but then his expression changed. In one swift move he yanked open the cutlery drawer, from which I'd just taken a teaspoon, and grabbed one of the sharp knives, a lethal-looking serrated number that I'd last seen Alvin use to cut up chorizo for the MA cheese and wine party ... I even remembered Alvin commenting on the wisdom of keeping sharp knives so accessible, with all the teenage hormones flying around! That had been my mistake. I shouldn't have let Adrian spot them.

But then, how could I have known that my friend, my lover, the one man in whom I'd been able to confide, had used me as much as Ed had?

I wanted to vomit, but there was no time for that. I needed to call the police, and fast.

I spun on my heel on the worn parquet floor and fled into the instrument store, which had a lock on the inside of the door, but as I was trying to slam it shut, Adrian jammed his foot in the doorway and forced his way in behind me. It was he who locked it, trapping me. We faced each other, panting, the bells and gongs of the gamelan between us like some sort of bizarre obstacle course.

This whole thing had been a set-up from the start.

'*You* sent me to spy on Ed! Fuck! Why? How did you know that I wouldn't get something on him?'

He gave a harsh bark of laughter, the knife steady in his hand. 'Isn't it obvious? Because I *knew* you. You were desperate for kids, for a husband, you were ripe to fall for someone. I'd known Ed since we were kids, I knew he'd be able to seduce you.'

I gave a sob of outrage. We were circling one another like tigers, but he made sure he kept himself between the door and me. There were metal security grilles on the windows. No other way out.

'You played me. You both did! You fucking bastards!' I paused, the full horror still sinking in now that my suspicions were confirmed. 'But why would you do that, risk everything, for Ed?'

'I owed him,' he said. 'We were best friends at school, then as adults too, family holidays together and so on, when the boys were little. He saved my arse once, gave me an alibi for when some stupid bitch accused me of rape, when Kit and Ben were five or six. We agreed never to see each other again after that. The kids forgot about their friendship; forgot they'd known each other. We didn't speak for years, until Ed came to me saying he'd accidentally killed Shelagh and it was my turn to help him. He threatened to go to the police and retract his alibi, get me convicted for that rape if I didn't. I found out that they wanted to send in someone undercover, and pulled a few strings to make sure it was you. You got nothing on Ed; and then we were eventually able to frame that homeless bloke...'

So it wasn't Ed who'd framed Garvey, it was Adrian. Poor Gavin

Garvey. Imagine confessing to something you didn't do, just for the sake of three hot meals a day and a prison bunk to sleep in – although, knowing Adrian as I now did, there had probably been some unpleasant behind-the-scenes coercion going on as well. And jail obviously hadn't been as much fun as Garvey had thought it would be, since he'd hanged himself.

'And it all worked out very well ... until now. Ed came up with that stupid dementia scheme and forced me to get involved again. I didn't want to. I told him I'd done my bit. But I needed the money, once I lost my pension. All because of what some bimbo sergeant accused me of doing to her.'

I knew it. I *knew* him getting booted out of the police had been something to do with a woman. Why had I not listened to my intuition?

'Ed *paid* you?' I couldn't prevent a moan escaping. 'So it wasn't an accident, us meeting at the Barbican?'

I didn't even want to think about what he might have done to the 'stupid bimbo sergeant'.

'Of course it wasn't an accident. He rang and told me to meet you there. That you needed a shoulder to cry on.'

'Did he ... did he know we slept together?' At that moment I couldn't imagine things being any worse.

'He suggested it.' Adrian's smile was cold. 'I did always worry that you might somehow recognise Kit. I knew you'd seen him once or twice with me back in Salisbury, and I had a photo of him in my office, didn't I? I told Ed to get rid of any photos of the boys together, but I couldn't be sure if he had. Did he not?'

'I ... I saw a holiday photo of them ... it was at Shelagh's sister's place,' I stuttered, barely able to get the words out.

The smell of Adrian's aftershave was toxic again, mingling badly with his sweat, almost choking me. He was stalking me now, the knife held high in his right hand. I realised only one of us would be leaving this room alive but I swore, on the memory of my dead child, it was going to be me.

'So when did you figure out that Ed really had killed Shelagh?' he demanded.

I was not going to die here. I would not. If only I'd asked Ellen who that boy was, when I saw the photo. I'd have remembered that Adrian's son was called Kit and made the connection straightaway. Then I would have known everything. Ed would still be alive. In prison along with Adrian, but alive...

'I never knew how he did it, or when. I just worked out what he must have done with her body. He put her into an acid bath at a door-stripping place, I'm sure of it. In fact,' I went on, holding his gaze, 'it was *you* who made me realise it. I'd forgotten who once said it to me, that if they ever killed someone and wanted to dispose of the body, that's what they'd do, but I remember now, it was you! I always felt creeped out by those door-stripping places after that. You suggested it to Ed, didn't you?'

I was gabbling. Adrian said nothing.

I felt around behind me for something I could use as a weapon. *Keep him talking,* I thought. 'Ed did a magazine article about his house renovation and said that he hadn't touched the stripped-pine doors, but I saw an old Polaroid from before the work started and all the doors were gloss-painted, so I knew he'd been lying about it. I just worked it out from there – although not till recently.'

Another brief snippet of memory returned to me. A dodgy-looking guy in stained white overalls once came to the front door of Ed's old house in Molesey, soon after we'd started dating. I was sitting in the upstairs living room learning my lines for the play and I'd seen the guy storm up the garden path, then pull the doorbell so aggressively that it jangled on for ages and ages. He'd definitely got out of a van bearing the name of a furniture-stripping company.

Ed hadn't come back upstairs after he answered the door, even though I saw the man climb back in his van and drive away. I went down to the kitchen and found him, Ed, standing by the Aga, an expression of utter shock and panic on his face. When I asked him what the matter was, he had snapped at me and pushed past me, the first time I had ever seen him lose his cool. Perhaps the guy had threatened to tell the police he knew Ed had been sneaking around his yard at night – or maybe he'd given Ed a key and then regretted it, or not been paid for his services...? I never saw him again. For all I knew, Ed killed him, too.

Turn it into rage, I urged myself. Don't let Adrian get away with it as well.

He nodded, looking briefly sorrowful. 'I wish it hadn't ever had to come out, Waitsey. We could have had something good this time, now that Ed's dead. But I can't let you go, not now.'

'Another relationship with another arsehole who's never respected me and never would? Thank fuck *that's* never going to happen. You must think I'm stupid – but I'm not that stupid. I'm going straight to the police. '

'You won't have the chance, I'm afraid,' he said, advancing on me, beads of sweat glistening on his bald head. 'Shame, Waitsey. I really was fond of you, you know.'

Where was everybody? I longed to hear the sound of the campus security van outside, or the uni's postman letting himself in, but the house was silent. My phone was in my jeans pocket. I slid my hand in to get it, and that was when he lunged at me across the gamelan's floor drums. I dodged out of the way, but he came at me again and this time the knife made contact with my side. I felt a sharp pain and then the sticky sensation of blood blooming on my white shirt, thick and hot, but I refused to look down. Instead, I yelled as loudly as I could, jumped over the drums and the bells and launched a kick at him.

If I missed, I really was dead.

I didn't miss. I'd been aiming for his groin but my taekwondo skills were rusty and I only connected with his thigh. It was enough to topple him, though, and he crashed to the floor, hitting his head on the metal frame of a gong.

This was my chance. I snatched my phone and dialled 999, shrieking 'POLICE' as soon as the call connected. Adrian was bleeding from his head, he'd dropped the knife and his eyes rolled back. I thought he was out for the count – but then he grabbed my ankle and tried to pull me down.

I wanted to stamp on him but if I lifted my other foot, I'd topple over. I cast wildly around me to try and find something to hit him with, but nothing heavy enough was within reach, except perhaps the double bass that I'd left leaning next to the door earlier that morning. Could I reach it? I wasn't sure.

I leaned as far as I could towards it and, grasping its slippery wooden sides like I was trying to heft a wide-hipped old lady into a car, I managed to get purchase on it, enough to lift it up, only then remembering that it rested on a long, lethal spike...

I raised it as high as I could. Realising what I was trying to do, Adrian let go of my ankle and attempted to roll away, just like Ed had managed to do when I'd held the ammonite over him. I wasn't going to miss a second time. I wasn't going to let another dishonest bastard get away with it. And I certainly wasn't going to die, not now, not after I'd survived everything else.

Screaming at the top of my lungs, I brought the instrument down on his face, its maple wood bulk mercifully shielding me from the sight of the spike driving straight through Adrian's right eye. His own scream did not drown out the squelching noise it made on impact.

Then everything was silent again, a sea of blood flowing across the carpet tiles just like the one in my recurring nightmare.

I stepped over his body, unlocked the door and sank to the floor to wait for the police. The last thing I remembered was the sight of my own, brighter, blood spreading slowly across the worn parquet of the corridor. I closed my eyes and saw my baby being swept away, anguish on its tiny face as it waved goodbye.

It was all over.

EPILOGUE
December 2017

I'm standing at the edge of the harbour in Alderney, and it's much colder than last time I was here. Wind reddens my cheeks and tips the waves with angry white crests, and I think briefly of the calm, turquoise sea in Mustique. Just briefly, though – I don't want to be reminded of *that*.

I am making a trip I've been putting off since I moved to Jersey. I lived with Maddie and Geoff for almost six months while the sale of the house went through, but it's only now I have my own place to go back to, a squat stone cottage in a green valley half a mile away from my friends, that I feel strong enough to face this meeting.

I turn and see Ellen waiting for me, no longer on crutches. She looks different, less harried than when I first met her. Her wiry grey hair has been cut short and looks far better, and she looks like she's probably lost a bit of weight – her bottom doesn't look nearly so massive. We go to a cafe overlooking the harbour.

'I'm so sorry for storming out like that last time,' I blurt, before our coffees even arrive.

She smiles, slightly tightly. 'I understand. He was your husband. Anyway, I asked you to leave. It's me who should apologise. I was worried for you – I know we didn't see eye to eye, but I really didn't want to read in the newspapers that you'd gone missing, or been found dead somewhere,' she said.

I'd forgotten about her accent, the way she had of saying 'r's as 'w's. *Somewhewuh.*

'I must seem so gullible to you.'

To her, to Surrey police, to Ed, to Adrian ... I still quiver with shame at the thought.

'No more than my sister did. Psychopaths are very convincing.' She looks down at the table and plays with a beaded silver bracelet on her wrist, twisting it around and around.

I point at it. 'Was that hers?'

'No, but it was a present from her to me on my thirtieth. I still miss her.'

'I'm sure you do.'

'How is Benjy?' she asks, and I start to laugh at her calling him Benjy instead of Ben, then stop. He *was* still Benjy last time she saw him.

'He's OK, all things considered. Devastated about his dad, but relieved that he won't have to watch his illness progress...'

And at least he doesn't know the whole truth. Like everybody else apart from me and April, he still believes that Ed threw himself off that cliff in Mustique. He doesn't even know that his dad had faked dementia for all those months, and I'm glad of it.

'Poor Benjy. And poor you. At least it's all over now.'

It's over, only my nightmares and a jagged scar on my side left to remind me. I had a tough few days being interviewed by the police as they tried to make sense of the whole story before concluding that I had definitely killed Adrian McLoughlin in self-defence and not pressing any charges. I claimed that he had gone at me with the knife after I rejected his advances. There were plenty of witnesses who'd seen us flirting in the pub that lunchtime, and the CCTV footage from the camera in the corner of the instrument store clearly showed him chase me in and stab me.

I said Adrian was an ex-lover I'd got back in touch with after my husband died. That he was bitter about women after his divorce and expulsion from the police and, in a moment of madness, hadn't wanted to take no for an answer. The original rape charges came out, the ones that Ed helped him wriggle out of all those years ago, and it also transpired that the reason he'd been fired from the police was indeed because he had harassed another young officer. The poor 'bimbo sergeant' he'd so scornfully mentioned, presumably. How had I not realised what he was really like?

I was on tenterhooks wondering if the detectives investigating would make the connection between Ed and Adrian, because if they did, I was screwed for not disclosing it. The whole sorry saga would come out. But the police made no connection between any of it – Mike's murder, which remained unsolved, Ed's 'suicide', Adrian's death. If they'd looked just a little harder they would have seen that it was me, and April, who were the connections, but with the CCTV evidence, they saw no need to dig deeper.

I wonder now if any other woman in the history of womankind has ever had such appalling judgement when it came to choosing lovers.

It is galling to me that April and the fake consultant, Bill Brown, both escaped without any sort of justice, but April has to live with her own conscience and the loss of Mike – and I don't give a shit about Bill Brown other than praying that he doesn't have a rush of his own conscience and go running to the police to confess. I suppose that this is an uncertainty I'll just have to live with.

'My poor nephew, losing both his parents.' Ellen's eyes fill with tears.

'But the good news is that he's going to be a dad himself – his girl-friend Jeanine is three months pregnant. They're thrilled. It's really helped, I think; given him a reason to look to the future.'

I suddenly want to tell her that she'd been right about everything; Ed *had* been having an affair. Ed *had* killed Shelagh, and Mike – but fortunately I stop myself. It's all in the past, and I am desperate to move on with my life now.

I will always wonder exactly what Mike discovered and blackmailed Ed about. I suppose it wasn't impossible that Mike, on his way to or from a night-fishing trip, might have spotted Ed's car and followed him to the paint-stripping yard out of curiosity, putting two and two together as I did much later, hugging the deadly secret to himself until he could deploy it to devastating effect. He had discovered about Ed's affair with April and decided that the best way to punish him was by hitting him where it hurt – his bank account. Particularly if, as April claimed, their show of wealth had been just that – a show. They both probably managed to piss hundreds of thousands of pounds up the wall with their debts and boats and swanky holidays. Mike had found a way to keep April, get more money *and* make Ed suffer, all at the same time. He must have thought it was a win-win situation – he wouldn't have wanted to continue the friendship anyway, once he knew Ed was screwing April. But he forced Ed to pretend that everything was normal.

Ellen changes the subject. 'So you're living in Jersey now – are you working?'

'Not yet. I've applied for a job in a school office and I've got an interview next week.'

I think back to my brief time at Hampton University. I don't particularly miss the job or Margaret and of course haven't ever set foot in Fairhurst again, but I do miss Alvin. He was upset when I said I wasn't coming back, but very understanding. He dropped round a couple of weeks later with an embarrassingly glowing reference for me in a white envelope.

'I'll email it to you as well of course,' he said. 'But I actually just wanted to see you, make sure you're OK. We're mates now, aren't we?'

'Of course we are. I'm, er, sorry for making such a mess of the instrument store. Please let me pay for—'

He cut me off with a traffic-stopping gesture. 'Certainly not. Please. That's what we have insurance for.'

I wasn't sure which of us was more embarrassed. In truth, I was slightly in shock at the sight of him, standing in my porch with his shoulders stooped so as not to bump his head, amongst my muddy wellies and all the old umbrellas and coats. His hair was sticking up all over the place like Krusty the Clown's, and I had to stop myself from hugging him round his pipe-cleaner-thin middle.

'Good,' he said, clearing his throat. 'Do keep in touch, won't you, Lynn? Let me know next time you're in the area, so you can come round for dinner with me and Sheryl? Or you and I could go out for a spot of lunch, if it's a school day, for old time's sake?'

He winked self-consciously, but all I could think of was that 'our' pub was now forever sullied by the memory of Adrian and me drinking rosé in the garden, right before he almost killed me.

'Sure,' I said, smiling at him – although now I'm in Jersey, I think it's fairly unlikely I'll be back over any time soon. Timmy the cat was willingly adopted by Naveeta and her girls. I've got Maddie and Geoff up the road, and Ben and Jeanine are coming to stay for a week as their next trip – a less challenging holiday than usual for them, in deference to her pregnancy.

'Sounds good,' says Ellen, about my interview. 'I come over to Jersey quite a lot. Hospital visits for my diabetes, and I have a few friends over there who I like to visit.'

'Well, I've got a spare room if you ever need one,' I say impulsively, immediately hoping that if she does take me up on it, it will only be for one night. I'm pretty sure we'll never be best mates, but at least I've done what I came to do, and it feels like a weight off my mind.

I've kind of run out of things to say to her now, but I'm glad I came.

'Thanks for agreeing to see me,' I say eventually, as we watch a fishing boat chug into the harbour, a cacophony of gulls swirling in its wake.

'I appreciate you coming.'

She nods magnanimously but I don't find, as I would have done last time, that I want to punch her in the throat. I wonder if she is less annoying, or if I was under so much stress back then that I was over-sensitive to everything? The latter, I'm pretty sure.

An hour later when Max the Cab arrives to take me back to the airport, I say to Ellen what I ought to have said when I first met her, instead of letting myself get so uptight: 'I'm really sorry for your loss.'

'Thank you,' she says, and we hug awkwardly. 'Please let me know when Ben's baby arrives. I'd like to send it something. Perhaps maybe even visit one day.'

'I will,' I say, and smile at her.

THE END

Acknowledgements

Never has a book taken me so long nor gone through so many drafts! Consequently I have people to thank:

TEAM ORENDA! The amazing, legendary powerhouse that is Karen Sullivan, of course, surely the hardest-working woman in publishing, who made it all possible, and who makes a lot of other stuff possible for many other people too. It's greatly appreciated. Big thanks also to West Camel, Sophie Goodfellow, Liz Barnsley, Luke Speed and to all the other Orenda authors for welcoming me in. I'm very happy to be part of the gang.

Huge thanks to Veronique Baxter and Laura West at David Higham for all their hard work and support, editorially and practically.

The Slice Girls: Susi Holliday, Steph Broadribb, Alex Sokoloff, Harley Jane Kozak and AK Benedict for sisterhood and encouragement in numerous different ways, but especially to Susi for specific pharmaceutical advice, and most definitely to Alexandra – AK – for being the first reader of the almost-finished version and giving me such detailed insightful and encouraging feedback – still can't believe you read it so quickly and thoroughly!

For various bits of research advice and/or emotional support: Hayley Webster, Will Franks, Amanda Jennings, John Rickards, Franco Iannelli, Chris Phillips, Nick Laughland.

The Lilies: Nik Waites, Helen Russell and Jenny Groome, but specially Nik for invaluable research help with this one.

The Alderneyites: Rachel Abbott, Tish McPhilemy, Alex Flewitt, Chris Rowley. Hope to get over to see you all again this year.

The Locals: Particularly Heath Jackson for friendship and boat inspiration and Simon Alcock, as always, for procedural advice, and also all my other local pals too.

My neighbourly neighbours Trish Hawkins and Andrea van der Schyff for printing stuff out for me when my elderly printer refused to.

All my crime-writer friends and colleagues, especially those of you in That Group. Ian Patrick, first reader of a very early version, for his encouraging and helpful words. And lastly, Tammy Cohen, for the best suggestion for a murder weapon I've ever used in a book.

What you see isn't always real...

house

'Disturbing but compulsive...'
Martina Cole

of

spines

michael j

malone

'Malone is a massive talent ... get on board now so you can brag you were reading his books long before the rest of the world' Luca Veste

Some secrets should never be kept...

a

suitable

lïe

michael j

malone

'Bristling with unease, this is domestic noir at its very darkest, twisting
the marriage thriller into a new and troubling shape' Eva Dolan

SHE LOVES ME.

SHE LOVES ME NOT.

EXQUISITE

SARAH
STOVELL

L V HAY

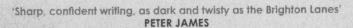

THE
OTHER
TWIN

in

her

wake

A perfect life ... until she
discovered it wasn't her own

Amanda Jennings

the

mountain

in my

shoe

LOUISE BEECH